NERVE DAMAGE

Tom Combs

Evoke Publishing

Nerve Damage

This is a work of fiction. All of the characters, organizations, and events portrayed in this novel are either products of the author's imagination or used fictitiously.

Published in the United States by Evoke Publishing

Author website: www.tom-combs.com
Email: tcombsauthor@gmail.com

ISBN-13: 978-0990336006
ISBN-10: 099033600X

Dedication

For twenty-five years I've worked the front lines of U.S. emergency care alongside police, fire/rescue, paramedics, EMTs, nurses, fellow doctors, technicians, air rescue crews, and the many others who respond when illness, trauma or tragedy strike. I dedicate this book to them – the special people committed to helping others when needed most.

Chapter 1

Wayzata, suburban Minneapolis, late afternoon

She basked in the Minnesota summer sun and the brilliance of her imminent triumph. The morning's pleasures had been just a sampling of what her future held. She lay on her stomach on the diving board over her pool. A bead of sweat tickled as it ran down her inner thigh. Her cell phone rested inches from her face, awaiting the call that would open the world to her.

Jester, her King Charles Spaniel, dozed atop the poolside settee. His head jerked as the ringtone trilled and the phone vibrated on the board's grainy surface. The caller's international exchange displayed. Closing her eyes, she gloried in the moment. From captive princess to ultimate victor—she'd have it all.

As she raised the phone to her ear, it dropped from her hand, bouncing off the board and splashing into the water below. The muscles of her forearms quivered as a freakish spasm coursed through her. Jester yelped and jumped from his perch. He crouched, whining at the pool's edge.

She struggled to her elbows as an impossible weakness claimed her. Strength dissolving, her arms gave way, and she slumped to the side. Her body rolled, as if in slow motion, off the board. Her choked cry died before she hit the water.

Her face plunged beneath the surface. Internal commands to swim and thrash yielded nothing.

The fresco on the bottom of the pool rotated through her frozen gaze as she spun and sank. Her mind filled with a white-noise shriek of terror and helplessness.

Water flooded her nose and mouth and bubbles streaked for the surface. The fluid advanced down her throat and balloons of air escaped, belching out and up. The reflex imperative to cough and gag demanded but her body would not react. *No!*

Water rushed into her windpipe, the dense and cool sensation terrifyingly foreign but unmistakable. It invaded her lungs like a first breath on an icy winter's morning. But it was not air. And it did not stop.

She heard and felt the back of her head clunk against the tiles of the pool's floor. Her body settled as if lifeless.

The frantic barks of Jester faded, water-muted and distant. Pressure mounted in her head and chest—like an overinflated balloon on the cusp of bursting. Time stretched.

No sound now but her heart's pounding frenzy and the sobbing within her mind. Awareness drifting…fading.

Fingers clamped onto her arms. Her body pulled upward. Hope surging. Her head and face launched free of the water.

The breath she must take would not happen. *Please, God!*

Agony expanding. Vision narrowing. Her body dragged over the pool's edge. A man's creased face looming. Eyes. A voice…the words melting. *Breathe!*

Her mind wailing, begging, shrinking.

Blinding brightness. Everywhere white.

A thought stuttering and lost.

A blink to black and the pain was gone.

* * *

Hennepin-North Emergency Room, Minneapolis, Minnesota

Dr. Drake Cody passed the suture needle through the tissues of the ER patient's forehead. The gaping skin and deep tissues came together as Drake secured the first stitch. As he advanced the needle for the next, the Air Care emergency flight pager sounded.

Drake set down the needle holder and placed gauze over the wound before silencing the beeper.

The grey-faced Alzheimer patient's eyes fluttered open. He groaned and struggled to rise.

Drake placed his hand on the man's frail chest and crouched so their faces were level.

"It's okay, sir."

The wide and jittering eyes probed.

"I promise." Drake smiled. The pounding palpable under his hand slowed.

The man settled back.

Drake tucked a blanket around the thin shoulders, raised the safety rail, then dashed into the crowded hall of the ER.

Dr. Michael Rizzini exited an exam room down the corridor. Drake caught his rangy, fast-moving friend's eye and raised an arm, making a twirling motion with his finger. Rizz diverted and jogged to Drake's side. Drake spoke over the ER din, providing thumbnail reports on his five current patients as they dodged stretchers, carts and personnel en route to the flight elevator.

"...last is cart fourteen. He's an Alzheimer's patient with a facial laceration. He's snoozing, but if he wakes and gets scared just talk to him. He'll be numb for at least an hour. I'll finish his repair when I get back."

Rizz halted at the open flight elevator doors.

Drake stepped inside and hit the button for the high-speed trip to the helicopter deck.

"No worries, partner." Rizz gave a mock salute. "I'll watch over your old-guy buddy and leave his repair for you. Odds are I'll have all your other patients cured and sent home by the time you return. Don't be ashamed. We can't all be exceptional."

Drake hated giving his smart-ass friend encouragement, but he couldn't avoid grinning.

His smile departed as the elevator doors pinged shut.

As he accelerated towards the rooftop helipad, Drake took a big breath then blew it out hard. He shook his arms loose like a boxer before the opening bell.

Any paramedic, EMT, fireman or policeman within a one-hundred-mile radius could summon the Air Care helicopter if they judged the situation desperate enough. The adrenaline-stoked challenges made his heart race and his throat clench. When he arrived on the scene, the life or death responsibility was his alone.

Responsibility—a focus of the psychiatrist's damning testimony years before. "The accused assumes unrealistic responsibility and—" Drake slammed shut the memory.

Now is what mattered.

The elevator doors slid open to the jet-fuel smell and hurricane roar of the high-performance rescue helicopter. The helipad shuddered with the twin engines' power and was awash in their driving heat. Drake held his stethoscope secure from the gale-force rotor wash as he scuttled under the blades and across the vibrating deck to the open copilot door.

He nodded to the pilot as he climbed aboard. Drake strapped in and affixed his headphones as the pilot initiated the helicopter's power-takeoff dive.

His stomach plunged and then rebounded as the craft dove, then accelerated forward and up. It felt like a runaway carnival ride.

Hennepin-North Medical Center sat on the edge of the Minneapolis downtown district's collection of older stone giants and newer glass and steel towers. The low afternoon sun fell flush on the copter as they flew out from the buildings' shadows and into the open corridor over the Mississippi River. The Minneapolis/St. Paul metropolis sprawled to the horizon in all directions, the brawny river separating the sister cities. The copter banked over the surging water of St. Anthony's Falls.

As they gained altitude, the pilot swung the stick to the west and into the sun. A chain of large lakes shimmered into view amidst the greenery-rich cityscape. Four years in Minnesota, and Drake still gaped at the beauty.

The Air Care dispatch operator's report crackled through Drake's headphones. "Adult female. Suspected near-drowning. CPR ongoing. Flight time, eight minutes."

They raced over highways, woods, marshland, and increasingly impressive neighborhoods. The glittering expanse of massive Lake Minnetonka's eastern reach came into view. As they neared the exclusive lakeshore, the homes became estates and the yards grounds.

Drake shifted as they passed over a lakefront retail district to open water. The area seemed familiar and a sense of unease kindled as the copter sped over the waves.

The pilot turned shoreward and elevated to clear towering lakeside oak trees, bringing into view the rear of a white stone mansion with a garden terrace and a large pool. A manicured lawn ascended from the shoreline, its green velvet gashed by coal-black ruts tracking to a police car and an ambulance, both with doors hanging open and emergency lights flashing.

The copter spiraled in over the pool, approaching a flat section of lawn clear of the trees. The rotor wash buffeted the surface of the pool as the helicopter passed over. Drake caught a glimpse of the splay-limbed, motionless, bikini-clad victim whose head and chest were hidden by the backs of two paramedics performing CPR. He glanced at the house again as the craft hovered before touching down.

His unease became a flood of dread and disbelief. He'd visited this property just once, during the winter more than a year ago, but he was certain. His friend, research partner and fellow ER physician, Jon Malar, lived here.

Was the stricken woman Jon's wife, Faith?

Please, God. No!

Chapter 2

Drake jumped from the helicopter as the skids touched down. He sprinted in a low crouch through the gale of the rotors and up the slope towards the poolside resuscitation. The stink of exhaust lessened as he neared the laboring paramedics. They looked up with grim expressions and a glimmer of relief as Drake arrived.

One paramedic squeezed the airway bag while his partner performed chest compressions, their actions coordinated. An IV access lay in the slim, unmoving arm in the midst of scattered spent vials and medical debris. The men's sweat-soaked white shirts clung to their backs.

The lead paramedic spoke, his report delivered between compressions of the airway bag. "A Mexican worker-guy pulled her out of the pool. No evidence of trauma. Unknown downtime. Call came 4:31. Police on scene 4:35. We arrived 4:37. Initially V-fib on the monitor. We've given it a full go. Defibrillation attempts times two. Intubated with good air movement. Full drug resuscitation and good compressions. She went flatline almost immediately. We got nothing."

The second paramedic's thick hands and knuckle-scarred fingers compressed the chest with piston-like precision. He gave an *unhh* in synch with each effort. The defibrillator monitor showed an unbroken horizontal line.

The paramedic's report, the cardiac monitor flatline, and the time passed without cardiac activity made the possibility of resuscitation remote.

The waiting helicopter's engines idled, its rumble resonating in Drake's chest. With cresting dread he directed his gaze over the airway mask. Gray-cast skin, open, unseeing, nightmare eyes—Faith Reinhorst-Malar.

Drake fought for breath, his legs weak. *No!*

His professional discipline held. He searched for any spark of life, moving through the checklist hardwired into him through medical school and his four years of advanced emergency medicine training.

His stethoscope confirmed adequate ventilation. Her pupils were blown wide and unresponsive to light. He lightly touched gauze to an eye—no blink. No pulse and no cardiac activity on the monitor with leads in position and the device functioning.

There was no doubt.

Faith was dead.

"Stop CPR, guys. She's gone." Drake's words formalized what the rescue workers already knew. "Time of death, four-forty-seven p.m." *How would he tell Jon?*

The paramedics were wordless, breathing hard from their efforts. Drake rested a hand on each of their sweat-soaked shoulders.

"You gave her every chance."

Their drained expressions and defeated postures eased slightly.

Drake took his stethoscope from around his neck. Clipped to the device's tubing hung a two-by-two-inch laminated photograph of his children. The image, from a trip to the zoo, captured the kids after four-year-old Kristin had mimicked one of the baboons, sending her and her six-year-old brother Shane into hysterics. Drake could not look at the picture without smiling. He had no smile now.

"Dr. Cody, maybe you should talk to the worker guy," said the lead paramedic. "He's the one saw her go down. The police are with him." He nodded towards the canopied area on the side of the pool nearer the home. "He was clawing at my shirt yelling, 'She alive but no breathe.' Speaks English pretty good but he was really upset. Not just sad, but I dunno…totally freaked."

Drake turned towards the witness. His mind churned.

Air Care protocol demanded he fly Faith's body back to the ER. Jon would be on duty now. There'd be no way to prepare him. His introduction to the death of his wife would be seeing her lifeless body rolled off the flight elevator.

Jon worshipped Faith. He was the proverbial "crazy about her" husband. Rizz said Jon was "so whipped, the woman could set him on fire and he'd thank her for the match."

Drake turned back to the paramedic. "Please radio Air Care dispatch and tell them the flight is a stand-down." He paused. "I'm going to ask you guys to stay with the body. Flying will provide her no benefit."

Drake would tell Jon upon returning to the ER and then help him as best he could. The Morgue was only five blocks from the hospital. Jon could be brought there to see the body. *My God, those eyes.*

How could an athlete like Faith drown?

Possibly an aneurysm, a heart problem or a seizure? Perhaps a fall and head injury? Something. The paramedic handed Drake a clipboard with the declaration of death form.

He was avoiding the thought, but he had to consider drugs or alcohol.

The trust-fund beauty and daughter of one of Minnesota's wealthiest men had a history. Before her marriage to Jon, Faith made the gossip columns regularly. Drake had heard plenty of stories. Rizz, a native Minneapolis resident, stayed clear of her. Unusual for a guy drawn to beautiful women like steel to a magnet.

Drake wrote the time of death and signed. He handed the clipboard back to the paramedic.

Drake approached the shaded poolside table where two police officers stood next to a seated older Hispanic man who held his head in his hands. His hair and denim work clothes were soaked. A small spaniel trembled at his feet, its gaze furtive. "Sir, I'm Dr. Cody from Hennepin-North hospital. I'm sorry, but Mrs. Malar did not make it."

Sad eyes in a weathered face turned toward Drake. "You say Senora Faith es muerte?" He nodded. "I know this. I see her go."

"You found her?"

"Yes. My name is Hector. I am caretaker here."

"The report I was given said she drowned."

"She no drown." His voice rose and he colored. "I save from the water. She was no drowned." He continued, more subdued. "I talk to her but she no move and no breathe. I see her in eyes." He hesitated, appearing almost overcome. "She is alive but she can do nothing."

"Do you know how she ended up in the water?"

"I old but I watch her. She laying on board for diving. Fall into water, slow. She make scream. Her Jester…" he gestured towards the dog that flinched with its name and remained pressed to the ground trembling. "He barking crazy."

He indicated an adjoining veranda separated from the pool level by a set of stairs and some distance. "I working there when she go in. I run and I jump to her. I pull her from bottom. She no move, no breathe, but she is alive. In her eyes. She see me. So scared—and me also. I call the nine-one-one." He made the sign of the cross. "I see her die." He placed his face in his hands. "Madre de Dio."

Drake rested a hand on the caretaker's shoulder. "You did all you could."

He then bent to comfort the dog but it shrunk back with its tail between its legs.

The caretaker's report did not fit a typical drowning. Drowning victims invariably lose consciousness at the time their breathing stops. The possibility of drugs or alcohol pushed once more into his thoughts.

Faith had sent out wild vibes. At last year's ER department gathering, Drake could have sworn she was hitting on him. In the end he figured it was the alcohol, but it had been intense. Faith was—had been—one of the most arresting women he'd ever met. The face of an angel, yet she radiated sexuality like molten steel gave off heat. Her attention had been stirring—a primal force.

Rachelle had been pissed. Drake had acted innocent but knew he'd flushed guilty red.

He strode towards the idling Agusta but stopped alongside the paramedics standing next to the sheet-covered body. He picked up the clipboard. In the space under "Cause of Death," he wrote "Uncertain–possible drowning" and assigned the death as a priority Medical Examiner's case. He asked the nearest officer to inform Homicide of the death and its ME status.

Police and the medical examiner were notified of all accidental deaths or those of unknown cause. In routine cases, the assessments were cursory. Assigning the death as a priority case assured timely and focused attention. Drake handed the clipboard back to the paramedic, then hurried to the idling helicopter.

The craft powered into the late afternoon sunlight.

Faith was an attorney. Jon said she got her law degree to fight the restrictions of the incentive trust her father had set up for her. Nonetheless, she'd volunteered to handle the startup of NeurVitae, the business that Drake, Jon and Rizz had formed in hopes that their research would someday yield something of value.

Now that they'd made the breakthrough, she was gone. Could her death compromise things?

She'd only dealt with the business side. The science was what mattered. D-44's results were solid.

The course of his thoughts struck him and his cheeks burned. *Damn, what's wrong with me?*

Faith's body was still warm and his thoughts were on the research.

The pitch of the engines altered as the copter entered the corridor over the river and snaked around the city's skyscrapers. The aged hospital came into view. Hennepin-North sat like an old stone fortress just west of the river on the edge of the downtown giants. Atop its weathered south tower perched the gleaming steel superstructure of the helipad.

They would land in seconds. After an elevator descent to the ER, Drake would have to tell Jon that the woman he worshipped was dead.

The copter set down hard.

Chapter 3

Hennepin-North ER

Drake found his friend within seconds of exiting the flight elevator.

Jon frowned in concentration as he applied the finishing touches to a wrist cast for a patient seated on a cart in a crowded hallway. The hospital PR people always came to Jon first when they needed a doctor for marketing photos or TV interviews. His face mirrored intelligence, sincerity and caring. It was an accurate reflection.

"Jon, we need to talk. Can you give me a minute?" Drake turned to the patient. "Excuse us. A nurse will be with you in a bit."

Jon got to his feet, pulling off plaster-smeared gloves. "When I got here, you were on the Air Care run." He flushed and looked down. "There are things I need to tell you."

"Sure thing, Jon. In a minute." Whatever Jon wanted to say couldn't matter in the face of Drake's news.

He led Jon into the minor procedures room, his mouth dry at the thought of the message he had to deliver. The yellow-tiled walls formed a backdrop to racks of sutures and chrome instruments.

Drake's stomach clutched, his breath came hard, and his palms were moist. He pulled over a chair for Jon, then took a seat facing him.

He leaned forward.

"Jon," he said, "Faith was the patient for my Air Care flight."

Jon straightened, raised his eyebrows, and cocked his head to the side. His mouth opened but he made no sound.

"I'm so terribly sorry to have to tell you that Faith is gone. She was found in the pool with no signs of life. She couldn't be resuscitated. Faith is dead."

Time stretched. The ER's raucous hum sounded in the background. Drake's eyes filled. He readied to support his friend.

Jon sat back, looked away, and slowly nodded his head. He sat, dry-eyed, hands folded on his lap. He closed his eyes.

The fluorescent lights flickered and the banana-like odor of benzoin solution hung strong in the room.

Jon spoke with his gaze directed to the ceiling. “It doesn’t feel like I thought.”

Drake nodded. “It’s unbelievable.”

“That’s not it.” Jon stopped and lowered his eyes to Drake’s. “The part that’s not right…” His expression darkened. “The part that’s wrong,” he looked away, “is that I don’t feel anything at all.”

Drake felt off-balance, as if he’d been leaning against a wall that gave way.

He put a hand on Jon’s shoulder. “It’s too much. It hasn’t hit you yet.”

Jon remained silent, his position unchanged.

Chapter 4

Washington, DC, early evening

The offices of Reinhorst Associates, LLC, were within a polo field's length of the US center of power and influence. Andrew Reinhorst had captured this office space four decades earlier. He'd known, even then, the importance of securing political favor and influence. He'd succeeded beyond his wildest imaginings.

This evening the offices were almost empty, as the youthful-appearing sixty-six-year-old business giant and political goliath was engaged in some decidedly nonpolitical maneuvering. He had a twenty-seven-year-old nakedly ambitious—and now mostly naked—brunette law intern bent over his desk. The black mahogany desk had reportedly been used by FDR. On the wall hung handshake-and-smile photos of Reinhorst with many of the most powerful men and women in the nation.

He very much enjoyed his position at this particular moment. On this very desk he'd penned the speech outlining his party's campaign platform of "Family Values and Timeless Morality." His worn leather-bound Bible sat adjacent to his computer.

As he approached consummation of his current venture, his private cell phone sounded and vibro-danced on the desktop, inches from his hand.

"Damn it to hell!" He corralled the phone without giving up his position and snatched it up. "Whatever it is will wait. Call the desk, damn it." He initiated the move to slam it down but was jerked, as if by a leash, by the words his top Minneapolis assistant rushed over the line.

"It's Faith, sir. Your daughter—they say she's dead."

Chapter 5

Hennepin-North ER, early evening

The waiting room now stood more than thirty patients deep. Drake's flight and his time with Jon had contributed to the backup. Seriously ill patients could not wait.

Patti had charge-nurse responsibilities this shift, and he left Jon in her hands. With fifteen years of ER experience, Patti had insight born of daily exposure to tragedy, yet somehow maintained the caring exuberance of a candy striper. He couldn't wish for anyone better to support Jon.

As Drake hurried towards the central station, he heard the overhead signal for a "doctor to the radio." The signal indicated that paramedics needed immediate orders for treatment of an incoming unstable patient. Rizz came out of an exam room moving fast. He looked Drake's way.

"Drake, I'll grab the radio. Your old guy's been sleeping. The others are history. We're swamped. Dive in." He stripped off surgical gloves as he passed near. He paused. "I heard about your flight. How's Jon?"

"He's pretty messed up."

"She drowned? Bizarre." He tossed the gloves into the waste receptacle. "Just when we're finally in position to make a move with the research. I'll bet she was high." He hustled away.

Drake stared after him. His reaction seemed cold. Rizz sometimes acted the hardass, but Drake believed otherwise.

When Drake next noted the time, two and a half hours had passed. He, Rizz, and their colleagues had treated the rush of sick and injured patients with speed and skill. The critical and high-risk patients had been cared for. The half-dozen or so remaining had issues of low urgency such as probable joint sprain, minor lacerations, and the like.

Drake learned that Jon had refused to leave until he'd cared for all his patients. He'd rejected an arranged visit to the morgue. Patti had the on-call priest come in, but Jon wouldn't speak with him. Surprising for a guy who made the Pope seem like a casual Catholic.

Jon's parents had been contacted and they'd left right away from Duluth—only a couple of hours away. Hopefully they were with him now.

Drake reached for the phone, his first chance to call Rachelle since Faith's death. As he picked up the receiver he sighed. Their last exchange had been painful. He should have handled things better.

Sometimes he felt more like Rachelle's doctor than her husband—and his treatment wasn't helping. She walked an emotional and mental health tightrope.

The news of Faith's death would not help her balance.

Chapter 6

As Drake entered his home phone number, he heard himself paged to the ER main desk. He looked at the phone, then hung up and headed down the corridor.

The rank odor of a hemorrhaging ulcer patient's bloody stool permeated the area around the Crash Room. Drake had stabilized the bleeding patient and transferred him to the Intensive Care Unit fifteen minutes earlier. The patient had left but the stink remained. Orderlies wrestled with two large oscillating fans they were setting up in an attempt to clear the odor.

The Crash Room sat directly across from the central desk. The room contained the ER's four most specialized treatment bays. These bays were designed and equipped to deal with catastrophic illness and injury. Only the most critical, every-second-counts patients were placed there.

Next to the central desk stood Aki Yamada. The thick-chested Japanese-American appeared to be reading the wall-mounted display hung there. He looked out of place standing immobile in a dark blue suit among the bustling white-coated or scrubs-wearing ER personnel. As he turned, Drake saw the gold badge flash from his belt. The detective looked tired.

"Hey, Doc, it was me that paged you. Geez," he waved a hand in front of his nose, "are you treating skunks now? That is nasty."

Detective Aki Yamada worked major crimes/homicide. He'd arrived in Minneapolis just months before Drake. The victims and perpetrators of violent crime had brought them together multiple times in the intervening four years. They got along, though Drake never let down his guard around the detective.

The forty-year-old policeman also knew Jon and Rizz. He referred to them all as "Doc."

Aki pointed at the information mounted in front of him. The four large posters described the spinal cord injury research of Drake, Rizz and Jon.

"It says you're the 'principal researcher.' Wow. I don't know what half of it means, but it looks big-time."

Drake felt his cheeks flush. The display summarized their previous month's presentation to the regional Society for Academic Emergency Medicine. Their work had received a special commendation as "research effort of greatest promise."

"Thanks. We're hopeful." Drake's low-key response hid his true feelings. Every time he thought of the breakthrough, fireworks went off in his head.

The detective turned from the display. "Doc Malar's wife—really bad news."

"It's brutal," said Drake. "I expected one of you guys earlier."

"Really?" Aki's brows arched. "I was upstairs on a shooting follow-up when I got a call from downtown. My report said a routine Medical Examiner case." He backed up as an empty stretcher and two paramedics rolled through between them. "I hurried down to catch you so I can put it to bed fast. Quash publicity and whatever. She drowned—right?"

Drake moved closer and lowered his voice. "I'm not sure. There are questions. Something feels off."

Yamada straightened up like a bird dog going on point. "Questions? Are you shitting me?" He pulled a pen and tattered notebook from an inside pocket. "I should've been called right away."

"Weren't you? I asked the uniforms to notify your department. I made it a priority ME case."

"Damn, Doc." The detective frowned. "No call—at least not to me. The report I got said accidental death. Those are a touch-base and sign-off for us. Jesus Jones." He gestured with the notebook. "This could be huge. She's a Reinhorst, right?"

"Well, yeah. Her father—"

"Yeah, everybody in the state knows who Andrew Reinhorst is. We've got to be all over this double now." He mouthed a silent expletive. "Gimme what you got, Doc."

Drake paused, feeling air movement and noting that the fans were now operating. "I talked with the caretaker who saw her fall into the pool. He's the one who pulled her out and called nine-one-one. He's the only witness I'm aware of. He swore Faith was alive when he pulled her out of the water. He said she was conscious and he watched her die. That doesn't fit with a simple drowning."

The detective pointed his pen at Drake. "The caretaker—is he a suspect, y'think?"

"I doubt there's anything to be a suspect for." He paused. "The man was shaken up and English is not his first language. I may have misread him."

Drake waited as three nurses passed. "Even without his story it's hard for me to imagine Faith drowning unless something medical contributed. A heart problem, an aneurysm, a seizure, something."

The detective scratched entries into his notepad.

Drake lowered his voice. "There's also the possibility of alcohol or drugs."

Aki shrugged. "It happens."

"I left a message for the ME to call me as soon as he gets in tomorrow. I'll share—"

"Yeah, you do that, Doc." Aki spoke quickly. "This is going to be a media shitstorm. Her father is a political heavyweight. The pressure on this will be incredible. Our every move will be—"

"Aki," Drake locked eyes with the detective, "Don't tell me about pressure on your department or any political bullshit. This isn't about that. Jon's wife is dead." A wild yell came from the area of the psych room then quieted. "I have a responsibility as a physician and a friend to find out what happened. So far, we have an odd story and my gut feel. It may be a simple drowning but I need to be sure."

Aki arched a brow. "I hear ya, Doc. I was just thinking out loud."

"Sorry if I sounded pissy."

"It's personal for you." Aki rubbed his chin. "Someone on my team dropped the ball. Now I'm stuck playing catch-up." He looked at his watch. "How long will you be here?"

"A couple more hours tonight and then back in the morning."

"We'll talk tomorrow." He handed a card to Drake. "If you come up with anything, the circled number will always get me." He pocketed his notepad. "The Medical Examiner's report will be key. Maybe it tells us this gut feel of yours is just indigestion."

"I hope so, Detective." A steel band tightened around Drake's chest. No one but Drake could understand how desperately he hoped so. If the ME ruled the death suspicious, a full-scale investigation would ensue. Detective Aki Yamada would turn over every stone.

And what he might find could shatter Drake's world.

Chapter 7

Wyndham Grand Hotel, Minneapolis, evening

Legs screaming. Lungs scorched by every breath.

Meryl loved it.

The mirrored walls of the luxury hotel's workout room revealed a crowd of predominantly young and affluent fitness buffs. Evening hours generally attracted only those serious about their workouts.

Meryl had started with two miles of treadmill at a six-minute-per-mile pace. She moved to a lifting rotation, ripping through repetitions of bench press, pull-downs, curls, and squats at weights greater than many men could one-time. Then three quick sets of twenty incline sit-ups with a twenty-pound weight held to her chest. Now she exulted in the exquisite burn of cycle spinning at twenty mph.

The exclusive hotel's clientele reminded her of the in-crowd that had infested her high school. Meryl's obesity, cheap clothes, and sexual orientation had made her a target back then. Poor, fat and a fag—it was as if there'd been a bounty on her.

She kicked up her cycling rate. Even after more than a decade, any of the old loser memories pissed her off. The indicator hung at twenty-four mph and she had more in reserve. The furtive awed and fearful glances coming from these hard-body boys and spandex girly-girls felt good. They were appropriate responses to her superiority.

Her watch-timer beeped. The mirror revealed engorged veins on slabs of muscle pumped rock hard. She surged on an endorphin and lactic acid high. The tailored Christian Dior workout gear highlighted her carved body. She smiled. Soon everything she owned would be only the very best.

She thought of the money. *Hot damn, it would be a lot of money.*

Twenty-five minutes later, she moved from the shower to the dressing area of her master suite. Holding a towel to her chest, she faced the full-length mirror. She let the towel fall. Raising a leg, she placed her foot on the ottoman there. Her taut skin and hyper-defined physique made each movement a rippling anatomical display. Her breathing accelerated as she picked up the syringe.

Keeping her gaze on the mirrored image, she placed the needle's tip on the skin of her thigh. She smiled into the black orbs staring back at her. *I just keep getting stronger.*

Her eyes widened as she buried the one and one-half inch needle into the mass of her quadriceps. She depressed the plunger. Twelve units of human growth hormone entered her body.

Ten minutes later, she sat dressed in front of her laptop, keying in the details of the day's workout and drug regimen. Tomorrow's steroid was Anabol. She was stacking hot and calculating dosages based on double her weight.

The amounts of the drugs she administered exceeded all recommended limits, but she understood the risks. Her body was far beyond normal, and when it came to pharmacology, she was an authority. More than that—she was genius.

Meryl didn't use drugs to get high. That was for losers. For her drugs were tools to increase her strength and cognitive performance. She was a test subject in her own revolutionary experiment. How far could the boundaries of her genius and physical development be extended under the influence of maximal drug enhancement?

The exactingly measured dose of the white crystalline powder sat on the compact mirror. She sculpted it into two tented lines using one of her business cards. She licked the edge of the card, glancing at it as the bitter taste faded and her tongue numbed.

Meryl Kampf, PhD/PhD/MSc
Chief Product Development Analyst
BioZyn, Inc., a Biomedical Ventures Enterprise

Using a rolled bill, she sniffed one line up each nostril. The pharmaceutical-grade cocaine fit perfectly as the newest addition to her pharmacologic palette. She envisioned her brain's neurotransmitters undergoing instantaneous amplification. *The better to think with, my dear.* She smiled. God, she loved the power of drugs.

Six weeks earlier, she'd quit the lithium she'd been poisoned with for years.

Lithium, the so-called "treatment" the physicians had prescribed. How had she allowed them to hold her down for so long? Medical degrees or not, they had a fraction of her knowledge of neuro-pharmacologic science.

Meryl rubbed her nose as her brain revved.

Stopping lithium and introducing cocaine had catalyzed her brain chemistry and enhanced her synaptic plasticity. It was the obvious explanation for her ascending brilliance. The drug-body-mind synergies she harnessed catapulted her beyond normal human capabilities—certainly far past traditional doctors and their pathetic, disease-focused thinking.

Medical doctors prescribed drugs in defense of "normal" health and performance. Meryl used drugs to leave normal far behind.

She felt disdain for all but one physician—Dr. Suzie Lind. Suzie's evident sexual leaning and attractiveness had initially caught Meryl's attention. But it was the psychiatrist's caring manner that persuaded Meryl to show up for follow-up appointments after her release from the hospital.

Dr. Lind agreed with the diagnosis of mania and emphasized the need for lithium. Meryl remembered the doctor's earnest warning. "Mania is diabolical. It hides itself from its victims. The greatest sense of well-being masks the most dangerously disordered thinking."

Pretty Suzie's diagnosis was absurd and her grasp of brain science pathetic, but she was well-intentioned. Meryl maintained a soft spot for the appealing but intellectually-challenged shrink.

Meryl hoisted her licensed transport valise to the tabletop. She glanced at the stainless steel tag attached: Designated Licensee – Meryl Kampf, Doctor of Pharmacology and Medicinal Chemistry. She opened the repository and stowed the steroids and syringe. She scanned her extensive array of drugs and smiled.

Leave it to a butcher to always have the best meat.

Chapter 8

Late evening

Detective Aki Yamada drove west on halogen-lit I-394 until he reached the Wayzata exit. He wound along narrow wooded roads, catching glimpses of the moonlit lake beyond huge homes and gated barriers. It didn't take a detective to know that none of his fellow cops lived in this neighborhood.

At the entry to a private drive, a sleepy-looking security guard waved Aki through. The headlights found the service road leading to the rear of the Reinhorst-Malar estate. He parked in the darkness. A lawn angled down to the vast moon-sparkled lake. The thump of his car door silenced a chorus of crickets. He stepped over two sets of deep ruts marring the turf and climbed a short set of steps to the pool level.

The submerged pool lights gave the water a green tint and the smell of chlorine tinged the air. The huge house was dark save for two shrouded windows on the upper level.

Damn, how do two people get by with only ten thousand square feet of living space? Aki pictured his modest one-story stucco in the southeast Minneapolis Nokomis neighborhood—it had been home to a family of three.

A hollowness filled his chest.

One night he brought his wife to the hospital. She went to the OR for surgery on what turned out to be a ruptured appendix. When she woke up, he wasn't there.

A snitch with info on an active case had paged him. He'd left the hospital to meet him.

That had been the last time she'd let him put the job first. After her hospitalization she'd taken their daughter and moved back to California.

Aki scanned the massive home once more.

He wished he'd had the chance to get a timely read on the husband. Dr. Jon Malar stood to inherit millions. Did his reaction to the news of her death reveal anything?

Playing catch-up meant Aki had missed the opportunity to find out.

Dr. Malar had been working in the ER when his wife died. Dr. Cody's poolside witness said that no one had been near Faith Reinhorst-Malar beforehand. If it was murder, it was accomplished indirectly. The doctor's presence in the ER would not eliminate him as a suspect.

Aki had learned that the uniforms at the scene had contacted Homicide immediately, but Newton Farley, the homicide rookie, had fielded the call. Aki's call to Detective Farley while driving the lakeside road had rolled to voice mail. Now he checked his contacts and entered another number. A sleep-fuzzed voice answered.

"Crime scene on-call, chief technician Dilger here."

"Ted—Aki Yamada. Sorry for the hour. Did you work the Reinhorst-Malar scene?"

"This isn't a call-out on a new case?"

"No. I'm playing catch-up on the possible drowning."

"I'm relieved." The phone muffled for a moment. "Okay. What do you need?"

"Tell me what went down at the scene."

"My team arrived and started processing as per protocol for a priority ME case. Your new guy, Farley, showed up a little later. He talked to the uniforms, spent a minute talking to the caretaker, and looked over the body just before the coroner's crew loaded her up. Anyway, next thing I know Farley, kind of formal-like, announces to us all that he thinks the death is accidental. Then he left."

Aki's gut dropped. *Damn.*

"I figured he'd never handled a priority ME case before. The guy looks like he just got out of high school, but he's got the gold shield so I didn't challenge him. But I made sure we worked everything to the nines just in case."

Aki let out a big breath. "Strong work. This case could end up biting us in the ass. What'd you find?"

"Nothing incriminating. We pulled a cell phone from the bottom of the pool and a towel from the diving board. I personally checked them both for any trace of foreign substances. They were negative. I sent the cell phone to the lab to see if anything can be salvaged from its memory."

"The site was clean?"

"We worked it A to Z. No evidence of foul play. Unless the ME comes up with something, your rookie looks to have called it right."

"Sounds good. Get some sleep." Aki disconnected.

Detective Newton Farley had a total of nine days experience in Homicide. Reportedly the chubby, young cop had been a star in the white-collar crimes division. White collar was the realm of desk jockeys and paper-pushers. Homicide was a different animal.

The rookie's premature assessment as accidental explained why Aki was contacted late and misinformed about the status of Faith Reinhorst-Malar's death.

He ran a hand over the sandpaper-like surface of the diving board. Maybe it had been a simple drowning—no evidence suggested otherwise.

Aki pictured Doc Cody's piercing eyes. He'd said the death gave him "a bad feeling in his gut." The ER doc was good. His impressions on other cases were always solid.

Damn. The doctor had infected Aki with his gut feeling.

The detective surveyed the pool area. A wealthy and beautiful young woman had died here only hours ago.

Doc Cody had mentioned the possibility of drugs or alcohol. A medical event, booze or drug use wouldn't make the young woman's death less tragic—but it would keep Homicide's—and Aki's ass out of the fire.

The Police Chief's signature had barely dried on the reprimand Aki had been hit with. Aki had apprehended a man in violation of a restraining order filed by his ex-wife. The ex-husband had been abusing her for years and had previously broken the woman's jaw. When she finally reported him, the protective order was all the law could provide. Its violation was not a jailable offense.

As Aki had uncuffed him, the brute smiled. "That bitch still got an asskicking coming."

The man then *accidentally* had his head slammed against the hood of a car. Aki let him know that worse accidents would occur if he came within a mile of the ex-wife.

The Civilian Review Board had pursued the asshole's claim of brutality.

The Chief's formal reprimand left Aki's job at risk. He couldn't afford to lose his detective's shield. Nailing murderers was his passion and paycheck rolled into one. Hell, he'd do it for free.

He descended the poolside steps to the lawn. The scene yielded no evidence of wrongdoing. Farley's assessment had been hasty, but could be right.

On the other hand, the dead woman's father was a political powerhouse and big-time wealthy. If the ME found evidence of anything hinky, the department's actions would receive OJ-like scrutiny. The initial mishandling would fuel a front-page barbecue. The Chief would make somebody pay.

Crossing the tire-scarred turf, he pulled out his phone. His stomach churned. He hated playing catch-up.

Chapter 9

Wyndham Grand Hotel, late evening

Meryl sat in the hotel's lounge at a table near the bar, enjoying the pleasant heaviness of her well-worked muscles. The patio doors hung open to the night's breeze. Her laptop lay on the table.

"I heard the server address you as doctor. Can I schedule an appointment?" The tall good-looking, thirty-something man posed at her tableside, expensively dressed and dripping confidence.

Meryl's V-necked top revealed the only softness of her body. She sipped her tequila before looking up. "Not that kind of doctor, boy. I have doctoral degrees in pharmacology and medicinal chemistry." She raked him with her eyes, blowtorching his bravado. "I have zero interest in any kind of appointment with you."

He deflated and skulked away. She smiled inside.

The TV mounted over the bar was tuned to the nightly news. The screen filled with an image of Faith. Meryl sprang to her feet and moved closer.

"…a society-pages regular and trust-fund beauty. An attorney married to an emergency physician but best known as the daughter of wealthy, political powerhouse Andrew Reinhorst. Faith Reinhorst-Malar pronounced dead today due to a suspected drowning in the pool of her Wayzata estate."

Meryl closed her eyes and controlled her breathing. She pressed her hands flat on the bar's surface.

Faith.

A tide of images flooded—the matchless face, the voluptuous yet athletic body, silk-soft golden skin, and eyes bluer than seemed possible. Meryl hugged her arms across her chest. It was as if she could still feel her, just as she had this morning.

Meryl found herself back at her table.

The first touch of Faith's hand had been like the rush of some incredible drug. The following weeks a dream.

Now Faith was history.

She took a generous sip of the tequila and let the liquid heat bathe her tongue.

Faith's beauty and sexual magnificence had made Meryl want to believe that what they had went beyond pleasure and personal gain. *Absurd.*

She damn well knew better.

Emotions were nothing more than the product of transient neuronal output. Countless synapses relayed sensory information into the most evolutionarily ancient portion of the brain. Neurotransmitters triggered cellular activation with the output perceived as emotion. These primitive "feelings" stimulated behaviors that improved early man's likelihood of survival.

The notion that such neurochemical-phenomena represented "love" or any other such noble fiction was a delusion of the scientifically ignorant.

Meryl used a spoon to push a segment of Mandarin orange about the small bowl. She admired the rippling muscles of her forearm.

Two days earlier, she'd answered one of Heinrich's calls and learned that Faith had begun negotiating directly with a Swiss pharmaceutical firm. She'd been attempting to double-cross BioZyn and reap all the riches of drug D-44 for herself.

Faith—damn her greedy, perfect ass.

Meryl swirled her drink, staring at the circling liquid. She raised the glass in a silent toast. A tear traced her cheek. She wiped the wetness away.

The screen of her laptop blinked. She returned to the email intended for Heinrich.

It had been two years since Heinrich had persuaded Meryl to join BioZyn. Technically, he was her boss. Even more ridiculous, he considered himself her superior. The increasingly annoying German answered only to the Board.

News of Faith's death would fluster him. Faith had completed her essential assignment. Meryl would handle all the rest. Nonetheless Heinrich would bitch. It was his way.

Continually dealing with people of lesser intelligence challenged her patience. Working with a dullard that presumed superiority seriously pissed her off.

She finished the email and hit send.

Her role could be described in one word—mastermind. Heinrich and the BioZyn board were riding on her brilliance.

She spooned a section of orange into her mouth and savored its sweetness. Smarter, stronger and better than those around her—and soon she'd be set-for-life rich. Meryl would not allow Faith's betrayal or Heinrich's nagging to drag her down.

She scanned the lounge.

The stereotypes of lesbian life made her laugh. Androgynous or dumpy women in sweatshirts holding hands and sharing cozy, placid relationships. As if sex wasn't even a part of it. As if they were all the same.

She scanned the lounge again. No more Faith. Meryl had needs. She rolled her neck and flexed the muscles of her arms and shoulders. *Cozy this, bitches.*

Chapter 10

Southern Andes, Argentina

The powder billowed at waist-level above Heinrich's skis as he sliced a sinuous trace down the sun-bathed slope. He relished his skilled negotiation of gravity, snow and speed.

Trailing above and behind, leaving halting tracks, were his three heli-skiing guests and the Argentine guide.

The helicopter perched on the ridgeline below, near the slope's junction with the tree line.

Heinrich's thighs burned and his lungs hungered as he drove hard. Nearing the helicopter he could see where the rotors had blown away the snow, forming a shallow bowl. He carved a power stop at the depression's apex. His chest heaved as he scanned the slope above him.

The trailing skiers traversed the deep powder making frequent stops in the high-altitude thinness. His guests were the product acquisition heads of their respective non-U.S. based pharmaceutical firms. Two of the men were European and had purchased pirated drug research from BioZyn before. The third represented a newer Malaysian firm.

Their halting trails bisected Heinrich's S-shaped trace, forming in some places what looked like dollar signs. He smiled.

World-class heli-skiing followed by wine and fine dining would put the executives in an expansive frame of mind. All was going according to plan. Heinrich loved it when things went according to plan. This deal would dwarf the total of BioZyn's previous schemes.

The rest of the day progressed successfully. Now, late in the evening, Heinrich sat alone in his suite in front of a raised fireplace. He set down a large snifter of cognac as he accessed his laptop.

While awaiting the encrypted uplink, he considered the responses of the pharmaceutical executives to his post-dinner overture. He smiled and took a sip of the Remy-Martin.

His presentation of the results and potential of the NeurVitae spinal cord injury drug had provoked wide eyes and sidelong glances. Each executive had tried to conceal from the others their lust for such a product.

BioZyn's pharmacology consultants all agreed with Meryl's assessment. The young ER doctors had somehow come up with what could be the most promising drug in the history of neurologic care.

Heinrich had recently reviewed the sales of Rituxan, a drug used in the treatment of some lymphomas; annual sales exceeded $6 billion dollars. If D-44's promise were realized, it would eclipse that total. Downstream payments based on D-44 revenues would be a part of their contract.

The BioZyn board, Heinrich and Meryl would all reap fortunes. His neck and shoulders tingled and his breath came fast. This deal was the one. He'd be rich beyond his dreams.

His laptop beeped as the link completed. An email sent from "Mastermind" with the subject "obstacle management" grabbed his attention. He hit open.

> *NeurVitae attorney dead today in reported drowning. Legal instruments for product transfer intact and in-hand. Complete research protocols and required documentation are secure. The molecular identity and synthesis pathway for D-44 are not yet in my possession. I have assured acquisition in the near term.*

Faith Reinhorst-Malar had died and D-44 was not yet in their possession. *Gott verdammt!*

Heinrich clenched his teeth. His excellent mood had crashed like a downhill racer losing a ski at high speed. Meryl had assured him she'd have the drug information days ago.

Without it, they had nothing.

Could he trust her newest assurance? Heinrich had used intelligence, experience, and attention to detail to craft a virtually risk-free plan.

The reckless American bitch had run his plan off the tracks. Things were getting messy. He hated messy.

At least the double-dealing attorney-wife had produced the needed documents before she died. The setup for transfer stood ready, but they had to have D-44's molecular identity and synthesis pathway. Soon.

He took another large swallow of cognac.

Heinrich had revealed BioZyn's clandestine research theft enterprise to Meryl several months after her hire. Did it matter to her that BioZyn engaged in biomedical research theft, stock market manipulation, and extortion?

"It's an open door to serious money. I want in," she'd responded. The bizarre but brilliant scientist craved wealth as hungrily as Heinrich did.

He bent and placed a split cedar log in the fire.

BioZyn had the U.S. Food and Drug Administration and its absurd policies to thank for their illicit and highly profitable enterprise. In the U.S., the NeurVitae doctors' successful animal results would require a minimum of three years and millions of dollars in additional studies before human testing was allowed. Even then, the U.S. restrictions and litigation risks were extreme.

The FDA's obstructionist policies crippled American research efforts—they were fools.

In Europe and Asia, successful animal research could advance to human testing in less than six months. The costs and liability risks were a fraction of that in the U.S.

These realities created a raging overseas market for promising U.S. research. Heinrich loved exploiting the researchers and the U.S. system. His elegant theft strategies were based on the manipulation of human weakness. Blackmail and extortion were his favored schemes. Violence was the tool of failed intellect and one that he worked to avoid. His BioZyn successes produced the same kind of thrill he'd felt as a youth chess champion outwitting tournament opponents.

He sat back and watched flames dance along the top of the log.

His ski partners and their multibillion dollar firms didn't care about the origins of the promising new drugs BioZyn provided. They cared about profit.

The announcement of a drug with the potential to treat spinal cord injury would skyrocket the acquiring company's stock value. BioZyn would provide documentation establishing a legitimate-appearing basis for the transfer of ownership of the researchers' intellectual property. The pharmaceutical corporation would have no incentive to look further. Their profits would be secure.

Heinrich looked into his drink. Should he notify the BioZyn board of Meryl's failed timetable and growing impertinence? The thought made his gut roil.

Meryl's failure would be his failure.

BioZyn's network of agents had already executed millions in anticipatory stock purchases and stock options in one of the European firms. The Board had decided before bidding was initiated which firm was positioned to yield the greatest returns.

If the selected firm didn't announce acquisition of the investigational new drug by the thirteenth of the month, the jump in their stock price wouldn't happen before the options expired. Missing the deadline would strip BioZyn of a portion of their anticipated gains.

The fire swelled, glowing hot on his face. He leaned back.

Heinrich picked up a walnut from the tabletop dish. Meryl no longer answered his calls. He used the gilt nutcracker and broke open the woody husk. The sound triggered thoughts of the BioZyn board and those who disappointed.

* * *

It was winter in Paris. Heinrich was nearing completion of his first special assignment. The French pharmaceutical giant, Aristan, had purchased the rights to a pirated U.S. developmental drug.

The BioZyn board discovered that an attorney, one of the French firm's agents, had diverted money into his personal account. The Board labeled the attorney's actions as "disappointing."

They instructed Heinrich to arrange a private meeting with the attorney.

He arrived at the man's office at nine p.m., as scheduled. He sensed the attorney's unease in his nonstop, forced chatter. The Frenchman's cluttered office reeked of body odor and cigarettes.

The three BioZyn operatives burst into the room five minutes later. They duct-taped the whimpering man to a chair and gagged him. Workmanlike and without reaction to his muted screams, the leader used a pair of pliers to sequentially break each of the fingers of the attorney's left hand. The muffled howls did not cover the sound of the bones breaking.

Heinrich jumped with each startlingly loud "sna-crack." The ruined digits were left grotesquely deformed. Blood oozed and bony shards protruded.

Heinrich's stomach contents hit the floor at the same time as the first drops of blood.

* * *

The fire popped and an ember jumped onto the tabletop next to Heinrich's laptop. If Meryl failed to obtain the D-44 information before the deadline, BioZyn's returns would be diminished.

The Board would be disappointed.

Heinrich shivered.

Chapter 11

Northeast Minneapolis, rental townhome

Rachelle Cody feared she was losing her mind—again.

The clock ticked 8:31, and the odor of dinner lingered. Dirty dinner plates and cookware lay on the kitchen counter with grease congealing. The sky peeking under the kitchen curtain had shifted to gray. Time moved as if she were on death row waiting for them to come for her.

Thwack! The noise blasted from the speaker of the audio monitor. Rachelle flinched. The monitor amplified the sound of six-year-old Shane's hockey stick scraping along the unfinished basement's floor.

Thwack! Another slap shot smacking the plastic hockey puck off a concrete wall. Rachelle reached to the shelf above the computer and turned down the volume of the basement monitor. The upstairs monitor continued its soft hiss.

Four year-old Kristin knelt on a chair at the kitchen table, bent over her drawing paper.

Rachelle closed down the computer. She'd scanned hundreds of searches but found nothing helpful.

Earlier, she'd tried to convince herself that the coming crisis might yet be avoided. Now she considered only how and if they could withstand the fallout.

Rachelle rolled one of her pills, one of the red ones prescribed "as needed for anxiety," between her fingers. Today it should read "as needed for when you are going to lose everything."

The doctors labeled her as PTSD with anxiety disorder and depression. She'd occasionally overheard the mental health clinics and agency workers use the diagnoses interchangeably with her name. "We have one left to see—the anxiety and PTSD."

She wanted to resist the drug, but it was as if she had already slipped into its soothing fog.

The ceiling fluorescent shined feebly in the evening's descending darkness. The worn, rental townhouse unit looked particularly shabby in the artificial glow.

Thwack! She pictured Shane, like a little Drake, strong and quick with eyes locked in concentration. Work or play, Drake never lost focus. He flew in helicopters and saved lives. His research sought to make the paralyzed walk.

She worked at getting dried macaroni and cheese out of pants pockets and rescuing Barbie doll accessories from the garbage disposal, all the while struggling to avoid falling apart—her memory a storehouse of proof that terrible things could happen.

She slipped the pill into her mouth. Did a child-proof bottle and prescription really make it any different than street drugs?

Weren't they both just ways to cover the fear?

It was likely one part of why painting meant so much to her. Standing at an easel outdoors, she could lose herself in beauty and the dynamic of light. Her attempts to capture it transported her. She forgot her fear.

They'd found a middle-aged baby-sitter that met Rachelle's fanatical reliability assessment and allowed her to occasionally get out.

This morning the sitter had freed Rachelle for a couple of hours. It seemed forever ago.

She slid into the chair next to Kristin. Rachelle fought to keep her arms from trembling as she gave her little one a hug. Kristin spoke as she continued her artwork.

"Here's you and me, Mommy. That's Shane. See? You're doing vacuum." Off towards the edge she drew more. "This is Daddy. He's going to the hospital to save people. But he has to stop and take care of his cats. Look. That's him going away again."

"Yes, honey, I see." Rachelle's voice broke. "He's going away." Her vision fuzzed and hot tears wet her cheeks.

She and Drake had fought two nights before. Sometimes it felt like she existed only to help him achieve his goals. Her resentment had boiled over. She'd wanted to fight.

Now it was a gnawing regret. It wasn't just *his* goals—it was *their* dreams.

Kristin saw Rachelle's tears and her eyes went wide. Her lips pursed then she nodded. "Is it your sadness again, Mommy?"

Rachelle wiped her eyes and hugged Kristin tight. "I'm okay, my little love."

A mother must protect her family. That responsibility stood first in Rachelle's mind—she prayed she could hold herself together. She was drowning in doubt.

Kristin rested her cheek against Rachelle's. "You can't be sad, mommy."

Rachelle fingered the wedge-shaped patch of thick, deadened tissue overlying her neck and shoulder. Sometimes she woke up screaming.

Yes, my baby. Mommy can be sad.

Chapter 12

Drake glimpsed the wall clock as he passed the Crash Room. Almost midnight—his scheduled shift had ended fifty minutes earlier. Just two patients to finish up and he'd be free.

The ER continued to hum. As Drake began an entry on one of the remaining charts, an angry, inner-city voice cut through the din.

"Fuck that I-bu-pro-feen shit. I ain't leaving without some Oxys, Percs or something heavy. I got me a toothache."

Drake turned. A large black guy in a do-rag, Oakland Raider's jersey, and low-rider pants leaned over Patti. They stood in the corridor at the door to a nearby room. Patti held discharge instruction and prescription print-outs in her hand.

He looked to be early twenties, gold chains and gang-tattoos visible over the strained tendons of his neck.

Patti held the discharge and prescription sheets out. "Sir, this is what Dr. Rizzini prescribed—antibiotics and ibuprofen. I also have a referral to the dental clinic for tomorrow morning. I heard Dr. Rizzini discuss this with you."

"You ain't hearing me, bitch." He slapped the papers out of her hand. They fluttered to the floor as he pushed even closer. "Get me a subscription for the for-real shit. I ain't playing."

Patti shrunk against the wall.

Drake spoke over his shoulder to the secretary as he moved. "Security. Now." He took quick strides and called out, forcing a smile and holding his hands wide and palms up. "Whoa. Hey, hey, partner. I can talk with you. Let's give the lady some space."

The drug-seeker turned, his face a snarl. He looked Drake up and down. "Kiss my ass, white bread. You s'posed to be a bad boy? And I ain't your damn partner, faggot." He faced Patti. "And I ain't leaving till this bitch," he rapped Patti hard in the chest with his knuckles, "gets me my—"

The heat flared fast and red. "Don't touch her again. For real," Drake said, prison-hard, as he moved closer. Drumming began in his head. His vision sharpened. The smell of booze, body odor, and menthol cigarettes flooded in.

The patient cocked his hand back again and started it forward. Time slowed. Before the hand hit Patti, Drake deflected it. The big man spun, fast-balling a fist towards Drake's face.

Drake's senses hummed, his movements reflex-fast. He slipped the punch and fired his right hand into the man's ribs. The gang-banger grunted, lurching sideways but maintaining his feet. He launched another swing.

Drake beat the punch, burying his left fist in the guy's gut. The brute doubled over, his face pitching forward into Drake's upward slashing elbow. The bone and cartilage made a sound like snapping celery as the nose flattened. The man moaned. Blood jetted from his face.

Drake turned and moved Patti clear. The banger bellowed and lunged. Drake shifted and whip-kicked his right foot into the man's groin. The hulk dropped to his knees. Drake slid behind and locked his arms around the thick neck in a posterior chokehold. He squeezed. The drumming in his head drowned all sound. He faintly registered thrashing resistance and clawing fingers. The body went limp.

And still Drake squeezed.

He felt pounding on his back and shoulders. New hands pulled at him. The drumming began to slow and fade. Rizz's voice penetrated. "No, Drake. No."

Drake let his arms go. The weight fell away.

The burly body slumped to the floor at Drake's feet.

Exhilaration bathed him—the satisfaction all-absorbing. The threat was gone and everything was fundamentally right. It was beyond any drug and as intense as sex, yet not at all sexual. Something primitive and savage, yet noble and just.

Rizz bent over the unmoving thug. "C'mon, asshole. Breathe." He ground a knuckle into the man's chest without a response. "Aw shit." He looked up. "Someone grab me an airway and bag."

As Drake watched, the downed body bucked and gave a snorting gasp. Bloody spittle flew on the exhale. Lost eyes opened, blinking wildly. The whites showed blood-shot pink. He looked to be somewhere far away.

Patti stood pale-faced, her palm rubbing the center of her chest.

Drake turned to her. "Are you okay?"

She looked at the downed man. "That was way scary." Her gaze met Drake's. Unease showed in her eyes. "Were you going to kill him?"

Drake felt himself flush. He looked away.

Rizz spoke to the two security guards as they arrived and stood expectantly on either side of the bleeding offender. "Let's lock this guy in room fifteen until the cops get here. And check him for weapons, will ya?"

Rizz grabbed a clean towel and flipped it onto the lap of the bleeding man. "I'll have to examine and treat him again. I did a pharmacy search on him earlier. Twenty narcotics prescriptions filled from different doctors in the last thirty days. He was busted six weeks ago with a forged script for fifty Oxycontin. And he was picked up for selling narcotics last fall, but got dumped right back on the street. Maybe an assault conviction will change that."

The gangbanger now sat on the floor with his back against the wall, holding the towel to his nose. His words came nasal and grim as his eyes aimed ugly at Drake. "You gonna pay." The attacker hawked and spat blood.

The discharge instruction and prescription papers lay crumpled on the floor.

Chapter 13

Drake entered 2121 Sumpter Lane, Unit C. Spackle-patched walls separated the aging two-level townhouse from identical units on either side. The wall clock read 12:25 a.m. An overhead circle-tube fluorescent illuminated the small combination living room and kitchen. The odor and humidity of macaroni and boiled hot dogs hung in the air. A plastic garbage bag gaped overfull next to the back door. Toys were stacked in a jumble next to the stairwell.

Drake smiled at his son's hockey stick, left beside the door for ready access in the morning. Kristin's prized Big Wheel sat next to the stick. Her rainbow-colored helmet rested on the seat.

Their little one's reckless, high-speed inclination assured plenty of bumps and scrapes. She was one part Fashion Barbie and two parts Evel Knievel. He checked Shane's hockey stick for splinters and Kristin's helmet to see that the strap and pads were intact. He resisted the urge to run up the stairs and awaken them.

He hungered for Rachelle and the kids.

Even now, in his fourth and final year of Emergency Medicine specialty training, the hours were inhuman and the pay paltry. Drake had been a fully licensed physician for four years and he still didn't make near enough to pay the bills. He'd averaged more than eighty hours per week in the hospital for the past four years. And their debt load continued to grow.

Rachelle carried the burdens of home and child care alone while he was forever gone.

Drake wet a dishrag and began to clear and wipe down the counters. He came to a stack of mail. On the top envelope was written in Rachelle's cursive, "What are we going to do about these???" He put down the rag and flipped through the stack. Car insurance, rent, payments on his mortgage–sized total of undergraduate and medical school loans, healthcare expenses for his mother in Ohio, credit card bills for their multiple maxed-out accounts and, last, a printout of their checking account balance: $37.00.

Drake dropped the stack of bills onto the tabletop. The hot dog and macaroni aroma persisted. He picked up the rag and finished the countertop, then grabbed the garbage bag.

He and Rachelle were in the middle of a rough stretch. Two nights earlier they'd quarreled and it still gnawed at him.

He'd come home late after a brutal shift.

A thirty-one-year-old mother of two had the onset of a headache at the grocery store. She collapsed and was raced by ambulance to the Crash room. An aneurysm had ruptured in her brain. Drake could not save her.

A forty-three-year-old worker was blown thirty yards in the air by an exploding industrial fuel tank. Drake arrived on the scene by helicopter. The man suffered severe blunt trauma and third-degree burns over eighty-five percent of his body. Drake injected the man with hospice doses of narcotics and held his hand in flight. He agreed to the man's request to deliver his message of love to his wife and three children. The worker's last breaths came as they exited the flight elevator.

Drake made two trips during that shift to the windowless Family Room adjacent to the ER where loved ones waited, sick with apprehension.

Drake tried his best to deliver the message in the least painful way, but the reality defied anesthetic—*the person you love is dead.*

Anguish and tears.

He had answered questions but mostly held hands and hugged the devastated friends and family of people whose lives had been cruelly ended.

He'd driven home with no memory of seeing the road. Hours late, and he'd forgotten to pick up the milk that Rachelle had requested earlier. He'd also failed to call.

Rachelle's angry greeting still stung. He'd not picked up the milk or called because he didn't "give a damn" about her or anyone else, and nothing mattered to him but "the ER and your damn research."

As they talked past each other, he realized that he'd somehow spaced out the lab and animal cares. He had to leave. The research meant everything.

He'd tried to apologize as he went out the door.

Rachelle had been in tears. He'd felt like shit. There'd been no opportunity to patch things up since.

Rachelle couldn't know what he experienced on the job. He occasionally related the happy outcomes, the funny or interesting things, but he kept the dark side to himself. She'd had enough pain.

Drake carried the bag of garbage out the back door into the night. He passed through their eight-by-eight fenced enclosure to the alley's collection of garbage cans. The night was hazy, the moon full, and the temperature had cooled to the humid mid-seventies. As he opened the garbage container the stink caused him to draw back. He tossed in the bag and closed the cover. He turned and looked over their shoddy rental property.

Rachelle struggled with emotional and mental health burdens that weren't helped by his prolonged absence. His mother lived damaged and alone back in Ohio—she was an ultra-Catholic like Jon. Her religion delivered her more comfort than anything Drake provided.

He was torn but he could not compromise the life-or-death demands of the ER or his vital research. No matter how hard he tried, he couldn't meet all his responsibilities.

The tone of his thoughts broke through. *Lighten up, whiner.*

He stopped next to the tiny garden plot that Rachelle had shoe-horned into their enclosure. The fragrance of mint and basil purged the odor of the garbage containers. The plants thrived.

Next year would be better. The marathon schedule of his Emergency Medicine training would be history and he'd start getting paid well. He'd be nearer to his dream of helping those with spinal cord injury, and NeurVitae might be a source of income rather than just a legally registered pipe dream.

He'd provide his mother the best care possible. Rachelle wouldn't have it so hard and would use less medication. She'd be able to paint. They'd have more time as a family.

He would make it all happen.

In spite of the tragedy of Faith's death and the problems he and Rachelle faced, when Drake thought of the research he soared. The possibilities were the stuff of his dreams—the answer for all who counted on him.

As he reached to turn off the kitchen light, Rachelle's note and the stack of bills caught his eye. He picked up the note and the neighboring pen. He wrote, *Expecting loan check next week!* He drew a smiley face and a valentine heart.

He hoped she'd smile.

Chapter 14

1:05 a.m.

Drake flipped the light switch, leaving the unit's ground floor in darkness. The stairs creaked as he crept up the stairs.

He stopped in the hall at the top of the stairs and cracked the door to peek in on the kids. Kristin lay curled in the midst of her gang of stuffed animals. Shane lay on his side with his hockey gloves beside the pillow. He watched their gentle breathing.

He closed the door, feeling like a lottery winner.

His cell phone sounded. He cuffed it silent, slipped back down the stairs, then answered as he moved toward the kitchen. "Drake Cody here."

"This is Dr. Dronen, a pissed off Medical Examiner here." The voice was strikingly high-pitched and nasal.

"Kip, I planned on calling you first thing in the morning." Drake felt relief. Although Kip Dronen was arrogant and a social cripple, no one was better at determining cause of death. "Are you working?" Drake flipped on the kitchen light.

"Am I working?" Kip mimicked Drake like a bratty child. "No, I'm calling you in the middle of the night to confess my flaming man-love." His whine returned. "Hell, yes, I'm working. Thanks to you."

Kip Dronen was in his early forties and married to his profession. Drake talked with Kip when following up on ER fatalities and had once helped the morgue-based pathologist with a study of trauma deaths. Kip had chosen the right specialty based on his sensitivity—he had none. He lived and breathed death and its causes.

"What the hell went down, ER guy? The story I've got is a chick splashes into her pool and doesn't come up. You copter to the scene and it's the wife of one of your own." He paused. "Son of a bitch. That must've been intense." Kip sounded envious.

When they first met, Drake thought the skeletal-appearing medical examiner was putting him on. Kip spoke construction-site crude and his remarks were often glaringly inappropriate. The Chief Medical Examiner position was a political appointment. Kip, in spite of his medical brilliance, had been stuck as "associate" chief for over a decade. Drake believed Kip did not have a clue why he was repeatedly passed over. If political incorrectness were a sport, Kip would be an Olympian.

"Yeah, Kip. My friend's wife. It's terrible."

"I looked at your Air Care report and declaration of death. It doesn't say jackshit. It couldn't possibly be any less helpful."

"I wrote what I knew and that wasn't much. It looked like a drowning. She was pulled from the bottom of a pool. But a witness said she was looking at him as she died—*after* he'd pulled her out of the water. She was an athlete and the same witness saw no trauma. It's hard to figure her as a simple drowning." Drake moved a jar of peanut butter from the kitchen counter to the cupboard.

"That's why I assigned it as a priority ME case. I suspect something else contributed—aneurysm, cardiac, something. Possibly even drugs or alcohol. I spoke with the police, but I didn't think I'd be hearing from you tonight."

"Didn't think, huh? Effing try it next time. You got my ass dragged out of bed. The district attorney, the mayor's office, a homicide detective, and Andrew Reinhorst's executive assistant are all on my ass. Son of a bitch, I hadn't even laid eyes on her carcass and they were screaming for answers. You can't imagine the pressure I'm under." His whine grated.

"Kip, I spoke with Detective Yamada. And Andrew Reinhorst is her father. He—"

"I know who Reinhorst is. Shit, everyone knows who Reinhorst is. Why do you think my lame-ass chief called me in? He's on call tonight, but he knows he's not effing good enough for a VIP. A fat-cat daddy means this soggy wench has gotta have the best." Kip managed to sound resentful and smug simultaneously.

"C'mon, Kip, show some respect. Her husband is my friend. I knew her."

"Excuse me all to hell. Pretend I'm saying something sensitive now." He paused a moment. "Okay, that's long enough. I'm not into the grief-and-feelings drama. It's not rational. Death I understand—death makes sense."

Drake sighed. "Can you keep me updated on what you find?"

"I'm already running the standard toxicology screens but the autopsy is where it's at. With all this pressure, I'll have to slice and dice her tonight. If she had an aneurysm, a heart issue or whatever, I'll find it. And there are distinct findings in drowning but they aren't specific. Most any death that results from lack of oxygen shares similar features."

"Are you saying you might not be able to tell if she drowned?" A silence hung so long that Drake thought he'd been cut off.

"I said it *could* be tough to tell. Most pathologists would miss the distinction—like, for instance, the hack that holds the Chief position." His tone rose. "But I'm sure as hell not most pathologists—am I? Christ sakes, ER, show me some effing respect." His whine hit helium heights.

"Sorry. I know you're a genius and definitely the man in forensic pathology." Drake paused after the ass-kissing. He pictured Kip nodding in agreement. "Can I call you later for your preliminary findings?"

"Totally against policy," Kip said and Drake drooped. "But," he added, "for someone who's sharp enough to recognize I'm the man, what the hell?" He chuckled. "I haven't forgotten you helped with my trauma study. That baby made The Journal of Forensic Pathology. Impressive, huh?" He sounded like a bragging parent. "If you want I'll even call you, but it won't be until afternoon."

"I appreciate it, but let me call you. I'll be in the ER and it's hard for me to take calls or talk for more than a second."

"Damn, that must suck. My patients are never in a hurry." He snickered. "But they definitely are dying to see me."

Drake rolled his eyes as the connection ended.

He entered the bedroom. Rachelle slumbered on her side. Her sheet-draped body lay silhouetted by the glow of the parking lot light penetrating the shade. She had the modest but perfect curves and lithe frame of a modern dancer. Her dark hair and olive skin lay in shadow. He sat at the bedside, watching her as he removed his shoes. As his eyes adjusted to the low light her loveliness showed more clearly.

Viewing her never failed to move him.

Other than their love of the kids, their sexual connection was the most powerful. Two guarded people who, due to chemistry or whatever controlled such things, reveled in one another. Clichéd as it sounded, Drake believed they were meant to be.

It seemed against the odds.

He slid into bed next to her. She slept quietly. Too many nights she writhed and cried out. He hoped she hadn't used any of her "as needed" medications tonight.

Drake hadn't been free to call her until very late. He'd shared the bare-bones report of Faith's death.

Initially she'd said nothing, leaving him off balance. Then he'd recognized the sound of muffled crying. Thankfully, her reaction hadn't been worse.

Rachelle's breathing altered. She rolled onto her back. Her thick, black hair fell away from her neck and left shoulder. The scar started just below her ear and extended down her neck, broadening and dying out at the point of her shoulder. The tissue lay thick and cruelly twisted. In the subdued light it looked like a darkened flow, as if of molten wax.

Only he ever saw her so exposed. She never spoke of the injury other than to say it was a childhood accident. Her self-consciousness dictated high collars and the artful placement of scarves and hair. He traced the outline of the scar with his fingertips, his throat clenched as he imagined her pain.

She stirred and draped a hand across his chest, then started awake. "Oh, Drake, how's Jon?" She clung to him with her cheek pressed to his chest

"Pretty rough." Drake stroked her hair.

She held him tight without words for some seconds then lifted up on an elbow. "Where was he when she died?"

"In the ER. I told him as soon as we landed." He sighed. "His folks were driving down from Duluth. I'm sure they're with him now."

"You told him in the ER? It must have been horrible."

Drake kept Jon's puzzling reaction to himself.

She laid her head in the angle between his arm and chest. "I saw Faith yesterday. She brought NeurVitae papers here for me to sign." She put a hand on his chest. "It doesn't seem real she's gone."

"It's unbelievable." Drake brought his arm down around her. "There was another issue tonight."

"After Faith's death, what could there be?"

"A patient assaulted Patti and I had to take him down."

Rachelle got to her elbow again. "Are you okay? Is Patti okay?"

"He scratched my arms, got some of his blood on me. Patti is sore but okay."

"Oh, Drake, is he an addict or sick? Could he give you AIDS?"

"Rizz drew blood from the guy for testing. The risk is small."

"The risk is small." Rachelle said, her voice tight. She stiffened and pulled back. "That scares me."

"You're safe." He hugged her close. "I can't possibly be infectious yet." He tried a smile.

"That's not funny," she said, but nestled closer.

"We kid about ER shifts from hell," said Drake. "This was the real thing."

Drake thought of the heat, the drumming in his head and how incredibly right it felt standing over the gang banger's slumped body.

He'd felt that exhilaration before. The first time had been in Cincinnati years ago. He'd ended up sprawled on a section of cracked sidewalk near injured bodies with the taste of blood in his mouth and the sound of approaching sirens. They'd abused his younger brother, Kevin.

Drake had done what he knew was right.

It had ripped their lives apart.

Chapter 15

River apartments, downtown Minneapolis, 4:42 a.m.

Michael Rizzini gasped awake, covered in sweat, fear-sick but with a hard-on so intense it hurt. His dream was lost, but pieces of his encounter with Faith picked up in his head.

She'd had a key, surprising him as she opened the door to the lab. In recall, he could see her position her shoulder bag on a table top.

He'd vowed to never be alone with her again. There was nothing good that could come from it.

She turned from her bag, holding a bottle of red wine, her smile a gloat. He kept the lab table between them as she poured two glasses full. She sipped the wine, set down her glass, then slipped off her silken top.

His breath and all sensible thought left him. *How can anyone be so beautiful?*

A joint materialized in her hand and she snapped a lighter, then inhaled. She flashed a triumphant smile through the smoke, her eyes already celebrating his surrender.

He'd been diamond-hard as she rode him, her flawless face lost in private pleasure. Her body enveloping him in velvet fire—a partner unlike any other. Then, for an instant, her face morphed, like the perception flip phenomenon of the drawing of the woman/old hag. He'd glimpsed ugliness—a monster. It had freaked him and, at the time, he'd thought it was due to the drugs he'd so recklessly tried.

Afterwards he'd submerged into a pool of self-loathing. Jon's wife—it was so wrong.

Rizz climbed out of bed, bumping the bedside table, knocking his cell phone to the floor, and nearly tipping a half-filled glass of whiskey. He crossed to the door then stepped onto the balcony of his fourth floor riverside apartment. His gut remained knotted as he looked down and made out the milky whiteness of the rapids in the pre-dawn blackness.

The next day Faith had contacted him with her blackmail demands. She'd secretly videotaped their betrayal and his drug use.

"I own you." She'd demanded he turn over the breakthrough drug information and bragged about her unstoppable scheme.

He'd delayed by handing over pieces, but not the entirety of the research while desperately seeking a way to escape her grasp.

Now she was gone.

Stepping to the deck railing, he clenched it with both hands. He closed his eyes and took deep breaths while tension drained from him like water from a wrung sponge.

Faith is dead. I'm free.

* * *

Still an hour before sunrise, but Rizz couldn't sleep. He'd dodged the worst for now but feared he might yet pay a higher price.

He powered up his laptop and reviewed the initiative he'd developed to help welfare ER psychiatric patients who were not ill enough to require hospital admission.

Currently, they were discharged back into their often hellish social situations with no access to help. Rizz had engineered a program that used Social Services and the University's resident physicians in Psychiatry for follow-up. It would ease a lot of suffering.

He shook his head. Even this didn't feel as good anymore.

His guilt caused him to find an ugly side to even his best deeds. The most meaningful moments of his life were those he spent helping the sick and injured in the ER. The work he shared with Drake and Jon meant more to him than anything.

It didn't take a shrink to see his ER efforts provided salve for a challenged conscience. Out of control partying and sex had led him off a cliff.

His recent sins would require more than salve.

The cell phone sounded. The caller screen showed *blocked.* He checked the time. No one who knew him would call this early.

"Michael Rizzini here."

"Good morning, Dr. Loser." It was a woman's voice but harsh. "Our beautiful Faith is gone but we have the video. No more stalling. Get us the information today or we will destroy you. Keep your phone handy—you'll be called with further instructions."

His stomach heaved and he could not catch his breath.

Faith had not been working alone. Her death hadn't changed anything. *You fool!*

He sank to the bed, clutching his head.

He was end-it-all screwed.

* * *

Drake awoke and turned off the alarm two minutes before it was set to sound. Rachelle continued to breathe deep and rhythmic.

In the dawn light she looked even more beautiful.

They'd made love before they slept, and it made everything feel so right. It happened like that for them, from angry to incredible in a blink. Perhaps it was their shared concern for Jon, the shock of Faith's death, or shared regret for their previous fight. He hoped things were as good as they'd seemed.

He climbed out of bed and into the shower. After toweling off, he put on a clean pair of scrubs and slipped downstairs. Even with little sleep, he felt rested. He was grateful for his physical gifts. He slept little, didn't get ill, and his strength and energy never let him down.

Rachelle came down as Drake stood at the counter eating cereal. Shane and Kristin spilled down the stairs behind her. They frolicked around him like puppies.

He wrapped them in a spinning hug. They giggled and screamed. He set them at the table and reached for bowls and spoons.

Rachelle appeared relaxed.

Most days her fears regarding the kids' safety bordered on phobic. She rarely let them out of her sight and insisted on audio monitors on every floor. Drake knew a stream of scary "what ifs?" tormented her.

This morning she looked clear-eyed. She seemed stronger. Seeing her at ease made him smile.

He wanted to stay but could not. He kissed and hugged Shane and Kristin and tried to store some of their loving magic.

Rachelle hugged him but he felt hesitation. When their eyes met, she looked away.

The issues had not disappeared.

As Drake closed the front door behind him, a police car rolled into the parking lot. He held his breath.

The squad car turned and pulled up in front of his unit. Two officers, one with a clipboard, climbed out while looking Drake's way.

Son of a bitch. No.

He stepped off the stoop and approached the officers the way his time behind bars and barbed wire had taught him worked best.

Straight up, bold-faced and ready to lie.

Chapter 16

Drake exited the highway near the research lab. The roads were free of the worst of the morning rush. He'd slipped away from the police quickly. He'd showed respect, acted calm, and stretched the truth like pizza cheese.

Smiling, he'd shown his hospital I.D. while feeling as if he might vomit. It had taken all he had to maintain outward calm.

The police told him the offender from the ER had used his one call to contact a well-known activist attorney. The attorney had contacted the media. The mayor had been challenged as to why a vicious racist attack on an ill black man had occurred at the Hennepin-North hospital ER. And how and why did the *victim* end up under arrest?

The officers acted sympathetic but advised Drake they were required to question him as a suspect in a possible offense.

A possible offense? Drake had the stomach-falling-down-mine-shaft sensation he'd experienced in his previous dealings with the law.

He'd told them he was needed at work. He hadn't mentioned his shift didn't start for one and a half hours.

Drake mentioned he was working with a Homicide detective on a case. They were to meet at the hospital shortly. Might it be possible for the detective to complete any questioning at that time? He was sure that his friend, Detective Yamada, would vouch for him. The officers had made a radio call and let him go.

As Drake drove away, he'd been so freaked he tasted bile. Unexpectedly, he felt a flicker of pride. The violent juvenile offenders locked up in the Scioto correctional facility would have given him a nod for his smooth slide.

Drake needed to check on the research animals and then get to the ER in time for his shift. Yamada had said he'd be following up with Drake sometime today. Would Aki let the political and media pressure influence him. A six-foot-four, two-hundred-fifty-pound gangbanger had demanded drugs and struck a one-hundred-pound nurse. If sanity prevailed, the questioning would be a formality.

Drake slowed as he approached the lab's parking lot. The University Chemical Storehouse building had been built pre-World War Two, a couple miles off campus in Minneapolis's north side. Neither the neighborhood nor the two-story brick structure had aged gracefully. The building lay surrounded by decaying gravel-covered blacktop.

A wire fence separated the parking lot from the adjacent multi-unit complexes containing hundreds of subsidized housing units. The area was known citywide as the projects. Sirens and police visits were common.

The first floor of the university's building had been renovated for administrative office space in the mid-nineties. The windows were barred, and the offices always emptied before dark.

The second floor housed the lab space Drake, Rizz and Jon had been renting for the past four years. It had a separate entrance and stairwell. Drake pulled his rusty Dodge into the nearly empty lot. Even this morning, his pulse quickened as he anticipated the possibility of further progress.

A red Audi sat parked in the lot. It looked like Rizz's car. Drake looked twice. Rizz never came to the lab in the morning.

Drake closed the Dodge's door and strode across the lot.

Dr. Michael "Rizz" Rizzini combined equal parts bad boy and brilliance. Many considered him the department's rock star. Though three years younger than Drake, Rizz had started working as a paramedic just out of high school and had four years of in-the-trenches paramedic experience by the time he completed his pre-med studies.

Rizz had blown the top off the Medical College Admission Test and then led his medical school class in spite of what his advisers charitably called a "wild streak." Every surgical and medical specialty tried to recruit him. His choice came easily. He was born to be an Emergency Medicine physician.

Doctors, nurses, paramedics, orderlies, secretaries and patients loved Rizz. People of all stripes were drawn to the cocky and unflappable jokester.

Drake climbed the stone stairs to the second floor. The door out of the stairwell was heavy and fire resistant. It shut with a soft clank.

Drake moved through the hall towards the lab door. It dawned on him that Rizz might have ended his evening here. Perhaps he had company on the foldaway cot? A distinct possibility. His relationships with women were like fruit flies—numerous and short-lived.

Rizz and Jon were the only people in Minnesota Drake had risked letting get close. His friendship with the two very different men had been forged in the shared life-and-death experiences that were part of their medical training.

Jon was the straightest of arrows and Rizz the doctor most likely to be arrested for drunk and disorderly.

Drake opened the lab door a crack. Sunlight streamed through multi-paned windows illuminating high ceilings, a warped parquet floor, and several slate-topped work tables. The walls were crisscrossed with exposed pipes and ductwork. It wasn't fancy, but the space accommodated the cat kennels, lab equipment, and needs of their research activities.

Rizz sat at a table beside the open data storage cabinet. He was hunched over the laptop with the data entry book open alongside. Drake stepped through the door.

"The planets are in alignment, sunspot activity is flaring, and Michael Rizzini is in the lab at seven a.m. Talk about amazing phenomena."

Drake awaited a smart-ass comeback but instead Rizz punched a few keys and closed the laptop. He shut the leather-bound data entry log and clambered to his feet. He put his hands in his pockets, removed them, and then crossed his arms.

"Why are you here?" Rizz asked. "You're in the ER at nine, right?"

"Why am *I* here? You can't believe *I'm* here? Michael Rizzini in the lab before ten is a reportable event. But seven a.m.? You must be on drugs." Drake smiled in anticipation of a Rizz witticism.

"Drugs?" Rizz glared. "Kiss my ass. I came to check some data. This research is more than just you, hotshot." He leaned forward, fists clenched.

Drake was caught between a smile and a surge of anger. *What is this shit?*

Drake raised his hands, palms out. "Lighten up, amigo. I'm just bullshitting you. What's the deal?"

A brief chorus of groans and whooshes emanated from the exposed pipes. The odor of cedar shavings and cats drifted from the cages.

Rizz's face lost all edge as he shook his head, closed his eyes, and slumped back into the chair. Drake noticed Rizz's shirt was wrinkled and his face unshaven and puffy. The bitter scent of body odor mingled with the smells of the lab.

"I screwed up, Drake." Rizz's face crumpled. "I so totally and completely screwed up." His head sagged.

"What do you mean? What'd you do?"

"Faith," Rizz shook his head, his eyes averted. "I couldn't stop myself."

Drake's breath caught. He clutched at a chair and collapsed into it.

"My God, Rizz." His voice wavered. "What're you saying? You're freaking me."

A lone, soft yowl floated from the cages.

Chapter 17

Hennepin-North ER

Drake made it to the hospital ten minutes before the start of his nine o'clock shift.

His drive from the lab was a fog. *Faith and Rizz. Damn.*

An ugly morning—and it wasn't likely to get easier. Jon had been scheduled for an eight a.m. to eight p.m. shift. Physician staffing of the ER was tight in the best of times. Now was not the best of times—two senior ER residents were out on maternity leave and a second-year had quit the program with stress-related difficulties. The odds of a doctor having been found to cover Jon's shift were remote.

Drake shrugged. Working shorthanded had become a familiar burden.

He gave a thumbs-up to the security guard as he swiped his I.D. card through the access reader. Every time Drake entered the ER, he felt a tightness in his chest. It reminded him of the mix of excitement and apprehension he'd felt during the birth of his children.

People lived or died based on his actions. Some talked about doctors as "God." Drake figured God would have things under more control. God wouldn't finish a shift revisiting all His decisions or calling vulnerable patients at home to assure all was well.

Taking care of patients was only partly science and assuring the future was beyond human ability. Diagnosis and treatment were as dependent on communication and judgment as knowledge. Uncertainty was an unavoidable reality.

Drake found comfort in the simple vow he made at the beginning of each shift and whenever things got ugly: *I'll give all I've got and care for every person the best I can.* It felt hokey but he meant it.

The security guard waved Drake over. "Dr. Cody, there's rumor of protests about the arrest last night. Let us know if anyone gives you trouble."

Drake nodded while wincing inside. More attention directed his way. "Thanks." He entered the main ER.

Standing out in a pin-striped suit amongst the scrubs and white coats was Tim Tommins. Tim was a middle-aged physician who for the past three years had worked full-time as a hospital administrator. His position as head of Medical Affairs put him in the hot seat for all complaints concerning physician misconduct, real or perceived. He stood at the counter near the central secretary's station, then stepped forward as Drake approached.

Shit.

"Drake, can I steal you for a minute? We need to talk." He motioned for Drake to follow him down the hall. Tommins entered a cubicle in the farthest corner of the ER. He pulled the curtain closed behind them.

"First off, I want to share my condolences on the death of Dr. Malar's wife—tragic."

"Thanks."

"I don't know if you're aware, but the assault incident in the ER last night is big news."

Drake swallowed hard but remained silent.

"The mayor called our CEO an hour ago and the CEO called me. The media are painting this ugly. Community activists are jumping on board. It's being played as a racial thing. The police have questioned Patti Verker, your buddy Rizzini, and several other staff. What can you tell me?"

Drake's stomach knotted as he considered his stained past and risk of discovery. He thought of the asshole's abuse of Patti and shook his head.

"Come on, Tim, this is crap. The jerk wrote his own ticket. He demanded narcotics and laid hands on Patti. That's what happened. Race had nothing to do with it. He assaulted a nurse and deserved to be arrested."

Dr. Tommins frowned. "That sounds reasonable, but the guy has a broken nose and a couple of rib fractures." He sighed. "The newspaper and TV posted his booking photo and it looks like hell. His attorney and community leaders are representing it as a hospital and police beat-down of an innocent and ill black man. He claims he did nothing and you attacked him."

"All lies. He hit Patti and then swung on me. I protected her and myself. He deserved what he got. You're a doctor. You know the shit we take in the ER from drunk and offensive patients. ER nurses and doctors put up with verbal abuse and the threat of violence every shift. That's routine for us. But this guy went way over the line. You need to stand up for us."

"Whoa." Dr. Tommins raised a hand. "Nobody said we aren't going to stand up for you." He moved closer and spoke just above a whisper. "We have to deal with certain realities. The media loves the hype. The attorneys love money and attention. The activists often have a legitimate but unrelated ax to grind. The politicians all try to see who can look the most politically correct. Everyone has an agenda. The truth is secondary for many of these people. The best thing that can happen for us is that it just goes away."

"How's that going to happen?"

"Number one is we don't do anything to make it worse. Be friendly and say, 'No comment' to any and all media. Cooperate fully with the police. Can you do that?"

"We need to tell what really happened."

"Let me take care of that. The facts are in our favor. He has a history of abusing women. He's a confirmed gang criminal and drug pusher. They can't hide him or his record. He's seriously bad news." Tommins paused.

"Second, and damned lucky for us, is that it happened in the corridor. Dr. Rizzini figured it might be caught on the hallway camera. He salvaged the video last night. It shows the big guy striking Patti and swinging on you. His injuries are explained. Risk management and the hospital lawyers think things should die-down fast. It looks like a loser for the attorney and the activists. The hospital doesn't want the bad PR. We need the media to let it fade away."

Drake felt some relief. If the story died quickly he might avoid attention. He knew he should let it go.

"Would you and the hospital have backed me without the tape?" Drake looked Tommins in the eye. The administrator blinked.

"I'd like to think so." Tommins adjusted his coat. "But I've learned that justice does not always prevail. I wish it did."

"In this case, what's right is in the hospital's best interest."

Tommins shrugged. "One could say that."

"I appreciate the honesty." Drake extended his hand. "No comment and friendly to the media. Full cooperation with the police—consider it done." They shook.

Dr. Tommins slipped through the curtain.

Drake had heard a paramedic radio call overhead and sensed activity in the front of the ER while he and Tommins spoke. It was time to forget his problems and start his real work. *I'll give all I've got and care—*

The cubicle's curtain ripped back, support hooks clacking. Drake flinched. A nurse gripped the still swinging curtain, her eyes urgent and arrowing to Drake's.

"Dr. Cody. The Crash Room. Hurry. Dr. Malar needs you. A baby in trouble."

Chapter 18

Lab, 9:00 a.m.

A scattering of *meows* came from the kennels as Rizz reentered the lab. Facing Drake had been the last thing he wanted. Telling him the partial truth about his hook-up with Faith made it worse.

Lies on top of lies—everything was spinning out of control.

If he'd been thinking straight, he would have anticipated Drake's lab visit and dodged him. Drake's commitment to the research matched his loyalty to friends. His trust made Rizz's deceit even sleazier.

At least Rizz had come through for him last night. Drake had left the ER by the time Rizz thought of the observation cameras. The cameras covered only the main hallways and weren't continuously monitored.

He had security show him the image replay setup. While the guards were on their rounds, Rizz hunted.

One of the cameras had captured the drug-seeking shithead's actions front and center.

Rizz had saved the stretch from before the asshole hit Patti to where Drake put the dude down. He'd deleted the section where they'd had to pry Drake's hands off the unconscious jerk.

The system stored images for three hours before auto-deleting. If Rizz had not thought to check, the evidence would have been lost.

He'd helped Drake last night but what he was attempting today would crush him.

The climbing sun angled through the windows.

Faith's partners demanded Rizz turn over the breakthrough drug.

In the past hours he'd focused so hard on finding a way out that his head throbbed. He couldn't string them along as he had Faith.

He either screwed his best friends or lost everything.

He opened the lab's data locker and scanned the underside of the shelves for the hidden information.

Drake used coded designations for each test drug. The blinded approach made bias impossible during the testing, as not even Drake knew which of his biochemical creations was D-44. The protocol key held the answers.

Where had Drake stashed it? Before Drake's awkward visit, Rizz had turned the computer, records and laboratory inside out.

Now time was running out and he was checking sites he'd already hunted through.

Self-loathing boiled in his gut. Betrayal of Jon, now working to steal Drake's dream. *Rizzini, you are scum.*

He could still tell the blackmailers to kiss his ass and pray he survived or—he flinched as his cell phone sounded. The caller identification was blocked.

"Dr. Michael Rizzini here."

"You better have what I need."

Rizz closed his eyes as the cruel voice continued.

"Faith is gone, but her sex-and-drugs video is alive and well. Understand, Dr. Co-Star?"

"Don't call me on this line." Rizz got up and checked the lab door. "You must be an idiot."

"Watch your mouth, little man," she said. "Well, perhaps little isn't accurate. The camera doesn't lie." She chuckled.

He bowed his head.

Her tone sharpened. "It's time to hand over D-44."

"I'm trying. I've searched the laptop, the documentation logs, and the entire lab. It's not here. Drake has the information hidden somewhere else. There's nothing more I can do."

"There had better be, boy. You will deliver D-44's molecular identity and synthesis pathway or I will destroy you."

"But I—"

"Your video will premiere on Hennepin-North hospital's ER intranet, with copies to Daddy Reinhorst, Faith's husband, and the Minnesota state board of medical practice."

A siren's wail sounded from the neighborhood outside the lab.

"Regarding my call to you—this cell is encrypted and untraceable. Some of us know how to avoid leaving evidence of compromising activity. You, as has been shown, are not that clever."

"Go to hell," Rizz yelled. He glared at the phone. Silence. As the seconds ticked by, his fighter's stance wilted. He slumped against the table.

"I'm so impressed." Her words dripped with disdain. "By the way, have you heard from Antonio lately?"

"A-Antonio? Who do you mean?"

"You know who I mean, Mikey. Although he's spent most of his time locked up. Good old dad, two-time loser, Tony Rizzini."

Rizz's right leg began pogo-bouncing, his heart filled his throat.

"We found him. Tony likes to buy, sell and use cocaine, doesn't he? We gave him a business opportunity."

Rizz's face burned. *The stupid bastard.*

"The third time's the charm for cons, Mikey. His video isn't as interesting as yours, but it clearly documents a felony. Strike three means he goes away forever. And it was nothing to get him to bite. He's another loser. What's with your gene pool, anyway?"

Rizz leaned forward, free hand flat on the table top, his stomach hollow and his legs weak. He opened his mouth to respond but could not. He slumped back in the chair.

His father—a lifetime of hurt and shame. *Damn him…and damn me. Maybe it is our worthless genes?*

"Get me D-44's molecular identity and synthesis pathway. You have until tomorrow morning or Daddy goes away forever and your video goes viral."

"I've done all I can. Please. It's out of my control."

Silence.

She'd severed the connection.

Chapter 19

Hennepin-North ER

"Dr. Malar needs you. A baby in trouble."

The nurse's words slammed Drake into overdrive. He moved fast, sidestepping the carts, stretchers and people that crowded the path to the Crash Room.

As he raced he processed the fact that his friend Jon was in the ER—taking care of patients. *Insane.*

Drake knifed through the swinging doors into the space containing the four bays of the Crash Room. The walls and ceiling glistened with the array of specialized medical instruments hung and shelved there. Patients rushed to these bays were fighting for their lives.

His urgent summons meant the current battle was being lost.

The throng of caregivers clustered in bay two hid the patient from view. Drake moved past the ambulance stretcher that lay abandoned to the side. A tiny, red athletic shoe and a doll-sized oxygen mask lay on the rumpled sheets there. His stomach clenched.

Dr. Jon Malar, less than twenty hours after his wife's death, stood grim-faced at the head of the bed.

Above Jon, the bay's wall-mounted life-clock flashed the time elapsed since the paramedic's incoming call. For these patients, every second without successful intervention brought death nearer.

The life clock displayed foot-high, glowing red numerals as in a major league sports arena. It showed *3 min. 25 sec.*

Drake moved to the head of the bed across from Jon. The surrounding faces were fearful, eyes flinching, as if trying to avoid being witness to an unfolding ugliness.

Drake's first glance told him the blond-haired baby boy was dying.

In that instant Drake's focus locked and the rest of the world fell away. The only thing that mattered was saving this child.

"What do we know?" Drake said, pulling on gloves.

Jon swiped his forearm at the sweat on his forehead. He spoke rapid-fire with his eyes on the baby. "Fourteen-month-old. No history. Mom called 9-1-1. Baby couldn't breathe. Paramedics arrived. Cyanotic and oxygen levels nothing. Lights and siren. He's crashing. Needs to be intubated." Jon held the metal laryngoscope and the straw-thin five-inch plastic endotracheal tube he readied to pass through the mouth and between the baby's vocal cords into the trachea. "Not asthma. Not allergic. I checked for a foreign body but his airway looks clear. Nothing makes sense." He ripped the plastic wrap off the tube.

The respiratory therapist held an oxygen mask and bag over the babe's mouth and attempted to support breathing.

The baby was blue. His eyes were shut and he lay motionless except for dwindling fish-out-of-water gasps. Each effort caused the tissues of his chest to retract, outlining his tiny ribs. A face-painted rainbow and a spray of silver glitter mini-stars stood out on his right cheek. Drake placed his stethoscope on the palm-sized chest. Silence—no air movement—the quiet of death fast approaching.

Possibilities raced through his mind liquid fast. *There is no magic test, there is no time.*

"Quick onset?" Drake asked.

"Real fast," answered a paramedic. "Mom said he was okay minutes before." The big man clenched and unclenched his hands, leaning forward, shifting from foot to foot, eyes on the dying baby.

The life clock clicked: 4 min. 04 sec.

Drake took the laryngoscope from Jon's hand. He snapped open its articulated metal blade and placed it in the baby's mouth. Crouching, he manipulated the light-equipped instrument to examine the recesses of the throat and airway. The fleshy epiglottis and the glistening white vocal cords guarding the entrance to the trachea were clear.

He peered deeper, a keyhole peek through the chink between the cords, as small as the gap between his six-year-old son's front teeth. He glimpsed something far beyond where the device typically allowed one to see.

"Orange. I saw orange." Drake moved quickly. He thrust the laryngoscope at Jon. "Respiratory, a forceps for Dr. Malar. Now." Drake picked up the dying toddler, and flipped him over in his arms.

He laid the baby across the lower corner of the bed between his hands, the blond head over the edge face downward. One of Drake's hands supported the toddler's chest and stomach; the other covered the now ink-blue back.

"Jon, scope his cords. Have that forceps ready." Drake nodded towards the stainless steel, oversized tweezers-like instrument the Respiratory therapist held out to Jon. Understanding lit in Jon's eyes and he dove to his knees under the table facing the baby.

The life clock flashed 4 min. 28 sec. The baby lay limp and purple in Drake's hands. The gasps were no more.

Drake compressed his hands together as one might try and pop a paper bag.

"Nothing," said Jon, his voice strained. "Again."

Drake repeated the forceful squeeze.

"Saw it. Lord, yes. Orange," Jon's words racing. "Again."

Drake compressed. A beat of silence.

"Got it. Got it." Jon's voice bursting. "Get him up. Oxygen."

Jon, on his knees, held up a small, uninflated orange balloon at the end of the forceps. It looked like a Chinese dumpling in a pair of chopsticks.

Drake rotated the baby in his arms and positioned the oxygen mask over his face.

The little one's chest did not move.

Drake lifted the baby, supporting the limp body with his right arm and the head with his left. He placed his mouth over the mouth and nose and blew steady but controlled. He felt the chest rise.

Drake paused and repeated. The chest expanded once more.

As he prepared to give a third breath, he sensed movement. He applied his stethoscope as Jon scrambled up off his knees.

Drake listened. Air. Moving air.

Before the stethoscope lifted off the chest Drake heard a wondrous sound—the amplified bugle of the toddler's cry.

The chest rose and fell, stronger with each breath. The little one's nightmarish blue color melted away.

Relief washed over the room. In a matter of thirty seconds, a pink-faced baby boy looked about, crying and flashing blue eyes.

"Can someone grab a warm blanket?" Drake cradled the naked baby to his chest.

Jon's face flashed relief, then joy, and ended blank with eyes fixed on the balloon.

"Past his cords. Down his trachea," Jon said as he fingered the religious medal he wore on a chain about his neck. "If we'd intubated him, the balloon would've wedged in his trachea and killed him. If we hadn't got it out, he'd have been dead within a minute. You popped it back up through the cords. Jesus Lord."

The heated blanket appeared and Drake draped it around the baby. The toddler's crying slowed and he settled his head against Drake's chest. Drake rested his cheek against the baby's scalp. He stood motionless, sensing the blanket's dry warmth, the smell of baby powder and the vital stirrings of the saved child. He stashed the moment away.

A nurse entered the Crash Room with a blond-haired young woman clinging to her arm. The woman wore a Happy Birthday T-shirt and had tear-tracked glitter stars on a face white with apprehension. Drake stepped towards her. Her eyes found the baby and she cried out as she lunged for her son. She enveloped him in trembling arms.

Jon stood blank-faced in the relative privacy near the Crash Room entrance. Dark patches marked the chest and armpits of his scrubs.

"I was losing him, Drake. Something was off but I didn't know what." He still clutched the religious medal.

Drake looked toward the baby. "The face art. It reminded me of a case report I read a few years ago. The same circumstances—a party and a baby.

"That doctor did everything he could and still the baby died. They found the balloon at autopsy. No one could have known. The textbooks say babies can't get something that size past their vocal cords." Drake shook his head. "Some babies don't read the textbooks. I looked deep and we got lucky. Getting it out was even luckier." He gave Jon a wink. "Strong work, partner."

The emergency caregivers all beamed as the mom shared her son with the team that had saved him. The toddler would be one hundred percent okay. Drake knew he was wearing a giant grin. Inside he was dancing.

Jon stood to the side, his earlier smile gone. Pouches showed under sunken, red-rimmed eyes. He stared toward the mother and child. "I couldn't have gone on if we'd lost him."

Drake guided Jon to a spot behind the adjacent bay's curtain. Jon moved woodenly and smelled of sour sweat. Drake put a hand on each of Jon's shoulders and faced him.

"You just lost your wife. You're so exhausted you can barely stand. The other docs and I will handle the ER. Give this mom and her little guy a hug and then get yourself out of here. Please."

From down the corridor the cry of a child in pain rose. Drake looked through the glass partition of the Crash Room wall. A Somali woman standing outside the orthopedics room raised her hands to her face and wailed in response. A nurse attempted to console her.

Jon looked off and his eyes appeared to lose focus as he fingered his wedding band. His eyes sharpened and his expression tightened as he turned back.

"I have things to tell you." His eyes met Drake's. "Terrible things. About Faith." He twisted the ring. "And me. Shameful, horrible things." His eyes were moist and his voice broke. "Lord in heaven, Drake. I didn't even know who she was."

Damn—does he know about Faith and Rizz?

Drake put a hand on Jon's shoulder once more. "Go home and get some rest, Jon. Your parents are there, right? When I'm done here tonight, I'll call you from the lab." He gave Jon a gentle shake. "You're hurting, friend. Please think of yourself for once."

Jon opened his mouth as if to say more, then shook his head and moved off. He looked lost.

The child down the corridor cried out again, the mother's wail an echo.

Chapter 20

Hennepin-North ER

An hour passed. Patients were lined up at the triage desk in the packed waiting room, and ambulances pulled in like taxis to an airport. Drake used the hallway to speed treat some of the patients with simple problems. The sounds of voices, medical devices, phones, and overhead pages swelled. As he moved down the corridor, he heard Patti call his name. He stopped and turned. Charge nurse responsibilities included triage and management of patient flow. He did not envy her. It was like trying to direct traffic in a demolition derby.

She approached with a smile. “Great job on the little guy. When we make a save like that, it makes it all worthwhile.” Her expression sobered as she lowered her voice. “I was told not to talk about that guy last night.” She touched his arm. “But I never thanked you.”

“Are you okay?”

“My chest is bruised, but it scared me more than anything.”

She shifted her clipboard. “A couple of minor things. There’s a woman in twenty-two with a cough—she isn’t very sick but she’s upsetting people. She hasn’t been seen by a doctor yet and she’s walking out of the room and yelling about people doing ‘jack shit’ while she waits. Can you see her before too long? And that elderly lady with diverticulitis from the night shift—her room upstairs still isn’t ready and her family is pissed. They’re giving us the evil eye. You know about the waiting room, right?”

Drake arched his eyebrows at her. “Are we having fun yet?”

She smiled.

"Please tell the nasty cough lady to kiss your ass and let the diverticulitis lady's family know that she's already being fully treated. She'll go upstairs as soon as the room is available. If I get a chance I'll stop in and grovel, er, I mean talk to them." He winked. "You know I'm kidding about the kiss-your-ass part, right?"

She shook her head, still smiling. "Someday I'm gonna say it." Her look turned serious. "I do need you on someone right away. I mean—can you? The paramedics just rolled in with the Captain. He's a mess."

The good-natured, homeless man was an ER regular. "Is he hurting? Does he need the Crash Room?"

Patti's brow furrowed. "I think he's probably okay—for him. He's unconscious and has a nasty facial slash. But I've seen him a lot worse. His vitals are good. A jogger found him down by the river. He smells like he's been marinating in booze. Can you look at him? The nurses and EMTs are just placing him now. I know he's your buddy, and if another doc sees him he ends up getting a thousand tests and admitted to the ICU. My guess is it's just this bad laceration and he's dead drunk."

Drake relaxed a bit, knowing Patti's instincts were superb. "I'll see him right away. If anything looks funky, we'll Crash Room him."

"Perfect. That's what I hoped you'd say."

Two paramedics with an elderly patient on oxygen and a cardiac monitor rolled past. Patti looked at her clipboard and jogged after them. "Hey, guys. Where're you going with that one?"

A few minutes later, as Drake stood at the Captain's bedside, an aide approached with two phone-book-sized volumes of records.

"These are the two most recent charts. He fills up a shelf in Medical Records all by himself. Glad we're going electronic." She smiled.

Drake knew the history. Multiple episodes of critical illness, trauma, bad luck and self-wrought catastrophe—the Captain's survival defied all odds.

His birthdate showed him to be in his early forties, but the tall, gaunt, black man looked to be in his sixties. He lived schizophrenic and alcoholic on the streets, parks, and byways of Minneapolis.

The Captain had presented to the ER with so many life-threatening issues that some suggested he be given a medical professorship based on the training he provided the physicians treating him.

Other than the gaping laceration extending from his temple to near the corner of his mouth, the Captain appeared, by his unique standard, generally okay. He was not bleeding and a period of observation was needed to see how he progressed. Drake ordered a fingerstick blood glucose check and a blood alcohol level.

Some minutes later as he exited another exam room, the secretary flagged him. "The lab called a critical result."

The Captain's blood alcohol measured 0.52%. His level was more than six times legal intoxication and would be fatal for 99% of people—for him it likely meant a coma-deep nap.

An hour later, Drake stood gowned, masked, capped, and gloved beside a tray of chrome instruments. The passed-out homeless man's face lay centered in the surgical light, prepped and surrounded by blue drapes. Patti stuck her head in the door. "He's okay?"

"Your impression looks to have been dead on. No evidence of other problems so far."

"Dr. Cody, Detective Yamada is here and insists you need to talk. Okay if I let him in while you work?"

Drake went cold. "Sure."

Detective Yamada slipped into the room. He hung back from the bright light and sterile drapes.

"I'm okay here? Not gonna get him infected or anything?"

"You're fine. Are you okay with the sight of blood?"

"I'd say yeah. I made it through the autopsy with that associate medical examiner." The detective looked as if he'd slept in his clothes and he had bags under his eyes. He leaned forward, peering at the Captain's exposed wound. "Ouch, that's wicked."

Drake interrupted his exploration of the wound. "Did Kip give a cause of death?"

"That doctor," the detective shook his head, "is beyond weird. Isn't a personality assessment part of getting into medical school? Or has he watched too many TV shows showing bizarre MEs?"

"It's no act." Drake said. "He's strange but knows his stuff. What'd he say? "

"He tossed around a lot of big words but wouldn't commit to a cause of death. He said his work is a little more complicated than handing out traffic tickets or taking a rubber hose to suspects." He inched closer as Drake worked to control a small bleeder.

"He said he'd give a report later. But the fact that he wouldn't or couldn't give a cause of death is unusual." Yamada took out a pen and frayed notepad. "I need to proceed as if it's a homicide."

"Homicide?" Drake straightened, pulling the instruments back. He'd felt there was more to it than a simple drowning, but suspected a medical event or drug and alcohol involvement.

"Yes, homicide—until proven otherwise. That means the truth and nothing but the truth. You got that, Doc?"

"Of course, Aki."

"Don't give me 'of course.'" Aki's voice had an edge. "And call me Detective or Officer Yamada. We're working here."

Drake glanced up.

Aki's chin jutted. "I received a call before seven this morning from a squad following up on an assault complaint. Imagine my surprise when I learned it involved my 'good friend' Dr. Cody, who had to get to the ER right away to save lives and help me with a case. I got here at seven thirty and learned you weren't on till nine. Understood, Dr. Nothing-but-the-Truth?" His gaze sharpened. "We'll deal with that later. First you need to tell me about Faith Reinhorst-Malar. Who do you think might want her dead?"

What the hell? Drake was thankful the surgical mask hid his face. He concentrated on aligning the deep tissues of the wound. He placed the first buried suture.

"What about the doc? Any hint of troubles?" Aki said.

"Who?"

"Don't play dumb. Your buddy, Dr. Jon Malar. He stands to inherit millions."

"Come on, that's absurd. Jon worshipped her. He's a choir boy and Eagle Scout—the kindest, gentlest guy I know. I've never even seen him angry. Working around here, that's saying something."

"The word I'm getting is his wife was no Eagle Scout."

"What are you saying?"

"You never heard any stories?"

Drake said nothing. The truth could wrongly put his friends in harm's way. He placed a second deep suture.

"What about this research? Didn't you tell me Faith did the business and legal work?"

Did I share that with Aki? The detective had already been turning over stones. Would he uncover Drake's history? His mouth went dry.

"She volunteered to represent us and registered the business. NeurVitae is the name. She made sure our intellectual property rights were protected in case we develop something marketable." He identified the parotid duct and tracked its course. "She handled the paperwork. All we needed to do was sign. But we haven't done any actual business. NeurVitae has no money."

Aki nodded. "What about sex? Do you think she was fooling around?"

"Are you serious?" Drake kept his eyes on the wound. "This is starting to feel like gossip time at the beauty shop." Sweat trickled down his temple.

"I got news for ya, Doc. Gossip is often true. What about Rizzini? I've heard he's a bit of a hound."

Rizz's confession was stuck like a tack in Drake's mind.

"This is getting ridiculous." He used the tissue forceps to expose a section of the facial nerve. He placed another suture, careful to avoid entrapping any nerve branches.

"Don't get huffy on me, Doc. I'm just asking questions here. That's the way an investigation works. If she was murdered, no one gets a pass."

"I can't believe it's murder. Kip's going to find something medical." Drake locked his focus on the wound.

"We'll see. It would make my life easier." Aki looked at his notepad. "Why would a drug company have called her? Their call came within minutes of her death." He looked at the notebook again. "Ingersen Pharmaceutical in Switzerland. We only have the main exchange, so we haven't been able to find out who wanted to talk to her or why. You say this NeurVitae of yours doesn't have any business yet, right?"

Drake straightened up and again backed the suture needle away from the Captain's face. "None. I have no idea why they would call her. They're a huge company. Maybe she was making some contacts for down the road. If it was anything more, I'd have to know."

"She called your home number two days ago. Why?"

Drake went blank for an instant. "Oh yeah, Faith got together with Rachelle. She needed a signature—legal stuff. Rachelle had to sign off so there couldn't be any spousal entanglements. Like divorce, I suppose."

The detective craned his neck, moving closer to the circle of light centered on the Captain's face. "Okay, that's it on the death for now. I'm hoping you're right and the M.E. finds a medical explanation." Aki flipped his notepad around and opened the back flap. "Now there's this assault mess you dragged me into."

Drake cringed inside. He placed a last deep suture, completing the union of two sections of transected facial muscle. The large skin defect now aligned evenly and lay ready for surface closure.

"This should have been completed by the squad this morning, but you lied your way out of it. I'm stuck completing a PPA assessment. PPA stands for Possible Pending Action, as in, do we need to place you under arrest, slide on the silver bracelets and process you downtown?" The detective looked pained.

Drake's chest clutched. "I needed to get to the lab."

The Captain made a snoring sound and started to raise an arm toward his damaged face. Drake blocked the arm with his gown-covered elbow, keeping his gloves and the operative zone sterile. The Captain settled and his breathing evened.

"I'm sorry I got you involved, Aki," Drake said. "I did not commit a crime."

"I'll decide that. Tell me what happened."

"Late in my shift I heard a patient yelling at a nurse. He demanded narcotics and cursed her. When I approached, he struck her and swung at me. That's it."

"Some people are demanding you be arrested," Aki said.

Drake's knees went weak.

"The complaint states the patient ended up with fractured ribs and a broken nose. He alleges assault. His attorney claims his client nearly died. They say he came to the ER hurting and upset due to a toothache and you attacked him. What do you say?"

"It's a lie. He hit Patti and when I stepped in he took a swing at me. I defended myself. It's clear he's lying if you look."

The detective glanced up with a raised eyebrow.

Drake read the look. *He's seen the tape.*

He opened a packet containing finer suture material for the skin closure. He fit the needle into the teeth of the holder.

"Okay, for the record," Aki's manner went formal, "your statement is that the arrested individual verbally abused a nurse. He demanded drugs and then struck the nurse. Correct?"

"Yes."

"You attempted to intervene to protect the nurse, and the individual attacked you?"

"That's what happened."

"You defended yourself and the nurse, necessitating laying hands on the attacker?"

"Yes."

"You observed no mistreatment of the prisoner by police?"

"Correct."

"There was no discussion of race, no name-calling or bias motivating your actions?"

"Absolutely none. Afterwards he threatened me. He said, 'You're gonna pay.'"

"I can't address that right now." Aki lowered the notepad. "They're alleging racism and police brutality. Those are high-octane issue in this town, and the media have already painted us guilty. You have no idea how damaging this could be for me."

"I really am sorry, but I didn't cause this."

"Yeah, whatever." Aki sighed. "You're in the clear on the possible assault. Witness interviews, your answers and video evidence," he shot a look at Drake, "don't support charging you with a crime."

Drake felt like a drowning man thrown a line. He kept his eyes on the Captain's face. He aligned the flesh and placed the first skin suture.

Aki continued, "But Doc, a heads-up. This may not be over for you." His voice lowered. "I did a check on you. As you no doubt know, you have a record—in Ohio. It's a juvenile case and it's sealed."

Drake's gut plummeted. His vision fuzzed and he pulled back the needle.

"Theoretically, the details are locked away, but reality is otherwise. It can't be used in a court action, but I could call Cincinnati police or track down the prosecutors and find out pretty easily what went down."

Drake felt momentarily lightheaded. He checked his hands for steadiness. The detective could have no idea of the impact of Drake's criminal record becoming known.

It would smash through his life like a wrecking ball.

The alcohol and musty odor seemed stronger. The Captain mumbled but remained still. Sweat ran into Drake's eye. He blinked his vision clear and locked onto the repetitive steps of his task—align tissue, pass needle, tension suture, tie, cut. Did his dread show in the portion of his face visible above the surgical mask?

As he passed the needle through the weathered blue-black skin, the words that could destroy him loomed.

The question printed in bold-faced type on his medical school application, on his petition for his MD degree, and on the forms he submitted requesting the federal and state licenses that allowed him to practice medicine and engage in medical research. The section wherein he'd documented a barefaced lie over and over again:

> *Have there ever been any criminal charges filed against you? This includes whether the charges were misdemeanor, gross misdemeanor, or felony. This also includes any offenses which have been expunged or otherwise removed from your record by executive pardon.*

Misrepresentation of answers will result in revocation of licensure and the fullest permissible professional and legal action.

Discovery of his record would strip him of his medical license, his MD degree, and any possibility of continuing to work as a doctor. Exposure would destroy all he'd worked for, crush his family and end his dreams.

"I was sixteen years old. I'm not a criminal. Please don't mention it to anyone. Please." Drake held his breath. The greater likelihood of being found out in Cincinnati had triggered his application for training in Minnesota. Even here, he kept people at a distance to lessen the risk of being found out. He felt Aki's eyes on him.

"That was the court's intention when they sealed your record. I'll honor it—for now." Aki pointed his notepad. "I'll track it if I feel you're holding back on me." He shrugged. "But I can't stop the media or attorneys. If they find out, it'll be everywhere."

Drake swallowed and locked his attention on the Captain's repair. He placed the final superficial sutures, completing the transition of the ugly gash into a precise tented ridge.

When Drake looked up, he found the detective studying the big man's face.

"I've never seen how you guys do that. Very cool." He pocketed his pen. "We'll be talking." He slipped out of the room.

Drake cleaned and dressed the wound. His neck and shoulders were still in knots as he removed his mask, cap, gloves and gown. *Will I lose everything?*

A nurse passed as he discarded his surgical gown.

"Geez, Dr. Cody. Did you go for a swim?"

Drake puzzled for an instant before realizing that his hair and scrubs dripped with sweat.

Chapter 21

Cincinnati, Ohio
Drake's childhood

Kevin Cody was born eighteen months, three days, two hours, sixteen minutes and some seconds after his big brother Drake.

When Drake was old enough, they explained that in the last minutes and seconds before Kevin's birth, part of his brain didn't get enough oxygen. His mind was good but the control center for movement had been damaged.

They called it cerebral palsy.

Drake walked at eleven months and rode a bike at four years. Kevin walked short distances, with specialized crutches, at five years and grinned hugely when he rolled forward on a specially adapted three-wheeler at age ten. His smile faced towards one whose grin shone larger yet—big brother Drake.

Kevin's body defied control and writhed and spasmed in synch with a rhythmless drummer. Only through iron resolve and grimacing will did Kevin complete actions others performed without effort.

Among Drake's early memories were his mother's words, "You've been given a gift—a blessing. You get to watch over your special brother. That's why God made you so strong."

For Kevin, speech was an agonizing, halting struggle. Walking a labor of flailing crutches and gravity-defying lurches. He fell frequently and visited the ER often. Drake, inseparable from his younger brother, helped with communication and care. Kevin continually suffered bruises, cuts and fractures. He never quit. He never cried.

Drake and Kevin communicated without effort, sharing laughing fits or pain, often without exchanging a word. From earliest childhood, Kevin was the largest and best part of Drake's world.

At the neighborhood playgrounds and the St. Stephen's grade school, episodes of childish cruelty and abuse occurred. Drake dealt harshly with anyone who wronged his brother—even those older and larger. The message quickly spread.

The small circle of the Cody brothers' contacts and schoolmates knew how cool Kevin was.

Other places, gawking and ignorant comments were the rule.

"I'm j-just t-too g-GOOD lookING! Th-they a-aren'T u-used t-to IT," was Kevin's standard response. He would flash his contorted grin.

Drake saw all and forgave less. The "talking down" speech and presumption that Kevin was mentally handicapped particularly maddened him.

"You're not talking to a beagle, lady," Drake had snapped at a clinic nurse when he was twelve years old. "He's way smarter than you are." His mother had made him apologize. Drake was not one bit sorry.

Kevin entered seventh grade at the same public junior/senior high where Drake was starting the tenth grade. On their third day, they waited next to the auxiliary parking lot off to the side of the main school building. Their mom would pick them up any minute.

Three slouching twelfth graders with shaved heads stood by a trash dumpster smoking cigarettes and talking loud. Drake knew of the three. They had a bad rep and were given a wide berth. Kids called them skinheads.

"C'mon Kevin, let's wait over there," said Drake indicating farther down the lot.

"B-but M-Mom s-said to b-be h-here."

"You're right, but she'll see us. C'mon." Drake put a hand on Kevin's shoulder.

"O-ho-KAY d-DRAKE." Kevin started his ungainly crutch flailing away from the dumpster.

"Hey! What the hell is that?" came the shout. "Can that thing fly? Looks like an almost-human helicopter." Coarse, biting laughter.

Drake slowed, muttering. "Brainless assholes."

"D-Drake, i-it's o-kay."

A second voice now, "What is it? A bird? A plane? No, it's Super-retard!" They backslapped one another and howled.

The harsh laughter echoed off the brick walls of the school. Drake's face flushed warm.

"I-it's o-kay D-Drake! C-c'mon!" Kevin worked his crutches, struggling to distance himself from the hyenas. Their braying surged and moved closer.

"Hoo-hoo-hoo. What've we got here? Its retard boy and his keeper," the largest and loudest of the three said as they stepped in front of the brothers. He stood bear-big, with a scraggly mustache and close-set piggy eyes. He finger-flicked his cigarette, bouncing it with a burst of spark at Drake's feet. "ARYAN" was tattooed on his forearm below a grinning skull with lightning bolts coming out of the eye sockets.

"You getting ready for take-off, retard?" said the vacant-eyed, second skinhead.

"I think I'll try out those sticks, spaz boy," said Aryan tattoo.

"Yeah. See if you can fly better than the wiggly retard," sneered the tough-looking third skinhead, pointing with his cigarette.

Drake stood on the sidewalk where tree roots had heaved the concrete. A faint drumming started inside his head. The jagged crack and an uneven step-off of the sidewalk lay under his feet. The smell of cigarettes grew stronger.

Kevin stood, crutch propped, and weaving, the skinheads laughing in his face.

Time stretched. Drake's vision tunneled and edges sharpened. The drumming in his head intensified. His face burned as though he was standing too close to an open fire. His reflexes were trip-wired. His body a bow with the arrow fully drawn.

Aryan stepped forward, grabbed Kevin's right crutch, and yanked, his laughter cruel.

Drake turned, grasped Kevin's shoulders, and smoothly lowered him to the curb. He took the left crutch strut, slipping the reinforced aluminum forearm ring free of Kevin's arm.

Aryan pulled hard on the right crutch, dragging Kevin.

Kevin's eyes pinwheeled, the whites showing large. His face contorted as he resisted. "Nuh-nuh-NOO!"

Aryan launched his leg, the sole of his boot driving towards Kevin's face.

The crutch whistled as it sliced through the air. The upper portion, where Kevin's forearm had worn the electro-plated blue to the underlying silver, struck Aryan in the middle of his face. The sound was that of an axe biting into a hardwood log. Aryan pitched backwards, his nose collapsed and his face a volcano of erupting blood.

Drake pivoted, shifting his grip, grabbing the now bent arm ring and driving the crutch, tip first, into the belly of the advancing second assailant. An explosive "Ooooffff!"

The skinhead jackknifed to the ground, arms hugging gut, legs bicycling in the air.

Drake glimpsed, too late, the third skinhead's incoming punch. The fist smashed into his face like a thrown brick. A lightning bolt of pain lanced his jaw and the taste of pennies filled his mouth.

He was on his back, away from Kevin. He slid toward unconsciousness, blackness reaching. The puncher straddled his chest and pounded his face.

Drake rallied, driving his hand through the storm of punches and finding the attacker's throat. His fingers closed. As the blows rained down, he squeezed.

A jolting impact and Drake's jaw shifted in a way that it could not. The pain doubled. Rage and instinct fueled his grip, his fingers hydraulic. His hand returned a sensation like that of twigs snapping and he heard a strangled bawl. The punches stopped. The drumming thundered on. Drake's arm supported a limp weight.

And still he squeezed.

A flapping, slapping on his arms, clutching fingers and Kevin's voice cutting through the drumming. "N-NOOO! D-draAKE! N-noOO!"

Drake released his grip, discarding the gurgling body. Turning, he saw the other two skinheads down and incapable of threat. He met his brother's wild eyes and wrapped him in a hug as they lay on the cracked sidewalk, Kevin's body quaking with sobs.

Drake held his brother tight to his chest. Pain spiked his jaw with each word. "I've got you, Kevin. We're okay, brother. We're okay."

* * *

Drake's jaw required placement of a steel plate and screws. He wore an ankle bracelet under house arrest for the three weeks between his discharge from the hospital and the criminal proceedings.

The Aryan tattooed assailant's face would be left with permanent deformity. The attacker that broke Drake's jaw had almost died. He was left with breathing difficulties and a voice that could not rise above a whisper.

At the trial, Drake's charges read "felony assault with weapon resulting in grievous bodily injury." The father of the assailant that had broken Drake's jaw was the largest highway construction contractor in the state. Drake's *victims* wore sport coats and ties. Their hair had grown to crew-cut length. Their past records were inadmissible as they were not on trial.

Drake's mother had no money. His defense lay in the hands of a novice public defender. The young attorney looked scared and his voice trembled on the few occasions he spoke at trial. He decided that Kevin's speech difficulties eliminated him as an effective witness. He allowed the prosecutor to introduce hearsay reports of Drake's previous "assaults" of those who "kidded" with his brother.

For Drake, it was as if the proceedings were a TV program—it didn't seem real.

The prosecution closed their case with a psychiatrist whose only contact with Drake was a ten-minute interview in a holding cell. Drake later learned that the "doctor's" only practice involved delivering testimony for pay.

The psychiatrist wore a fine suit, wire-rimmed glasses and a trimmed goatee. "The accused, though young, has demonstrated viciousness beyond his years. He uses a delusional sense of responsibility to legitimize a hunger for brutality. Innocent schoolyard horseplay provides an excuse for him to indulge his lust for violence. It frees him to engage in savagery."

The timid public defender did not even cross-examine.

When the verdict was read, Drake's mother fell to her knees, dropping the rosary she'd clutched throughout the trial. The bespectacled, balding black judge spoke over her quiet tears and the braying sobs and writhing protests of Drake's brother.

"You are convicted of one count of assault with a deadly weapon." He glanced at the trio of alleged victims and then at the rookie public defender. He gave an exaggerated sigh.

"The verdict disturbs me, but based on what transpired in this courtroom," he looked over his glasses at the public defender, "I have no technical grounds to reverse the decision. I must, by mandate, remand the defendant into custody for the minimum sentence allowable: twenty-four months incarceration in an Ohio juvenile correctional institution for violent offenders. I note, for the record, that this result offends my sense of justice." His eyes met Drake's. "I remind the convicted that he has the right of appeal." The gavel struck.

* * *

Drake entered the Scioto Juvenile Correctional Facility for Violent Offenders in Franklin Furnace County. The Scioto "Furnace" was documented to have six times the frequency of violent events as the worst of Ohio's adult maximum security prisons.

As a white boy alone entering an institution that was 85% minority, overwhelmingly gang affiliated, and a segment criminally insane, he was a dog among wolves.

He'd done what he'd had to do to survive. His capacity for violence had been the key.

The judge's on-the-record comments opened the door to action by a pro bono criminal justice oversight group aligned with the University of Cincinnati Law School. While Drake was incarcerated, the group worked to achieve his release.

Four months and seventeen days after being delivered into the hell of the Scioto Furnace, he walked out.

His release came twenty-one days too late to avert the worst. What he'd done still stalked the perimeter of his consciousness.

He was released from jail, but his sentence continued.

Chapter 22

One physician short and an incoming stampede of patients kept Drake running. An hour after he completed the Captain's facial repair, the big man was awake and talking. *Amazing.*

The Captain metabolized alcohol the way a flame burned paper.

Drake knew that inner voices directed the homeless man in his role as "Captain"—an alien scout assessing earth for possible colonization. His belief in the reality of his mission never swayed.

Despite the Captain's mental illness, profound alcoholism, and hard-luck life, he radiated kindness. He never showed anger. The closest he came to showing displeasure occurred when misguided nurses or doctors challenged the authenticity of his mission. Drake had overheard the Captain ending such contentious discussions with comments such as, "Do not fret, native. You are many generations from enlightenment."

Drake enjoyed the flustered sputtering of the tightly wound caregivers.

Five hours after the Captain's arrival unconscious by ambulance, he was able to stand, walk and talk. Drake determined the intergalactic explorer was safe for discharge and found him a sandwich and juice.

Later, the ER regular stood unaided as he pulled on the two full-length coats, stocking cap and fedora that made up his year-round outfit.

He raised a hand to Drake. "Your vital force protects and saves. You are highly evolved for an earth creature. This explorer salutes you."

Drake returned the salute feeling as if he'd received a prestigious award.

The Captain strode slowly down the hall.

As Drake turned back, a medical student in an ill-fitting white coat approached him. Her manner seemed weighty, and she twice squinted at his hospital I.D. tag. She handed him an oversized manila folder. "This is from Dr. Dronen in the Medical Examiner's office." She walked out.

Enclosed in the folder was a single sheet covered in precise, near-microscopic handwriting:

Observations – preliminary and incomplete

E.R. – I provide this to you as an immense courtesy. Do not share with anyone.

General:

Subject appears to have been in perfect health with no evidence of disease.

No evidence of stroke, seizure, aneurysm, cardiac disease, or precipitant health event.

No evidence of bruising, wounds, illness, or significant trauma.

No needle marks or visible injection sites. Stomach contents unremarkable (no pill fragments).

Trace of personal lubricant recovered from vaginal vault. Suggests pelvic pogo activity within 8 to 10 hours of death. No spermatozoa present. Brazilian pubic hairstyling noted.

Key finding:

Water in lungs: distribution reflects passive entry – not active inspiration (i.e. water flowed in – not actively inhaled).

Impressions:

Death due to hypoxia with resultant cessation of brain and cardiac activity. Basis of hypoxia uncertain.

NOT CONSISTENT WITH DROWNING.

Note – 98% of examiners would have errantly confirmed cause of death as drowning (including our so-called "Chief" M.E.).

Lab results:

Tox screen positive for cocaine. Blood level does not support as cause of death. No alcohol present. Trace level of marijuana. All other tests pending.

Comment – An annoying Japanese-American cop showed up in the middle of the night to observe the autopsy. There is mega-pressure on me from everywhere on this one.

Drake sat down.

He'd expected an aneurysm, a heart problem, or some other medical condition to be found. Drug use and alcohol had been on the ugly side of his list of possibilities. Kip's report was inconclusive. "Death due to hypoxic injury" was so nonspecific as to be almost meaningless. The note said primarily what the cause of death wasn't.

Drake's call was put through directly.

"It is I," announced the pathologist in his squeaky pitch.

"Kip, what are you saying in this note? Are you—"

"Whoa. Ease up, ramrod. How about 'Gee, thanks, Dr. Nice Guy. I can't believe you were good enough to send me the info on this soggy wench after slaving all night.' And, not incidentally, 'Man, are you brilliant.' How about a little love before you start gunning questions at me?"

"Kip, you're right. I appreciate the report. Sorry for being abrupt, but this death is about more than you. You're undeniably brilliant, but you can also be a pain in the ass. Can you deal with that?" Silence hung for an instant and Drake feared he'd blown it.

"Deal with it?" Kip said. "Hell yes, I can effing deal with it. 'Undeniably brilliant' you say. Hmmm. I really like that." He paused. "So, other than thanking me, why did you call?"

"Come on, Kip. She didn't drown, it wasn't the cocaine, and nothing else showed. You didn't answer the question as to cause of death. It's not like you to dance around."

"Back off, ER. I'm getting called every ten minutes from VIP types screaming for the answer. I've learned this is a fifty-million-dollar, headlines and TV question. I'm under more pressure than the effing San Andreas Fault. If I blow this, I trash my reputation forever. I won't rush this one. Don't push me."

"What's your best guess?"

"Damn it! I said don't push me," Kip shrilled so loud Drake flinched. "Jesus Jones, dude, I'm not in the effing guess business!"

"Sorry, I'm not looking to jam you. I know you're under the gun."

"No shit. This case has my nuts in a vise." Kip sighed heavily enough to be heard over the phone. "I'm not holding out on you, ER. I'll admit something to you in take-it-to-the-grave confidence. Part of my dancing is because I haven't completely figured this death out yet. It's a weird one." Kip sounded almost humble.

"If I can help with anything let me know."

"Ah yeah, thanks for the offer, ER." His arrogance was back and evident in his patronizing tone. "I'll give you one last thing. However this babe died, it's something I've never seen—and I've seen them all."

The connection ended. Drake stared at the phone, his thoughts tumbling.

Chapter 23

Purdue University Medical Center, Mental Health Services, 3:40 p.m.

Staff psychiatrist Suzie Lind took a sip of her mocha and pulled up the afternoon patient schedule on her desktop computer. Her three-thirty patient had not checked in. She shrugged.

In her early years, every missed visits had been torture. She'd imagine each no-show patient on the verge of suicide or committing horrible acts.

Now if the patient wasn't one of her few "red flag" individuals, she didn't sweat it.

The red-flag patients' missed appointments still kept Suzie awake at night. Her red-flag patients left her uneasy even when they did show up.

She accessed her email and scanned the in-box. Her mug set down so abruptly the hot liquid splashed and scalded her fingers.

Ex-patient Meryl Kampf had quit Suzie's care in a rage more than two years earlier.

> *Dr. Suzie –*
>
> *Greetings from the top. I decided to let you know all is well and your diagnosis and concerns about me were baseless. I'm strong, fit, and the picture of perfection in all respects. I eliminated the lithium and find myself improving without limit.*
>
> *On a professional note – I'd like to recommend some therapy for you. I've developed a regimen integrating cocaine's neurotransmitter impact with the effects of human growth hormone and anabolic steroids. I've found that limbic up-regulation linked with maximization of endogenous endorphins extends human boundaries in*

both physical and cognitive performance. I can provide you details. You would benefit.

On a personal note – I had to lose a beautiful someone recently but dealt with it magnificently. I'm expecting some tremendous professional success soon. I'm looking forward to wealth, travel and intimate fun. I'd love to share special times with you – no strings attached.

Yours for pleasure,
Meryl

As Suzie read, a knot formed in the pit of her stomach. Meryl without lithium and experimenting with cocaine—*please no.* It was like tossing a Molotov cocktail into a tinder dry forest. Grandiosity and delusion dominated the message. Meryl was in the grip of full-blown mania.

What could Suzie do? Meryl could be anywhere.

Suzie used a Kleenex to mop up the spilled mocha. Meryl's reference to "had to lose a beautiful someone" was awkward but seemed benign. For some reason the words chilled her.

She began typing a reply she hoped would persuade Meryl to restart lithium and seek help. Susie's knowledge of the illness and her ex-patient smothered any optimism.

She paused and cradled the cup of mocha, seeking warmth for hands that had turned ice-cold.

She pictured a red flag snapping in the wind.

Chapter 24

Andrew Reinhorst felt the Gulfstream bank and begin its descent into Minneapolis. Faith was dead and he needed answers.

He'd spent the morning pleading his firm's case before a Senate finance oversight committee. It was noon before he climbed into the high-tech office cabin of his corporate jet.

This had been his fourth Washington visit in the past three weeks. Each trip involved increasingly strident efforts to use his political influence to buy time. He'd failed. Reinhorst LLC balanced on the brink of collapse.

Cash was the only thing that could save his empire. His thoughts went once more to the fifty million dollars sitting in Faith's trust fund.

Reinhorst spoke to his Minneapolis-based assistant via speaker phone. "What have they learned about Faith?"

"Sir, the chief of police says he's giving it his personal attention. The Medical Examiner's office completed the autopsy this morning, but the doctor refused to give a preliminary report."

"Refused?" Reinhorst sat forward. "You accepted that?"

"Sir, he is a doctor and—"

"I don't give a shit," Reinhorst said. "The ME position is a political appointment. I can have his balls in a heartbeat." He paused. "Get me Rudy Michaels. Now."

"But sir, the DA is tough to reach. He—"

"God almighty—you're talking to Andrew Reinhorst! I put that hick in office. You've got five minutes to have him call me."

He disconnected. The afternoon sun strobed through the porthole-like windows as the jet banked. He pulled an ebony cell phone from his vest pocket.

The number he entered connected to Catalyst Consulting. Catalyst was actually one man. A man who made things happen.

"I'm on a pure line. What have you learned?" Reinhorst swiveled and looked at the small sculpture of Lady Justice. The bronze of the blindfolded, gowned woman with her balance scale sat mounted on the front corner of the desk. He stroked one of the breasts with his finger.

"The trust principal has grown to sixty-three million dollars," answered the man who was an attorney and much more.

"Excellent. We need to make sure that doctor husband of hers doesn't get his hands on my money." Reinhorst rotated his chair. "What are my chances in the courts if we play it straight?"

"Virtually zero. Whoever set up the trust was incompetent."

Andrew Reinhorst's lip curled. The Consultant knew Andrew had set up the trust. "Whatever. It's my money and I'll damn well get it." He rubbed his forehead. "I set it up so it reverted to me if Faith was convicted of a crime, or any number of other screwups. I barbwired that girl into something approaching Christian behavior. Smart as a whip, but just flat-out devil wild." He paused. "I did mess up on her death contingency. Who would have thought it would matter?"

"Any first-year law student."

Reinhorst could picture the man's smug expression. The condescending bastard pissed him off. "Her mother had me by the balls. Either I put fifty million dollars in trust for her sweet, little Faith or I fork over more than four times that in a divorce. It was a good business decision—plus it gave me some control over the girl."

He took a pen out of his pocket. "Now both of them are gone. Her mother's aneurysm was a miracle. This could be providence as well." He sighed. "God works in strange ways."

"The way you deal with your grief is inspiring."

"Don't be insolent." Reinhorst flushed and sat forward. "Of course it's a tragedy. And I'm just sick. She was such a sweet baby." He pulled a notepad across the desk. "But she grew up and hated my guts." He held his eyes closed for a moment. "None of that matters anymore. I need my money and I need it now."

He jotted something on the notepad. "If the courts won't do what's right, we need to do whatever it takes."

"So you're saying ignore the law?"

"I said—whatever it takes." He tapped the pen on the notepad. "You're the make-it-happen guy. That's why I call you. Just make it happen. Keep me out of it." *Why else would I tolerate your arrogance?*

"It's going to cost you."

"I'll pay."

"I'll let you know payment details as things develop. No haggling. I'll contact you." The Consultant disconnected.

Reinhorst shook his head. *The blood-sucking bastard.* He pocketed the phone.

A buzzing sounded and Reinhorst put on a lightweight headset. “Talk to me, Rudy.”

“Mr. Reinhorst, can you please let me get back to you. I’m in the middle of—”

“I don’t want to hear any ‘you’re busy’ shit, Mr. Big-Shot DA. The only reason you aren’t still doing farm foreclosures and chasing divorce cases in St. Cloud is because I made it happen. Now what in the name of sweet Jesus happened to my daughter?”

“I haven’t forgotten what you did for me, sir, and I appreciate it. I’m all over the investigation. The police chief and the ME think it looks suspicious. They—”

Andrew pounded his fist on the desk. “They *think* it looks suspicious? Lord in heaven—that’s no answer.” He looked at his watch. “Have the chief call me in one hour and you get back to me in no more than two. You have one job until I tell you otherwise. Find out if someone killed my little girl.” He severed the connection.

His left hand rested on the Bible, with the pen in his right he repeatedly underlined what he’d written on the notepad.

$63,000,000.

Chapter 25

Drake pulled into the lab building's parking lot, his headlights sweeping a late-model, black Suburban—Jon's vehicle. He'd planned to phone Jon, but it appeared they'd talk in person. Drake hoped his hurting friend was doing better. He exited the car to the sound of thumping bass coming from the project high-rises on the other side of the fence.

He climbed the stairs with the details of Rizz's confession returning. If Faith had presented herself to Rizz in the way he described, the outcome was foregone. Drake wished he didn't know of their ugly betrayal.

And Jon's words and manner in the ER were worrisome. Did he know about Faith and Rizz?

Drake opened the lab door a crack.

Jon sat at the slate-topped table with his head down, forehead on his arms. A five-hundred-milliliter beaker partially filled with amber liquid rested near his hands. A half-empty bottle of Johnny Walker Black sat adjacent.

Jon did not drink.

He raised his head, scanning about until his half-closed, reddened eyes found Drake. He raised an eyebrow, nodded and lifted one hand with index finger extended as if to provide emphasis. A lost expression slid over his face.

"How you doing, partner?" Drake said, crouching to Jon's eye level.

"Well, Draker, to tell you the truth—" He paused and cocked his head. "To tell you the truth…" His voice rose. "Ha, ha. How about—" Louder. "To tell you a lie. Ha. That's it. Nothing but lies. Shit, damn right." He tried to stand and pitched sideways, grabbing for the edge of the tabletop.

Drake caught him. "Easy, buddy."

"You're blessed. Y'know that, Draker? Children are a gift from God." His words were slurred. "I'm alone."

Drake guided Jon to his chair. "Let's sit. Okay?"

"Sit? I can sit. On command. Like a dog." He sat. "God damn—a tail-wagging, clueless puppy dog. Y'know that, Draker?"

Jon had never before sworn in Drake's presence, nor ever called him "Draker."

"Lighten up, Jon. You didn't do anything wrong."

"Wrong?" His eyes wide. "I didn't do anything wrong?" He shook his head. "Are you damn, shitting nuts?"

The pain in Jon's face tore at Drake's heart.

"I loved her—more than anything." He sat straighter though still weaving. "What a fool."

He reached for the beaker, missing and knocking it over. The scotch spread over the slate tabletop, aroma rising. He made no reaction, his eyes blank.

"She was so beautiful. Being with her was…" He clutched his temples, moaning, then began to mumble.

Drake strained to make out his words.

"I hated her. What she did." Jon slumped forward, his arms splayed on the table. "She made me. I had to."

His head drooped to his arms. His eyes closed and his breathing slowed. The spilled liquor dripped onto the floor.

Drake picked up the bottle and looked at his passed-out, hurting friend. Tipping the bottle back, he took a cowboy slug.

Lifting Jon off the chair like a jumbo-sized version of little Shane, he then laid him carefully onto the sleepover cot. He stood and scanned the cats' cages along the adjoining wall, then noted the time. He'd be hours late, with Rachelle left hanging once more. *Damn.*

Jon needed him, and the animals' care could not be compromised.

Chapter 26

Lab, evening, ***two months earlier***

"Rizz, are you sure this cat's deficit met protocol?" Drake opened the research log book.

"Absolutely." Rizz continued putting away equipment. "That's specimen D4, female, 2.1 kilograms, fully med checked. You performed the procedure at 0730 hours four days ago. I confirmed zero motor function at 1930 hours that evening, then infused study drug D-44 at 2100 hours." He mock-bowed. "I am a slave to protocol, research master."

Drake shook his head looking at the records. "I ask because I can't believe what I'm seeing." He indicated the smallish black-and-white cat positioned on the exam table. "She has function."

Rizz looked up. "No shit?"

"God, I hope it's not a technical error." Drake checked the strip of surgical tape covering the fur-shaved skin midway down the cat's back. "Maybe I messed up surgically?"

"Not likely," Rizz said. "Your surgical skills might be even better than mine, and I'm Michelangelo with a scalpel. Whatever screwed up, it probably wasn't your technique. And it wasn't me. It's something else." He went back to gathering his gear.

"I'll review the data trail and video records. If there's an error, it means this little one went through surgery for nothing."

"Don't beat yourself up," Rizz said with a shrug. "Remember these kitties were headed for the great catnip field in the sky before we gave them a last chance to help their human buddies."

Drake obtained the research animals from the to-be-euthanized queue at the city's Animal Rescue center. The cats he selected would've otherwise been put to sleep within hours. But it still bothered him. Sometimes the cats appeared in his dreams.

His exposure to the human suffering caused by spinal cord injury overrode his misgivings. He took care of the victims—individuals he spoke with and touched. He looked into their eyes. It was his responsibility to tell them they were paralyzed.

Then he had to confess that no treatment existed.

At the moment of their injury, every aspect of their life instantly changed. Paralysis, absence of sensation, urinary catheters, and an ever-circling wolf pack of complications became their reality. He knew what their injury meant. On each occasion it was a struggle for him not to break down.

Four years of research effort had resulted in the development of a solid animal testing protocol—and nothing more. The drugs Drake developed had showed no benefit. Zero, zip, nada, zilch.

But this night, everything felt different.

Drake's examination of the cat revealed movement—a slight twitch of the tail and claw extension on a hind foot. For a spinal cord injured animal, it was as if she'd done a back flip. Could it be real?

Drake revisited the methodology. The cats received the same anesthesia as human surgical patients. He would shave the fur over a two-inch section of the animal's mid-back, sterilely prep the skin, and open the tissue with a scalpel. He then meticulously dissected down to the thoracic spine, exposing the bony vertebrae. Using a miniature high-speed saw he painstakingly cut through the top layer of bone at the precisely identified level. The high pitched whining of the blade was accompanied by an odor like that of burnt hair.

Removal of the freed section of bone exposed the glistening white spinal cord.

The spinal cord, without its bony armor, was incredibly vulnerable. A nickel dropped from a height of six inches striking the cord would result in complete and irreversible paralysis below the point of impact.

This is essentially what they did in the next step of the procedure. A falling weight struck a specifically identified site of the spinal cord, creating a paralyzing injury. They used a blunt mini-guillotine-like device designed by Rizz to deliver the paralyzing injury to the exposed cord.

Drake then sutured the surgical wound closed and, after the anesthesia wore off, performed a neurologic exam documenting the location and degree of paralysis.

Then the code-labeled test drug was administered.

Drake examined the treated cats every day, looking for the return of movement. Over the previous three-plus years, none of the animals had shown any benefit. The drug-treated cats remained completely paralyzed below the cord lesion. With each successive failure, he wrestled growing doubt.

Drake now slipped his hands, with fingers spread, under the drape, lifting the black-and-white cat and placing her, as if made of crystal, into one of the kennels along the wall.

Rizz stopped his cleanup and looked across the table. “Drake, you knew going in that the odds against success were ridiculous. There’s never been a treatment that helps spinal cord injury. Never. I still can’t figure why you chose such a hopeless problem to work on.” His expression lightened. “Whatever. You’re the biochemist and principal investigator while Jon and I get research credit just for being Igors to your Dr. Drakenstein genius.” He affected a hunched back and claw-handed posture.

Drake looked at the cage where he’d just placed the black-and-white cat. “I have to try.”

“Hey, I respect that, partner, but just keeping it real. We’re like three guys in a garage trying to build the first supercomputer. Multi-million dollar labs at Pfizer, Genentech, and all the big boys have been trying to develop a drug that treats spinal cord injury for a long time. Newsflash—they haven’t come up with one. When the spinal cord goes down, it stays down.” He stuffed a last item into his backpack.

“I won’t quit.”

“No,” Rizz said, eyeing him. “You won’t.” He looked at his watch. “But I will—at least for today. I’m meeting someone a hell of a lot better looking than you or these cats.”

“Rizz, why not wait? I can double-check this pretty quick.” Drake picked up the test drug vial. The vial’s protocol label read D-44. Could it be the real deal?

Rizz slipped a backpack strap over his shoulder. "Dude, it's party-time. All work and no play—"

"If the video shows no errors, I'm gonna be super jacked. Keep your phone handy. I'll call you."

"Don't bother." Rizz gave a backhanded wave as he passed the cages heading for the door. "I can wait. Later." He pulled the lab door closed behind him.

Drake shook his head. Rizz had ceased believing. He wasn't remotely considering the possibility the result was real.

Drake dared to believe. He tried to control his excitement, dreading the likelihood that it was a technical error. He turned to the data records and computer with surging anticipation.

They maintained duplicate documentation and videotape records of every step of each procedure. Drake could double-check each step of the small cat's surgery and treatment. He held his breath as he assembled the materials for review.

First he opened the handwritten data log where each animal's drug treatment was recorded. He compared this with the duplicate computer data. They should corroborate one another. They did.

The lab's overhead lighting hummed. He smelled the mix of the cats and the fresh cedar shavings used as bedding. He heard the soft, quick paw pounces of the untested animals and a soft mewing from the upper cages. He began to fidget and bounce his leg as he reviewed Rizz's documentation of the cat's pre-drug paralysis. His leg stopped. Rizz had not made an error—the animal's findings were complete.

Drake soared inside as he accessed the video file. He selected *Surgical Record: Cord exposure and lesion induction, treatment protocol D-44, Subject D4*. The wall clock ticked loud as he waited for the program to open.

The video image flickered. The gurgling sounds of water rushing through the building's plumbing started and stopped. His heart pounded as the video played. The images displaying his surgical treatment of the little black-and-white cat were clear.

His technique was without flaw.

He licked his lips and swallowed. Last to be reviewed, and most prone to error, was creation of the spinal cord lesion. The video showed the fall of the weight onto the exposed cord. Drake involuntarily winced just as he did every time he actually performed this harsh step. The digital readout of Rizz's device displayed the impact achieved. The values were correct.

The experimental record left no doubt. There were no errors.

Drake entered the review check-off and saved the data. He picked up a remote storage device and connected it to a USB port and backed up the experimental record. He carefully closed the laptop, slid it forward with both hands and stepped back from the slate-topped table.

He felt as if he might float away, static charged, his scalp tingling. In his dreams of a breakthrough he jumped into the air, screaming his joy. Tonight he placed both hands over his face and slumped to the floor with his back against the ancient iron radiator. The unyielding flanges dug into his back. He heard the scattered soft mewing, the ticking clock, the hammering of his heart.

He looked up and out the upper panes of the streaked and vine-latticed windows to a brilliant full moon. Absolute confirmation would require repeat trials. But inside he knew.

It was real.

Chapter 27

Lab, present

Drake wiped up the spilled scotch while keeping an ear on Jon's breathing.

Jon was a twenty-seven-year-old ER doctor but tonight he was as vulnerable as a first-time drunken teenager. His breathing was noisy but regular. The odor of alcohol had strengthened.

On that incredible night two months back, Drake had broken out Rizz's Wild Turkey and celebrated the black-and-white cat's miraculous gain. Since that night, Drake spent every spare moment in the lab.

They'd informally presented their preliminary results at the spring meeting of the regional Association for Academic Emergency Medicine. Faith completed the legal work that established NeurVitae as a business and protected their intellectual property rights.

He estimated he needed three more weeks to complete the study. If all went well, they would then begin venture capital acquisition—what Rizz called "chasing drug money." With funding, they could apply for FDA acceptance as an investigational new drug. It was the first step in a costly, multi-year process.

Jon groaned from the cot.

Drake noted the time and reached for his phone. He kept it turned off in his locker while in the ER and had forgotten to turn it on. Seven missed calls – three from Yamada and four from Rachelle.

Rachelle answered before the second ring.

"Rachelle. I'm sorry I'm so late. Things—"

"You should've called. Or at least answer your phone." Her voice cracked. "A detective has called—twice. You have to call him right away. He sounded upset."

"Don't worry. I'm sure it's routine." *Nice work, Yamada, you inconsiderate prick.*

"Do you even think about me and the kids?" She sounded near tears.

Drake's shoulders slumped. "I'm a jerk. I should have called. I couldn't get the lab work finished this morning." Rizz's ugly confession flashed. "I'm stuck doing it now. And Jon's here. He's going to need me for a while."

"Jon? Oh Drake, poor Jon. How is he?"

Drake looked at his friend crashed on the cot. "He's a wreck."

"That was the first thing the detective demanded—did I know where Jon was? What's going on?"

"I'll call the detective right away. Don't worry." He kept his unease hidden. "Are the kids okay?"

"I heard them on the monitor talking and giggling before they fell asleep."

"You're a great mom. Thank you." He waited but she stayed silent. "Don't wait up. I should have called earlier. I'm sorry." Drake cupped the phone in both hands. "Are you okay, Rachelle? You know, really okay?"

She answered just above a whisper. "The detective scared me. I wish you were home." Silence. "I miss you. Take care of Jon."

"I will. I love you, Rachelle."

She disconnected.

He pulled out the detective's card. Why was Aki tracking Jon? He dialed the circled number.

"Homicide. Detective Yamada here."

"This is Drake Cody."

"Damn. About time. Where're you at? Do you know where Malar is?"

"I'm at the lab. My phone was turned off." *Which is no excuse for hassling my wife, asshole.*

"The lab?"

"Our research space."

"Got it. The spinal cord stuff. You may not have heard, but your ME buddy released a preliminary report declaring the death suspicious for homicide."

"Suspicious for homicide?" Drake frowned. "I bet he's just covering his ass. He's going to find a medical explanation."

"Maybe so, but the mayor, district attorney, and Reinhorst's people are all over my chief. Her death is the department's number one priority. I need to find Malar. Even his parents don't know where he is. I hope to hell he's not on the run."

"God's sake, Aki," Drake said. "Jon's not on the run. He's here with me. He's drunk and passed out. I'll have to haul him home."

"We'll come and pick him up."

Aki seemed a decent guy, but foremost he was a cop. If he suspected a crime, he'd go wherever his instincts led. What would he make of Rizz's sex-confession and Jon's drunken ravings?

Drake's stomach knotted.

"Aki, please. He's totally wasted. Let me take him home. Watch his place if you want. He's not running anywhere, I guarantee you. Talk to his folks. Let them take care of him tonight. You can talk with him tomorrow. It would be a kindness."

"Kindness doesn't play a big part in the investigation of a possible homicide, Doc." He paused. "But I'm gonna trust you. Take him home. You're not screwing with me?"

"I'm telling you straight."

"We'll talk tomorrow."

"Thanks for treating Jon right." Drake braced a hand on the lab table. "One last thing and no disrespect intended—any time you spend looking at Jon as a suspect for anything is a waste."

"Back off, Doc. It's nice you believe in your friend, but there's a lot you don't know and ain't none of it pretty. I know what I'm doing." He disconnected.

Drake looked up at the clock. The animals needed care and he had one miserable and very drunk friend that needed help.

As if on cue, Jon groaned, flung an arm across his chest, and hung his head over the edge of the cot. A mop-bucket splash of scotch and stomach contents splattered onto the floor. Jon raised an ashen face.

"No, no, no," he moaned. "Why?" He slumped, ending twisted and face down on the cot.

Drake cleaned Jon's face with a hand towel and spread two lab coats as a blanket over him, wishing he could somehow ease his friend's pain.

Drake opened a window wide. What did Jon's drunken words mean? If the police heard anything similar, there was no doubt what would happen.

Drake's past had taught him that the criminal justice system was a machine that grabbed, held on, and shredded lives.

As Aki said—kindness played no part in it.

And, Drake knew, sometimes neither did justice.

Chapter 28

11:10 p.m.

Alone in the deserted homicide room, Aki disconnected with Doc Cody and pocketed his phone. His eyes felt raw and he squinted in the harsh fluorescence. Maybe he'd be able to steal some sleep tonight after all. Malar wasn't going anywhere. Aki trusted Drake Cody on that—but nothing more.

His years on the job had trashed his faith in those he was sworn to "protect and serve." He'd been let down too many times.

He moved to the kitchen cubby and poured a cup of coffee. It tasted bitter. The death had not been officially confirmed as murder but he'd been operating as if it were from the start. It was the only way to keep his ass, and the department's covered.

Aki had sent an exhausted Farley home just minutes before Doc Cody's call. Aki held the report that summarized the results of the pudgy young detective's investigatory efforts.

When Aki had tracked down the rookie early this morning he'd been ready to rip him a new one.

"Shit, kid. A doc on the scene assigns the death as a priority ME case and she's a VIP besides. You declare it an accident and don't call me? Are you on drugs?"

The baby-faced detective went pale. Hell—he looked like he might cry.

"I'm so sorry. Damn me. I thought I had to make the call and I was trying not to look weak. I messed up." He wrung his hands, looking away. "How can I make it right?"

Farley's remorse was so genuine Aki's anger bled away.

"Always call, Farley. When you don't know—call."

"Have I totally screwed things?" He looked ill.

"We'll try and make it right. It's not certain there's been a crime, but things are pointing that way. If we're damn lucky the ME's suspicion is wrong and he finds a medical cause."

"What can I do?"

"Research Faith Reinhorst-Malar. Consider her death murder and find out everything about her you can."

Farley dove into the work like a man fighting to save his soul.

It was thirteen hours later when Aki finally sent Farley home. The earnest officer's desk was covered with crumpled snack bags, candy wrappers and Mountain Dew cans. The rookie had hammered the computer and performed phone interviews non-stop. He looked exhausted when he handed over his report on Faith Reinhorst Malar.

Aki leafed through the pages. "How'd you get all this stuff?"

"People talk to me." The young detective had lowered his gaze "And I'm a computer geek. I started hacking as a kid—ended up in front of a judge. He let me off easy and told me I should use my skills for good. That's what I do. I stay out of trouble and still get to do my thing. You have to be careful though." Farley had looked a bit guilty. "There can be admissibility issues. Unless you check with me, you should consider my stuff for investigational use only."

"Go home and get some sleep. I'll study this," Aki had said. "Hopefully the ME will know more by morning."

* * *

Aki leaned against the counter as he studied Farley's typed and hand-annotated pages. It summarized what he'd dug up on the twenty-seven-year-old woman whose death was "suspicious for homicide."

Andrew Reinhorst was her rich and powerful daddy, and mommy had been a country club socialite. Faith was a poor little rich girl raised by nannies and corralled in private schools. Farley's reports from his conversations and electronic data tracking showed Faith Reinhorst-Malar had been a wild one.

Media stories, police documents, and phone inquiries showed a pattern of reckless behavior smoothed over by Daddy's money and influence: At age fourteen, Faith had crashed Mommy's Mercedes en route to a concert with a car full of stoned friends. At seventeen, she engineered a credit card scheme resulting in theft of more than twenty thousand dollars. Quick payoffs and her father's influence staved off prosecution. At age eighteen, she was ticketed at two a.m. driving half-naked while doing a hundred. A thirty-two-year-old Minnesota Vikings wide receiver was in the car, and police reported seeing powdery material flung out the window.

Aki moved to the sink next to the coffeemaker. He set the reports aside and turned on the cold water, then splashed his face and the back of his neck. He used a paper towel to pat himself dry, then went back to the file.

Several years back, Andrew Reinhorst had placed fifty million dollars in an incentive trust for Faith. She started receiving disbursements from the endowment at age twenty.

Aki knew a bit about incentive trusts but went online and reviewed. It was as he thought. Faith had to live by the rules her father wrote into the trust or she kisses the money good-bye.

Aki paged to another sheet of Farley's report. He'd somehow unearthed the terms Daddy Reinhorst had written into Faith's trust.

The stipulations showed Reinhorst to be a world-class control freak. Faith had received a comfortable but surprisingly modest baseline monthly payout. A long list of behaviors would cost Faith part or all of the money: arrest, substance abuse, smoking, tattoos, and many more. Reinhorst had used the trust to fence his daughter in tighter than a dog in heat.

Some of the terms rewarded Daddy-approved behaviors. The pay-out increased when Faith completed college, entered law school and graduated. The final monthly increase came when she married—as her husband met the requirements of being employed, a church-going Christian, a college graduate without criminal record, and Caucasian.

Aki huffed. *How do you feel about Japanese-Americans, you bigoted turd?*

The media reports and risqué stories dwindled after the trust took effect.

Farley had printed a photo from the Minneapolis society section from four years previous. The husband, Dr. Jon Malar, all-American handsome, looked transfixed at her side.

Faith was gazing off over the crowd. Aki took a second look—the face of a goddess and the curves of a bikini model.

Grisly images from the autopsy flashed in his head. He went to Farley's next sheet.

The terms of the trust would keep Faith comfortable financially until the age of fifty. At that time she would finally get the big money. It had to suck to be unable to touch the massive wealth that was supposedly hers. Several of Farley's sources volunteered that Faith hated her father.

No shit! I haven't met the prick and I can't stand him.

They'd had no reported contact, other than via the courts, in years. He hadn't been invited to her wedding.

Aki pulled out a pack of Rolaids and chewed three of the chalky tablets. He washed them down with coffee, the aftertaste metallic and nasty. The dysfunction in the Reinhorst family made Aki think of the mess he'd made of his life. His wife and daughter were living back in Los Angeles. "He's married to that damn job," she'd said at the divorce proceeding.

A lump formed in his throat. *Low pay, high stress, and now alone—way to go, genius.*

He picked up the next sheet.

Faith's law career was more appearance than fact. She had an office without staff that she leased in an exclusive building near downtown's Loring Park. Apart from the reported NeurVitae efforts, her total legal activity involved a string of unsuccessful individual and summary challenges to the restrictions of her trust.

Farley had somehow tracked expenses routed through her legal practice. These included a surprising number of daytime check-in metro-area hotel and motel stays. Aki had seen this pattern before—typical of philandering husbands. Damn—this gal was a risk-taker.

Aki sipped the coffee. Farley had documented his call to her office building's security desk and transcribed the exchange. The daytime guard had reported that Faith came to her office daily, her appearances being a highlight of his day.

"That woman was just flat-out hot," was the quote. The guard noted that her clients were almost exclusively men. "But lately she's been in and out a few times with a woman—dark hair, totally buff, but kinda scary. A ball-buster, I'd guess."

Doc Cody said the husband, Eagle scout Dr. Malar, "worshipped Faith." Frequent hotel visits, going to work daily without any record of paying clients. Who visited her office? And why? Worship might not be what this wife had coming.

Farley's report finished with information on her finances. How had he accessed this?

Aki zeroed in on a transfer of $75,000 to Faith's business account. *Double damn.* The anonymous deposit occurred four days before her death. They would need a court order to track the origin of the deposit. Farley had written that he would pursue this when the banks opened in the morning.

Farley's efforts impressed Aki. Last night it seemed Farley should be fired—tonight Aki felt the rookie and his computer skills were a special asset. He'd delivered a week's worth of shoe-leather investigation in one day.

Aki dumped the remainder of the coffee and pitched the Styrofoam cup into the waste basket.

Most homicide investigations were slam dunks. The mindless and common drug- and alcohol-related killings were self-evident and could be solved by a chimpanzee. Even for the much less frequent premeditated murders, basic inquiry generally pointed the way. Love, hate, sex, money or power—most murders arose from one of these.

Faith Reinhorst-Malar appeared to have been living a life awash in them all.

Detective Farley's investigative efforts convinced Aki that Faith Reinhorst-Malar had been a woman who liked to play with fire.

His instincts told him she'd been burned.

Chapter 29

After disconnecting with Yamada, Drake mopped up Jon's mess and began the lab tasks. Jon's drunken snoring rasped like a saw.

The sixteen cages were stacked four across and four high on a platform two feet high. Currently nine of the cages were occupied. Five of the cats had been operated on and treated with D-44.

Drake pulled on rubberized cleaning gloves and dragged out the service cart with its two fifty-five-gallon plastic drums. One was waste and the second held fresh cedar shavings, a large water bottle, and a bag of cat chow. The cats' sensed his attention and began their typical chorus of yowls and mewing.

Over the past few years, he'd become fond of the cats. His current and all-time favorite was subject D4, the little black-and-white female. The miracle.

When Drake's schedule allowed, Rachelle and the kids accompanied him to the lab on non-operating days. Rachelle had enough medical knowledge to assist with routine medication administration and cares.

Kristin loved the animals and drew dozens of pictures of them. One showed the black-and-white miracle cat jumping over a fence. Drake thought the fence looked like a hurdle and named the cat FloJo, after the historic female U.S. track star.

The cages, made of plastic mesh with a collection tray underneath for spent shavings, were high-tech and equipped with automated food and water dispensers. Drake daily emptied each tray and replenished the shavings, food and water.

Every day, he documented a precise neurologic assessment of each of the five current study animals. The surgically-induced spinal cord injury left them unable to walk or stand on their hind legs.

FloJo and each of the four subsequent D-44 treated specimens showed evidence of regained function. The gains were small—most were just twitches and faint tremors of movement. FloJo showed the greatest improvement. She was now slightly over two months post D-44 treatment. Six days back she had raised a paw. *Incredible.*

Even the slightest recovery could transform the life of a spinal cord injured person. If D-44 allowed a totally paralyzed person to regain the full use of one finger it could mean the difference between institutional living and considerable independence.

Drake's dreams extended far beyond one finger.

He stared out the vine-stippled upper windows. A siren wailed somewhere in the distance. Jon's booze-sick smell was blunted by the aroma of the cedar shavings. Drake bent to pull out FloJo's tray. Her cage sat on the bottom of the second stack from the end.

"How's my Flo?" As he pulled the tray he glanced in. He did a double-take.

He stepped back, rechecked the cage position and crouched once more.

The smooth-furred female with black patches on a white coat gazed at Drake. She poked out a pink tongue then gave a soft *mew*. His breath caught. He dropped to his knees. Then to all fours, his eyes inches from the cage.

His face split in a smile and he laughed out loud.

FloJo, research specimen D4, was *standing upright* in her cage.

Chapter 30

Wyndham Grand Hotel, 11:47 p.m.

Meryl had slept less than four hours in the past three days.

She leaned forward from the couch and lifted the cover off the room service tray. Mandarin orange segments in a china bowl on white linen—perfect. She plucked a segment from the bowl and popped it into her mouth—ideal fuel for a kick-ass brain. Her naked, carved body still glowed from the workout she'd completed fifteen minutes earlier.

Meryl picked up the syringe and speared the one-and-a-half inch needle into her thigh. She drove the plunger home and withdrew the needle. A bead of blood formed on her skin at the injection site.

She couldn't recall the dose of Anabol she'd loaded today. Recording her regimen no longer mattered. People like her didn't have upper limits.

She was free-styling in the genius zone.

Meryl had read Dr. Suzie's email before drawing up the steroid injection. According to the fetching psychiatrist, Meryl was in the throes of uncontrolled mania and needed to resume lithium and immediately seek psychiatric help.

Meryl laughed out loud. The doctor hadn't even responded to Meryl's intimate invitation or her breakthrough thoughts on drugs and the advancement of human physical and cognitive performance. *It's clear who has the thinking disorder, pretty Suzie.*

Meryl used her fingertip to dab the bead of blood off her thigh. She touched her finger to her tongue.

Doctor "swinging-dick" Rizzini had yet to produce the molecular identity and synthesis pathway for D-44. Meryl didn't believe he could—regardless of his motivation. She smiled as she recalled his pleading.

The doctors underwhelmed her. They'd been as trusting as sheep regarding Faith and their legal work. The supposed intellectual hotshots deserved to be ripped off. They were all fools compared to her.

The idea that there was something noble about doctors, nurses, or any of the so-called "caring" professions was a joke. Their "commitment" was the result of the same instincts and neurochemical physiologic processes that caused a rat to push a bar for a food pellet.

The caregivers' prestige, power, and personal rewards were nothing more than rat chow. Their accomplishments linked to their sexual pairings and survival much like the flaming red ass and canine teeth of baboons impacted their reproductive success.

The notion that they were motivated by some selfless ideal was a moronic fiction.

Whatever his motivations, this Dr. Drake Cody was problematic.

Despite the flashy academic pedigrees of Drs. Malar and Rizzini, it was the low-profile family man from Ohio who drove the research.

Faith had shared an impression of him as something of a rebel. Perhaps, but he showed no suggestion of outlaw in his adherence to blinded protocol and scientific method. Where did the troublesome bastard have the D-44 identification information stashed? How could she get her hands on it?

Meryl opened her laptop and found another of Heinrich's increasingly dramatic communiqués:

From: Heinrich Pater, President – BioZyn, Inc.
Subject: Product acquisition
You have failed to produce the needed information.
Board advises deadline must be met or grave consequences.
I cannot overemphasize the gravity of this advisory.
I will be arriving in Minneapolis with operatives ASAP.

Meryl gave a huff and slapped the laptop shut, shoving it back on the table top. Screw Heinrich. She'd made assurances—that was true. But he'd set the timeline.

The deadline must be fast-approaching. The Board was displeased—whatever. Deal with it, Heinie.

Faith was history. Dr. Rizzini inept. Shit happens and one does what needs to be done.

Faith had directly approached the Swiss firm. A complete betrayal, but so outrageously ballsy that now that Meryl's fury had cooled, she couldn't help but smile. The erotic beauty had been like no other. Meryl's body responded to the thought of her. *Damn, we had it happening, girl!*

Faith's blackmail of Rizzini had provided them NeurVitae's research documentation and results. Coupled with the legal documents Faith had constructed, Meryl had everything needed to complete the transfer. Everything but the key—drug D-44's molecular identity and synthesis pathway.

She popped another segment of mandarin into her mouth.

Heinrich would bitch and wring his hands. Meryl would take care of business. Weaklings whined while Meryl did what needed doing. She'd learned early it was one of the ways she was special.

* * *

During Meryl's junior year in high school, Grandma got sick. They moved her into Meryl's room with a welfare-provided hospital bed and a grocery bag full of medicine.

The pill bottles came in all shapes and sizes: some were plastic cylinders, others amber-colored with white covers. Still others were rectangular and white with fluted tops and complicated twist-off caps. A few were brown glass and tiny, with metal caps that unscrewed normally. The dressing table's mirror doubled the medicines in its reflection.

Meryl fell in love with the pills. The long names and precise information printed on the labels fascinated her. She researched them. Studied what each medication did and how many and when they should be given. She learned of their life-and-death power.

Her parents couldn't even read the names. Meryl took control of administering Grandma her medicines.

Grandma was weak. Spidery blue veins ran along the surface of her arms. Her skin was bruised, scabbed and tissue-paper thin.

From the start, Meryl noticed that Grandma smelled. The source of some odors was obvious, but even when Grandma was cleaned up, Meryl sensed a lingering foulness. It reminded her of when her mother had left raw hamburger in the refrigerator for too long.

Almost daily, her parents would wring their hands and talk about Grandma's suffering. They said it would be a blessing if she slipped away.

But they didn't do anything.

Meryl liked Grandma before she'd become sick and moved into her room. Back then, she'd open her carpetbag of a purse and pull out orange candies. Now Grandma did nothing and smelled bad. Meryl did not like that.

Her mother made Meryl responsible for Grandma's cleaning as well as her pills. She really did not like that.

Meryl did what needed to be done. No one cried at the funeral.

It was a blessing.

* * *

Meryl picked up the scrolled twenty-dollar bill. Heinrich was pissed off and coming to check on her ASAP. Screw him. He and the big, scary BioZyn board could kiss her buff and luscious ass.

She was done taking shit from inferior minds.

A knock at the door interrupted her thoughts. She checked the time—right on schedule. It would be the "young and adventurous female, likes discreet fun w like-minded ladies" from the internet escort service.

"Just one minute." Meryl bent over her well-used compact mirror. Two big sniffs of cocaine passed through the rolled bill. Seconds passed as her head buoyed up like a hot-air balloon.

She slipped on her teddy, noting her nipples standing sensitive and tall through the sheer fabric. *Time to give the pleasure centers some serious up-regulation.*

Moving toward the door, she stopped. Her cheeks stretched into a smile. A plan for getting the D-44 information had burst full-blown in her head like fireworks.

Brilliant and fast—she'd likely complete the job before Heinie touched down.

Damn, girl—you're one diamond-hard bitch. A superstar.

"Coming," Meryl called as she put her hand on the handle to admit her girl-toy. She so hoped her request for a tanned blonde that could role-play had been met.

Meryl would call her Faith.

Chapter 31

Germany, thirty kilometers SW of Munich

Heinrich drank from his second glass of scotch as sunrise peeked into the drawing room of his Lake Starnberg villa. Out the wall of windows, the snow-covered peaks appeared next-door close in the alpine clarity. The low-angled sunlight on waves created a field of dancing jewels. He took no pleasure in the beauty.

Heinrich had lunged awake hours before dawn, soaked in cold sweat. He'd wakened his Filipino live-in and sent her away. She didn't interest him now. Another female dominated his thoughts.

Meryl—damn the arrogant American. Her last communication was defiant and she'd ignored his subsequent calls and emails. She'd wrested control of the NeurVitae operation and had them headed for disaster.

He checked his in-box every few minutes, hoping for word that she had D-44 in hand.

If she didn't succeed soon, they would both pay. The BioZyn board did not address failure with an entry in your file and a caution to do better in the future.

The Board scripted unsatisfactory performance reports in blood and punctuated them with the snapping of bones.

The negotiations initiated in the Argentine mountains had yielded spectacular bids from each of the three pharmaceutical companies.

This would be just one component of BioZyn's anticipated returns. The Board had decided beforehand, based on stock market analysis, to award the drug to the Danish firm. Based on Meryl and Heinrich's assurances regarding D-44, BioZyn had, through shadow buyers, secured millions in stocks and stock options.

Further negotiations would ratchet up the bids and BioZyn would award the deal to the Danes at an incredible price.

Upon completion of the deal, the financial media would announce the arrival of the breakthrough drug in the Danish firm's development pipeline. The value of their stock would take off like a Trident missile.

The BioZyn "investment" in shares and options would be worth many additional millions.

But until Meryl succeeded, BioZyn could not complete the transfer. No announcement would be made, and the investment in stock and expiring options would return little or nothing.

A beep signaled an incoming email. Heinrich sprang to the computer in hope. *Scheisse!*

Not Meryl. A message from the Board:

> *Re: Product acquisition*
> *Transfer to be completed within seven days or stock options expire and part of our investment will be lost.*
> *Satisfactory performance is required.*
> *Oversight is being arranged.*

Heinrich swallowed. His eyes stuck on one word—oversight.

He would never forget the declaration the pliers-wielding BioZyn operative had delivered to the terrified French attorney.

"There are issues. We have been sent to provide oversight."

Chapter 32

5:55 a.m.

Drake climbed into the old Dodge, a cup of coffee in one hand and a bagel clenched in his teeth. Heavy dew covered the windshield and he flicked the wipers on for a few passes. The eastern sky brightened in the predawn coolness.

He'd delivered Jon to the care of his parents shortly before midnight. When Drake arrived home, Rachelle was asleep. She'd not stirred despite his purposely noisy entry. He wondered if she'd taken something.

She and the kids slept as he awoke, dressed and slipped out the door in the a.m. darkness. He wasn't sure if Rachelle knew how much it hurt to see so little of her and the kids. *Next year will be better.*

The news of FloJo's miracle improvement remained his alone. As he drove, he imagined doctors in ERs diagnosing spinal cord injury, then telling the patient of *the possibility for recovery* as nurses administered D-44. His imaginings had leapt far beyond reality, but even the sadness of his morning's first business couldn't rein in his dreams.

Drake slowed the car. The low-slung, almost windowless sandstone building sat surrounded by blacktop. He turned into the morgue's parking lot. A fluorescent orange Hummer sat in the parking stall nearest the front walkway. The license plates read "IC-DEAD."

Drake resolved he wouldn't let the associate ME's manner get to him.

He entered the autopsy theater where Kip Dronen's gaunt body hunched over a stainless steel table. His surgical mask hung loose beneath over-sized wire-rim glasses and Einstein hair. The cloying odor of formaldehyde hung heavy. Underneath, Drake registered the sewer-air tinge of dead flesh.

The brightly lit corpse of an elderly black male lay on the table. The standard Y-incision exposed the contents of the chest and abdomen. Kip wrestled a knobby softball-sized organ from the abdominal cavity. He plunked it into a basin dangling from a scale just above table height.

"Son of a bitch, ER, sneak attack at dawn, huh?" squeaked Kip. He toed a foot pedal, turning off the microphone he used to record his findings. "See this?" He held his hands towards the body. "I'm under nut-crushing pressure on your celebrity crump and I still have this bullshit to deal with."

He lifted the dark-colored organ out of the basin. "Check out this hunk of alligator hide—a cirrhotic liver. Tough as a boot. This dude was hardcore. Found null and void last night in an alley on Nicollet Island. Unknown cause so he rates an autopsy—a waste of my skills. An old drunk dies—big mystery."

Drake thought of the Captain ending up on a table here someday. He buried the flash of annoyance he felt towards Kip. "Detective Yamada told me you released a statement."

"I had to." Kip's eyes darted about. "They were ripping on me like hyenas."

"Did the toxicology screens show anything?"

"Nothing but the recreational level of cocaine and some weed. Of course, only the routine poisons and drugs are detected by the screening tests. Beyond that, I have to run individual substance-specific assays. If you don't specifically test for it, you won't find it, and the number of toxins is huge."

Kip turned back to the corpse and picked up a scalpel. "But I've run her for damn near everything our lab can check, and I haven't turned up what killed our smoking-hot wench."

"So now what?" Kip's disrespectful language irritated.

"The tests didn't spit out an answer, so I revisit the pathophysiology." He shrugged. "She died from lack of oxygen. That's beyond question. *How* is unclear. She either couldn't breathe or wouldn't breathe."

"Wouldn't breathe? You mean like an overdose? Or mixing tranquilizers and booze? She became so sedated she quit breathing?"

"Don't forget Propofol and Michael Jackson." Kip mimed a clumsy moon-walk. "Possibly something like that, but this is much more complex. This is ninja level." Kip spoke faster as he warmed to the discussion of death, his favorite topic. "Here's what we know. The autopsy pulmonary pattern doesn't fit a drowning—she has the wrong water distribution."

"You said that the water in the lungs looked like it just flowed in," Drake said.

Kip sawed free something in the chest of the dead man, then set the scalpel on the adjacent tray. "Exactly." He continued in lecture mode. "When people drown, eighty-five percent of the time their lungs contain water—what we call wet drownings. The drive to breathe becomes so overwhelming that, in the end, they actually do. They breathe water. Effing radical, huh?" He gave a twisted grin. "The inhaled water distributes in a characteristic pattern within the lungs. Also, if one looks, you can find froth in the trachea and bronchi. They churn the water in and out so frantically it turns to froth. How intense is that?" Kip spoke as if he were describing a sporting event.

"This babe had water in her lungs, but in the wrong distribution and no froth. So she didn't drown." Kip reached both hands into the chest and lifted out the man's heart. "I've never seen her pattern before. I don't think it's ever been reported." He plopped the heart into the hanging basin.

"Just for completeness, I'll tell you that the other fifteen percent of the time drownings are dry. When people are forced underwater the vocal cords reflexively close. In wet drownings, as I described, the cords open as they're dying and they try the water breathing thing. In dry drownings, the cords stay shut even after they die. No one knows why. In those cases, the lungs have virtually no water in them." He paused. "That clearly was not the case here."

"I'm with you. It doesn't fit either a wet or a dry drowning. Besides which, the caretaker said Faith was conscious when she came out of the water."

"That," Kip said, "definitely doesn't add up." He frowned in concentration.

Drake folded his arms in the meat-locker coolness.

"Son of a bitch," Kip straightened. "I should've nailed this earlier." He faced Drake. "The babe had water in her lungs. The only way that could happen was if her vocal cords were open. If her cords were open underwater, she'd either be doing the water breathing thing, or gagging and coughing. Unless…"

"Unless what?"

"Unless she couldn't." Kip gave a snort. "Unless she couldn't close her cords and couldn't breathe! You get it?" He laughed. "Aha!"

Kip lifted the heart out of the basin. "What I'm saying is, if your witness is right, somehow she must have been paralyzed—completely paralyzed." He grinned and gestured with the heart. "Paralyzed vocal cords allowed water to flow in and paralyzed muscles prevented her from gagging, prevented her from coughing, and prevented her from taking a breath."

He set the heart down and held his hands wide, his shrill voice jubilant. "No froth, passive water distribution, and she checks out from hypoxia. It all fits." He slapped a gloved hand on the corpse's thigh. "Damn. This is effing awesome. When I nail this and write it up it will be the cover article in *Journal of Forensic Pathology*." He cackled and gave a fist pump.

"Damn it, Kip." Drake banged his fist on the metal instrument stand.

Kip flinched at the echoing crash.

"End the celebration. Now." Drake leaned forward. "We're talking about the death of my friend's wife."

Kip huffed and shot Drake a frown. "Jesus! Lighten up, man." He turned back to the corpse. "I told you before, I'm not into the feelings shit." He lifted a lung free of the chest cavity, the surface scarred and blackened. He held it aloft. "Check out this coal sack. The old drunk was a smoker. Color me surprised." He flopped the organ into the basin. "You don't find my emotional sensitivity acceptable, huh, ER? Well, excuse me all to hell. Who are ya, effing Oprah?"

Drake closed his eyes. Each medical specialty tended to attract certain types. Drake fought to save lives—Kip dealt with nothing but death. He hadn't talked to or treated a live patient in a decade. Perhaps his detachment was explainable.

"This is personal, Kip. Are you saying she was murdered?"

"I'm close, really close, to nailing this, feelings-guy." He shrugged. "What I do know for sure is that this death is so awesome it's giving me a hard-on."

Drake looked toward the ceiling. This wasn't a specialty thing—Kip was uniquely messed up. Drake pictured him as Chief ME making a similar statement to the press.

Kip bent and reached into the body. "The rapid onset of paralysis in this setting doesn't fit a natural process. It looks to be murder—or, less likely, suicide. I'm convinced the chick died from a drug or poison." Kip squinted as he strained with something. A soft pop sounded and he rocked back. He straightened, holding up the long, whitish Y-shaped structure that comprised the trachea and main stem bronchi.

"I don't know yet what substance killed her, but I'll figure it out." He grasped the trailing portion of the trachea. He fit the organ into the basin. "And ER, I gotta admit—your input helped. I'm listing you as a secondary author when I nail this and publish." He nodded. "Murder or suicide—either way it's effing great."

Drake hung his head. *He's in his own world.*

"It ain't great, Kip. It definitely ain't great." Drake started walking out then stopped, still facing the exit. "Kip, if you really want the chief ME position, you need to tone yourself down. Being a cheerleader for death doesn't go over well."

"Hey, ER, check this out."

Drake turned.

The scrawny, grinning doctor had his arms extended, displaying raised, gloved and blood-smeared middle fingers.

* * *

Drake looked across the ER corridor to the clock mounted above the central secretary station. Nine-forty a.m. Detective Yamada should arrive any minute. Drake's shift started at ten.

He couldn't imagine Faith committing suicide. He didn't want to believe she'd been murdered.

Could Kip be wrong?

"No, No. Please, sir. Stop!" The urgent female cry came from the cubicle adjacent to the counter. "I need help here! Please." Drake jumped up and hustled into the cubicle.

A large, dark-haired man sat naked on the bed, his gown on the floor. He held Julie, a short, red-haired nurse, by both wrists. She struggled to get free, her eyes wide. A bandage covered the man's forehead and he had a blackened eye. A Harley-Davidson tattoo crossed his chest and road-rash abrasions covered his left leg and hip.

His eyes were open and unfocused, his face a blank. An IV lock lay taped in the muscular, tattooed left arm.

Drake spoke softly over his shoulder to the personnel he sensed collecting behind him. "Let's get one hundred fifty micrograms of Fentanyl and two milligrams of Ativan, please." He turned to the man.

"Hello there," Drake spoke slowly and calmly as he glanced at the patient's wristband. "Robert. It's all okay. No worries, it's all good." He placed a hand gently on the big man's shoulder. "This little gal is just helping you out. How about we ease up on that grip? You're a strong dude. You don't want to hurt her."

Drake made eye contact with the nurse and spoke just above a whisper. "Don't struggle. Just be loose. I've got you. You'll be okay."

She stilled.

The big man still looked vacant but the muscled cables of his forearms appeared looser. A nurse materialized next to and behind Drake. She flashed two syringes.

"Robert, we're going to give you some medicine to help you out." Drake picked up the IV access port and held it towards the nurse behind him, and whispered, "Fentanyl, one hundred fifty micrograms

She accessed the port and slowly depressed the syringe's plunger.

"You're doing great, Robert. Just relax, big guy. Let's just loosen up that grip and let this little lady help you out." To the side he whispered, "Two milligrams of Ativan."

The nurse switched syringes and pushed the Ativan. The patient slowly turned his head towards Drake, looking at him without expression.

"Thank you, Robert. We appreciate it." Drake rested his hand on the burly man's shoulder. "Can you let go with your hands now, please?"

The man looked at his hands and popped them open as if surprised they'd been holding anything.

"Thank you, Robert. Thank you. How about let's just have you lay back." Drake leaned over and with a hand on both shoulders, eased the man back onto the bed. "Just relax, Robert. We'll take care of you. It's all okay."

An intern hustled up. "What happened?" he whispered. "I was taking care of him. Is he okay?" The first-year doctor was in the midst of several weeks of training in the ER.

The red-haired nurse responded, "I went to cover him up. His gown had come off. He grabbed my wrists. Really hard. He had that blank look. Scared me." She looked sheepish.

Scaring an ER nurse, thought Drake, is like lifting an elephant—very hard to do.

The intern spoke to Drake. "He came in about an hour and a half ago. Dumped his Harley. Low speed. No helmet. No reported loss of consciousness. Awake and alert. Neuro intact. He's got a head gash, facial bruises, and some road rash. A nice guy. I finished sewing up his head twenty minutes ago."

"Wasn't drinking? No pain meds?"

"Nothing. Sober and he refused pain meds," said the intern. "This is a big change. Should I get him to CT and scan his head?"

"Immediately," Drake said. "Stay with him. Stand next to the radiologist and call neurosurgery immediately if a bleed shows up on the scan. He may have an epidural. Be ready to get him to the OR fast. Let me know if any issues."

"For sure." The intern nodded. "Thanks for getting him settled down." He eyed the dozing big man. "If he'd stayed combative, you'd have had to put him down and intubate him. That would've been the only way to get the CT, right?"

"Yes. And if he's bleeding in his head, struggling would be the worst thing for him." Drake froze, his mind running.

Julie, the red-haired nurse, rubbed her forearms. "Thanks for helping so quick, Dr. Cody."

Drake heard her but it took a moment for him to respond. "Oh. Of course, Julie. You're welcome."

He faced the adjacent Crash Room. The life clock displayed "0 mins, 0 secs." Racks of endotracheal tubes and intubation equipment hung mounted behind the head of each cart.

If Drake had not succeeded in calming the Harley man, they'd be in the Crash Room now. On Drake's order, the nurse would inject the drugs necessary to keep the agitated biker from moving. The drugs that would allow Drake to place a tube into the man's airway to breathe for him as they kept him motionless for the CT scan he so urgently needed.

The clattering of the lab results printer and the overhead pages continued in the background. The odor of the antiseptic that had cleansed the man's wounds lingered.

"...would have had to put him down and intubate him," the intern had said.

"...must have been paralyzed. Paralyzed vocal cords allowed water to flow in and paralyzed muscles prevented her from taking a breath." Kip's determination of Faith's mechanism of death.

What Kip didn't know was what had caused such paralysis.

Drake felt himself go weak, he leaned against the wall, hand on forehead, stomach queasy.

He knew, oh God. He knew. And what he knew sent his world wobbling on its axis.

Chapter 33

Loring Park office building, morning

The evidence tech continued to chuckle as she snapped photos of the contents of Faith Reinhorst-Malar's law office.

Farley knew he'd turned beet red when he'd pulled the jointed sex toy from the leather athletic bag. He'd almost thrown the item in shock. He ended up holding it, at arm's length, pinched between gloved finger and thumb like a soiled rag.

His first search warrant as a homicide detective and he was already about to become part of department comic lore. Why was it that he always ended up looking like a clown?

The search warrant described entry, examination and seizure of any and all contents of the law office of Faith Reinhorst-Malar, deceased.

The outer room had proved to be a typical professional's office with stylish furnishings, file cabinets, a desktop calendar, and a PC. Farley had found some provocative information on his quick perusal of those items. He was eager to get into the computer but had to wait until the hard drive could be cloned downtown.

He'd opened a door to what he thought was a closet or office restroom. His jaw had dropped at the sight of the king-sized bed with satin sheets and the mirrored walls and ceiling. The inner sanctum was a lavishly appointed sex pad.

The tech had poked her head past his stunned immobility and whistled. "Toto, I don't think we're in Kansas anymore."

They found a fully stocked bar, glassine packets of white powder, and a supply of condoms and other sex paraphernalia. Lying on the bar was the leather athletic bag. It contained the lesbian sex devices that startled Farley.

"Hey, I've heard about getting screwed by lawyers, but this office takes it literally," the tech said.

Farley blushed.

"Hey, detective. Give me a smile." Farley turned and she snapped a photo of him holding a bizarre strap-on contraption he'd just catalogued.

"That's definitely not your style." She giggled.

Farley didn't laugh. He felt afresh his embarrassment regarding his initial mishandling of Faith Reinhorst-Malar's death. He'd tried to display initiative and a take-charge attitude when he'd stood poolside and declared the death accidental. Instead he'd compromised the investigation and looked like an idiot. He was such a fat-assed screw-up.

Money, adultery, deceit, sexual debauchery and drugs—what hadn't this woman been involved with? The more Farley learned, the more shameful she became. Imagine having been her husband?

The poor bastard.

Chapter 34

ER, 9:45 a.m.

The intern and a nurse rushed Harley-man towards CT as Drake spoke with Kip. He ended the brief call and hung up the cubicle's phone.

The conversation reinforced his certainty. Kip said he'd fast-track the needed drug assay. "Damn—you were thinking like me. Not bad for an ER guy. We nailed it."

Yesterday Kip had overnight-expressed specimens to the FBI lab in Virginia in anticipation of further testing. The Virginia Beach facility had the most extensive forensic laboratory capabilities in the nation. A pathologist colleague of Kip's held a key position there.

"He's okay. Not a complete hack." Kip believed they'd be able to get the analysis result soon. "These assays are quick, and the dude owes me. I taught him every clever thing he knows. Besides which, there's big juice from everywhere on this case."

Detective Yamada was due any minute. Should Drake wait for the test result before sharing his theory?

"Hey Doc. Sorry I'm late." Yamada approached from the central corridor.

Drake did a double take. Aki wore a pin-striped suit, a tie knotted in a perfect Windsor, and a silk shirt. And a barber, or perhaps a stylist, had him fashionably shorn. His expression matched his new appearance. He looked cutting-edge.

"Where can we talk?" Aki asked as he looked about the bustling ER. "Privately."

Privacy could be hard to come by in the busy department.

"I've got a spot." Drake gestured down the hall. "Thanks for helping me with that assault thing—and for treating Jon right last night." They moved down the corridor.

"Don't know how much thanks I deserve. The security video saved your ass." Aki shook his head. "Without it, I don't know what I would have been forced to do."

Drake stopped in front of the Air Care elevator and swiped his ID card through the access. "Why are you so duded up?"

"I was told to look good." The doors slid open and they stepped in. "This case is high profile."

As the elevator ascended, Drake considered everything at stake.

What should he say to the detective? What shouldn't he say?

If he shared what Jon and Rizz had said, the suspicion would focus on them. It would lead the investigation off track and Drake knew too well that people could be ruined by accusation alone.

The doors slid open, revealing the helipad and the glistening, flame-painted helicopter. A pilot stood alongside an open engine compartment holding a clipboard. He gave Drake and Aki a nod and returned to his task.

A concrete slab formed the central portion of the flight deck. The east and west aspects consisted of sections of steel mesh that extended over the building's edge like gilt wings. Walking on those sections provided a through-the-mesh view of the eight-story drop to the ground below. It made Drake uneasy.

He stopped on the edge of the concrete slab, crowded by the copter, but just clear of the see-through steel section.

The morning's sunlight glowed warm and golden. St. Paul's downtown skyline rose out of the metro expanse a few miles to the east.

"Wow," said the detective, taking in the view for a moment.

"Doc, I just had a thirty-second conversation with the ME. He'd just hung up with you. He says you guys nailed it—some weird drug. The FBI lab is testing for it as we speak." Aki placed a hand on Drake's upper arm.

"Doc, if you're right, this confirms murder." He drilled Drake with his eyes. "Now it's time to tell me everything you know that could relate to the death of Faith Reinhorst-Malar. And I mean everything. I think you've been holding back on me."

Drake's mouth went dry. His thoughts skipped to his vulnerable friends, his record, and the destructive potential of the criminal justice system.

"I'm concerned some things may seem suspicious—might get you looking in the wrong direction."

Aki frowned. "Let me worry about that." He pulled out his tattered notepad. "Start with this drug that you think killed her."

"Succinylcholine. A neuromuscular blocker—that's what fits."

"A neuro what? Spell that. What does it mean?"

Drake spelled it and continued, “It’s a drug that paralyzes—it causes a complete but temporary inability to move or breathe.”

“Why the hell would you want that?”

“It eliminates the cough and gag reflex. It’s necessary to allow intubation of patients. Otherwise reflexes slam the vocal cords shut, blocking the trachea. Like the way a blink protects the eyes. The drug is injected before every major surgery to allow the breathing tube to be put between the open vocal cords into the trachea. The inability to move lasts only minutes. Often the patient needs to be kept motionless longer, so the dose is repeated for as long as the surgery, tests, or other care require.”

“So you drug them and jam a tube into their throat?”

“The drug is injected. Within a minute, every muscle twitches, then becomes completely paralyzed. The tube is slipped between the paralyzed vocal cords into the trachea. It must be done quickly to prevent the patient from dying because they can’t breathe. The tube is connected to a ventilator. The machine breathes for the patient.”

Aki looked doubtful. “So you think someone knocked her out with this drug?”

“The drug doesn’t knock you out. We always give another drug beforehand to sedate the patient. The tox screens proved Faith did not have any sedatives in her system. If this is how Faith died, she remained completely alert and felt everything. But she couldn’t have moved. Not even a blink.”

Drake looked down through the adjacent steel mesh deck to the ground far below. His equilibrium shifted and he felt himself sway. “If this drug killed her, she would have died whether she had fallen in the pool or not. No matter where she was, the drug would have made her unable to move or breathe.” His view began to spin. He stepped back and raised his eyes. The horror of such a death hadn’t previously registered. Faith would have been helplessly aware of each excruciating second.

Aki clenched his teeth, lips drawn. “Nasty. I guess that pretty much rules out suicide—unless she wanted to go out suffering.” He shrugged then flipped a page in his notepad. “How would the killer get it? Is it a drugstore kind of deal?”

“No—definitely not. But it’s used in every hospital and operating room.”

“So we’re looking for a surgeon or someone who works in surgery?”

“There are a lot of circumstances where a patient needs to be temporarily paralyzed in order to help them. It’s also used in ERs. Oftentimes patients are so out of it they can’t cooperate and they fight the efforts to save them. The temporary paralysis and intubation are life-saving."

"Okay. So OR people and ER people are the ones who can get the drug?"

"In the ER, it's the nurses who handle the drugs, but the pharmacologists, pharmacists, technicians, and aides also have access. The drugs are monitored to some degree, but not like narcotics. I'm not sure how hard it would be to get some."

"So basically the whole damn hospital can get their hands on it?" Aki looked pained.

"It's also used in some animal research projects on campus."

"Damn, that's great. Everybody can get it." Aki rubbed his chin. "How easy would it be for Doc Malar to get it in the ER?"

"Jon?"

Aki shot a hard look at Drake. "Yeah, Jon, the husband—the one who stands to inherit millions."

"It would be difficult for a doctor in the ER. Easier for the nurses because they handle the drugs." Drake pursed his lips and rubbed his ear, avoiding Aki's eyes.

Aki leaned forward, his voice rising. "What is it? What aren't you telling me?"

"NeurVitae. The spinal cord injury research that Jon, Rizz and I are working—"

"Okay. The research. And…?" Aki squinted.

"We use succinylcholine when we operate on the animals. We don't track it. We just make sure to order more before we run out."

"Your lab? No shit." Aki rolled his eyes. "You bullshit for ten minutes listing all the nobodies who might have access to the drug before you mention that the husband handles the stuff daily? Jesus, Doc." Aki looked skyward, and his chest swelled in a series of deep breaths.

"This NeurVitae is the research that the victim was handling the legal stuff for. Right? Where's this lab at? Why do you have the drug there?"

"The cats are intubated for their surgery. We also have anesthetic and painkillers there. We keep all the drugs locked up."

"But you all have access, right?"

"Jon, Rizz and I…yes."

"Did Faith have access?"

"It's locked up. I can't imagine Jon would share the combination with her." Drake had a stray thought but let it go.

"Doc, do you have any idea why Faith would have $75,000 deposited in her account four days before her death? Could it be related to your business?"

"I know nothing about her personal dealings, but our company is just now in a position to try and drum up venture capital. Up to now we're just three ER docs doing research in a beat-up lab. We have huge potential, but as of now, NeurVitae is broke."

"Venture capital?" Aki checked his notepad. "We just came across something like that." He checked his pad. "BioZyn, Inc. They're listed as a biomedical venture company. Is that what you mean?"

"We're planning to approach firms like that, but we haven't yet. I've never heard of BioZyn."

Aki tapped his pen against his chin, frowning.

He tilted his head and pointed the pen towards Drake. "I have a reportedly straight-arrow husband who stands to inherit millions. The victim, his wife, is no angel. She's killed at their home. Likely with an exotic drug the husband is swimming in. Is this what you're talking about as 'sounds suspicious'? Or is there more I should know?"

Drake felt cornered.

At that moment the pilot waved the clipboard at them, signaling by twirling his hand with one finger raised in a circle above his head, then covering his ears. He pointed from them to the shelter at the apex of the elevator.

Drake put a hand on Aki's arm and guided him to the concrete vestibule next to the elevator doors. The electric whine of the starter engine cranked, followed by the starting blast and shattering roar of the main engines. The lieutenant slapped his hands over his ears, his notepad held pinched against his head. Heat and engine exhaust buffeted them.

Drake swiped his card through the access and the elevator doors slid open. They climbed inside. The door closed and the noise faded as the elevator dropped.

Drake punched the stop button and their motion halted, a tinny electronic buzz sounding continuously. "Lieutenant, I've told you what I know. My shift is starting and I'm needed. Despite how things look, there's no way Jon killed Faith." Drake pulled his stethoscope free from under his belt and hung it around his neck.

"You've already shared that opinion, Doc, but there are things you don't know. Things your friend had to deal with. Things that would test a saint. You—" The lieutenant's ringtone sounded. He reached into his pocket.

"Detective Yamada." His listened for a moment then nodded. "How long will that take?" Another pause and nod. "Call me as soon as you know." He grimaced. "Okay, I mean please. Can you do that?" He reached with his free hand into his jacket and pulled out his notepad. "Tell him what?" He listened. "Okay."

He turned to Drake. "That was Dr. Weirdo. He's excited. The FBI lab proved you guys right." He pocketed the phone. "He said now the question is how the drug got into her." His brow furrowed. "Couldn't it have been slipped into something she ate or drank?"

"No. It can't be given orally because then the drug is digested and has no effect. In the ER and lab we inject it intravenously."

"Hmm. Yeah, the lab." He scratched an entry. The tinny elevator alarm continued to sound. Aki gestured with the notepad. "Doc, without your gut feeling and medical smarts, this killing would probably have been missed. Someone might have gotten away with murder. I credit you that."

His expression shifted. "But this is the last time you act dumb or play bullshit word games with me. Why are you working so hard at holding back? Does this have something to do with what happened back in Ohio? Because if—"

"This isn't about me. It's about keeping Jon from getting ripped apart by the system. You know it happens. He doesn't deserve that. I'm just trying to keep you from heading in the wrong direction."

"Damn." Aki glared, shaking his head. He pointed with his pen. "Your arrogance is unreal. Do you think you're the only one who knows how to do his job?" He flipped the notebook closed. "Murder is motive, method and opportunity. The person that fits is Jon Malar."

Aki jabbed his pen into his top pocket. "I let your friend sleep it off, but now it's time for answers." He crossed his arms. "Is there anything else you want to tell me?"

Jon's drunken ramblings and Rizz's ugly confession flashed through Drake's mind. *Shit.*

"No, detective."

Aki hadn't asked what Drake knew about Rizz's involvement with Faith, or if Jon had said anything regarding Faith or her death. He'd asked if there was anything else that Drake *wanted to tell him.*

No, there was not.

Drake hit the button and their descent resumed. The detective reached up and slapped the button. The elevator halted again, the alarm sounding.

"I shouldn't have to tell you this but I'm going to, anyway. Do not share anything I've said with your friend. Do not interfere with this investigation in any way or there will be consequences. Understood?"

Drake flushed hot. "I hear you." He locked eyes, sure that the detective had no idea of the emotion raging in his heart. "But carve this in your head, *Officer* Yamada." He reached past Aki and punched the button, resuming the elevator's descent. "Don't let the system destroy my friend. He's no killer. It's on you. Don't let it happen."

The elevator reached the ER and halted, causing the detective to sway. The doors pinged open and the bustling din invaded.

Drake headed down the corridor breathing hard. He rubbed his neck, trying to unravel the knotted muscles there.

Chapter 35

Jon slumped behind the wheel of his Suburban. He was nauseated, his head pounded, and a greasy sweat clung to him. His father had dropped the car off in the police parking lot with the keys in the driver's side wheel well. Faith had leased the high-end vehicle as a gift. "Now you can get rid of that clunker of yours. What an embarrassment," she'd said.

His parents had scrimped to purchase the used car they'd proudly presented to him as a medical school graduation gift. He missed his old Buick. Everything connected to Faith seemed poisoned now.

His parents had not initially grasped the reason for the police visit. Jon had come down the stairs after his father woke him with the message that "the police are here." When the officers said they "needed to bring him downtown for questioning," his mother had gasped. His father had become red-faced.

"What are you suggesting? He's grieving. You…you idiots! This is inhuman."

Jon calmed his father, phoned a defense attorney, then went to the bathroom and threw up. Brutally hungover and sick with fear, he'd climbed into the back of the squad car.

The attorney met him at the station.

Thank God his parents had not witnessed the questioning.

Detective Yamada's recounting of Faith's actions felt like a public flogging. The details of each deceit, betrayal, and infidelity cutting into him like a lash.

Jon followed his attorney's advice and kept quiet. At one point he'd had to excuse himself, then went to the restroom and dry-heaved until he produced bitter, yellow bile.

Before his recent soul-crushing discoveries, what the police had revealed about Faith's actions would have been beyond belief. *How could I have been such a fool?*

He checked his mirror's adjustment and signaled the turn as he pulled out of the lot. The sunlight jabbed his headache.

It was clear they were convinced he'd killed Faith. The police chief and assistant District Attorney had only grudgingly agreed to Jon's attorney's demand for release.

They'd let him go but ordered him to remain in the city.

Jon responded with "Thank you, Detective Yamada." He'd held the door for the short, frowning assistant DA.

Internally, he burned with rage and shame. How could Faith have done what she did? What she planned to do?

After listing Faith's sins and outlining Jon's humiliation, Detective Yamada had sighed. "Doctor, we know you're a good man. Your wife lied to you, cheated on you, she did you wrong in every way possible. No man could endure that." He'd looked at Jon and continued in a voice filled with pity.

"She was cruel, dishonest, and unfaithful." He'd leaned forward and rested a hand on Jon's forearm. "You stand to inherit a fortune, but I know that's not why you did it."

Jon's vision had blurred and he'd fought to avoid breaking down.

"She abused you, Jon. The jury will take that into account."

She *had* abused him. And they didn't know the worst.

A horn blared. Jon flinched and swerved back into his lane. He rubbed his eyes.

The gift of children had always been his greatest dream. Faith had fanned his enthusiasm. She'd set up a nursery next to their master bedroom shortly after the honeymoon. "Just the basics," she'd said, "we'll have to see if our first is a boy or girl before fine-tuning." He'd been so happy. Then came the months, and then years, of prayers and disappointment.

She reported her fertility workup showed no issues. Jon was evaluated as well. No explanation could be found, so they were both undergoing repeat evaluation. Or so Jon had thought.

Three days before Faith's death, Jon was looking for a pen and opened her purse. He found birth control pills. He stood staring—it couldn't be.

Later he called the dispensing pharmacy, claiming an insurance issue. The pharmacist identified that Faith had been receiving the pills uninterrupted for at least eight months.

The following day, when he arrived home, he spotted her phone on the entryway table. She was upstairs. As he scanned through her messages, he lost whatever hope he'd held.

It was all so very much worse.

A text from a blocked number dated two days earlier. "11 a.m., your playroom. can't wait. business first, naked next!!" The phone shook in his trembling hand.

"Just the office and clients," she'd said that morning. How many days had she said that? His legs had turned to jelly and he sat on the stairs. *Oh my Lord.*

He checked the phone's camera function. Twenty-three images logged. The photographs were close-ups of NeurVitae research summaries. He'd occasionally brought such documents home. Why would she want the information? He deleted the message and images from her phone. Why the research?

Why any of it?

He'd explored further in the following days. What he learned could not be erased from his mind. What she'd done.

Damn her. Damn her soul to hell.

Chapter 36

Reinhorst LLC offices, IDS building, Minneapolis

"Twenty-eight million dollars." The chief financial officer of Reinhorst LLC laid the report down on the massive mahogany table. "As you know, we've investigated every possible option for relief."

The participants in the one p.m. emergency meeting in the thirty-sixth floor executive board room held their breath. Andrew Reinhorst looked past them and out the floor-to-ceiling glass to the chain of metro lakes that stretched from the edge of downtown into the distant suburbs.

"No alternatives?" He knew the answer.

"None, sir. The appraised value of the San Diego marina property has dropped to three hundred million. No lender will put up more than seventy percent of value. That's two-hundred and ten million. We're holding a two-hundred thirty-eight million dollar note that's due the end of this quarter. We need twenty-eight million in cash to keep us out of receivership. All of our loans are cross-collateralized and coming due. If San Diego goes down—they all go. Like dominoes."

Reinhorst rubbed his forehead.

"Sir, the twenty-eight will only cover the first wave. The Omaha ethanol plant note is due in the fourth quarter. That's another twenty million. Forty-eight million would allow us to cover both notes. We could stay above water for at least a year. That assumes values don't fall any further. If that happens, I see no escape. We're in too deep."

"How much time do I have?"

"At the outside, two months. The courts are aggressive. The perception is that our type of, er, strategy is unethical."

Reinhorst sat at the head of the table, chin on fist. He grit his teeth as he gazed out the glass wall. A 757 banked from south to east against a backdrop of towering cumulus. He stood, placing both palms on the table.

"Twenty-eight million now and another twenty million by the fourth quarter—cash money or I'm done." He swiveled his head, looking each of them in the eye. "I will not let what I've built disappear." He slid his hand to the worn Bible in front of him. "I'll find a way."

"But sir, it's imposs—"

Reinhorst slapped the table top; the executives jumped. He dead-eyed them with his lip curled. "I said I'll find a way. I'll get the money. Let the banks know. Meeting adjourned." He snatched up his Bible, then strode through the door linking to his private office.

He jabbed the intercom. "The district attorney. Route him to my cell. Now."

He'd been pushed to the limit before. He'd always operated on the edge. But never had he been in a position to lose so much—to lose it all.

The ringtone sounded, the caller ID displaying "DA."

"Rudy. Who killed my daughter?"

"Mr. Reinhorst, sir, this process takes time. And I need to respect the investigation's confidentiality. When I spoke with you earlier, it had only just been confirmed as murder, and, again, my sympathies to you, but—"

"Rudy, I don't need your phony, butt-kissing sympathy. And don't talk to me about confidentiality. I put your country-bumpkin ass in that job—now you damn well better do it. Was it the husband?"

"Sir, please. This is privileged. If it gets out that I discussed an active investigation with you, I'm done. Not just as DA—I'd be disbarred."

"Stop your whining. What've you got?"

There was a long pause. "Theoretically I might have just spoken with the police chief and my assistant. They were in on the questioning—"

"Geez, you're pathetic." Andrew snorted. "Okay, to the best of your knowledge, *theoretically,* the questioning of whom?"

"The husband—Jon Malar. The one you asked about. You must know him."

"I know of him. My daughter hasn't allowed me in her life for several years. I wasn't at the wedding but I researched him. Did the bastard do it?"

"He was picked up and interrogated."

"He's in jail?"

"No. We don't have enough. Not yet."

Reinhorst pounded his fist on the desk top. "Damn it, Rudy. Is he the guy?"

"They found…well, there was some stuff that was not so nice."

"God in heaven, spit it out."

"Sir, there was adultery and lying. Er, I should say allegedly. On your daughter's part. There appears to be plenty of motive. And now we know the drug that killed her. Very sophisticated. The killer has to have familiarity with medications. The husband uses the drug all the time. He has access to it in his lab."

"His lab? Isn't he an ER doctor?"

"Yeah, but I'm told Hennepin-North ER program is big on experimental research. Faith's husband and a couple of other ER docs rent an old lab on the north side. We served a search warrant and found the drug there."

"And you let him go? Good God, Rudy. He did it!"

"It's all circumstantial. And the guy is squeaky clean. He's like some kind of saint. Plus he was working when she died—though that doesn't rule him out. Fact is, the chief and my assistant think he's the guy."

"He was at work when she died?"

"Yes. But no one was anywhere around her when she died. Whoever killed her somehow got the drug into her without being around. No one has figured out how yet. So it could be him. He had motive and means."

"Hell yes, it could be him. He's a doctor. Of course he could figure a smart, sneaky way. And motive? Good God, Rudy. Sixty-three million in motive."

"Yes, sir. It's a lot of money. He's definitely the prime suspect."

"There are others?"

"The investigation is ongoing—"

"Damn it, Rudy. Don't give me your press release bullshit. Is there another suspect?"

"No. Not as of now, but—"

"Don't screw this up. Do you hear me? Nail his ass."

"Yes sir. When we arrest him, we'll make it stick. We're being careful. He's got a good attorney."

"Call me immediately with any developments." Reinhorst's volume rose. "This damn doctor can't kill my daughter and steal my money. That's not going to happen." He broke the connection.

He felt the urge to smash something. *God damn it.*

He had to get his money.

As his mind probed, he stared into his office aquarium. A mid-sized tiger Oscar flashed out from beneath a rock arch and inhaled a neon Tetra. The Oscar settled back into his hidden nook.

Less than a minute later an idea sparked. As he considered it, it grew into a plan. A damn good plan—righteous action and fundamental justice. Like Solomon in the Good Book.

He took out his phone and entered the Consultant's number.

"Meet me in thirty-five minutes at the Lake Calhoun lot—you know the one. I've found a solution. We need to move fast." He disconnected.

This order needed to be given in person. And there could be no record.

Chapter 37

3:20 p.m.

Meryl pulled the van over at the point where the gravel road pinched between a riverbank concrete erosion levee and a cattail-filled culvert. She looked back through the dust at the site she'd spent the afternoon preparing.

Secure accommodations with all the necessities. And she couldn't have found a more striking setting if she were making a movie. She loved it.

The *Twain*, a paddle-wheeled riverboat permanently moored along the Mississippi river flats near the university. It had been a restaurant and event site, but was now out of business and for sale or rent. It was ideal.

The shielded walkway and enclosed space were ideal for managing her cargo without attracting attention. It was only minutes from downtown, yet isolated. Perhaps best of all, it was funky and dramatic.

She checked her cocaine stash— still more than one hundred grams. Nice.

A breeze wafted, and the fish and muck scent of the riverbank registered stronger. The road dust left a chalky taste in her mouth. The sounds of traffic from the I-94 bridge came over the water as a hum.

She checked the interior of the vehicle. The rental van had tinted one-way windows and a sliding panel separating the front seats from the rear compartment. More than enough room and well-insulated for sound containment. *Perfect.*

She gripped the wheel as thoughts streaked into her mind like insects striking the windshield of a speeding car. Talk about a natural high. No one had a mind like hers.

It was all so incredibly cool.

Would it get physical? She flexed and felt her muscles strain the fabric of her shirt. *Bring it on!* Her nipples went hard.

When the curtain rose, Dr. Drake Cody would be in the ER. Meryl would take the stage in the starring role.

She hadn't felt this exquisitely jazzed since Faith.

Chapter 38

Early evening

When the jet of blood tracked across Drake's chest and neck, the first sensation was heat. The warmth of human blood always startled.

He'd pulled back the make-shift dressing to examine the patient's chainsaw-injured arm and been nailed by the spurting artery. Drake had controlled the bleeder and repaired the wound.

Now as he entered the tiny physician locker room, he stripped off the bloody scrub top. He pumped the wall-mounted dispenser and painted antimicrobial foam across his neck, chest and abdomen, then leaned against the counter, giving the chemicals time to wage war on any infectious agents that might be present.

The sounds of the frenzied ER carried through the door.

Structural inadequacy.

The words described one of the challenges of emergency medicine. The hospital staffed the ER to cover the "average" number of patients with the "average" level of acuity. The average was made up of times of fewer patients with relatively minor problems and periods like today—an impossible-to-predict flood of patients, many with severe illnesses or catastrophic injuries.

Complicated and critical patients like the elderly person in septic shock or the child hit by a speeding car took more than an average amount of time. A day such as today required the ER doctors to see, diagnose, perform procedures and treat patients faster than was humanly possible. Include the similarly stretched nursing, lab, support personnel and physical resources, and the entire system became overloaded. Structural inadequacy.

As he waited, his skin itched from the foam's sanitizing action. The ugly chain of recent events gripped his thoughts:

Faith murdered with succinylcholine.

Rizz and Faith naked in the lab just days before her death.

Faith in contact with both a pharmaceutical and a biomedical venture firm. Why? How could he not know of it?

Jon as Aki's prime suspect. Would the system destroy him?

The gangbanger who struck Patti—would Drake's assault conviction be discovered? On the verge of realizing his dreams, he'd lose everything.

The patient whose blood had splashed Drake denied any habits that placed him at risk for HIV, hepatitis or other infectious blood-borne conditions. Of course, Drake had never yet had a patient admit, "I'm a promiscuous homosexual and I shoot IV drugs." Yet some were and did.

He trusted this patient and believed the danger was remote.

He would skip the hospital's "body fluids contact reporting protocol." His HIV status was already being monitored due to the blood contact with the gangbanger who'd assaulted Patti. There were too many seriously ill patients waiting for care to take the forty-five minutes in paperwork and blood draws the protocol demanded. The contact was low-risk and his monitoring would assure Rachelle was safe.

Rachelle. He'd not yet told her that Faith had been murdered. A lump lodged in his throat.

He checked the linen shelf for a clean scrub top. Rachelle...his thoughts skipped to that first day. It was while he was in college working as an orderly in the University of Cincinnati ER.

* * *

He'd been restocking linens when paramedics raced the adult Down's syndrome patient into the Stabilization Room. The head-turning young woman ran beside the stretcher. The patient appeared elderly by Down's standards—affected individuals rarely lived beyond their mid-forties. Even to Drake's untrained eyes, it was evident the man was deathly ill. The gray and gasping man clung to the hand of his stunning escort. She wore scrub-type pants and a collared shirt with a neck scarf.

Drake helped shift the patient to the ER bed. He applied cardiac leads to the patient's sweat-soaked, heaving chest. Drake worked around the linked arms of the ill man and the distraught beauty. The ER doctor's questioning revealed she worked as the patient's personal care attendant. The patient had a history of mental retardation, seizures, and severe heart disease. His name was Drew.

She stroked the man's brow and spoke softly to him, her bond as visible as the cable linking him to the heart monitor.

"Does anything hurt?" the doctor asked.

The struggling patient directed his answer to his dark-haired companion.

"Drew… bad… sick."

Drew had developed chest pain and shortness of breath. She'd administered nitroglycerin tablets under his tongue, then called 911.

The doctors and nurses examined Drew and administered medications via his IV line. His features eased but his breathing did not improve.

A stack of records appeared at the nearby desk. Drake overheard snatches of the hushed exchange: "End-stage cardiomyopathy. Unbelievable he's lasted this long. His Living Will says comfort cares only. No intubation or ventilator. His heart is done—poor guy."

His color worsened and his eyes grew dull. A sob escaped his aide, wrenching Drake and silencing the caregivers.

She leaned her forehead onto the failing man's shoulder.

He rallied for an instant, a glimmer in his eyes. "Drew…love…Rachelle."

She lowered the side guard rail and climbed onto the cart, laying next to and curling around the fading Drew. The doctors and nurses stood clear. Drew nestled his head against her. He was quiet, his mouth a small smile.

Her face—sad, knowing and indescribably lovely.

The cardiac tracing became a flat-line and a soft continuous beep sounded.

The raven-haired attendant's eyes shimmered huge and dark. Her sorrow lay so naked Drake felt his viewing was a violation.

He could not take his eyes off her.

* * *

Wounded and tormented by worry, but kind, beautiful, and the loving mother of their precious children—Rachelle.

He toweled off the antimicrobial cleanser then picked up a scrub top. A page sounded overhead. "Dr. Cody, line two. Dr. Cody, line two."

He grabbed the wall phone. "Dr. Cody here." He pulled on the scrub top while juggling the phone.

"This is Yamada giving you a heads-up. A TV reporter caught your egomaniac ME buddy coming out of the morgue. He bragged about his discovery of the drug that killed Malar's wife. He announced the murder details to the world. The station broadcast the clip. It's a feeding frenzy—Hold on."

The phone muffled for a moment. “Okay, Doc. A warning I didn’t think I needed to give your ego-freak colleague. Say nothing to anybody about the death or investigation. Nothing.”

“Understood, Aki.”

“Gotta go.” The connection ended.

Drake had to tell Rachelle before she learned of the murder via the media. He bit his lip and began dialing. *I should be with her.*

The paramedic call signal sounded overhead. A doctor was needed immediately for another incoming critical patient.

He hung up the phone, grabbed his stethoscope, and raced to respond.

Chapter 39

Heinrich looked out the jet's window as the black Citation banked a lazy south-to-north arc as it neared Flying Cloud airport in suburban Minneapolis. The sky was orange-tinged and cloudless, save for a brush stroke of cirrus high above the setting sun.

The beauty of the Minnesota countryside surprised him. Forested hills, rich farmland, marshes, and sun-sparkled lakes were everywhere. The views were appealing. His situation was not.

Fastidious in appearance and habits, today he noted fingernails chewed to the quick and a stubbly patch on the underside of his chin he'd missed shaving. He found himself in a state of apprehension that his Aryan discipline could barely contain.

Meryl had sent an email.

From: Mastermind
Your complaints are tiresome and inane.
I contribute only solutions. You and the Board ride on my genius.
D-44 will be mine—soon. I am in control.
Stay where you are. I will do what needs to be done.

Heinrich's subsequent emails and calls had gone unanswered. Time was running out and Meryl was running wild.

Intrusive visions of what would happen if they failed left him nauseous.

The two BioZyn functionaries the Board had assigned to accompany him were asleep. They'd hardly spoken. The lean, hard-eyed men's exchanges identified them as Croatian.

Childhoods filled with the atrocities of war forged unique specimens. Heinrich had no doubt what they were capable of. He thought of them as guard dogs on loan. They followed his commands, but he was not their master.

The jet banked and Heinrich glimpsed sprawling cityscapes stretched along a gleaming river. Would Meryl be waiting with D-44 in hand?

His mouth went dry and his stomach knotted. His future, perhaps his life, depended on a woman he feared was going insane.

The engines changed in pitch. They were on approach.

Chapter 40

8:30 p.m.

Rachelle feathered in flecks of cadmium yellow, striving to capture the vivid colors of the scene she'd started at Lake Calhoun the previous week.

Her second-hand easel stood chipped and paint-spattered, its tripod legs resting on newspapers spread on the kitchen floor. The canvas showed the fiery hues of the setting sun bracketed by purple-black thunderheads reflected in the lake's mirror-like surface.

Her initial outdoor session had been ended abruptly as the winds leading the coming thunderstorm had whipped the water to froth. Her visual memory of the once-in-forever scene directed tonight's efforts to complete the painting.

She stepped back and assessed the image. It was one of her best. She set down the brush. The tension that had afflicted her for the past days had eased.

The audio monitor from the kids' room broadcast a soft hiss. They were asleep. Drake would not be home for hours. The quiet felt nice.

The jangle of the phone caused her to jump. She wiped her hands on her smock as she moved to the wall-mounted handset.

"Hello."

"Rachelle, are you okay? Have you heard any news?"

"I'm good, Drake. News? I've been painting and—"

"I'm sorry, but I have bad news and I don't have any time."

Rachelle's sense of well-being evaporated.

"It's about Faith," Drake said

Rachelle raised her hand to the receiver. "Faith?"

"The police are investigating her death. She was murdered."

It was as if she'd been punched in the stomach. "No. That can't be." *An investigation?* "You said she drowned. The TV said she drowned."

"It looked that way. We found a killing drug in her system. She didn't drown."

Rachelle began to pace. The air thinned. *No!*

"I'm sorry I can't be with you."

"The kids are sleeping. I was painting. A sunset before a storm." She raised a hand to the thickened, irregular tissue of her neck.

"It's a bad time, but I have something good to share with you about FloJo and the research."

"What?" Rachelle stopped pacing. Her hands trembled. She slumped against the wall.

"Last night at the lab, FloJo—"

"An investigation? Murder? No, Drake, no. I can't listen anymore." She hung up.

The pushy detective had called last night, looking for Drake and tracking Jon. *Lord, no.*

She took a step back and knocked over the tin of mineral spirits she used to clean her brushes. Falling to her knees, she used her painter's rag to try and control the spill. The fumes triggered shadowed memories of glue-sniffing and foster homes. Bounding fear and flashes of past ugliness flooded. Tears blurred her vision.

A pins-and-needles numbness enveloped her hands. She needed more air. Her heart hammered. The panic surged. *Please no!*

Her strength bled away. Struggling she stumbled to her feet. The hunger for air grew. She bumped against the kitchen table and then the countertop as she made for the uppermost cupboard. She banged it open. Clumsily she reached and grasped the prescription bottle on the top shelf.

Her hands began to spasm. She was breathing way too fast. Control lost, she breathed even faster.

Her panic-attack medication was similar to Valium, but stronger. The drug was like Drew's heart pills—it absorbed more quickly if put under the tongue. She clawed at the childproof cap while falling to her knees. The cap popped off with pills scattering across the floor.

She sprawled toward the blue tablets and raked one across the floor with hands now cramping and claw-like. The certainty that things were end-of-the-world wrong consumed her. Using her lips, she took in the medication and maneuvered it under her tongue. *Too late!*

Her desperate gasps did not slow. Her hands, arms and legs contracted like burning bacon

The shadow of imminent doom engulfed her.

She whimpered as she slid into blackness.

* * *

Twenty years previous

The Cincinnati newspaper pieced together the story from interviews of those involved.

A moonlighting Family Practice doctor was staffing the tiny northern Kentucky hospital's two-bed ER that Sunday.

When the badly burned, eight-year-old girl arrived, the young physician knew to stabilize and arrange transfer to the burn center in Cincinnati. She hadn't known how to address the girl's glassy-eyed unresponsiveness. "She stared straight ahead, blank. Didn't react to anything. Not even a blink at the needle stick for the IV. It was like she was somewhere else."

The EMT team that had transported the girl from the injury scene communicated grim particulars. They'd met the sheriff and fire rescue at the rundown homestead located far off Highway Forty-one. "Beyond the boondocks," one of the EMTs had said.

The fire truck and sheriff's vehicle were parked near a rectangle of blackened rubble and smoking timbers located forty yards behind a ramshackle farmhouse. A volunteer firefighter with a mask on his face placed a hazmat warning sign as the EMTs arrived. Debris was scattered widely around the destroyed building.

A bicycle lay on its side near an upright Harley Davidson and a Big Wheel tricycle. A weathered, sleeveless biker's vest lay draped across the motorcycle; cinder-scorched but the gang letters and symbol still clear.

The sheriff had arrived at the property first and too late.

He reported that he recognized the site as the scene of a meth lab explosion. The caustic burnt toast/ammonia stink, the biker gang jacket, the remote locale—it was a near-perfect match of features described in a DEA informational video. The spread of such operations to rural locales was a new but growing phenomenon.

He'd explored the wreckage. He found the charred bodies of an adult man and woman. Seconds later he'd spied the scorched leather of a baseball glove. A prod of the ashes with his boot revealed it to be fused to the hand of a body— a small child burned charcoal-black and twisted in the rubble.

The EMTs found the sheriff red-eyed and dry heaving.

The house looked a mess and stunk of garbage. Drug paraphernalia lay in plain sight. The sheriff reported feeling sickened at the thought of the deceased child being raised in such squalor. That was when he found the survivor.

The dark-haired girl lay fetal-curled on a filthy carpet. Her hands were blackened and blistered, and a severe burn extended over the left side of her neck and left shoulder. Her eyes were open but she was unresponsive and mute.

She stared blankly during her ambulance trip to the tiny rural hospital and her subsequent transfer to the city. The follow-up articles reported that she did not speak for eighteen days. The specialists at Cincinnati Children's Hospital said she suffered from post-traumatic shock.

On the nineteenth day, she said, "Billy," and tears ran down her cheeks.

The newspaper chronicled her plight. The young girl, now an orphan, was another tragic victim of drugs and the erosion of the family.

The Cincinnati paper ran a special Sunday series on the epidemic growth of drugs and crime in the rural areas of northern Kentucky and southern Ohio. The series ran for four weeks.

When the series ended, the girl had been discharged from the burn unit after completion of two skin grafts.

She'd been made a ward of the state and transferred to the full-time care of mental health and social service professionals. These caregivers acknowledged to reporters that they had no graft procedure to mend her inner wounds.

The newspaper started and ended its series with the heart-strings tug of the eight-year-old—the burned, glassy-eyed girl whose younger brother and mother were killed in the explosion of a rural meth lab.

Would there be more who suffered like Rachelle X?

* * *

Rachelle lifted her head off the floor. Newspaper clung to her cheek, and the scent of mineral spirits was thick.

Storm clouds threatened and the sun threw no heat. Her painting lay angled against the wall in front of her eyes. The easel likewise knocked to the floor. She dragged a hand across her face, clearing the paper with fingers numb and stiff.

Feeling began to return to her hands. Her tortured muscles loosened. Doctors had told her the panic attacks could not harm her. It felt otherwise.

The pill and the effects of the attack left her dazed. Awareness flashed and her throat clenched—*the children!*

The soft hiss of the audio monitor reassured. She checked the clock. It had been only minutes.

She climbed to her knees, bracing herself as the room spun. Her head began to clear and her hands steadied.

A level of calm accompanied her post-panic exhaustion. She'd experienced this with past attacks and supposed it to be something like the after-effect of electroshock therapy.

Ten minutes later, she'd collected the pills from the floor and checked on the kids.

She stood in front of her canvas. The ceiling-mounted fluorescent fluttered. The kitchen window glowed a soft orange.

The sense of foreboding provoked by Drake's call had not disappeared, but she felt more focused.

It's what mothers must do. They hold themselves together and take care of their family. Her fingers trailed over her scar.

She was nothing like her mother.

Chapter 41

Jon guided the Suburban out of the drive of the Wayzata estate, his mind turning like the wire-rimmed wheels. He gripped the steering wheel so tight his hands hurt. The headlights tracked along the curving lakeside road.

His attorney had called. The police and DA had strengthened their case. They'd executed a search warrant at the lab and found succinylcholine. Witness reports established Jon as the last person known to be with Faith before her death.

The attorney communicated "as was his obligation" that a DA's offer of a plea bargain was "always worth listening to." Jon understood the unspoken message within the lawyer's words.

His attorney believed they would convict him.

He'd brushed his teeth multiple times since the questioning and he still tasted bile. His drinking had been pathetic. He'd done everything wrong.

He imagined steel shackles on his wrists and a guard leading him through a gauntlet of accusing eyes into a courtroom.

They'd all learn how Faith had lied to him, how she'd betrayed him, how she'd abused his love.

And the money—he'd have millions.

Succinylcholine. Goodness. How many people on the planet had ever heard of it? Every day he had access.

The facts would make murder easy to believe. *Please, God, spare me.*

His vision blurred as he guided the vehicle off the exit ramp into the zone of failed businesses and graffiti-tattooed buildings in North Minneapolis. It shamed him that he still longed for her. Every memory brought a tightness to his throat and an ache deep within him. He mourned his loss but did not grieve her death. *Could that be?*

He turned onto Jader Avenue. The majority of streetlights were broken, and intact windows were rare. He neared the darkened lab building and pulled into the crumbling, asphalt parking lot. The moon glowed dim behind massing clouds. The only cars ever in this lot after dark were Drake's, Rizz's, or his own.

Tonight he saw a dark sedan parked in the back row across from the lab entrance. Likely a first floor, daytime office worker's vehicle had been stranded.

The hospital paging text message had said to meet Drake at nine. Where was his car? Jon checked his watch: nine-fifteen. He turned off the car and opened the door. Unusual silence ruled. Even the projects were muted. The crunch of gravel under his foot was amplified in the stillness. The slam of his car door reverberated.

Before the door's echo died, the parked sedan roared to life. Jon's head snapped in reaction. The car's engine surged, wheels clawing.

The vehicle lunged forward, lights blinking on.

Jon broke for the lab's door. The car reached him instantly, so near he felt its heat.

Tires locked and gravel crunched as the car lurched to a halt, cutting him off.

"Police. Homicide. Dr. Malar, I need a word," came from the open passenger window now just feet from Jon's hip. Dust rose like gritty steam in the headlights' glare.

Jon halted. *God Almighty!* He sagged—his heart pounding and breath short.

"Come on," Jon said, angry and loud. "You scared me half to death." Flushed and taut, he stepped to the open passenger window. He leaned his face toward the darkened interior and the lone driver within.

The silhouetted driver moved, an arm extending, a glint.

What the—?

Thunder stuttered and lightning flashed. *Boom-Boom.*

Fire bayoneted his chest.

Hurtling back. The *tha-crack* of his head impacting asphalt.

Ears pinging and vision a blurred glimmer. A car door opened. A shadow loomed.

Voices?

The shadow, a man, stiffened and turned. A car door *whump* and the engine roared. Tires screeched and spun. Lights faded in stinging gravel and the stink of burnt rubber.

Pain. *Oh God.* Dying.

Fading…blackness.

Chapter 42

Projects, 9:12 p.m.

The paramedic team manning ambulance 725 had been on for seven hours of nonstop calls. They'd barely had enough time to wipe down and restock the rig between runs. Now they had a call for "can't breathe—dying" from a projects apartment. It could be anything.

They responded Code 3 with lights and siren, then hustled their stretcher up three flights of stairs to find a twelve-year-old boy who had got his hands on some high-potency marijuana. He'd gotten scary high with two buddies, then freaked out and began hyperventilating. One of the boys made the panicked 911 call.

The two veteran paramedics did their job. They settled the boy down, got him to slow his breathing, and discerned there was no major problem. His mother showed up from another apartment. She'd been drinking but wasn't impaired. She did not want her son transported to the hospital. The team agreed, then collapsed the stretcher and headed back to their rig.

* * *

9:16 p.m.

Dewayne ducked as two shots rang out. "Muthafu—"

"It going down right here." Antonio crouched, reaching under his Chicago Bulls jersey for his nine millimeter. He'd seen the flashes from the lot just forty yards away. "We all be good?"

"We all here 'cept Deed and Punto, and Deed be wit' his bitch," said Danton from behind the others.

"Aw shit. Those cocksucking Chicos coulda shot Punto. Nine-eleven it, Dewayne," Antonio said. He then yelled towards the lot. "Punto! You there? You aw right?"

Dewayne pulled out his cell phone.

A roar and screech of tires marked the fishtailing exit of a late-model sedan from the lot. It passed under an intact streetlight, moving away fast. The crew looked at one another and ran towards the lot. Dewayne connected with 911 as they reached the shadowed mass. A body lay motionless next to a black rig.

"It ain't Punto. A white dude," Dewayne said.

"This is the 911 dispatcher. Do you have an emergency?" came from the phone.

Danton rifled through the man's pockets. The others were swiveling their heads with weapons at the ready.

"It not be my emergency, but a white dude got hisself shot. Parking lot of…" he looked up and saw the dimly lit name of the building above the doorway, "University Chemical building. On Jader. He look dead but it ain't be us. Probably them muthafucking Chicos." Dewayne ended the connection as Danton stood up, waving a wallet and a cell phone.

The crew sprinted off.

* * *

9:19 p.m.

"This is 911 dispatch to police-paramedic response. Man down. Reported gunshots. Parking lot, University Chemical storehouse building at 2114 Jader Avenue. Do I have a confirm?"

"Police squad four-two-two. We're on it. ETA one minute."

"Second that. Dispatch, this is Paramedic seven-two-five. Just had a no-load right on top of that. Two minutes. Is the scene secure?"

* * *

9:21 p.m.

The police cruiser came in fast and dark, vaulting into the lot then screeching to a sliding halt. Their headlights flashed on, capturing a downed man in the beam.

The two police spotlights scanned a three-sixty without revealing a shooter. The first officer jumped out and approached the parked vehicle in a crouch with a Maglite and gun drawn. He jump-flashed the car's interior, keeping his body protected. He signaled his partner with a one-hand-slashing safe sign and turned to the downed body. The second officer, with gun drawn and radio in hand, reported in, "Paramedic 7-2-5, this is PD 4-2-2. Site looks clear. Keep your head down." He flipped the emergency flashers on.

Fifteen seconds later, Ambulance 725 careened into the lot with siren screaming. They braked hard alongside the two officers, one of whom was at the downed man's side while the other scanned the perimeter. The siren yipped to silence.

"Looks like a citizen. Gunshot chest. Maybe multiple," said the first officer as the paramedics jumped from the rig. The police and ambulance lights and emergency flashers combined to make the scene a crimson-tinged stroboscopic light show. The police and paramedics' movements looked jerky and fast-motion.

The paramedics were instantly at the victim's side with stretcher ready.

"Not breathing. Two shots to the chest. A weak pulse here," said the lead medic, his fingers on the man's neck. "Load and roll. His only chance," he yelled to his partner. "Haul ass."

He grabbed the downed man's shoulders and, coordinating with his partner's quick snatch of the legs, heaved the limp body onto the stretcher. "Bag breathe or tube en route, man. Three minutes to the ER. Heading in hot, brother."

They launched the stretcher into the rig, with the second medic climbing in and placing a bag mask over the downed man's face, initiating efforts to breathe for him. The lead medic jumped behind the wheel and floored the powerful truck while keying the radio.

Tires spun, the siren came to life, and the rig rocketed out of the lot. In the back of the rig the second medic had trouble getting the air mask to seal around the ashen, dark-haired man's mouth and nose. He tried to reposition the mask at the same instant a chilling knowledge hit him. He shouted to the driver over the sound of the engine and siren.

"Holy shit, bro. Holy shit. It's the doc. It's Doc Malar."

* * *

9:25 p.m.

The ER was jam-packed and wild. Drake rushed into the radio room silencing the overhead bleating of the paramedic call signal with one hand as he hit the transmit button with the other.

Just what they didn't need—another incoming critical patient.

"Doctor Cody here, over."

"7-2-5 here. Two minutes out. Gunshot wounds chest. Adult male. Not breathing. All bad." Some static interposed, then a raised voice,

"He's intubated now. No pulse. We got nothing. And he's—" Static drowned out the end.

Drake, up and leaning, spoke into the mike. "10-4, see you in the Crash room." He released the transmit button and sprinted, calling out to the station secretary who stood ready with her headphones on and a finger poised over the paging control. "Trauma team. Crash bay three."

Drake heard the trauma call overhead as he grabbed a prepackaged tray of specialized surgical instruments off the Crash Room supply rack. He ripped open the sterile wrapping, then tore open a second plastic-wrapped pack and removed and threw on a protective gown, mask, eye gear, and sterile latex surgical gloves. He selected a large scalpel and a second stainless-steel instrument that looked like foot-long needle-nosed pliers.

Drake and Rizz called the wicked-looking thoracostomy device a vamp, short for vampire because its function required it to be driven into the chest.

Drake placed the scalpel and the device on the open, sterile tray at the bedside.

The trauma team, including two nurses, two orderlies, and a respiratory therapist, raced to the bedside and began to make ready. The Crash Room life clock displayed *1 min 34 secs* since the call. *How long had the patient been down before the call?*

Drake addressed the mobilizing team as they prepared. "7-2-5 is seconds out, gunshot chest, male patient. Pulseless and unresponsive. He's intubated but otherwise nothing."

Based on the bare-bones report, Drake anticipated tension pneumothorax. Untreated, the condition meant death. The lung collapses, and breathing and the heart's ability to circulate blood ceases. The only way to avert death is to decompress the lung by creating an opening into the chest and inserting a large bore tube between the lung and chest wall. The tube is connected to suction to remove the blood and air that shut down the vital structures.

Drake would have seconds to, at most, two minutes to return circulation before death or profound brain damage would result. *2 min 14 secs* flashed on the life clock.

He spoke to the trauma team. "Insert large bore peripherals if you're able. I'm going to scalpel slash and slam a tube into his chest immediately. May need to go bilateral. If no air rush and no response, I'm going to crack open his chest and look for a wound to the heart. Have the sternum cutter, chest spreader, and full thoracotomy tray open and ready. Two number thirty-six chest tubes on my call, and have suction up and ready now. Be quick but don't hurry. Look out for sharps. None of us gets cut or contaminated. No AIDS for us today. Everything clear?"

As the team members nodded, the Crash Room doors exploded. The 725 crew ran the stretcher through the swinging doors like a wheeled battering ram. The lead paramedic, drenched in sweat, was performing CPR on the run. He spoke rapid-fire and breathless, "Bullet wounds left and right chest. We lost his pulse en route. Tubed him but he's bagging hard. He's got nothing."

The patient was lifeless and gray on the cart. The airway bag obscured the face. While the team smoothly shifted the man to the trauma bed, Drake pushed in next to the paramedic to check the ET tube position. The respiratory therapist took the bag from the paramedic as Drake glanced toward the patient's face.

Time froze. *Oh God. No.*

The team sliced off clothes and applied monitors, airway support and oxygen within seconds. The tension level in the Crash room rocketed with the recognition of the patient as physician, coworker and friend.

The flesh felt cold to Drake's touch as he splashed and quick-wiped antiseptic solution across the naked chest.

The life clock flashed *3 min 04 secs.*

Bloody craters of torn flesh on each side of the chest gaped at Drake as he raised the scalpel. He stole one more glance at the face of his good-hearted friend.

He carved the scalpel into Jon's left chest, the blade opening the skin like a zipper, with the bloody and glistening deeper structures bursting into view. The metallic-tinged, raw smell of blood and tissue filled the air.

Drake exchanged the scalpel for the vamp device and placed its tip immediately above Jon's exposed seventh rib. Shifting his feet for advantage, he plunged the stainless steel through the deep tissues into the chest cavity with a fleshy *tha-pop*. Jon's inert body lurched with the impact. Drake spread the pliers-like handles wide, resulting in a large rush of escaping air and jetting blood.

He removed the instrument and forced his gloved finger through the blood-warm track he'd hewn into his friend. He digitally assessed the anatomy. The collapsed left lung began to expand, nudging his fingertip. Redirecting his digit Drake could just reach Jon's heart. He felt the organ begin to pulse—weak but each beat stronger than the last.

"Tube to me now, then suction and tape it down. Soft restraints now," Drake directed the orderlies. He guided the tube into the chest as he spoke. Blood surged through the transparent hose.

"Fluids wide open. Two units of O-negative blood," Drake said to the trauma nurse as he vaulted to his friend's right side.

"I think I got a faint pulse," said the paramedic, holding a finger on Jon's neck. Drake saw the life clock blink *3 min 44 secs*.

"Tension pneumothorax. Probably bilateral." Drake raised the scalpel to Jon's right chest. The scalpel carved deep. He grabbed the vamp and muscled it into the chest. Again a strong rush of air and a surge of blood erupted. The finger exam and tube placement were repeated and suction established. The blood that had collected in Jon's ravaged chest coursed through the tube like a garden hose.

"Follow those two units of blood with two more. Wide open and pressure bag 'em."Drake noted that the chest tubes' blood output was slowing after the initial 600 ml rush.

"Watch that output," Drake directed one of the orderlies. "Don't take your eyes off it and sing out if it hits 800 ml. You with me?" An earnest nod in response.

The paramedic, fingertips still at Jon's neck, brightened. "Definite pulse now."

Drake saw the life clock blink *4 min 34 secs*. His gut clenched.

"Pulse 120 and pressure 100," the trauma nurse said with disbelief in her voice. Smiles rippled through the team and the group of ER and hospital personnel that had accumulated outside the Crash Room.

Drake took a large breath. His friend had a chance.

His relief was tinged with dread. Jon's brain had been blood- and oxygen-deprived for too long a time. If he survived, would his brain be intact?

Sweat ran down Drake's back and his scrubs clung. He performed an ultrasound assessment and examined Jon from head to toe while nurses and orderlies finished cleaning and dressing his wounds.

The findings were grim.

Drake stripped off his gore-soiled gloves and removed his bloodied gown. The sterile, white orderliness of the Crash room was now a blood-splattered bomb site. Used instruments, linen, soiled dressings, slashed clothing, and medical debris spread from the epicenter. Jon's body rested at ground zero, incongruously immaculate with spotless linens and clean dressings. He looked like an offering on a sacrificial altar.

Chapter 43

Kenwood district, Reinhorst estate, 9:40 p.m.

Andrew Reinhorst rested his frayed Bible on his lap. As he sat in front of a fire in his oak and leather appointed library, he considered that he'd caused a man to die this evening. Actually, no. Faith's husband bore that responsibility himself. His sin demanded the Lord's justice.

Reinhorst's now-deceased wife had once said he could legitimize anything if you gave him the Bible and fifteen minutes. He would review, select and cull scripture, much as he researched and drafted his legal arguments. He hadn't needed to open the Book tonight. The applicable Old Testament law was as familiar and oft-quoted as it was clear. "An eye for an eye, a tooth for a tooth."

With the husband's passing, the trust fund money would revert to Andrew. Sixty-three million dollars—he would have it in time to make his empire safe. He settled back into the stuffed chair, closed his eyes, and let his muscles loosen. *Trust in God and he will make you free.*

The buzz of the chair-side intercom startled him. The panel indicated a call from his security supervisor. Reinhorst leaned forward, frowning as he toggled the switch.

"I left instructions not to be disturbed."

"I'm sorry, sir, but there's a gentlemen at the gate. Says he's with 'Catalyst Consultants.' He's quite insistent."

Here? Is he insane?

"Sir, should I have him brought up?"

His hands clenched the arm rests. "Ah, er, yes, bring him up." He stood and began to pace. Something must have gone wrong. But why come here?

Was this just the arrogant prick screwing with him? Could he have bailed out on the job, looking to jack up the pay-off? Reinhorst sat down.

Damn the shifty bastard—the visit couldn't be anything good.

He turned his head and flinched.

The Consultant had materialized beside the chair.

"God in heaven. You spooked me."

The Consultant wore a blue pinstripe suit, yellow dress shirt, and a red silk tie. Despite his attire, the man had the look of a pudgy-faced, balding peasant. This guy was a Special Forces veteran? A top-of-his-class law student?

Andrew knew that underestimation of the ordinary looking man's capabilities—physical and intellectual—had been the ruin of many.

The Consultant remained silent. He crossed to the liquor cabinet and poured a glass of Andrew's thirty-year-old scotch. "Is this area clean?" He scanned the room with ferret-like eyes.

"It's swept twice daily." Reinhorst rose to his feet. "Why the hell did you come here?"

The Consultant, drink in hand, settled into the armchair adjacent to the fireplace. He gazed into the dancing flames. He raised his drink, his cufflink catching the flickering flames. "Mission accomplished." He sipped.

"So, it's done?" Reinhorst stood with Bible in hand in front of the seated man.

"Two shots, chest, point-blank." The ice clinked as he took a deep draw of the scotch. "But a bit of trouble." He glanced down.

"Did you screw up? Besides coming here, that is. Damn." Reinhorst assumed his disapproving chairman posture. He loomed over the seated man.

The Consultant tilted his head, his fleshy face and narrow-spaced eyes somehow looking lean and predator-like.

Reinhorst stepped back. "What kind of trouble?"

The Consultant held his gaze a moment longer. Reinhorst had to look away.

"Punks showed up. Ghetto trash. I had to take off. I didn't get a chance to take his wallet or phone." He swirled the cut-crystal glass and stared into the liquid. "No matter. In that neighborhood they'll still blame it on gang criminals. We're in the clear."

"So why are you here? Don't you see that if anything is found out, your visit ties me to you? My staff will remember." Reinhorst hated the whine he'd let crawl into his voice.

The man stood and adjusted his tie. He walked to the liquor cabinet and turned towards Reinhorst. "We better make certain nothing focuses attention on either of us. Understood, Mr. Chairman? By the way," he looked at Reinhorst over the top of his glass, "if I disappear or have an accident, a packet of information will be electronically delivered to the police and media." He shrugged. "A simple measure to assure I don't have any accidents. I'm sure you understand." He placed the glass on the cabinet. "Thanks for the drink."

"He deserved to die." Reinhorst raised the Bible. "It was justice, considering what he did. He—"

"Whatever, Andrew. Sure." The man waved a hand in dismissal. "Just make sure to transfer the remainder of my fee." He exited the library, the door yielding a soft closing click.

Reinhorst looked into the fire. He hated the smug, scary bastard, but the man was capable. Justice demanded the doctor should die, and God worked in mysterious ways.

He opened the Book to his favorite verse in Proverbs. *Wealth and riches are in his house and his righteousness endures forever.*

The trust money would be his. He closed the Book.

Chapter 44

ER Crash Room

Drake pinched Jon's toe in a neurologic test assessing one of the brain's most basic responses—reaction to pain. His foot did not withdraw—instead his body contorted in the freakish reflex Drake recognized as decorticate posturing. He almost moaned in response to the brutally ominous prognosis this held.

The prolonged shock state had starved Jon's brain of blood. His reaction confirmed severe neurologic insult. Would enough cells survive for him to recover?

Brain tissue can't be replaced. The brain, heart, and spinal cord uniquely share this vulnerability. New cells do not arise to replace those lost.

Adding to Drake's desperation was his knowledge that cell death was continuing. Injured brain tissue triggers destructive inflammation. What was his friend losing right now? His ability to walk or speak, his intelligence? Perhaps his kindness or his ability to forever overlook the bad in people?

Drake had to act.

He'd recently learned of an experimental treatment for brain injury—induced hypothermia. It involved lowering the patient's body temperature. The lowered temperature slows the brain's metabolism and reduces cell injury. More brain cells survive. *That was the theory.*

Induced hypothermia had been tried in patients whose hearts had stopped. These were people who had collapsed with what the media described as heart attacks. They had CPR until paramedics arrived and shocked the hearts back to beating. Many times in these circumstances, although the bodies were resuscitated, the minds did not recover. The patients were left in a vegetative state.

Experimental hypothermia had been used in a number of these rescued heart patients, and it appeared to help more minds survive.

Hypothermia in a trauma patient had never been tried. Could it be done? Among its possible complications was poor blood clotting – Jon would be at risk of uncontrollable bleeding.

If hypothermia worked, it would give Jon the best chance to awaken as the man he had been.

If uncontrolled bleeding developed, it would kill him. Drake's throat knotted.

Jon's parents had been called immediately upon his arrival to the ER and Drake was told they'd just arrived. He hurried to the family room located next to the ER waiting room but stopped at the door. He paused, hoping he could avoid overwhelming Jon's parents with the urgency he felt. They needed clear heads for the wrenching decision they faced.

He'd met Jon's folks on a visit to their modest Duluth home two years earlier. His mom was a petite, easy-smiling woman. She fluttered about her only child, extending a continuous stream of inquiries as to what she might get him. Jon had been visibly embarrassed by her doting. When he'd given in to her offer for a cup of coffee she'd lit up and hurried off to the kitchen. When she delivered the cup, she put her hands on his shoulders and glowed.

Jon's dad worked in a foundry. For over thirty years, he'd poured molten steel. He was slim, like Jon, and looked to be made of whipcord. He was graying and distinguished, with a thoughtful manner like Jon that would lead one to think he was a college professor or, perhaps, a man of the cloth. He radiated pride when near his son.

Drake hugged Mrs. Malar, her cling desperate, her tiny frame rigid with tension. Her red-rimmed eyes did not meet his. It seemed as if she were ashamed of her grief and fear.

Mr. Malar gave a firm handshake that belied the lost and desperate cast of his eyes. Jon's parents sat side by side on the family room couch and Drake pulled up a low stool facing them. As clearly and kindly as he could, he informed them of the cruel realities. He presented the grim threat of brain damage and the gamble of induced hypothermia,

"Jon says that you're the best." Mr. Malar put a hand on Drake's forearm. "Tell me what we should do. The cold gives him a better chance not to be brain-damaged, right?"

Jon's mother sat, head down, with a dark blue rosary clenched in her hands. She advanced the beads singly, at intervals, as if tallying the depth of her dread. She never looked up.

"I believe it gives him the best chance of full recovery. But it involves risk." Drake's mouth felt so dry he could barely speak. "There's a greater risk of Jon dying using the hypothermia." He paused, working to keep his voice from breaking. "But using the cold gives him the best chance of surviving with his mind intact—of Jon being Jon."

The scent of Mrs. Malar's floral perfume hung in the air. The murmur of voices penetrated from the ER waiting room.

"No matter what course we take, Jon may die. Or, what may be worse, be alive with no consciousness, no awareness. Severe brain damage." Drake swallowed. "What some people call being a vegetable."

There was a sharp intake of breath from Jon's mom. Mr. Malar looked down at his calloused hands. "Lord, help me. I don't know what we should do. I'm not smart enough to know."

He snaked a hand to the side and it found his wife's, her other gripping the rosary. They clenched tightly and released. Her hand slid back to the beads.

"Starting hypothermia involves me putting a large needle into a blood vessel in Jon's groin. The needle is hollow and I slide a thin cable through the needle into one of Jon's veins. Part of the cable within the vein is a cooling element. I remove the needle, and as his blood flows over the element, it is cooled. Putting in the cable is routine." Drake repositioned his chair. He placed a hand on Mrs. Malar's knee.

"Lowering Jon's temperature is the big risk. It can cause increased bleeding and other problems we may not be aware of. No one has ever done this in a situation like Jon's. Increased bleeding could kill him. It's only because of how bad Jon's condition is that we are even discussing it." He held his hands open. "Have I explained things well enough that you both feel you understand?"

Mr. Malar's eyes glistened. "Yes. I follow." His face showed anguish. "But I don't know what to say."

The wail of an approaching siren grew louder, then abruptly stopped.

"Sir, nobody knows. The key, I believe, is what you think Jon would want."

Mr. Malar clenched and unclenched his fists, then ran trembling fingers through his hair. "I can't hardly breathe, let alone think."

Drake took Mr. Malar's work-hardened hands in his own. "I could talk science, but I don't think that will help us. What I can tell you is that if Jon was my brother or my son, I would risk it. I'd try the hypothermia—the cold. That's what I'd do. And sir," Drake's voice thickened, "I feel for Jon like a brother."

Mr. Malar's eyes probed. A large vein stood out as it tracked down his creased forehead, fading out just above his graying right eyebrow. He shifted his gaze to his wife, whose head remained bent over her rosary. She did not look up but must have felt his eyes. She nodded. Jon's father faced Drake.

"Do it, Drake. Do it. We want our Jon."

* * *

The life clock flashed *47 min 19 secs* as Drake started the procedure.

Jon's flesh looked drawn and ashen. The internal bleeding that had been draining via the chest tubes appeared to have almost stopped.

Utilizing a four-inch specialized needle, Drake penetrated the skin in the crease of Jon's left groin. He guided the needle by using his gloved fingers to feel the adjacent femoral artery's throbbing pulse as a landmark.

The rush of dark venous blood into the syringe confirmed he'd entered the vein. He removed the syringe from the needle, carefully maintaining the needle's position in the vein. Purplish blood welled from the needle's open hub. Drake felt the heat of Jon's blood as it flowed over the fingers of the surgical gloves. An awareness of the enormity of what was at risk washed over him. His chest knotted. *Am I doing the right thing?*

Drake slipped the guide wire through the font of blood into the hollow needle and fed the wire into the vein for a distance of six inches. He removed the needle, then threaded the hollow, specialized plastic catheter over the wire and advanced it into the vein. A knitting needle-thick section of the catheter two inches in length contained the cooling element.

Drake advanced the catheter into Jon's vein, then removed the guide wire, leaving the catheter and its cooling element within the vein. He connected the end of the catheter to the power and control hub of the bedside cooling module.

He set the temperature parameters on the control panel of the module's console. He flipped the switch.

Please. Make it work.

As Drake removed his bloody gloves, the graying nurse working as charge approached.

"Dr. Rainey is the admitting doctor for trauma," she rolled her eyes. Bartholomew Rainey was a giant of a man with an ego that was larger. The nurses called the massive, dark-haired physician "Black Bart" behind his back in reference to his temper. "He was finishing up a case in the OR, but the trumpets should announce his arrival any moment."

The admitting surgeon would typically be responsible for all medical decisions involving Jon's care beyond the ER. Drake's actions were contrary to usual procedure.

He went to the family room to inform the Malars that the procedure had gone well and the cooling had begun. They would be able to see Jon soon.

Drake returned to the Crash Room. Dr. Rainey had arrived. The towering surgeon approached with his chief resident and two interns trailing. He puffed up his six foot ten inches and waved a finger. "What you've done is outrageous—probably malpractice." He spoke loud enough for all to hear. "Hypothermia in this setting is a death sentence. Lowered body temperature impedes clotting. I'm going to try and reverse the damage when we get to the ICU but you're responsible if he dies."

The hospital personnel froze in stunned silence. The rhythmic click-hiss-blow of the cycling ventilator took center stage. All eyes were drawn to the machine and its charge.

Drake met the surgeon's glare, then switched his gaze to his stricken friend. "His parents are willing to risk the hypothermia. That is the decision, and yes, I am responsible." He placed a hand on his friend's forearm. "I pray I've done the right thing."

The bandages, tubes, wires, and lines shrouded Jon, who lay still as death but for the machine-driven rise and fall of his chest.

Chapter 45

Rachelle jerked awake to the sound of pounding on the kitchen door.

After picking up her pills and checking on the children, she'd collapsed on the couch and dropped into a coma-like slumber. The clock read 9:17—less than an hour since panic had overwhelmed her. The frantic hammering on the glass pane of the door repeated.

Any visitor after dark frightened her. This night her heart was in her throat.

Bracing a foot against the base of the door, she switched on the outside light. She pulled the curtain aside a crack and peeked out.

A dark-haired woman in a windbreaker who looked to be around thirty fidgeted at the door. She swiveled her head looking over her shoulder with her brow furrowed and rapped hard on the door once more. A yellow van sat in the darkened alley space beyond.

"What do you want?" Rachelle's voice cracked as she spoke through the door's pane.

"Please. Please. I need your phone. I hit a dog with my van and he's hurt. My cell phone is dead." She waved a small device. "Oh please." She clasped her hands prayer-like in front of her.

Rachelle moved her foot aside, turned the deadbolt, and swung the door open. "Is it a black lab?" She worried about a neighborhood dog that the kids played with.

"Yeah, I think it's a lab. He's hurt bad. Where's your phone?" asked the woman, her dark features knitted.

"Over there, on the wall, next to the table." Rachelle took a half-step back and looked towards the alley as the woman brushed passed her.

"Did he run off or—?" Rachelle felt herself yanked back, her legs swept from under her. She hurtled down. Her body slammed and her head smashed into the floor.

The door banged shut.

The dark-haired woman held a cell-phone-sized device pointed towards Rachelle. Rachelle looked up, taking in the surprising bulk of the woman's shoulders and the inky intensity of her eyes.

"What do you want? Please—"

"Shut up, little Mommy."

"What do you—?"

The woman sprang forward, kicking Rachelle in the ribs. Rachelle doubled up, unable to breathe.

"Where are the children?" The woman pulled a large plastic zip-tie out of the windbreaker pocket. She had the freakishly huge muscles of a bodybuilder. "Kneel and put your hands behind your back. We're going for a ride."

Rachelle fought for breath as her mind pinwheeled. A survival course commandment—don't allow yourself to be taken. Never get in a vehicle—scream, fight, do whatever. You must not let them get you in a vehicle.

"Move it." Another kick landed.

Rachelle struggled to her knees. She put her hands behind her back, head bent forward as if praying. She felt the woman move behind her, heard the soft rustle of the windbreaker material. At the instant fingers touched, Rachelle whipped her head back as fast and hard as she could. Her skull slammed into the woman's face.

Rachelle stood as she screamed. "Run. Kids! Outside! Get help!" She pivoted, looking to press her advantage. A fist blasted into her face like a sledge hammer. Rachelle crashed against the wall and crumpled to the floor. She looked up.

The woman crouching over her looked like a rabid beast. Blood gushed from her nose. Her teeth showed in a silent snarl. She held the small black device underhand, brandishing it like a knife fighter.

The muscled woman's eyes sparked. She swiped a hand under her nose and glanced at the blood. An electric crackling ignited as her arm shot forward. The device bit and held.

Rachelle convulsed in agony—her last awareness the smell of burning flesh as the world went dark.

Her little one's cry—Rachelle willed herself from the blackness. Her breathing difficult, something wedged in her mouth. Face against the linoleum. Her whole body hurting.

"Get your hands back here." A zipper-like sound and Rachelle heard her Kristin whimper once more.

Rachelle lay on her stomach, her hands pinned behind her. She fought to turn her head and saw the woman checking the placement of a plastic lock-tie on Kristin's wrists, her little arms trussed behind her like Rachelle's.

Her Shane sat slumped on the floor. His arms were behind him and a plastic tie creased his mouth and cheeks, encircling his head as a gag. His left eye was swollen.

Please, God. This can't be happening.

The woman removed her windbreaker. Her arms hung with slabs of muscle like an ape's. She stuffed a rag into Kristin's mouth and positioned the plastic tie. The zipper sound repeated and the cruel bit cinched tight.

"Hey, lookee here. Sucker-punch mommy is back with us. You thought you could throw down with me?" The woman's features twisted in disdain. Bloodied wads of Kleenex protruded from each nostril, her nose swollen and discolored. "Now that you're packaged, we're going to the van."

Rachelle's head reeled. *No.*

The woman glanced toward the kitchen counter. She reached over and grabbed a bag of M&M's lying there. She opened it and spilled the contents out. She sorted, separating some and popping them into her mouth. "M and M's—thoughtful of you. I love the orange." She chewed. "Hey, prom queen, what did you think of my hurt-doggie act? Outstanding, huh?" She ate another candy. "I was in school plays. They were too stupid to give me good roles. The idiots. I'm a star."

She glanced about the cramped kitchen and rundown living room. "This place is a dump." She walked over and peered out the back-door curtain. "I'm going to take you guys out this door and into the van. If anyone makes noise or misbehaves…" she said this last part with a theatrical trill, "yooou'll be sorry." She stared into Rachelle's eyes. "Check this out, cheap shot. Your little tough guy thought he could fight me, too."

The woman raised the shock-device. She clicked it and blue arc crackling began. Leaning over, her eyes never leaving Rachelle's, she touched the device to Shane's shoulder. His body snapped like a sprung mousetrap. Rachelle screamed against her gag. Shane lay slumped and motionless.

"Don't go getting all worked up, Mommy." She smiled as she displayed the device. "That was just a baby jolt. You got twenty times that."

Shane lolled to his side. His lost and fearful eyes met Rachelle's. Her heart pained.

The woman gave her big shoulders a shrug. "Screw up and you fry. Behave and we can have some fun."

She turned to the two bound and gagged children. "We're going for a ride, kiddies. It'll be cool. Front row seats watching a star in action—a superstar." She flexed her arms like a pro wrestler.

"Okay, juicy Mama. Let's get this hot body of yours on wheels."

Rachelle felt her wrists in a strong grip, her arms levered up behind, forcing her to bend forward at the waist.

The woman drove Rachelle, like a human wheelbarrow, out the door. A whiff of garbage filled Rachelle's nose. The woman controlled Rachelle one-handed while sliding the van's side panel open.

Their kidnapper loaded them into the van. *Jesus, no!*

Rachelle sank. She'd failed the critical survival commandment.

She had failed her children.

Chapter 46

Finally, Drake had a moment to make the call he did not want to make. He closed his eyes and rested his forehead on his hand. Rachelle would still be reeling from news of Faith's murder. Learning of Jon's condition would crush her.

ER caregivers observe that shot or stabbed drug dealers and hard-core criminals often survive injuries that would kill most others. As one of Drake's mentors had once stated, "Assholes are hard to kill."

Drake reached for the phone. *Please, God, save one of your good ones.*

As he entered his home number, an overhead page directed him to line two. He disconnected and took the incoming call.

"Dr. Cody here."

"Dr. Cody, this is Tracy from ICU. Dr. Rainey ordered me to call. Dr. Malar's bleeding heavily and he's looking bad. Dr. Rainey tried to stop the hypothermia. Mr. Malar refused unless the order comes from you." The nurse softened her voice and Drake strained to hear. "Dr. Rainey's really angry. He was rude to Dr. Malar's father."

"I'll be right up." Drake heard the concern in the nurse's words.

He bit his lip. The fear that the big surgeon might be right caused his gut to tighten. *Is my treatment killing Jon?*

The glowering doctor confronted Drake the moment he arrived in the ICU. They stood in the middle of the bustling nurse's station.

"I warned you," Rainey broadcast for all to hear. "Your bullshit treatment impedes clotting. I won't be a partner to your malpractice. His parents are too clueless to listen—stop the damn hypothermia now. The man is bleeding to death."

The normal background exchanges of the nurse and secretarial working exchanges ceased as if a mute button had been pushed. The awkward human silence left the technology chorus center stage. Monitors beeped, the lab results printer chattered, and the phones buzzed.

Jon's parents must feel as if they were being torn apart. Rainey had been rude to Mr. Malar, the nurse had said. *Bastard.* Drake felt the rush of heat. His vision sharpened. Pounding began in his head.

No. He took deep breaths and forced himself to slow. His muscles loosened.

He focused on what mattered. Jon's life hung in the balance.

The big surgeon was scared—afraid he'd be blamed if Jon did not survive. Drake understood the surgeon's fear. He knew about blame—and guilt.

He knew the judgment that truly mattered came from the court of his own conscience.

The Malars trusted him with their greatest treasure—their son's life. He forced down the knot that had formed in his throat. He needed to think quickly and clearly. Jon's life was draining away.

"Tracy, will you please get me Jon's chart and the most recent labs?" He turned towards Jon's bay.

The station was made up of an open central work space with desks and counters surrounded by fifteen ICU rooms arranged like the spokes of a wheel. Jon lay in bay number four.

He looked still as death, the ventilator breathing for him. His color matched the hospital sheets. Drake laid a hand on his friend's chest, the cold striking. He forced himself to maintain his clinical focus. Why the ongoing bleeding?

A unit of blood hung above Jon, the crimson column of the IV line linked to his right arm. The monitor displayed his vital signs:

Blood pressure: 80 over 40. *Too low.*

Pulse: 130 beats per minute. *Too high.*

Temperature: 92 degrees. *Damn cold, but the best chance for his brain to survive.*

Jon teetered on the verge of irreversible shock. He was dying.

"Can you give me the chest tube outputs?" Drake asked of Tracy as he looked at the lab results. Jon's hemoglobin had dropped to 8.0 g/dl from an earlier 11.5 reading. This was in spite of the transfusions.

"The total is 1600 mls," she said.

Drake looked up sharply. "1600 mls?"

"Yes. I haven't done a breakdown. Dr. Rainey demanded I get you on the phone as soon as he heard the total."

"That's my point," Rainey interrupted as he arrived at the bedside. "Your insane cool-down is causing platelet dysfunction and he's bleeding out. You're killing him."

Drake ignored the big man. "Tracy, how much blood has he had transfused?" He could not allow anything to dislodge his focus. Evaluation of Jon's course, physical exam, labs, X-rays, and astute clinical reasoning were what would help his friend.

"That's the sixth unit hanging now. Two were given in the ER. So that's a total of eight."

"Thank you and damn," Drake said. Eight units equaled more than half of Jon's total blood volume. Large transfusions of blood correlated with low survival.

"Is there a repeat chest X-ray?" asked Drake.

"You're wasting time," Rainey interrupted. "Stop your murderous experiment and let me take care of my patient."

"I'll get the film, Dr. Cody," Tracy said. Dr. Rainey shot her a glare.

As she retrieved the X-ray, Drake pulled back the sheet to examine Jon.

"What the hell? There's a new chest tube on the right." Drake turned, open-mouthed. "Good God, man. What else haven't you told me?"

The surgeon made a huffing sound and gave a half-roll of his eyes. "Your chest tube looked poorly positioned to me, so I had my chief resident put in another. And it's good he did, because it's draining a lot of blood. As I suspected, your tube was placed incorrectly."

Drake was expert and had never had a failed chest tube. He didn't care about Rainey's insinuation that the tube had been positioned poorly. This wasn't about ego. This was about his friend suffering the pain and possible harm of an unnecessary procedure.

Heat and redness flared. The impulse for violent response fired. His fists clenched. *No*.

This was not the Scioto Furnace. Violence was not the answer.

Jon needed him. He looked at the sunken eyes and drawn flesh of his friend's face. His heart skipped. *Find the answer now or Jon will die.*

"Here's the chest X-ray, Dr. Cody." Tracy positioned the film on the wall-mounted view box.

Drake looked. "This tube has a lot of subcutaneous air tracking around it. Dr. Rainey, did you oversee the procedure? Were there problems?"

"Ah...yes. Yes, I did." Dr. Rainey said. "There were no problems."

Drake glanced up, finding Tracy staring at the big man with her mouth agape.

"That's not right," she said, shaking her head. "I was in here when your resident doctor did the procedure. You were on the phone. The whole ICU overheard you complaining to the head of surgery about the hypothermia."

"Be quiet, nurse. This is between doctors." Rainey said, scowling down at her.

"I will not," Tracy said red-faced. "This is about a patient and his care. I absolutely will not be quiet." She stood, jaw thrust, with her five-foot-two inches and one hundred-some pounds facing the massive doctor.

He drew back, his brow furrowed.

Tracy turned to Drake. "I've assisted on a lot of chest tube placements, and the resident had some trouble. He couldn't get the tube to advance into the chest. He had to go back with the scalpel a second time."

Drake palpated Jon's chest and carefully pulled back the tape around the new chest tube. Each tube was connected to suction. Any blood that had pooled or accumulated in Jon's chest due to ongoing bleeding flowed through the tubes. Each tube had a separate collection chamber.

"The left tube has no more blood than when he left the ER. The new tube has almost 700 mls." Drake turned to Tracy. "The bleeding increased after the new tube, correct?"

Tracy nodded as she looked at her documentation. "Yes. It picked up after the new chest tube."

Drake closed his eyes and took a deep breath. "Rainey, this is not a complication of the hypothermia." *Son of a bitch.* "There's a bleeder in the right chest cavity. Your resident probably inadvertently cut an intercostal artery when he placed the new tube."

Dr. Rainey's eyes swiveled between Tracy and Drake.

"No, I don't think so," he said. "It could be the clotting problem."

"If it was a clotting problem, Jon would be bleeding from all his wounds." At the thought of Jon's suffering with the pain and damage of the unneeded tube, heat welled. "Damn it, Rainey. Poor clotting wouldn't be localized to one site."

"That's right," said Tracy, as if to herself. "I should have noticed. But as soon as I reported the total, Dr. Rainey demanded I get you on the line."

"Why don't you just shut up and do your job, *nurse,*" Dr. Rainey said with a sneer.

Drake reflexively considered several moves that would drop the big man. The IV alarm sounded.

Tracy readjusted the tubing. The alarm silenced. Drake gained control of his mounting anger and maintained his focus on what mattered.

"Tracy, please ask the secretary to STAT page Dr. Peter Kelly for me. And let's hang two more units of blood." If a surgical arterial injury had occurred, it meant there was a possibility to control Jon's bleeding.

Tracy's communication had pointed the way. He had a hard time finding the words. "Tracy, Jon is so very lucky to have you watching over him. Thank you."

She flushed. "I'm just doing my job, but you're welcome." She slid the glass door closed behind her.

Drake heard her call out to the paging secretary.

Dr. Rainey pulled himself to his full height. "Who do you think—?"

"Shut up and listen," Drake said. "You screwed up. Probably because you were too busy pissing about hypothermia and worrying about blame."

The big doctor's face reddened.

"Rainey, you're off the case. Fired—as of right now. Got it? You'll apologize to Tracy in person and in writing. Your treatment of her is a disgrace. As a physician, I'm ashamed."

Rainey raised a hand and waved it at Drake. "You can't kick—"

"Damn it, Rainey. I can and I have. The Malars asked me to oversee Jon's care and direct things the way I think best. I'm certain that you are not that. "

Rainey held up a fist. "I'm going to report—"

"Son of a bitch, Rainey, shut up! I'll be doing the reporting. Apologize to Tracy on your way out, and do not push me. All that matters to me is Jon. I'm going to ask Dr. Kelly to take your place."

Drake took a deep breath. How could this doctor not recognize that they all wanted the same thing? Why treat people so badly?

"Rainey, you have a reputation as a competent surgeon but you're an asshole. You bully people. I know you feel a ton of pressure, but that's no excuse. You're a doctor. You need to treat people with respect. Saving lives is a team effort. None of us do it alone."

Rainey remained silent. The huge doctor's shoulders were slumped. It was apparent he recognized he'd screwed up. Drake's words had let the surgeon know he would face peer review discipline, at least—and possibly legal action. He faced Drake.

"I was doing what I thought best. I truly thought the problem was the hypothermia." He dropped his head and took a step toward the door. He stopped and turned. "An intercostal artery injury makes sense. You and Dr. Kelly can try a Foley balloon tamponade of the placement track at the bedside. It might stop the bleeding and keep your friend out of the O.R. I hope he does well. I really do." He exited.

Drake found his anger fading. He thought of Jon's parents and what really mattered.

He stood alone beside Jon's savaged body. He grasped his friend's icy hand and a chill spread through him. Drake had seen people come back when everything said they couldn't. No one was more deserving than Jon. He bent to his ear.

"Keep fighting, brother."

Chapter 47

The bastard who'd killed his daughter and was trying to steal his money was not dead.

Andrew Reinhorst hung up the phone. Shot twice in the chest, yet still alive. A miracle?

No. An outrage—Faith's husband deserved to die. He should be burning in hell.

Reinhorst's hospital source said the doctor had not regained consciousness. And the odds were against it. But no one knew for sure.

He got to his feet and paced beneath the wall-mounted crucifix. The chapel was an addition Andrew had added when he purchased and remodeled the Kenwood estate. He'd installed a business desk with full tech capability beneath the four-foot-tall cross. In tough times he liked to work from here.

What would be the upshot if the doctor survived? What if he awoke and remembered details? Reinhorst went numb.

What if he survives but is severely brain-damaged?

Damn. Any law student could answer that. The doctor would get it. He'd be awarded the money, and a guardian would be appointed by the court—likely his parents.

Even if the murdering doctor was subsequently convicted of killing Faith, it would be too late. Like most states, Minnesota had a "no illicit gain" law. This meant as the convicted killer, the doctor could not benefit. The money would revert to Reinhorst.

But it would be too late.

The bankruptcy bomb was ticking. When it went off, it would leave his empire a pile of rubble. Only the doctor's death would assure survival of Reinhorst LLC.

The Consultant's failure had put everything at risk.

* * *

The Consultant pocketed his phone. *Shit!*

A nine-millimeter double-tap to the chest from three feet. Alive?

An agitated Andrew Reinhorst had just confirmed that the doctor was in the hospital—in critical condition. He might make it but, if so, likely brain-damaged.

He swiveled his chair to face the bank of windows. The leased west Bloomington property sat wooded and private. It was not a home but a base of operations.

He turned to face the side-by-side computer consoles displaying his current games. On the left he sat in a Texas Hold 'Em tournament with the winner getting a chair in a World Tour event. On the right he played in a private, big-money game.

A bad beat made the World Tour event look low probability, but he was up big money in the cash game. He'd discovered online poker six months before and played whenever possible. High-stakes competition based on the continuous calculation of risk and probability—he loved it. And he rarely lost.

If the doctor ended up alive and badly brain damaged, it meant no payoff. Alive and intact meant a witness and… *Damn.*

There'd been enough money to retire. He'd planned to quit but had taken the Reinhorst job regardless. Greedy. And now it was biting him in the ass.

He crunched a baby carrot as he tapped the keys at his main console. The veggies helped keep his weight down. His workouts kept him in shape. Strong and fit, but he had the fleshy features and jowls of a fat man. He knew people perceived him as chubby. They didn't get past the face.

He refreshed the console displays. His online name was "Smart-Play." He cashed out of the money game and forfeited his spot in the tournament competition. There would be no more games tonight.

If the doctor survived with brain intact, it could get serious. There'd been ghetto punks at the scene. The cops might sniff out his trail.

He didn't worry about Reinhorst. It wasn't loyalty but self-preservation that assured the pompous bastard wouldn't talk. It had been wise to let him know of the in-case-of-death packet.

He walked across the room and slid open the door to the deck. Hardwoods loomed in the moonlight. The marshy area at the margin of Hyland Park pulsed with noise—a cadenced, cricket-like chorus. It was some type of frog. He'd never seen one, but from the sound, there must be thousands.

He rubbed his forehead, then looked at his hands with fingers wide and palms up. They held steady.

Should he wait it out and hope the doctor dies? Or follow through and finish him in the hospital?

Reinhorst could be convinced to up the pay. The desperate power-freak would have no choice. The doctor was in intensive care and hospital security mattered nowadays. It would be a gamble—worse odds but a bigger pay-off.

The safe money said fold and run.

A flight to Costa Rica and he could be poolside in less than twenty hours. He'd have full access to his funds and no extradition. Able to indulge his passion for gambling full time and financially set for life.

All in or cash out and run?

Chapter 48

9:41 p.m.

Meryl signaled her turn. The van's headlights swept the secondary road paralleling the river downstream of the Washington Avenue Bridge.

As she drove, she shared the spectacular action within her head. She spoke fast and nonstop, the ideas and observations gushing like a wildcat oil well that had hit a deposit too rich to be contained.

After a mile, she turned towards the river, and within two blocks the surroundings looked like part of a different city. The headlights swung over dark areas of low cinder-block buildings surrounded by steel fences and dirt parking lots. There was no activity, and the only lights visible were at entryways and loading docks.

It looked like a setting from a thriller movie. She couldn't help but be the star.

Meryl loved drama. She created drama. Her thoughts were front-page news. If people could be in her mind for just one instant, they'd recognize her brilliance. Like no one else, ever. What could be cooler than that?

She glanced in the rearview mirror, catching a glimpse of little Momma's bound throat and paleness. The little girl continued to whimper like an annoying puppy. The boy's eyes were locked on Meryl. The restraints held them helpless in their chairs.

The road changed from narrow tarmac to rutted and weed-tufted gravel. She passed a No Exit sign, bent and graffiti-marred, standing sentry at the access road's origin. The headlights pitched skyward as the van humped over a spur of railroad track. The smell of the river flats rushed in her open window—mud, decomposing vegetation and fish.

"We're almost there, people. A riverboat. You're gonna love it." The paddle-wheeler stood silhouetted against the rippling silver of moonlight on water. Meryl saw the scene as if projected on a wide screen.

The road dead-ended at a cement apron that formed part of a riverbank levee. Mooring hawsers linked the boat to two thick pillars. A wooden shack sat adjacent to a walkway linking the dirt parking lot to the awning-covered gangway. The blue-haloed glow of a single light shone from atop a post at the gangway's base.

Meryl pulled onto the concrete. She inched the van close to one of the mooring pillars. The headlights fanned the concrete slab, showing three sets of narrowly spaced, crimson eyes positioned over a shapeless lump.

The rats scrambled over one another, disappearing over the concrete's edge. The gnawed carcass of one of their brethren lay centered in the beams.

She killed the ignition and lights, then turned to her prisoners. "We're home!"

Chapter 49

Farley's keyboard sat in a field of junk-food detritus, and fast-food wrappers littered the floor around the wastebasket.

His first homicide case and he was not in control of his emotions. *Unprofessional.*

He took out the society pages photo he'd printed. Faith Reinhorst-Malar had been turn-every-head-in-the-room beautiful.

Yet everything he'd uncovered about her was ugly and cruel. He felt sorry for the husband. She'd wronged him in every way possible.

And now the doctor might die. He was about the same age as Farley.

Had Jon Malar killed Faith, as the D.A. and department brass believed? In the hour before the doctor was shot, they'd issued a warrant for his arrest. A cell was reserved and waiting. Dr. Jon Malar—murderer.

It felt wrong.

Yamada would be back soon. He'd instructed Farley to keep "working his magic" and focus on Faith Reinhorst Malar's death. Yamada said most murders are tied to love, hate, or money.

Love? Perhaps one of Faith's lovers rejected? Unquestionably, she had plenty—if what she'd engaged in could be called love. The trusting husband might as well have taken a number for service like a patron at a deli counter.

Hate? Hating Faith did not seem a challenge. Farley had yet to find anyone who liked her. The husband? She'd provided him more than enough fuel for hatred.

Money? With Faith dead, the trust fund millions would go to the husband.

And what if he dies? Something to check out.

Faith had a law practice. And she represented her husband and his partners' research company. Farley checked his notes—NeurVitae. Reportedly, it had done no business but had potential. Sketchy, but it warranted further checking.

And where did the $75,000 deposited to her business account four days before her death come from? Farley had also discovered an additional $100,000 transferred to her personal account less than seventy-two hours before her death. The deposit amounts had been entered into her office computer, but their origin had not. Today he'd obtained court orders for access to the bank records but would get no information until tomorrow.

Farley stood, then paced back and forth behind his desk. On each pass he fed a potato chip into his mouth. *What drove this twisted woman?*

He considered what he'd learned of her behavior. Money and sex were her passions. It was likely one or the other got her killed.

Her sexual activity appeared too indiscriminate to track but money had to have a source.

He sat at his computer and his fingers flew over the keyboard.

* * *

Two hours later

Detective Aki Yamada entered the Homicide room, running on five hours sleep in the past forty-eight. He needed a shower.

A bleary-eyed Farley looked up from among the wrappers, pop cans, and printouts spread over his desk.

Yamada shrugged off his wrinkled sport coat, hanging it over the back of his chair.

"How's the husband doing?" Farley asked.

"Bad. Real bad."

The young detective grimaced.

"They say he was gone. No vital signs." Aki undid his tie. "Doc Cody brought him back, but there's a good chance his brain is gone. I'm headed to the hospital next to see what I can learn."

"It sounds grim." Farley hung his head.

"I want you to stay focused on the wife's killing. Okay?" The news had clearly upset the rookie. The kid was learning he wasn't in white-collar crimes anymore. "I caught up with Dr. Rizzini just before the shooting. He's got a rep as a hard-partying type. Looks to be true—he was half in the bag when I talked with him. He's got access to the paralyzer drug and admits he didn't care for his friend's wife."

"I'm finding that's a common feeling." Farley rubbed his eyes.

Aki slipped off his tie. "On the other hand, I don't see that he has any motive. We need to check it out but I think he's clean." He stretched his neck. "As I was leaving his place, the call went out on the doc's shooting.

I diverted there. The 911 tape sounded like gangbangers. That area is Vice Lords territory and the caller said the shooters were 'chicos'. That's what the Lords call the Hispanics. The Vice Lords and the Latin Kings have been banging in a turf war.

"The doc's wallet and phone were taken and triangulation of the phone shows it's still somewhere in the projects." He sat down at his desk alongside Farley's. "I've got the gang task force shaking the trees. It looks like the Doc's shooting might be a *wrong place at the wrong time* kinda deal."

"There's no doubt the guy is seriously unlucky," Farley said.

Aki looked over his shoulder and lowered his voice. "I just left a private meeting at the DA's office. Me, the chief, the DA and, get this, the victim's father—Andrew Reinhorst. It was my first meet with our new DA." Aki looked around again. "The man is a certifiable tool. He bowed to me when we were introduced. You know, like a Japanese thing. He talked slow and loud to me as if I might not understand English. I was expecting him to ask me to show him some karate or fold him up an Origami swan."

Aki had felt like returning the bow to the DA and then kicking him square in the nuts.

He reached into his draped coat and pulled out his notepad. "I didn't volunteer anything with the father there. Why would a family member be part of an after-hours meeting with the DA in the midst of an active investigation? Hell, the guy could be a suspect. Some seriously weird shit is going down."

"That sounds messed up." Farley said.

"Bottom line—the DA and the department brass are ready to close the case on Faith Reinhorst-Malar's murder. They have their man. They've decided the husband's shooting is unrelated." Aki set his notepad on the desk. "According to them, it's some type of karmic closure. The mistreated doctor kills his rich, wayward wife, and then he's a victim of random violence."

He rubbed his face with both hands. "Hell, maybe they're right. It all fits. But..." He looked at Farley. "You found anything?"

Farley gathered several sheets. He rolled his chair next to Aki's. "I've been chasing the money. The trust fund is the big payoff. It's over fifty million dollars. It goes to Doc Malar if he survives. If the doc dies it goes back to Daddy Reinhorst." He lowered the sheets. "Would Reinhorst kill his daughter and then her husband for money? Seems cold—and complicated. If he were gonna kill them both, why not take them out together? On the other hand, I found a business article suggesting that Reinhorst's business is on the verge of bankruptcy."

Aki shook his head. "And the DA has this guy sitting in on a meeting related to the investigation?"

Farley picked up another page of notes. "I looked at other possible money angles—her law practice and NeurVitae, the doctors' research company. I went through her office records. I didn't find evidence of any meaningful legal work other than the basic NeurVitae stuff she did.

"I found the $75,000 deposit to her business account that I already told you about and a separate deposit of $100,000 to her personal account about seventy-two hours before her death. I haven't been able to find where the deposits came from. I have the court orders, but we won't have answers any earlier than tomorrow morning. She may have just been moving funds around. She's not poor."

Aki nodded. "Worth checking—no doubt. Anything else?"

"I found a name in the appointment calendar and a matching business card in her desk. Meryl Kampf. She's with that BioZyn company I mentioned to you. They invest in the development of new drugs. It's privately held and registered in Mauritius with its main office in Berlin. Mauritius is a dodgy site but lots of companies register there for tax reasons. I haven't found much on them." He pulled loose the next sheet.

"I tracked Meryl Kampf's education and professional history. She's a pharmacology and science wizard. She holds two PhDs and is an expert in drug development. She's been with BioZyn for just under two years. Faith's calendar showed the appointment almost a month ago. Since Faith had the BioZyn business card, I figure the meeting took place."

Farley scanned the sheets in his hand and reshuffled their order. "And I dug up this." He handed a page to Aki.

Aki scanned it, then frowned. "A health insurance claim? This is five years old, right? The name is blacked out."

"That's Meryl Kampf's record. It's from her university student health insurance file. I couldn't hack into her hospital or medical records, but the insurance files are a piece of cake. This was during her first year of post-graduate work. Look at the diagnosis and admission sections."

Aki squinted and read aloud. "Diagnosis code: Acute psychotic break – undifferentiated manic decompensation." He trailed a finger down the sheet. "Admission criteria: emergency hold – risk to self/others. What does this mean?"

Farley handed another sheet forward. "Five years ago, she was psychiatrically hospitalized against her will as a risk to self or others. Acute mania. The insurance records show she was on the drug Lithium for at least the duration of her schooling—another three years. That's pretty heavy duty."

He pulled out another sheet. "I researched acute mania. From what I find it's not a condition you typically get over. It requires lifelong control, and manic folks are prone to stopping their meds. They believe they're A-okay and everyone else is screwed up. Here's a description."

He read aloud, "Inflated sense of self, delusions of grandeur, excessive energy, pressured speech, emotional volatility—euphoria may alternate with irritability or rage—diminished need for sleep, marked sexual excess, bursts of artistic creativity and genius." He raised a finger as he read the next. "Lack of judgment, engagement in high-risk activities, distrust of others, and a penchant for violence." He lowered the sheet. "I figure someone with that potential is worth checking out."

"Definitely," said Aki. "Any evidence she was around for anything more than an appointment a month ago?"

"I pulled up a photo from her university identification and text-mailed it to the security guy at Faith's office building. He says this is the gal he saw with Faith several times. She's real muscled up now, but he says the scary eyes are a for-sure."

"We need to talk with her." Aki frowned at the print-out of Meryl Kampf's old photo. "Those are some kinda eyes."

"I've been trying to track her down. I contacted BioZyn headquarters and got a secretary. She said Dr. Kampf's whereabouts are…" he checked his sheet, "'confidential, due to the sensitive and competitive nature of BioZyn's business.' I left my number. She said she'd inform her superiors."

Aki rubbed his forehead, then looked at Farley. "The brass are convinced Faith Reinhorst-Malar's murder is solved. They have their man. The Doc's shooting will go to a back burner as a case of random gang related violence—which it looks like it may have been. Unless we find something significant soon, we're gonna be pulled off these cases."

Farley frowned. "I wasn't going to say anything yet, but I'm tracking something else."

"Don't hold back. We might not have a later."

"It's about the call at the pool—the one from the Swiss pharmaceutical company around the time of her death."

"Yeah. We couldn't determine specifically who called her. Right?" Aki said.

"That's right. But I learned the call was routed from the executive offices of their acquisitions section. That's the department that purchases new drugs for their development pipeline. It theoretically could be a money angle, but I'm pretty much just fishing."

"I asked Doc Cody about that call." Aki shrugged. "He knew nothing about it. Said she might have been checking out things for the future."

Farley crumpled an empty chip bag into a ball. “The way I see it, Faith Reinhorst-Malar is the knot at the center of a tangled mess. I don’t understand half of what she had going on.” He shot the wrapper toward the waste can like a basketball. It bounced off the rim. “Shutting this case down now feels like a rush to judgment.”

“The more media and political pressure,” Aki rubbed his temples, “the bigger the rush. Welcome to Homicide.”

He collected Farley’s notes. “Maybe the brass are right,” he tapped the sheets on the desktop, squaring the edges, “and maybe not. Jon Malar as a murderer doesn’t sit right with my gut—but I’ve been fooled before. Ministers, teachers, social workers—sometimes it’s the straight arrows that snap.”

Farley’s brow furrowed.

Aki looked at the clock. “I’ve got to get to the hospital.” He held the pages up. “Farley, this is great work. I mean it. Keep digging.”

The rookie blushed. “Thanks.” His face turned pensive. “My gut agrees with you. About the husband being innocent, I mean.” He picked up another loose wrapper and crumpled it. “The more I learn about Faith Reinhorst-Malar, the nastier she looks. The woman seems to have lived her life screwing everyone over.”

Farley shot the paper at the waste can and hit dead center.

Chapter 50

9:46 p.m.

Rachelle and the children were lashed to captain's-style chairs in the back of the van. The woman had looped plastic ties around their necks and pulled them tight around each chair's headrest. Their bound arms were pinned between their backs and that of the chair. Restraints also secured their ankles to each chair's floor-mounted swivel post.

Rachelle's wrists burned. The zip-tie restraint cut like wire. Her hands felt dead. She wiggled her fingers every few minutes trying to maintain function if the woman gave her an opening.

Their kidnapper was clever and strong. More than anything, she was scary. Very scary.

Rachelle's mind boiled with frantic imaginings of what was going to happen to them. Another survival commandment came to her. *Do not panic.*

She could rotate enough to see each of the children. Kristin had been making a gag-muffled mewing but sat silent now. Wide-eyed and tear-streaked, she shook her head in response to Rachelle's gaze. Rachelle so wanted to hug away her little one's terror.

Turning further, she glimpsed Shane. The sight of his bruised and swollen eye sickened her. His gaze remained locked on the back of their captor's head. When he turned, catching Rachelle's eyes, he quickly responded to her nod. He looked angry. Good.

Their captor had left the sliding panel between herself and the rear compartment open. She talked nonstop as she drove. At times she hummed and laughed. Her tone sounded chatty, as if they were friends on a trip. Not victims she had kidnapped and brutalized.

Rachelle had way more experience with mental illness than she wished. She recognized one thing with chilling certainty—their kidnapper belonged in a locked ward.

The vehicle slowed and made a number of turns in succession. She heard the sound of tires on gravel, and the van clumped unmistakably over railroad tracks. Rachelle's nose told her they were near the river.

What? A riverboat. That's what the woman said. A boat?

The van stopped. Their captor was silent for a few moments and then Rachelle heard the prolonged sniffs. *Oh God.* The door slammed.

The van's side door ripped open. The woman had her jacket off and stood grinning with her muscled arms held out in a *Ta-da!* gesture.

"Awesome, isn't it? A boat that used to be a restaurant and now it's your home away from home."

Rachelle's chair faced the open door. A single light illuminated concrete, a mooring post, and a section of the multi-decked craft. Craning against the neck restraint, she could make out a canopied walkway bridging from cement to boat.

The woman used wire cutters to snip the children's ankle and neck restraints. She lifted them out of their chairs as if they weighed nothing, then held their rear-pinioned arms in either hand and steered them as they stumbled forward, bent at the waist. Rachelle watched helplessly as they were driven up the walkway. They disappeared into the massive boat.

As they left her sight, something collapsed inside her. The fear she fought to control burst into flame.

Her breathing accelerated. Bound and alone, her children in peril.

Do not panic. Do not panic.

Movement caught her eye. A shadowy form advanced down the hawser securing the boat to the pillar next to the open van door. The grayish shape came into focus as it crept down the braided surface. Glistening black eyes probed at her from behind a long snout, the nose raised and sniffing. The lips and jaw grotesquely nibbled the air as the creature advanced towards her.

Rachelle strained against her restraints. The rat moved closer, so near she could hear its moist snuffling. The animal stopped, went silent and jerked its head toward the sound of steps on the walkway.

It reversed and slithered away, trailing a hairless tail.

The freak was coming for her.

Chapter 51

Intensive Care Unit, 11:24 p.m.

Drake stood gowned, gloved, and masked by the bedside of his pale and motionless friend. Bleeding to death is quiet. There is no outward evidence of suffering or struggle. Life steals away in silence.

Dr. Peter Kelly, the surgeon now caring for Jon, cut the anchoring sutures and slid out the suspect chest tube. Drake then fed a finger-thick latex catheter with an inflatable balloon at its tip through the surgical track into Jon's chest cavity.

Using a large syringe, Dr. Kelly injected fifty cc's of sterile water into the catheter inflating the in-chest balloon to the size of a small lime. Drake exerted traction on the catheter, pulling until resistance told him the balloon was lodged snugly against the inner aspect of the chest. The surgeon secured it there.

If their assessment was correct, the in-chest balloon was now pressing against the artery that had been cut when the unneeded chest tube had been placed.

Drake fidgeted as they waited and monitored the result. Ten minutes seemed like forever.

Dr. Kelly looked at Drake and smiled. It was clear—the bleeding had stopped.

They had, at least temporarily, slowed Jon's slide toward death.

Drake blew out a huge breath and returned the smile. Inside he was soaring.

* * *

Minutes later, Drake sat alone at the small wall-mounted desk outside Jon's room with the phone to his ear. The nurses had the central lights turned low, and voices were subdued. The line rang again and again. He still hadn't told Rachelle about Jon. It clicked to message.

He checked the clock: Eleven twenty-five p.m. He'd hesitated to call so late but felt he had to try. She must be asleep. Hopefully without having had to take one of her pills. The non-answer made him suspect otherwise. The phone usually woke her. *Damn—I should be with her.*

The ICU secretary called to him from the nurse's station. "Dr. Cody, I have a transfer from ER. The person has called a few times but we didn't put it through because, well, y'know, you were kinda busy."

"Yeah, for sure. Thanks." He tried to smile. "I'll take it. What line?"

Drake punched the blinking line five. "Dr. Cody here." There was a pause, static, then a low buzz. "Hello, Dr. Cody here. Hello?"

He heard a click, more static, then a mechanical sounding voice.

"Dr. Cody, do not show alarm or behave—"

"What? What are you say—"

"Quiet!" snapped the voice. "Listen or your family dies."

His skin went cold. The words sounded unreal, a buzzing tone of varying pitch. Like one of those voice scramblers like in a movie when...*Lord, no.*

"Do what I say," the voice said, "and I'll let them live." Static and feedback squeals followed.

He got to his feet and turned his back to the nurses' station.

"What do you want? This is Dr. Drake Cody. I haven't done anything to you. This must be a mistake." Drake thought of the gangbanger from the ER and his threat, *You gonna pay.*

"I don't make mistakes. We've got your family—Momma and your two runts. Listen to this." There was a buzz, then a click.

"Daddy, I'm so scared." It was the terror-filled voice of his Kristin. "She hurt us and—" The buzz returned.

Drake's chest caved in. He grabbed at a chair and collapsed into it. He fought for air.

"Still think I made a mistake?" A harsh laugh. "Do not contact the police. If you do, we will know and I will kill your family. "

Drake struggled to speak. "Why? Why are you doing this? I don't have any money. Do not hurt my family. I'm warning you—"

"I do the warning, boy," roared the electronic voice. "You have three hours to hand over research drug D-44. You will provide its molecular identity and the step-by-step blueprint for its synthesis. Three hours. Fail and they die." The phone buzzed and crackled.

His thoughts shrieked and crashed like cars in a highway pile-up. He felt lightheaded and realized he was breathing way too fast. *Slow down. Get it together.*

"I'll give you what you want. Just don't hurt them."

A part of his self stabilized amidst his shock. He clung to it. A faint drumming arose in his head. *Bastards!*

"I'll get it for you, but I can't get it within three hours. It's locked up. The information is at the bank in a safety deposit box."

The device buzzed. "Do not screw with me."

"I'm not. It's a blinded study. Even I don't know which one of the drugs I created is D-44. The identification key and synthesis information is locked away. That's protocol. It's technical but you have to believe me." He gripped the phone like a lifeline. "Did you hear me? I can't get the information until the bank opens tomorrow."

"Shit. Shit. Shit. Yes, I heard you." The device rumbled. "And don't talk to me like I'm a dumbass. I know more about drug research protocol than you ever will." A static-filled pause extended for some seconds.

"New plan. Be ready for a call on your home phone at seven a.m. No cops. No tricks. My phone is blocked and untraceable. We'll know if you contact police. Do exactly what I say and you will see your family again. Anything else and they die. We're watching you. Your party-boy partner knows I mean what I say."

A buzz, a click, and the connection ended.

Drake hung up the phone, feeling as if his insides had been ripped out. He kept his face hidden from the nurse's station.

Rachelle, Shane, Kristin—his everything. As he struggled to stand, the ICU secretary called out again. "Dr. Cody, you're popular. Another ER call. It's a Detective Somebody, line three."

Yamada. God, not now.

"Thanks." He faced Jon and the bank of monitors as he picked up the phone. "Dr. Cody here." His voice caught.

"Doc, this is Yamada. Is he gonna make it?"

"Jon is bad. Real bad."

"Damn. Doc, we need to talk. Can you come down?"

Drake bit his lip.

He checked the monitor screen. Jon's vital signs had improved. His temperature was being maintained without complication. Now it was a matter of time and the resilience of the millions of threatened brain cells.

Dr. Kelly would be in the hospital overnight. Drake trusted the surgeon—and Tracy. Jon was in expert hands.

"Doc, you hear me?" Yamada's voice came distant and small from the phone's speaker.

"I'll come down. Give me a couple of minutes." He hung up.

The ventilator cycled. Jon's chest rose and fell. Drake picked up his stethoscope. The happy expressions of Shane and Kristin, his life's magic, faced him from the photo on the instrument's tubing. He imagined the look on their faces now.

A silent scream filled his head.

Chapter 52

Hennepin-North Hospital, 11:41 p.m.

Meryl couldn't feel her nose. It had hurt like hell when little Mommy had connected with her cheap shot. Meryl had gushed blood all over the cheap-ass kitchen.

Once again, cocaine had come through—it was both a topical anesthetic and a vasoconstrictor. The bleeding had slowed and her face had gone numb. She removed the Kleenex she'd packed in her nose.

The bleeding had stopped. She tossed the Kleenex out the parked van's window into the hospital parking lot, but kept the dish towel handy.

She touched her swollen nose. An ER visit was an annoyance, but everything possible must be done to protect her incredible beauty. And even this development was more awesome drama.

Meryl had shown Miss Sweet Tits who the stud was. It had been smoking hot fun with her alone in the van—until it got weird.

Hot little Mommy had bucked hard as Meryl stripped off the blouse and bra, unveiling those perfect breasts. Faith had told Meryl that Dr. Drake Cody's wife was yummy. Faith had said she'd sensed the uptight little momma might enjoy a walk on the wild side.

The scar looked wicked, but somehow it seemed to accentuate what was otherwise perfection. Meryl had stroked herself to a double supernova as she tongued the all-world nipples. The doctor's wife hadn't fooled her—no doubt the babe had been digging it. Pink tissue doesn't lie. But then the fun ended. The little momma had flipped out.

For a moment Meryl thought the scarred beauty might die. She started huffing like a train and spasmed up like burnt bacon. Meryl cut the neck restraint because Momma's breathing got freaky. Those big brown eyes bulged, and then rolled back. The chick went somewhere else.

Meryl had put Momma's clothes back together, cut her free of the chair, and hauled her onto the boat. By the time Meryl dumped her on the galley floor, the wench was breathing better.

Whatever. She'd survived. It was clear Basket-case Momma wouldn't give her any more trouble.

Meryl found the irony of a visit to the emergency room amusing. Two minutes earlier she'd ended her call to *Dr. Daddy*. She'd made him listen to the "proof-of-life" recording. She chose the little girl because her pleading sounded so damn pathetic. It was such a blast putting doctors in their place. These supposedly "best and brightest" were village idiots compared to her.

She put the scrambler and phone in the glove box and climbed out of the van. She crossed the parking lot and entered the ER waiting room. Judging from the crowd, she'd have a long wait.

Meryl felt a rush as a scheme jumped from among the thoughts streaking through her mind. She raised the blood-soaked towel to her nose and rushed up to the triage desk.

"I need help. Oh please. I was in a car accident and my nose got smashed. I can't stop the bleeding. My blood doctor says I should always go to the ER if I'm bleeding."

The graying triage nurse straightened in her chair, craning her head forward and looking over the tops of half-frame glasses. "Blood doctor? Why do you have a blood doctor? Do you have any other injuries? Can you breathe okay?"

"Oh, no. I'm not hurt. Except my nose. I have hemophilia so…" before Meryl could continue the nurse got to her feet, grabbed a wheelchair and came around the counter with it.

"What was the accident like? Did your airbag inflate?" The nurse seated Meryl in the wheelchair and affixed a blood pressure cuff.

"Really it wasn't much, but my head kind of whipped forward and I think I hit the steering wheel." Meryl felt a surging sense of pleasure. "I still feel blood running down my throat." This was so much better than any school play.

After a few more questions, the nurse wheeled her towards the inner ER doors, past the crush of sick and injured. The security guard slapped the button opening the doors in time for them to swoop through. Meryl controlled the laugh that wanted to escape. She felt like a Hollywood celebrity being rushed past the long line and velvet ropes of a popular night club.

And why not? She was a star. Her grin stretched wide behind the rag she held to her face. As she rolled past the secretary's station she saw him.

Her online research had included a newspaper photo from a helicopter rescue of a pregnant patient. The sturdy build, thick hair, and piercing eyes were unmistakable. He looked fatigued in blue scrubs as he approached an Asian guy in a rumpled suit holding a phone to his ear.

The nurse slowed at the entry to a cubicle a short way down the corridor. The level of noise and bustle in the ER surprised Meryl.

"Nurse, I think I know those guys," Meryl said nodding towards the two men.

"Maybe so, honey. The solid-looking guy in the scrubs is our Dr. Cody. The other guy's detective something-or-other. One of our earlier patients was a crime victim. You still breathing okay? This band needs to stay on your arm." She wheeled her into the cubicle. "Please take your top off and get into this gown. I'll have another nurse in here straightaway."

Meryl changed into the gown and then stood by the cubicle entry, peering out at the doctor and detective. The doctor looked uneasy, but too little time had passed for the police to have traveled here since her call. Their meeting must be about another matter, as the nurse had suggested.

Meryl noted the thick forearms and worker-strong build of Doctor Cody. She knew the type. Put him in a gym and he'd lift as much as puffed-up hulks. His conversation ended. It did not look like the exchange that would have occurred if he'd talked.

A tall, athletic-appearing nurse came in.

"Please have a seat. Are you breathing okay?"

The long-legged brunette's questioning quickly cut through Meryl's scam.

"I think that other nurse misunderstood," Meryl said.

The nurse's eyes showed she had Meryl figured. "If you had hemophilia, your injury could be life-threatening. As a healthy person, I suspect you simply have a broken nose."

Meryl bristled. "'Simply a broken nose'? Look at my face, bitch! Would a hammer to the nose of the Madonna be *simply a broken nose?*"

The nurse's eyebrows went up. "Sorry. I'm going to give you an ice pack and take you back to the waiting room. We have to care for the sickest patients first."

Meryl stood and leaned forward. "Get a doctor in here now. I'm not one of your ordinary losers."

The nurse made no reaction.

"How long a wait?"

"It could easily be an hour."

"Not acceptable."

"I can only apologize—" started the nurse sounding unrepentant.

"Cut the bullshit, skank. What's the doctor gonna do when they finally see me?" Meryl glared.

The tall nurse looked at her, giving a long sigh. "Given that there is no ongoing bleeding and the alignment looks good, my guess is that the doctor will advise ice and medication for pain. It'll look worse before it looks better, but it should heal."

"Ice? That's it? For that I should waste my valuable time? I'm walking out."

"That's your choice. I do need to inquire whether you are a victim of domestic violence. Are you involved in a violent relationship?"

"Kiss my ass."

Meryl sensed the nurse was suppressing a smile. Meryl ripped off the gown revealing her naked breasts, thickly muscled torso and arms. She raised a finger and locked onto the nurse's eyes. "I'd like to run into you some other time, Nursey Hot-Shit. I'd enjoy ramming home a little discipline."

The nurse did not blink. "Any more crap and I'll have security toss you out on your ass. Have a nice day. I hope you can recommend us to your friends." She turned and hung her head out the cubicle calling down the busy corridor. "Cubicle twenty-nine is free. Please let triage know." She turned and began to strip the bedding.

Meryl pulled on her top. She'd received the medical opinion she needed.

Her anger had become something else. Her nipples throbbed. Her breath came short. The ballsy nurse turned her on.

God, she loved a hard-ass wench.

Chapter 53

ER, 11:47 p.m.

Drake found Aki standing near the secretary's station with his phone to his ear. He had his left hand shielding his other ear from the ER din.

The detective's collar hung open and his tie had disappeared. His suit was wrinkled and his face drawn. He raised a finger, making a combined greeting and stand-by gesture.

Drake wanted to tell the detective. Not telling is what the kidnap victim's family does in every schlocky TV movie. And it's always the wrong move. But no. Drake couldn't risk it—at least not yet.

Why did the kidnapper reference his 'party-boy partner'? It had to be Rizz. What could Rizz know?

Kristin had said "She hurt us." The mechanized voice belonged to a woman—a nasty and easily agitated woman. The woman had said "we"—"We will know…" She bragged about her drug knowledge. Had they killed Faith? Was his family in the hands of murderers? *Please, no.*

Drake scanned the ER, looking for anyone who stood out. He saw a typical middle-of the-night crowd—lots of drunks, druggies, and/or mentally ill joining the regular citizens who'd become acutely ill or injured. Late night in a major metropolitan ER brought together people who never came near one another elsewhere. Tonight they all looked suspicious.

Yamada pocketed his phone and turned. "Did Doc Malar say anything when they brought him in?"

"He was out and may not ever wake up. He's on a ventilator."

"Jeez, Doc. Rough." Aki rubbed his chin. "I gotta tell ya. At the time he got shot, he had a cell waiting. The DA had moved to indict."

"Damn it, Aki." Drake clenched his fists. "The DA can go to hell. Jon Malar did not kill Faith. Find who did, and find who shot him. Those are the bad guys. Not Jon."

The detective leaned back, eyeing him. “The DA and the department brass think your friend killed his wife. There are things I can’t share, but I’ll tell you this—he had plenty of motive. He looks good for it, but I admit my gut isn’t one hundred percent sold.”

“Listen to your gut, Aki. And find the bastard who shot him.”

“That’s why I’m here. What you can tell me? Physical evidence? Known enemies?”

“Shot twice in the chest at close range. He went down hard.” Drake scanned the department. “Enemies? No way. Everyone loves Jon. If you don’t, there’s something wrong with you. Have you got any idea who shot him?”

“It may be gang-related. You know that area. The Doc’s wallet and cell phone were taken. We have the phone company triangulating his phone and it’s still in that neighborhood. That’s our best lead. We’re chasing every way we can, but down there we get stonewalled. People are afraid. Nobody heard nothing, nobody saw nothing, and nobody knows nothing.”

Drake straightened. “You’re tracking his phone?”

“Yeah. If you have the cell number and the phone has power, they can track it. How tight depends on the area. In that neighborhood, maybe a couple hundred yards. Down there, that includes hundreds of apartments full of uncooperative folks—including a number of felons and repeat offenders.”

“Who does the tracking?”

“Either the phone company or 911 dispatch. Believe me, Doc, we’re doing everything we can.”

The menace of the kidnapper’s call echoed in Drake’s head. His palms were sweaty. “I need to get home.”

“You don’t look good. Are you getting sick on me?”

“You still have that same number?”

“With me all the time.” Aki patted his pocket. “Hey, one more thing. I mentioned BioZyn to you before and you knew nothing. How about the name Meryl Kampf? Or maybe Dr. Kampf—she’s a PhD. She works for them and we know she was seen with Faith. Ring any bells?”

Drake shook his head. “No. I don’t know the company or the name. It could be that Faith was checking things out for the future. If it was anything more, I would have to know.”

“Okay. Go get some rest.” The detective turned and started walking away.

A baby’s cry pierced the ER din. Drake’s mind flashed to Rachelle and the children—imagining their terror.

"Aki," Drake called out before he could stop himself.

Yamada turned. "Yeah, Doc. Something else?"

Drake stammered. "Ah, nothing." He rubbed his ear, avoiding Aki's eyes. His gut churned like molten lava.

The baby cried out once more.

Chapter 54

Her face pressed against coarse wood that smelled of grease. Rachelle recalled fragments—an impression of being carried, and moments ago the impact of being dumped on the floor. The image of the rat came to mind and she jerked her face upward. The stifling gag and her rear-bound hands heightened her helplessness.

The clanking and vibration of a heavy chain dragging across metal came from the opposite side of a set of swinging doors to her right. The sound of footsteps moving away.

A whimper caused her to turn. The kids were on their knees, cowering against one another, bound as she was. She struggled to her knees and crawled to them. They pressed their bodies to her and she rested her forehead on theirs. Fear radiated from them like heat off a bed of coals. Tears ran down her cheeks. *My poor babies.*

She'd broken a second survival commandment. Panic had overcome her in the face of the woman's depraved assault.

She saw her burden in her children's trembling lips and wide eyes. Mothers make things right. The care and protection of her children is any mother's greatest responsibility. Rachelle swallowed hard.

Her assault and resulting panic left her feeling too feeble to stand. Her life history had convinced her she was weak and cowardly. *I must not fail them!*

After her discharge from the burn unit, she'd survived a decade of institutional and foster care. Anxiety and panic attacks had crippled her. Counseling and hospitalization provided no relief. The doctors were quick to write prescriptions. Some of the medications seemed to help but most just made her numb.

She'd attempted suicide at age fourteen.

The psychiatrists diagnosed depression, anxiety with panic attacks, and post-traumatic stress disorder. The diagnoses provided labels, but no relief.

A deep horn blast of a river barge sounded. Her wrists, secured behind her back, were raw and her hands numb. She leaned a shoulder against the wall and used her legs to drive herself upright. The exertion left her gasping.

At age seventeen, she'd been staying in a homeless shelter. She'd fallen into a pattern of alcohol and drug use that scared her. A staff person told her about a job. The pay was bad, but room and board were included.

She'd never held a job, but she summoned the nerve to apply.

They hired her. Her assignment—to work as a personal care attendant for Drew, a severely handicapped man with mental retardation, a bad heart, and seizures. Training was piecemeal. The responsibility terrified her. She almost quit several times in the first days. But with each day she held on, she came to know and care more about Drew. That made all the difference.

She learned to administer powerful medicines, manage his seizures, and look out for him. Drew became much more than a job. Her relationship with him likely saved her life. Taking care of someone else made her feel different about herself. By the time she met Drake, she'd come a long way.

Now her children needed her like never before. Her stomach was a knot. It was all up to her and she'd panicked.

Shane and Kristin looked up at her. Their desperate dependence evident.

She feared she would fail her children—as her mother had.

* * *

20 years earlier, rural northern Kentucky

Grease showed under his fingernails. His teeth looked as if they'd been carved from rotting wood, and he smelled of cigarettes and body odor. Since big Joe showed up, Momma only laughed when she drank or they smoked the stinky pipe. Even then, Rachelle could see her peek at the huge man to see if it was okay. Even Momma was afraid.

Rachelle hated him.

Why did Momma let him live in their house and do what he did?

One day Joe couldn't find the TV remote. "Damn it!" His curse made them jump like the crack of a whip.

They all scrambled to find the remote while Joe steamed. No one wanted Joe mad. Rachelle was scared-sick but then she found it. It was in her little brother's baseball glove sitting right there on the couch.

Billy had just turned six years old and was her best friend. He didn't talk much anymore and had started to wet the bed.

"Here it is, Joe. It was sitting right here all the time." She was so relieved she laughed.

Joe ripped it from her hand snarling like a mean dog. "Funny, huh?" He looked at the glove, then down at her brother.

In an instant, Billy was flying through the air like a rag doll.

Billy smashed into the wall and screamed a bad hurt right away.

Joe tore after Billy, then stood above him all crazy-purple and yelling. He kicked Billy over and over.

Rachelle could not breathe.

Momma just stood.

Rachelle unfroze and ran at Joe.

He slapped her down.

They left her and took Billy to the far-away hospital in Oswalt. That wasn't smart. Rachelle knew there were two hospitals much closer.

She waited, scared and crying the hours they were away.

Finally, way past dark, they came back. Billy had a big cast on his arm and his face was all swelled and cut—it hurt for him to move.

Hours later, in the shadowy moonlight coming through the bare and dirty windows of their bedroom, Billy whispered, "Rae-rae." He'd known she was awake.

Rachelle slipped out of her bed and cuddled next to her brother's skinny, quaking body. His sheets smelled of dried urine.

"Joe told them I fell down the stairs." Soft, moist sobs sounded. "He said," his voice hiccupped, "he said unless I said it was true he was gonna hurt me real bad."

She laid a hand on his heaving chest. "Momma and I'll protect you, Billy."

"No." He moaned and a tear glinted in the moon's glow. "She won't." He turned to her, his eyes huge. "Momma told them I fell, too."

Chapter 55

Minneapolis, 12:59 a.m.

Drake crossed over the Mississippi, his tires drumming on the deck of the Hennepin Avenue Bridge. Thick fog swallowed his headlights and obscured everything beyond their limited arc.

His thoughts surged like people escaping a burning theater. The temptation to call the police pulled hard. The responsibility for his family's safety would no longer be his. But if the kidnappers found out… His throat knotted.

He pulled into the townhouse parking lot. The shades of their unit were down, but a light was on. Could it all be a cruel hoax?

The fear he'd heard in Kristin's voice made him believe otherwise.

He held his breath as he opened the front door. A kitchen chair lay overturned. The table was jammed against the wall. He sprinted up the stairs.

His returning steps were heavy.

They were gone.

Rachelle's easel lay on its side with newspapers spread beneath it. He smelled paint and mineral spirits. His ears buzzed and his chest grew tight.

Red splatters crossed the newspaper and the floor. He crouched and dabbed a finger.

It was not paint. *Oh, God, no.*

Blood marked the counter and saturated part of a crumpled kitchen towel. Pain gripped his chest and he slumped against the wall.

The wall phone rang a foot from his ear. His heart skipped.

He snatched the phone.

"Drake Cody here."

"You messed up." The rumbling electronic voice froze him. "You talked to the police. Guess which one of your family I killed?"

Drake dropped to his knees.

"Time's up. The winner is—envelope please—Shane Cody. You killed your boy, Doctor Hot Shit. I told you what would happen. I made it quick. He didn't suffer."

Something gave way inside of Drake. The phone struck the floor. "No, No, No," he moaned, his head hung. Nausea, weakness, and a razor slash of pain sliced to his core. He ended up on all fours, his chest and throat knotted, a scrap of bloody newspaper pinned under one palm.

Electronic tones warbled from the dangling phone. He seized it. "You will die!" He yelled so forcefully his vision flashed red.

A robotic-sounding chuckle came from the receiver. "Hey, I'm not done talking, lightweight."

Drake knelt, taking great rasping breaths. "I hear you, bitch."

"Your kid is alive. I didn't kill anyone—yet." She paused. "Just a lesson for you. I know you met with a detective but I also know you didn't blab. That's how plugged in we are. Do exactly what I say, when I say, or they die. No cops. Have a nice night." The connection ended.

Drake released the phone and collapsed onto his back, arms outstretched and chest heaving.

Chapter 56

Riverboat, night

Rachelle's muscles cramped and it took effort to remain standing. Weak and hurting but she had not quit. She put her doubts and the loathsome violation she'd suffered somewhere else.

Shane's and Kristin's helplessness and trust pulled at something deep within her.

She would do anything to protect her babies. *I am not like my mother.*

Rachelle blinked back tears. Find us, Drake!

Another directive of survival training—*if kidnapped, make every effort to escape.*

She looked about their prison. This had been the kitchen of the riverboat restaurant. The air hung heavy and smelled of grease. The room was about thirty feet by forty feet and low-ceilinged. The only windows were two portholes too small for even Kristin to fit through. The space had been stripped of everything that wasn't bolted down.

She took a few steps then slumped against the wall, fighting blackness. Her rear-bound arms made maintaining balance difficult.

A long stainless-steel prep table split the room's center, and ranges and ovens lined the outer walls. A sink was located against each wall, and across from her was the oversized door to a walk-in cooler. She saw only one exit—the large swinging doors. Rachelle had heard the rattle of chains from the other side as their kidnapper departed. She leaned against them and there was no yield. The floor was thick plank, and the walls solid.

A metal flange extended from one of the tables. She turned her back to it and sawed the zip-tie restraint against the flange. The exertion made her nauseous, and she realized that if she vomited with the gag in place, she could choke to death. As she sawed, searing pain and a warm honey-like stickiness coated her hands and wrists. Shane had awoken and stood next to her. She turned, showing him the restraint for a progress check.

He winced and shook his head, then leaned against her hip in an obvious effort to comfort her. Her heart swelled.

Kristin lay on her side, arms winched behind her back. She whimpered in her sleep.

The sparseness and metal tables reminded Rachelle of their family's visits to the animal rescue center. That site held animals until they could be released to a home. That is what Rachelle prayed for—the safety of their home.

The image of the vivid sunset descending into the lake flashed in her head. A coming storm…

Where are you, Drake? A bitter *Not around, like always* passed through her head. She regretted the thought. *Please God, help him find us.*

Their kidnapper had made no effort to hide or disguise anything. She bragged about her expertise in drugs and research. And flaunted her freakish body and appearance.

All of that would help the police when Rachelle and the kids told what they'd witnessed.

The realization snatched her breath like a plunge into icy water. She felt light-headed and as if the floor had shifted beneath her feet.

Not *when* they told the police but *if.* Their captor was not worried.

Rachelle's heart clutched. This wasn't just a prison—it was death row.

She's going to kill my babies. She's going to kill us all.

* * *

Rachelle startled awake, feeling lost. Reality snapped into place. She moaned. How could she have slept?

Exhaustion had overwhelmed her.

The kids lay sleeping alongside her. She sensed hours had passed. Earlier, they'd all had the humiliation of wetting themselves. Kristin had sobbed quietly. Shane had gone to the farthest corner of the room and returned with the telltale pattern of wetness.

Then Rachelle had moved to the corner and then returned with her jeans likewise branded. The kids held their heads down and looked away. She made a huff sound, corralling their eyes. She then looked at her own stain and gave a quick shake of her head and a shrug of her shoulders—no big deal.

Now Shane and Kristin lay awkwardly slumped with their cruel bindings in place.

Rachelle leaned against the walls and used her legs to drive herself upright. Her bound hands and arms were numb. She began another exploration of their prison. *Must escape.*

The galley had only two ceiling lights, with bulbs that cast a dim yellow light and created deep shadows. The tiny portholes showed inky black outside.

The boat had electricity as the lights proved. When she was in the van, Rachelle had seen a large tank mounted on the boat's middle deck. The galley had gas ranges.

Were the gas lines connected?

She moved to the nearest range and peered into the space between it and the wall. The range looked to be reasonably modern. She could see the gas line running to the back, as well as an electric cord. There was a gas shut-off lever valve on the wall behind the range, but out of reach. Was it on or off?

Rachelle moved to the front of the range, turned around, and got her hands to twist the knob. The clicking sound of an automatic igniter sounded, but she heard no hiss and did not smell gas. She left it on until she was convinced that no gas flowed. She went to each range, finding the same result.

Returning to the first range, she tried to reach the valve behind the range with her foot, but the space was too narrow.

Shane had awoken and followed her efforts. He stepped over and tried to reach the valve, but his leg was also too thick. Their eyes met and turned to the sleeping Kristin.

They woke her but she lay listless and droop-eyed. Through head shakes, muffled vocalizations and pantomime, Rachelle got her to rouse and understand the task. Kristin snaked her skinny leg into the space and shifted the lever with the sole of her tennis shoe. She brightened for the first time in hours as Shane and Rachelle gave gag-muffled cheers.

Would it light?

Turning and grasping the knob with slick fingers, Rachelle gave it a turn. She went past the ignite position with her clumsy and stricken hands.

But she smelled and heard gas flow.

She turned off the knob, let the gas clear, and attempted once again. The click-click-click of the igniter was followed by the *whump* of a flame's birth. Blue tongues of fire blazed from the burner. She tipped her head back and closed her eyes.

With head gestures and eyebrows, she herded the kids to the corner opposite the range and got them to sit on the floor.

Her beautiful children looked up at her—fear and puzzlement written on their faces.

Her heart pounded and she needed air. Memories of the pain that had forever marked her flared as if new.

She clenched her teeth and inhaled deeply.

With long strides she crossed the room. She stopped and turned her back and arms toward the burner's jetting blue-orange blaze. She swallowed. *Oh God, I can't.*

Mothers take care of their children. *She's going to kill my babies!*

Raising her rear-bound arms, she backed her butt against the front of the stove. Her trembling hands hovered over the flames.

Closing her eyes, she lowered her wrists.

She gasped, then gave a prolonged gag-muffled scream. The stink of burnt hair, the pops and crackles of incinerating clotted blood, and pain rocketing beyond her imagination.

She held her children in her mind's eye as she sacrificed her flesh to the fire. Torture without limit. Her face twisted and pulled. The smell of charring flesh, her muscles quivering, then involuntarily bucking as she willed herself to endure. Colors flashed in her head, her wrists a blacksmith's forge.

She strained at the restraint with all she had. Her vision raced to black and her moan expired.

She pitched forward to the floor.

* * *

Rachelle opened her eyes to the blanched faces of Shane and Kristin. She'd blacked out and fallen. Her wrists and hands shrieked in searing agony. The chemical stink of burnt plastic found her nose.

She tried moving her hands. They were free! The zip-tie had melted through. She looked.

Her wrists were blackened, palms whitish and leathery appearing. Skin at the wound margins bubbled like melting cheese. The remnants of the plastic tie were fused to her skin. The pain had no limit.

She heard animal whimpers. The sounds were hers.

When she'd been burned so many years ago, her awareness had disappeared. Her mind had escaped to somewhere else. But she couldn't fade away now—her children needed her.

Kristin cried. Shane crawled closer, eyes darting.

She pulled out the cloth gag and opened her arms. "My babies."

The kids clambered to her. She wrapped them in a hug challenged by their restraints and her scorched flesh. As she squeezed them her energy and resolve surged as if their love pumped fuel into her exhausted tank—her beautiful, magical babies.

They must get out.

Chapter 57

Farley awoke, his face plastered to the desk in a slick of saliva. He grabbed a napkin and swabbed his face, then scanned the empty Homicide desks, grateful there was no one watching. The moment echoed high school humiliations where he regularly dozed off in the midst of classes.

"Passed out, huh?"

Farley flinched and turned to find Detective Yamada behind him at the office mini-kitchen, unloading a fast-food bag.

"I must have dropped off."

"Understandable. It's almost two a.m. But you haven't been out long. You messaged me just ten minutes ago. I went through the drive-through and grabbed some chow." Aki held up a bag. "Carbohydrates, grease and sodium. You want some?"

"Sure. Thanks." He'd yet to find any fast-food product on the planet that he didn't find irresistible.

Aki reached into the bag. "Have you learned anything more?"

"That's why I called. The ME just called."

"At this hour?"

"He was excited because he figured out how the killing drug got into the victim. The drug doesn't work if it's swallowed, so it had to be injected or otherwise introduced directly into the blood. Remember the vaginal lubricant he mentioned in his first report? He had his FBI lab guy test it for the..." he read off his sheet, "succinylcholine." Farley eyed the food as Yamada set it on his desk.

"The drug was there big-time. They also found some kind of…" he checked his notes, "cellulose matrix. He says it's the stuff used to make the capsules for time-release medications. He thinks the succinylcholine was in some kind of time-release capsule placed in her vagina. He talked a mile a minute and used lots of technical terms. I tried to write down the key points."

Farley raised a drool-smeared page. He squinted. “The pH of the vagina would break down the capsule in somewhere between four and twenty hours. Then the succinylcholine would be directly absorbed into the bloodstream by what he called the ‘vascular mucosa of the vagina.’”

Farley looked up from the sheet. “He said it’s like rectal suppositories, or medicines that are given under the tongue. The capsule was inserted, after some time it broke down, and then the drug was absorbed straight into the blood, paralyzing her.” He looked back at his notes. “His exact words were, ‘Find who was getting down with this wench sometime in the twenty hours before she died, and you’ve found your killer.’”

Aki handed a fast-food bag to Farley.

“Damn, Farley—a bizarre drug, vaginal route, time-release matrix, mucosal absorption. This is not the work of a C student. It looks bad for Doc Malar.” He frowned. “He had the drug, the knowledge and, presumably, vaginal access.”

“Maybe.” Farley spoke around a mouthful of burger. “For sure it’s someone who knows something about medications. And someone who had intimate access to Faith Reinhorst-Malar. But from what I found at her office,” he shrugged, “the intimate part could be almost anyone.” He took another bite and spoke as he chewed. “Earlier, I found something that surprised me, but I don’t know if it means anything.” He fed in a fistful of fries.

“Jeez, partner, slow down on the chow and tell me,” Aki said.

Farley’s felt himself blush. “Sorry.” He chewed and swallowed. “Remember the security guard who helped us out by identifying Meryl Kampf from her picture? I text-imaged him a couple of others.”

Farley picked up his papers and rearranged them. “He recognized one as a visitor.” He slid the top sheet onto Aki’s desk.

Aki’s eyes widened as he stared at the enlarged hospital photo ID of Dr. Michael Rizzini.

Chapter 58

Night

Rachelle's hands and wrists shrieked as she teased the cloth gags past the zip-tie bridles girding the children's mouths. She hid the pain.

"Momma, I'm so scared." Kristin began to cry. Rachelle hugged her tight.

Shane laid his head on her shoulder. His lip trembled. "The bad lady will come back. We need Dad."

"Yes, she will come back. But we're going to get away from her. To do that, we have to be brave."

Kristin looked down, sniffling. "I-I'll try, Mommy."

"Good girl. We don't give up." Rachelle stroked Kristin's hair.

Shane stood hunched with his arms restrained behind him. His jeans had not dried. "I'll be brave, Mom."

"I'm proud of you. Proud of you both." She struggled to her feet. "I can't get your hands free. The ties are too strong." She looked to the sink. "I need to see if these faucets work."

"Oh yes. Please, Mommy," Kristin said. "I'm so thirsty."

The faucets worked. Rachelle ran cold water over her burns. She then used her hands to form a cup, allowing each child to drink. Their up-close exposure to her wounds caused them to cringe. After they drank their fill, Rachelle bit and tore the fabric that had been her gag. She fashioned bandages around the most damaged parts of her wrists and hands.

She moved to wash her bloodied face but caught herself as she considered the impact of a change in her appearance.

Rachelle climbed on top of the range, still warm after delivering its brutal benefit. She looked out the sealed landside porthole to the dark parking lot and the concrete apron below. No van. She guessed it was at least an hour until dawn.

She climbed down. “Kristin, you’re going to be our first lookout.” She lifted Kristin so that she stood on top of the range. Her head just reached the level of the porthole. “Keep checking the window. If you see any cars or people you let me know. Can you do that, sweetheart?”

Kristin nodded.

Rachelle’s energy wilted as the pain of her burns rebounded.

She went to the door to what looked to be a walk-in cooler. Earlier, with her hands bound, she’d been unable to open it.

She pulled the metal handle and wrestled the door open.

The cooler was about ten feet by twelve feet, the walls lined with wire shelves. A bare, yellowed bulb illuminated from the back wall. The space did not feel cool and had a musty, overripe odor. Thick plastic sheets lined the empty shelves.

Sitting against the back wall stood a white, six feet long, four feet tall, and three feet deep horizontal-opening freezer. Opening it, she found it icy cold but empty except for an inches-thick layer of frost. She closed the door.

There was nothing usable as a tool or a weapon. She saw no escape.

The pain of her wrists flared, and she moved to the sink for the cool water. As the water ran, she recalled seeing a video of an ice crystal forming in thirty-two-degree water. The first crystal triggered a chain reaction that instantly changed all the water to ice.

It was as if their world had transformed just as completely—everything had gone to hell. She barely had the strength to remain upright. Choking back a sob, she slumped against the sink.

I can’t do this.

Chapter 59

5:45 a.m.

Drake hung up the phone. The first hint of daybreak tinged the kitchen window.

As an Emergency Medical Services radio control physician at a regional level I trauma center, Drake stood fairly high up the ladder of the 911 and EMS operational chain. Even so, he could tell the 911 operator's responsiveness had more to do with her commitment to helping others than his position in the hierarchy. The lie he told took advantage of her dedication.

She'd guaranteed her best effort.

Drake set the notepad with her personal extension on the kitchen counter next to a scattering of M&Ms and a blood-soiled dish towel.

Would the technology work? He had little else.

Drake's mind riffled through cascades of complex analyses—similar to the way he diagnosed and treated critical patients presenting to the ER. This ticking-clock, do-or-die problem-solving ability was his greatest gift.

He went to the sink and splashed water on his face. Who or what might help him? The nightmare call he'd received after talking to Yamada proved police contact to be too great a risk.

Rizz wasn't scheduled in the ER for another eighteen hours. Drake's texts and calls had gone unanswered. Could Rizz be crashed out somewhere after partying all night? Though he'd seemed miserable about his betrayal of Jon, a night of excess was possible. Drake shook his head. Possible? Hell, it was damn near certain.

Drake was alone, and if the 911 technology failed, he had nothing.

He'd either have to hand over D-44 and trust the kidnappers to release his family unharmed or call in the police and hope for a miracle rescue. A rescue so fast and clean the kidnappers could not deliver on their promise to kill and disappear.

Both choices left him hollow. The fact that his actions would determine if his family lived or died held more threat than a gun to his head.

The wall beside the kitchen held photos. Drake's favorite of Shane and Kristin at the zoo hung in the center. The image that always provoked a smile now caused his chest to draw tight.

Two older photos were positioned on either side of the kids—one a close-up of Drake's brother, Kevin, smiling. The other was their mother standing in front of the tiny Cincinnati home where they'd lived. He couldn't look at the pictures without being seized by a deep and familiar pain.

He pushed the thoughts away.

Drake turned toward the kitchen table and turned over the canvas lying there. The paint at one edge had smeared. The flaming sunset grabbed him. He could feel the menace of the gathering storm. Rachelle had been painting when Drake last spoke with her. It seemed an eternity ago.

He had feared what impact the news of Faith's murder and Jon's struggle for life would have on Rachelle. What must she be battling now?

Fatigue and tension burned in his neck and shoulders. He had a little over an hour before the kidnapper's scheduled seven a.m. contact. Hundreds of nights on call had taught him that even minutes of sleep made a difference. He set the cell phone alarm and lay down on the couch, hoping exhaustion would shut down his mind and allow him rest.

Please God, don't take them from me.

Chapter 60

5:55 a.m.

As Drake closed his eyes and tried to sleep, guilt carved open his mind to the memories that always lay in wait.

He and Kevin had been closer than best friends, more than brothers. When Drake lifted or carried his brother's unruly body, Kevin would tickle or pinch him and laugh. Where others saw a handicapped person, Drake knew only a fearless and funny smart-ass. And he loved him.

The legal system had imprisoned Drake for the injuries he'd dealt the skinheads. They had abused Kevin—that caused the rest to happen. It was unfortunate they'd been injured so severely, but Drake had come to terms with that.

It was the consequences of a less dramatic act that caused him to lie awake nights, sick at heart. His remorse was a blade that never dulled.

It was one day—really just one thoughtless instant.

He never had the chance to make it right—to be forgiven.

His mother's plight was a continuous reminder. Her selfless acceptance made it worse.

* * *

Anna Cartabiano was new to the school and, unlike the other eleventh-grade girls, knew nothing of Drake's past. She did not know of the fight, his conviction, or his time locked up. It was her first day and she shared his study hall.

Anna had silken black hair and doe eyes that flashed when she laughed. Her flawless skin, fair and glowing, looked like the unbroken surface of rich cream. Her lips were rose-colored and full, one cheek dimpling with her frequent smiles. Her body was such that he had no words. He was breathless in her presence.

She had smiled and asked if he'd mind if she sat with him. He could initially only gesture, speech beyond him. Then they did speak. And she laughed and her eyes flashed.

He felt as if he must be watching someone else's life.

She'd asked about his classes. Were the teachers nice? Did he like music? She came from Indianapolis. Had he been there?

Then her face clouded. Sadness shadowed her face as her gaze shifted over Drake's shoulder. Partially turning, he glimpsed Kevin, whose face contorted with the effort of his labored, crutch-flapping struggle across the study hall.

Her wondrous features pained, Anna whispered, "I feel so bad for someone like that. Crippled and retarded. It's just not fair. I can't stand to look at them. It's just too sad."

At that instant Drake's sideward glance skimmed his brother's. Kevin brightened and made what only Drake could have recognized as a purposeful nod among his mutinous movements. Drake turned away, his back to Kevin and facing Anna, pretending he had not seen his brother.

In the after-image, Drake caught the flash of Kevin's perception and pain. Kevin had read it all in an instant.

Drake heard the slap, tink, slide and grunting utterances of Kevin's challenged trajectory. Veering away—keeping clear. Kevin had registered the message in his big brother's actions.

Drake, for the first time ever, had rejected his brother.

Drake did not speak with Kevin after the study hall. He did not ride home with Kevin and their mother that day. He met with Anna instead.

He sensed he'd hurt the person he loved most, but Anna's dizzying appeal overwhelmed his inner voice.

Their modified Dodge Caravan, the vehicle that Kevin called the "palsy mobile," was broadsided on the highway by a Coca-Cola truck two minutes from the school.

The Dodge had run a light, darting onto the highway. The truck driver did not have time to even touch the brakes. The mini-van had been almost ripped in two.

Kevin was pronounced dead at the scene, their mother transported by ambulance in critical condition.

A day later, she regained consciousness in the University of Cincinnati Medical Center's ICU. With consciousness came recall. She'd been distracted behind the wheel. Kevin had been unusually quiet when she picked him up. Minutes later he had started to weep. He never cried. In her distress she'd turned to ask what was wrong.

The answer never came.

Their mother's soundless tears had started before she received the other news. Her spine had snapped at chest level and the lower half of her body would never move or feel again.

She'd nodded and given a slight shrug. It seemed she accepted it as penance deserved.

Drake's brother and their mother—one dead, the other paralyzed.

Only Drake knew who was responsible.

* * *

Drake awoke on the townhouse couch, sweat-soaked and gasping. The wall phone rang a second time. He checked the clock: six forty-five a.m. He rushed to answer.

"Drake Cody here."

"Today you will make me rich," the electronically altered voice commanded. "First Minneapolis Guaranty opens at nine thirty. You will collect D-44's molecular identity and synthesis pathway and then be available with a car awaiting my call. I'll contact you with instructions. What's the number of your cell phone?"

Drake gave the number. "You need to prove to me that Rachelle and the kids are okay."

The voice surged. "I don't *need* to do anything for you, Daddy-boy. You do what I say or they die."

"Please. I'm doing everything you ask me. I'll do whatever you want. Don't hurt them." His voice was pleading but his mind was clear and his hands steady.

"Jesus. Don't cry."

Drake's grip on the phone tightened. He continued in a plaintive tone. "Just tell me what you want me to do. And you need to give me your number so I can reach you if I run into a problem." He held his breath.

"This number is blocked and I sure as hell will not give it to you. I know about signal tracking. Just make damn sure you don't have any problems." The electronics squealed. "I'll call at ten o'clock. Be ready to make me rich."

"You can have the drug. I just want them safe. Please." He kept his words begging as he imagined his hand clenched about her throat. "I'll do anything. Just don't hurt my family." He leaned his forehead against the wall. "I need to know my family is okay. Put them on during your next call. Please. I don't care about the drug, but I can't give it to you unless I know Rachelle, Shane and Kristin are okay. Please."

"Damn, you are a sniveling thing." A pause. "I'll put them on when I call. Ten o'clock. Be ready. Any bullshit and they die. " The connection ended.

Drake toggled the receiver and dialed the direct number the 911 dispatch operator had provided. *Could she help?*

She answered on the second ring.

The conversation lasted less than thirty seconds. Drake hung up the phone.

He bowed his head and clenched his fists. In the mix of exhaustion and dread he sensed something foreign.

He felt the tiniest flicker of hope.

Chapter 61

6:53 a.m.

The Consultant parked the rental van in the hospital lot nearest the main door. Workers streamed towards the entrance in the early morning light. He removed the four-wheel work cart from the back of the van and then began to fill it with equipment. He loaded both the tools for his real task and the props needed to complete his guise. His true tools included a Glock nine millimeter, to which he'd added a silencer, and his favorite, a needle-sharp five-inch ice pick.

Placed in the ear canal and plunged to its hub, the pick speared the brain's core, producing a clean and quiet death. The technique left a corpse without immediate or obvious evidence of injury. By the time the cause of death was discovered, the Consultant would be long gone.

He'd contacted Reinhorst and upped the fee by fifty percent. The corporate tyrant had squawked but had no choice.

A mouse of doubt scurried through the Consultant's mind. Why take such a risk now?

More money was always a good thing, but that wasn't all. It was the thrill. This would be his career finale, and what could be better than ending with a mega-stakes wager? He'd placed his bet—he was all in.

His scouting and staging visit to the hospital hours earlier had increased his confidence. Hospital security was looser than he had anticipated.

In this, the kill run, he was a technician with "Capricorn Diagnostics." On his cart was a volt/amp/resistance meter, electrical wire, and micro-components. The fictitious Capricorn supposedly had a new contract to service and quality-check patient monitors.

He wore an unmarked black ball cap, dark trousers, a crisp white shirt, and thick-soled, black shoes. He slid his Capricorn logo name tag into position. A plastic photo ID card with a magnetic strip hung clipped to his pocket protector.

A clipboard loaded with work-order slips sat atop the cart. The sheets listed the surgical ICU and several other wards with today's date and signature sites. A cliché but true – a clipboard conferred instant legitimacy.

Capricorn Diagnostics had come into existence late last night, after Reinhorst's panicked call. The logo-emblazoned pocket protector, the fake ID card, and the authentic-appearing work orders had been fabricated in the hours since.

After donning a pair of clear-lens glasses with thick black frames, he pulled his cap low. He affected a slouched posture as he pushed the cart across the lot. The Consultant rolled through the main entry to the hospital in the stream of day-shift workers. The tall, black female security guard caught his eye. He gave her a friendly nod. She reciprocated.

He took a service elevator to the sixth floor, then made his way to the hallway just outside the surgical ICU's card-controlled access doors. The passing workers and hospital visitors ignored him while he made notations on his clipboard.

The automated ICU doors swung open as a lab tech exited.

The Consultant rolled into the kill zone.

* * *

The ICU nurse stared at him, shaking her head. "You've got to be kidding. Right after shift change?"

"I'm sorry. I know you're nutso busy, but I'm good at getting in and out quick. At Capricorn, we say 'we monitor the monitors.' Heh, heh. Get it?"

"Uh, yeah. Got it." The veteran nurse rolled her eyes. "All right, but you do not enter a room until the nurse gives you the okay. Touch nothing. Understood?"

"You got it. By the way, we wear gloves like you guys," he held up his hands limply showing her the light brown latex, "and we don't touch nothing but the monitors. If I find a problem, it's mostly modular components so—"

She cut him off. "Yeah, whatever. Just don't bother any patients or nurses.

"I won't be any trouble. I do need you to sign here." He held out the clipboard and made an 'x' in front of the signature site.

"I don't authorize repairs. I'm a nurse. I take care of patients, not machines."

"Oh, not a problem. This here is just a check-off. Your signature just shows I was here. Believe me, you can't get in any trouble from this." He tilted his head back, smiling through the thick, black-framed glasses.

"Well, okay," she said as she signed. "You might as well start in bay eighteen. After that, just move down the line, but make sure you check with the nurse every time. Get me if you have an issue. I'll be charting right here." She indicated with a sweep of her hand the central station where thick patient charts sat in front of computer consoles. "The patient and nurse names are on the board there." She pointed. The name Malar was written in the space listed for bay four, with Tracy listed as nurse.

"I'll be quick and quiet. I'm very good at what I do." He let his chubby cheeks form a smile and pushed the drooping glasses back up the bridge of his nose.

* * *

He'd worked his way from patient bay eighteen to bay five. Things were all systems go, with zero suspicion. His target was in the next bay. He wet his lips, sensing a tingling in his neck and shoulders.

He reined in his excitement and reviewed his exit plan. Every job required a solid escape route and contingency plans. As the against-all-odds doctor lying in the next bay proved, one never knew what might happen. It all contributed to the incredible thrill.

Everything was green light and it was going to happen. *Hooyah!*

Cut-throat business deals were interesting, but they were a far cry from actually cutting throats.

Dealing death was the ultimate rush.

Chapter 62

Bluestone Restaurant, Eden Prairie, 8:17 a.m.

Meryl had ignored Heinrich's emails and phone calls for the past twenty-four hours. She undid her seatbelt. Why bother trying to enlighten such a limited loser? Her mind was a Ferrari, his a go-kart.

She scanned the restaurant parking lot for gawkers. None. She laid out cocaine on her compact's mirror and used her fingers to push it into two sloppy lines, then bent and snorted. She closed her eyes tight and leaned her head back. Anabolic steroids and cocaine—the breakfast of champions. She smiled.

D-44's molecular identity and synthesis info would be hers within hours. How would the-sky-is-falling Heinrich react to that?

Likely the delivery of the drug with multi-billion-dollar potential wouldn't be enough to please him. He'd find something to whine about. What would it be like to deal with an intellectual equal? She'd come to believe none existed.

This morning she'd sent Heinrich a text. "Meet me at Bluestone restaurant, on the patio, for breakfast at eight-thirty. My treat." She did have a treat for the loser. As usual, she'd done it all.

It was she who had found, developed, and executed everything of consequence to make this super-score happen. While he pissed and moaned, she took care of business.

Meryl had enjoyed the a.m. call to the hot mommy's husband. Dr. Daddy had almost begun to cry. His ass-kissing submissiveness proved him to be gutless. She'd expected more from him and found it disappointing— just another loser. *Is there anyone on my level?*

She checked herself in the powder-dusted hand mirror. Her application of makeup had done an amazing job of hiding the purplish discoloration centered about her nose and encircling her eyes. A skillful and subtle job—the way she did everything.

Meryl climbed out of the van and walked through the lot to the carpeted entry to the upscale Bluestone, Her first rendezvous with Faith had been for the brunch here. God, that day had been fantasy-like fun. Meryl felt a special tingle just walking in the place.

Her clothes screamed country-club chic—oversized Dior sun hat, a Prada leather bag, and a light, body-clinging sleeveless top with a flyaway mid-calf floral skirt and open-toed Gucci heels. She knew the outfit highlighted her body and accented her chiseled arms and buff legs. The look felt perfect for her triumphant meet with Heinrich. It would be hard not to gloat.

She'd reserved the same table on the patio, where she and Faith had celebrated the birth of their illicit venture—partners in business and pleasure. A pang of loss for what could have been washed over her, but just as quickly disappeared. *Either you hang with me or you lose.*

When she was shown to her table, she selected the corner seat, considering both her sight lines and her place in the composition of the scene. *Perfect.*

She smiled widely, overflowing with brilliance and anxious to lay it out for the full-of-himself Heinrich.

Chapter 63

Ignored.

Over the last twenty-four hours, Heinrich had sent Meryl texts, emails, and phone messages. No response.

Then this morning she sends a text message inviting him to breakfast as if they were chums on holiday.

The restaurant was part of an expensive-looking suburban shopping complex. As Heinrich turned into the parking lot, the two BioZyn associates sat in the back of the rental Escalade. They were attack dogs—two-legged Dobermans, physically imposing and hyper-alert. They did what Heinrich asked, but he sensed their menace.

They would wait in the vehicle while he met with Meryl. He didn't believe in God, but his hope for the successful acquisition of D-44 was as desperate as any prayer.

He stepped out of the car and into the parking lot. The sky was harshly bright, prodding his headache and causing him to squint. The aroma of cooking meat and baked goods grew as he approached the entry.

He informed the hostess he was meeting someone on the patio.

The outdoor space was surrounded by railings dense with flowers. About half of the twenty open-air tables were occupied. At the outermost corner stood a lone table on a slightly raised platform.

Positioned there sat Meryl. She looked dressed for a summer gala—Alice as she went through the looking glass. Her bare and rock-muscled arms looked like those of a shaved ape. She spotted him, stood, and performed an embarrassing curtsey. Patrons shot awkward glances.

He approached, taking deep breaths.

What happened to her face? She was severe-looking on a good day, but now? Her nose was deformed, with purplish discoloration visible under her eyes in spite of makeup that looked as if it had been applied with a trowel.

He pulled out a chair and sat facing her. The scent of her perfume struck him like a strong breeze.

"My God, Meryl. What happened to your nose?" He fanned a hand in front of his face. "Apparently, it affected your sense of smell. Did you put your perfume on with a bucket?"

Meryl's smile melted. Her eyes narrowed her lip curled.

Jesus! How to deal with a rabid she-wolf?

"I joke with you, Meryl. You look good. Nice outfit." He nodded towards her face. "A mishap?"

She put her elbows on the table and placed her hands together with fingers tented. Her eyes bore into Heinrich. "Yes. A mishap, little man." She exhaled audibly. "You're such a buzzkill. Even good news goes bad."

Heinrich sat forward. "Good news? You obtained the D-44 information? Do you have it with you?"

She leaned back, looking skyward, then huffed and shook her head. "I need a break. In the meantime lose your attitude, Hein-dick. Learn to respect those superior to you." She picked up her purse.

Heinrich swiveled his head, tracking her as she moved towards the restrooms.

A saucer of orange M&Ms and a small bowel of Mandarin orange segments sat on the table at her place. He rubbed his forehead as he considered how to handle this new, even more volatile, Meryl.

Heads turned and Heinrich looked up. Meryl swaggered back through the tables as if she were a body-builder posing.

Scheisse! What am I dealing with?

He'd have to humor the bizarre misfit. He had no choice.

She gave a sniff as she sat down.

"I'm sorry, Meryl. I was impolite. I felt angry with you for ignoring me these past twenty-four hours. If you obtained D-44, I can understand that you've been busy. How'd you get it?" He leaned forward with a forced smile on his face, his stomach roiling.

"It will be delivered later this morning." She held her head high. "Mission accomplished."

"Being delivered?" Heinrich's brow furrowed. "By whom? Can we pick it up? Let's get it right now."

"It's in a bank safe deposit box. This morning it will be surrendered to me at the place of my choosing." She radiated self-satisfaction.

He held his hands together as if praying. "Who is delivering it?"

She glanced over the railing. "The only thing I've eaten for the past few days is M&Ms and mandarin oranges. Did you know that glucose is the only energy source that the brain can directly metabolize? It's a fact. It makes sense that those of us with high-energy brains should provide it plenty of fuel."

M&Ms? He'd gone through the looking glass and found an Alice who made the Mad Hatter look sensible.

"Meryl, who is delivering the drug information?"

She looked at him as if he had just asked which way was up. "The doctor, of course. Who else? Dr. Drake Cody, his condescending, lightweight self. Can you believe he attempted to lecture me about research protocol?" She spooned a segment of the mandarin orange, eyed it, and delivered it to her mouth. "Fuel for the brain. Burn, baby, burn."

What? She was out of control. Was the NeurVitae drug information actually coming?

The waitress approached.

"Hein-dick, can I get you something? Perhaps some Mandarin oranges? I think your brain could use some glucose." She put a hand to her face too late to contain a snicker.

Heinrich waved the waitress off.

"Meryl, can you tell me why Dr. Cody is handing over the drug information?"

"Certainly. If you appreciated my abilities you wouldn't have to ask. The reason is—because I want him to."

He pictured his fist smashing into her face. "Okay, you want him to. Why does he want to?"

"He doesn't."

Heinrich grimaced. "You aren't making sense."

Meryl's smile dissolved. "Heinrich, you're so limited. It's almost impossible for someone of my intellect to explain things to someone like you."

Standing, she pushed her chair away from the table. She glanced around, appearing to take a second look at a recently seated trio of attractive and showily dressed young women.

She stepped clear of the table and off the low platform. "Pay the check, Heinie. I'll finish with you in the parking lot."

As he exited the restaurant, his eye caught motion. Meryl stood behind the open driver's door of a yellow van. He headed for her. The temperature had climbed and the whitewashed sky had grown brighter. Sweat ran down the middle of his back.

"Good work, Meryl." He forced a smile. "How did you persuade the doctor to give up his formula?"

She alternately covered each nostril with a finger, giving a quick sniff. "Got to keep the passages clear. Been an issue since that bitch—er, mishap." She scanned the sky, then glanced at her watch. "Oh, yeah. My *superior* asked me a question. Excuse my delay, Mr. Boss-man." She rolled her eyes. "The doctor is delivering the drug because I've got something of his he wants. I gave him no choice."

"I'm listening. What is it of his you have?" He again imagined his fist driving into her.

Meryl smiled and answered in a sing-song. "That's as easy as one-two-three—because I have his fa-mi-ly." She laughed.

Heinrich's stomach plunged. "You have his family?"

"Yes. One phone call and he'll fetch the molecular entity and synthesis information to me. If not, he loses his nut-job of a wife and two punks."

"No." His shoulders slumped. "Gott verdammt, no."

"I've got them stashed until whiney Dr. Daddy delivers the drug." She held her battered nose in the air as if she were royalty. "Now maybe you can quit bitching and show me the respect I deserve."

Heinrich clenched his teeth. The path she had started on led only one place. Once the drug information was in hand, her life was a loose end to be dealt with.

She lowered her chin and locked eyes on him from under an arched brow. "Poor dumb Heinrich. You just don't get it, do you? This is *my* show."

He looked away, his gut in knots. He was partnered with a lunatic—their failure a guarantee of torture or death.

And now a kidnapping, a capital offense likely performed as sloppily as she'd applied her clownish makeup.

Chapter 64

8:47 a.m.

The Consultant rolled his cart out of ICU bay five and made a phony entry on the clipboard.

"Excuse me, please. Are one of you Tracy?"

A petite, bright-eyed thirtyish nurse with a chart open in front of her turned towards him.

"I'm Tracy. Can I help you?"

"Yeah, please. Sorry to bother you." He adjusted his glasses and smiled. "I'm with Capricorn and I need to check the monitors in bay four. I won't disturb anything. Is it okay for me to go in?"

"Check monitors? That's new to me. But what the heck, I've only worked here nine years." She smiled as she set aside the chart. "I'll go in with you. He's my only patient right now and I'm checking him often."

"Yeah, like every twenty seconds," said one of the nurses, and the others smiled. "Better not breathe wrong in there, mister. She may be little, but she's fierce."

"Oh, don't listen to them," Tracy said, blushing. She came around the counter. "I took care of him when he came in and signed on for a double, so I'll be with him all day."

"Well, you don't have to worry about me. Like they said, I won't even breathe wrong."

The nurse pulled back the privacy curtain, the metal support rings clacking. He rolled his cart in behind her and positioned it to the right of the patient's bed, below the suspended monitor console. She pulled the curtains closed behind them.

The nurse looked, brow furrowed, at the dark-haired patient and then scanned the monitor displays. She approached the bed and began to check the collection of tubes, wires and devices.

The air smelled like raw meat and iodine. The patient, this doctor who wouldn't die, lay connected to a ventilator. He looked dead.

In addition to the regular monitors, a small rectangular console on wheels sat at the left side of the bed. "Is he conscious, nurse?"

"No, he's brain-injured and comatose. His body and brain are being cooled. He's strongly sedated."

One of her hands rested on the patient's chest while the other stroked his brow. "Later we may ease back on the sedation to see if he wakes up. We'll see what his doctor says." She picked up an oversized chart and began making entries.

The Consultant picked up his clipboard and made a couple of meaningless notations. The ice pick lay atop the cart under a blue utility rag. He wet his lips. A moment alone was all he needed to slam the steel shaft through the ear canal and into the core of his target's brain.

With the patient already unconscious and sedated, there would be no outward response to the lethal plunge. He'd have time to disappear before crashing vital signs and shrieking alarms revealed the doctor's death spiral.

Now if this pain-in-the-ass nurse would just leave. He fiddled with the monitor knobs. He could wait her out. Ten seconds unobserved would be enough.

His pulse raced, his mind in hyper drive, the beeps and clicks of the equipment marking the moments until he could strike. Could there be any greater thrill than balancing on this life-and-death tightrope?

The nurse set down her clipboard.

Finally she appeared to be leaving.

Chapter 65

9:07 a.m.

Aki stepped out of the Fifth Precinct interrogation room disheveled and worried. The call he'd received forty-five minutes earlier had awoken him from the lumpy couch in the Homicide room.

Initially, Jon Malar's stolen phone tracked to the projects. The 911 operators provided initial location intelligence, but when tracking became part of an ongoing investigation, the responsibility transferred to the cellular service provider.

At some time during the night the phone's position changed. The move was missed, and it was speculated that the phone company employee had been on break when the tracking software alarm beeped. The technician who came on at eight a.m. noted the blinking icon signaling the position change. The phone had relocated to near the intersection of Franklin and Lyndale Avenues. She dialed Homicide and was connected with Aki.

Aki had hung up from her call and immediately dialed the Minneapolis Fifth Precinct police station, which was located at Franklin and Lyndale. A Vice Lords gang member named Danton Robinson had been arrested during the night on charges of domestic assault. His possessions, including Doc Malar's stolen cell phone, were in the possessions lockup. Aki had raced across town.

Now he'd just completed his interrogation of the gang member.

He pushed a wrinkled bill into the Coke machine in the hallway. After the third try and some mumbled curses, the machine rumbled out a cold can. He gulped the Coke, then glanced at his reflection in the machine's glossy front. He looked like shit and felt worse.

The gang member's story left Aki sick-to-his-stomach uneasy.

Two gunshots had sounded as Danton and his "dogs" walked past the old building. They feared a rival gang had taken out one of their members. They'd yelled and seen the squealing exit of a "sharp looking ride." They discovered the white guy down, finished the 911 call, and Danton reported "finding" the cell phone. He swore that he and his crew did not shoot anybody.

The story made the "wrong place, wrong time" explanation for the doctor's shooting doubtful. If it wasn't a robbery or gang violence, who shot Jon Malar? And why?

Aki crushed the drink can and tossed it in the trash.

An evidence tech approached. "It's been dusted and backed up." She held out the cell phone. "It's okay for you to check. Do you know how?"

"Thanks. No problem." Aki scanned the recent calls then accessed the text messages.

He read the most recent. *Shit!*

He first trotted, then sprinted down the hall. Barely slowing for the stairs, he made it to the street and jumped into his unmarked Ford.

The tires of the five-liter performance engine vehicle squealed. He was electric with an adrenaline surge. Dread and self-reproach were riding shotgun as he raced down Lyndale Avenue.

Understanding had dropped into place like a roulette ball clicking into a winning slot. Only it wasn't a winner—anything but. The text message instructed Dr. Malar to meet Dr. Cody at the lab at nine o'clock.

Aki had spoken with Doc Cody at the hospital after the shooting. He'd been working in the ER all evening. Drake Cody hadn't arranged any such meeting.

Someone had lured Doc Malar to the lab and tried to kill him.

And now he lay in the hospital, near-dead and unprotected.

Aki radioed base and advised them to call the hospital and notify their security. He asked to have the desk captain arrange a police guard for Dr. Malar.

Aki would be at the hospital in minutes. So why did it feel as if his chest was being squeezed in a vise?

Because they'd dropped the damn ball, and his experience proved that was when things went really bad. He smacked the steering wheel so hard his hand hurt.

The car left the ground as it launched over the crest of a hill. Two black teens in baggy pants and wearing white ball caps were in the middle of the street. Aki buried the brake pedal. The car hood crouched in shrieking deceleration, the teens springing wide-eyed and blink-quick. One teen executed a defensive stiff arm off the lunging car hood flying upward then landing on his feet. The two bounded off like whitetail deer, ball caps flashing through the cityscape.

Aki tasted bile. His hands were clawed on the wheel. He put it in park and rubbed his face with both hands. If the two had not been athletes, the Crown Vic would have drilled them.

He looked at his watch: nine-nineteen a.m. Doctor Malar had been unprotected without incident for twelve hours. Surely Aki was overreacting?

He slammed the car into gear and floored it.

Chapter 66

Drake pulled into the lab's crumbling parking lot. His throat tightened. *Jon was shot here.*

Jon's wounds and the cold, lifeless feel of his flesh were fresh in Drake's head. The flat morning light showed spray-painted markers left from police examination of the crime scene. As he walked across the lot toward the lab entrance, he stepped around a darkened patch. His friend's blood marked the asphalt like a large oil leak. The fire door at the top of the stairs shut behind him. He unlocked the lab and entered.

Michael Rizzini straightened up from over the sink, looking startled.

Drake felt momentarily buoyed—his kick-ass friend an ally.

"Rizz, someone kidnapped Rachelle and the kids and is threatening to kill them. They want D-44. I'm scared sick. I need help."

Rizz blanched and ran a hand over his glistening brow. He leaned his head down, supporting himself on arms braced on either edge of the sink.

He looked like shit.

Drake spied a half-empty bottle of Wild Turkey on the slate table top. "You're hung over."

Rizz swayed slightly as he raised his head.

"Shit, you're still drunk." Drake grit his teeth and rubbed the back of his neck.

"Yamada questioned me." Rizz spit into the sink and wiped his mouth on a lab towel. "I think he's trying to nail me for Faith's murder. I turned off my cell and came here to hide out." He bent at the waist and dropped his forehead to the edge of the sink between his arms. "And now they have Rachelle and the kids? Jesus. I can't take anymore."

Drake stepped forward, grabbing Rizz's shirtfront. He snapped him upright and spun him face-to-face. "You said 'they' have Rachelle and the kids." Drake probed his friend's eyes. "My God. You know something."

Rizz's jaw moved, but no words came out. His eyes shone bloodshot and glassy.

Drake smashed him against the cages, triggering a hiss and the sound of cats scrambling. He held Rizz pinned by his shirt as drumming began in his head. Drake slammed him again. "Talk, damn it."

Rizz hung limp, his eyes downward. He stunk of whiskey, vomit, and body odor.

"Shit." He raised his hands to his temples. "I don't understand what's happening. I knew I was screwing you over—but your family?"

Drake released his grip. *Is this defeated drunk my tough and trusted friend?*

Rizz sagged to the floor, ending on his butt among papers knocked from the tabletop, his back against the cages.

Drake stood, clenching and unclenching his hands, wanting to make someone pay. Rage and fear filled his head with a roaring white noise. "God damn it, Rizz. What are you saying?"

"The other morning, when you found me here—I lied." Rizz kept his head down. "I wasn't working on the research. I was looking for D-44's molecular identity and synthesis information." Guilty eyes met Drake's. "They're blackmailing me."

"Who the hell are they?"

"I don't know. Until the morning after she died, I thought it was only Faith. She was twisted, Drake. She sold us out. Her trust fund was bound up and she had to have more. She rigged the legal work when she registered NeurVitae. The documentation gave her control of our intellectual property—including D-44. She said it was iron-clad. We were fools. She was going to get rich. We'd get nothing. She outsmarted everyone—bragged about it."

He stared off for a moment

"I didn't know any of that the night she came to the lab and we got naked. I didn't tell you she secretly video-recorded it. It was all part of her plan. She set me up and blackmailed me. That's when she told me all the rest."

"Damn it, Rizz."

"I'm sorry. I'm a loser and not worthy of your friendship. Or Jon's. God, that poor guy." He shook his head. "He was heart and soul in love and she was banging everyone."

His eyes roamed, when they met Drake's they deflected. "I tried to resist but it was no contest. She knew it from the first time I saw her." He dragged together several sheets of paper that had been knocked to the floor.

"I gave her copies of everything except the D-44 identity and synthesis pathway. I told her I couldn't find it, but I hadn't even looked. I was stalling while I figured out a way to stop her." Rizz rolled the papers into a tube and clutched them. "When you came back from that Air Care flight confirming she'd died, I thought my problem was solved."

"Jesus, Rizz."

He licked his lips and twisted the roll of papers. "Things were worse than I knew. The next morning I got a call from a nasty woman. She was the one who'd been telling Faith what to do. She's smart and part of a group that's organized and ruthless. They have Faith's video and more.

"They set up my dad, which ain't hard. They have slam-dunk evidence of him committing a felony. Besides being a jerk, he's an ex-convict. Two stints inside. Another conviction and he's locked up forever. I couldn't let it happen."

"So you sold out my family?" Drake's anger had become a sick dread.

"God, no. It wasn't like that." Rizz clenched the tube of papers. "She said it would all go away if I gave them D-44. Otherwise, they were going to show the video of Faith and send my dad away forever."

"Son of a bitch, Rizz. Why didn't you come to me? You know I would have backed you. You rolled over without a fight and now they have my everything."

"I fucked up big time, Drake. I'm weak. Just like my old man." He grimaced, looked at Drake and swallowed. "When Faith showed up here, she had more than wine. I used drugs. It was on the video. She knew it would cost me my medical license."

Rizz stared down at the scrolled papers. "I'm not like you or Jon. My work as a doctor is the only decent thing about me." A distant siren wailed. "I was going to give them D-44, but I couldn't find where you stashed the info. That must be why they took your family. They want the drug. It has to be them."

Rizz got to his feet, appearing more stable. "I've only had phone contact. The chick is smart and wicked." He paused. "She may have psych issues. That's everything I know."

Wicked with possible psych issues fit Drake's impression of his contact. Ruthless and possibly mentally unbalanced people had his family. *God help me.*

Rizz brushed debris off his pants.

Was Drake's messed up and buzzed friend capable of helping? Could he be trusted?

"Drake, I would never have knowingly done anything to put Rachelle, Shane or Kristin in danger. I'm dying inside." Rizz held the now tattered roll of papers in his left hand while he clenched his right.

His eyes looked steady as he met Drake's gaze.

"I'll do anything to make it right, Drake. Anything."

Chapter 67

Surgical ICU, 9:15 a.m.

Tracy had heard it from her earliest days in nursing school.

"You can't allow yourself to care too much," and "You have to stay detached or it will eat you up." It passed as popular wisdom. The public perceives that doctors and nurses get used to dealing with tragedy—that it doesn't affect them.

Tracy knew better.

You should care. And if you care, the bad things that happen rip you up. That never goes away. Sometimes you feel guilty or inadequate. You learn painful lessons. At times you can't sleep at night. But you keep on caring. That's the burden you accept when you do something that really matters.

The bedside light shined on Jon Malar's closed eyes. He probably couldn't notice, but she redirected it while touching his forearm.

How do you not care? Flip a switch in your head? Tracy didn't have any such switch. And she believed that the overwhelming number of nurses and doctors she worked with didn't have that switch either.

She hoped they didn't.

She moved through her nursing assessment—vital signs, oximetry, core temperature, ventilator parameters, checking rates and doses of all drips and lines, checking and recording the status and outputs of catheter and chest tubes, examining all skin sites and patient wounds. All highly complex tasks that were routine for her. Her practiced expertise allowed her mind to roam.

Something about this patient, this doctor Jon Malar, had her thinking heavy thoughts. She knew him, a little at least. Like she knew most of the ER docs, a little, but in some ways a lot. They were the physicians that responded to all code blues, the occasions when hospitalized patients' hearts stopped, they quit breathing, or were otherwise in the act of dying.

Every patient room, ICU and otherwise, had a code blue alarm switch mounted on the wall.

When a patient was crashing, a nurse flipped the switch and the code blue sounded. One of the ER docs would come running—racing from the ER to lead the resuscitation. They arrived fast, exertion evident, but the calmest, most together doctors you could hope for.

The ventilator readings told her that Doctor Malar's injured lungs were moving easier. The oxygenation was excellent. She would notify respiratory therapy and let them know they could ease off on the ventilator pressures per the standing orders. *Nice.*

She remembered Dr. Malar from code blues over the past few years. The other nurses always commented on his good looks. Tracy remembered him because he spoke softly and had kind eyes.

Dr. Malar and his friend Dr. Cody were the type of doctors you hoped for when things went bad. Just as impressive as their lifesaving efforts was their class and compassion in dealing with the families and loved ones of patients who did not survive. They didn't have an off-switch for their caring.

The chubby tech guy remained under the monitor console next to the bed. He'd been around for long enough. Friendly but definitely a putz. He made notations on his clipboard and mostly just stared at the monitor displays. He'd never make it as a nurse. It was as if he was just killing time waiting to actually do something.

Her patient lay motionless, save for the ventilator-driven rise and fall of his chest. His core temp remained at the targeted ninety-two degrees. The raw smell of his damaged flesh nudged through.

She knew that despite the outward stillness, inside his body a war raged.

His pallor matched the white of the sheets and contrasted with his black hair and sunken eyes. Somehow he kept hanging on—the past hour had been his most stable. Last night, she'd been certain he would die.

The tech stood with his clipboard in one hand, the other grasping something under the small rag on his cart.

It was time to go to the station, complete her notes, and call respiratory therapy on the vent settings. She set down the chart and readied to leave the room.

How long was it going to take this tech to do his job? *I don't want you around anymore, putzy guy.*

She hesitated.

The *tock-tock* cadence of the IV pump paced the slower rhythm of the ventilator's click-hiss-blow, and the musical beeps of the heart monitor. Small, silvery drops of fluid streamed into the IV line from the micro-pump.

Respiratory therapy was paged to the nurses' desk. Tracy could step out and catch them. She took a step in that direction.

Shrill voices pierced the curtain from the nurses' station. She heard movement and sensed the aura of alarm.

The curtain ripped open, causing her to jump back. An Asian-featured guy with wild eyes, rumpled hair, and a wrinkled suit stood breathing hard with his arm raised holding the swinging curtain. He looked deranged.

Tracy placed her body between the intruder and her patient. Several nurses stood open-mouthed behind him at the station.

"Is the doc okay?" The man reached to his belt and flashed leather with a gold badge. "I'm Detective Yamada." His eyes scanned Tracy and then the tech guy. "You his nurse? Who's this guy?" He pointed towards the bespectacled tech.

"Yes, I'm his nurse. What's going on? You scared me silly." She held an open hand to her chest. "This is a technician checking monitors." She turned to the putzy guy. "Who did you say you worked for?"

The detective stepped past her and stood next to the tech's cart and alongside the doctor's unmoving body.

"Golly, guys. Let me get out of your way. I'm with Capricorn Diagnostics…" As he spoke, he held the clipboard to his chest and slid towards the exit, trying to get past Tracy and the detective. "I see you guys have something going on …" He looked towards the patient and gave a start, eyes wide. "Oh my—"

Tracy and the officer turned their attention towards the patient. The tech's right arm slashed towards the detective, whose arm shot up in defense. The thrust of the ice pick directed at the policeman's chest entered his raised arm, penetrating to the handle. The tool tore free of the attacker's hand.

The tech bolted past Tracy and the writhing detective, out the open door of the ICU.

The detective attempted to get his gun out of a belt holster using his left hand. Pale and grimacing, he then tried to reach the handle of the ice pick lodged in the upper aspect of his right arm. He spoke through clenched teeth. "Someone pull it out."

Tracy stepped forward. She grasped the handle with her right hand, then placed her left hand on his shoulder and yanked. The pick tore free like a cork from a bottle of wine.

The detective ripped his pistol free as he sprinted from the room. Over his shoulder he yelled, "Call 911 and security. Tell 911 that Detective Yamada said to set up SWAT cover on all hospital exits. Give the description." He slapped the exit panel and raced down the hallway.

Tracy stared at the bloodied instrument. Her hands trembled. She deposited the weapon in a plastic bag and quickly washed and re-gloved her hands while keeping her eyes on her patient. His vital signs remained solid and his appearance unchanged. She drew the curtain.

Noise built from the station's core—security personnel talking into radios and terse, static-laden replies. The nursing staff's words were adrenaline fueled—high-pitched and loud.

On her side of the curtain, the vital signs held steady. She puffed out a big breath and swiveled her head and neck. A small thing caught her eye.

One of the pillows she'd positioned to support her patient's head lay out of place. The one nearest to where Capricorn man stood had been pulled away, leaving the ear and side of Jon Malar's head exposed.

She repositioned the pillow. The beeps of the heart monitor marched on. She gave his shoulder a gentle squeeze.

Chapter 68

Drake read off the cell phone GPS coordinates he'd just received from the 911 operator and Rizz entered them into Google Earth. They sat at the slate-topped lab table. The morning's brightness glinted through the multi-paned windows, making the image difficult to view. Rizz rotated the laptop, placing the screen in shadow, and the Google Earth image showed clear.

"Downtown, Drake. It shows the phone as being somewhere in the Wyndham Grand Hotel. That's five-star and high security. It makes no sense."

"No! I was afraid of this. We're tracking the phone, but I won't know for sure Rachelle and the kids are where the phone is until the kidnapper puts them on—if she does."

Drake put his face in his hands and rubbed his eyes. "Until then, anything I do risks tipping them off. She said they'll kill them and disappear." He clenched his fists. "I'm *hoping* the kidnapper keeps the same phone. I'm *hoping* she'll let me speak to Rachelle and the kids." He raised his head. "My plan is bullshit."

"No, Drake. The plan makes sense." Rizz indicated the laptop. "We're locked on."

"But there's a chance this freak might not honor her word. She might not let me talk with my family. If she ditches this phone," Drake pointed towards the screen, "or leaves it somewhere, we'll be following a trail to nowhere."

He got to his feet. "My wife and children are being held by a lunatic," he slammed a palm down on the tabletop, "and all I have is a half-assed plan based on hope and chance!" Startled cats rustled the cedar shavings and then silenced.

"It's gonna work, Drake." Rizz spoke softly. "We're gonna make it work. I damn well know it."

Drake took the measure of the sunken eyes and sallow cast of his half-drunk friend. The eyes were bloodshot, but the confidence and toughness were back. He wanted to believe in Rizz.

Rizz gestured with the cup of microwaved coffee in his hand. "Drake, minutes ago you told me what happened to Jon. Then you turn me around," he pointed the cup, "and show me Flo-Jo standing in her cage."

Rizz set the cup on the table and laid his hands flat on either side. "Don't you see? Two gunshots to the chest with no vital signs and Jon is alive. A spinal cord paralyzed animal standing unaided." Rizz's eyebrows raised and he spread his palms. "These are miracles."

He stood and placed a hand on Drake's shoulder. "Now you're gonna save your family. *We* are going to save your family."

"Christ, Rizz, if—"

Drake's cell phone sounded. He snatched it. "Dr. Cody here." He pointed at the computer letting Rizz know it was the 911 technician. "Thank you. Please keep me updated." He disconnected and fed Rizz the coordinates.

Drake's fabricated story of a mentally ill ER patient whose tests had come back positive for active tuberculosis continued to galvanize the 911 dispatcher's efforts.

Initially, when he told her the patient had a cell phone with an unknown and blocked number, she'd said there was nothing she could do.

When Drake shared that he anticipated receiving a call from the patient, her answer changed. She told him of a new technology. What she called a "toy." If she knew in advance the receiving number, then, prior to the call, locked the new "signal source monitor" on the exchange, she would be able to capture the incoming number.

She'd employed the technology on Drake's home exchange and obtained the "patient's" blocked number from the six forty-five a.m. connection. Since then, she'd continuously monitored its location.

Rizz rotated the screen of the laptop. "Eden Prairie. Take a look."

Google Earth displayed a shopping complex in an upscale southwestern suburb. The cell phone looked to be in or near a building within the development.

"Drake, I know that place. It's a restaurant and night club—Bluestone. I've partied there." Rizz hesitated, seeming embarrassed. "Anyway it's a busy and open area. Not a logical place to hold your family." He checked the time. "Could they be in a vehicle and on the move with the kidnapper?"

The lab's ancient pipes shuddered and banged. With each passing minute, Drake's apprehension grew. The only positive was that, given the time, wherever they had his family must be near the city. That was *if* the phone remained with the kidnapper and *if* she would call with his family at the time promised.

Now he had to wait.

Drake worked with materials from his chemical lock-up cabinet while Rizz drank coffee, looked at FloJo, then washed his face and hands. Drake fed and watered the cats while his mind scrambled for solutions. Having his family's lives on the line made his worst ER challenges seem like a holiday.

* * *

Rizz checked his watch. "Drake, you're cutting it close if you're going to get to the bank and be ready in time for the call."

Drake looked at the animal cages and fixed on Kristin's drawing of the black and white cat helping the stick-figure man to stand.

Rizz pointed at the clock. "No shit, partner."

Drake moved to the sink and splashed water on his face.

"C'mon, Drake. You should go, man."

"Hold on. I'm okay." Drake walked to the back corner and pulled out the lab's wheeled service cart with its twin fifty-five-gallon plastic drums. He picked up one of the drums and dumped it over. Shavings spilled across the floor, and the aroma of cedar wafted.

"Damn, Drake. Have you flipped out? What are you doing? You need to get your ass to the bank."

Drake lifted the drum free of the shavings, then bent, reaching his arm deep into the drum. He jerked and then stood up, holding a circular piece of plastic, the color and size of the drum's bottom. Taped to it was a clear plastic case holding a trio of memory-storage devices.

Rizz's eyebrows shot up. "No way. The D-44 information. Not at the bank. Right here." He shook his head. "Damn Drake, you stone-cold lied your ass off to her."

Drake pulled free the storage devices. "I checked out safety deposit boxes as a storage site but decided against it. I stashed all the information here and promised myself I wouldn't touch it until the study ended." He shrugged. "From the first minute of the kidnapper's call, I knew I couldn't trust them. Using the safe deposit box story gave me time."

"Einstein-level move, partner. Seeing you outsmart that bitch feels good."

Drake sighed and shook his head. "If I hadn't hid the drug info so well, you would have found it. Rachelle and the kids would've never been put through any of this."

Silence hung.. Rizz fidgeted and looked at the floor.

The ringtone of Drake's cell sounded. "Yes. Okay. I'm ready." He picked up the pen and jotted. "Thank you. We haven't been able to get to him yet. Maybe we'll get lucky on this location." Drake clicked off. "The cell phone moved again."

Rizz entered the coordinates and the laptop flickered.

"Bizarre. It looks like it's in the river." Rizz frowned. "Or on the riverbank." He altered the aerial photo image function and tapped his finger, waiting for it to reload. He angled the screen as the image appeared. His frown left. "I know this place." He pointed at the screen. "The old riverboat. This is it."

"A riverboat? Like a barge?" Drake said.

"Not a barge. It's a paddle-wheel riverboat that's been moored there for years. It used to be a restaurant. On my runs I cruise through there sometimes. The whole area is on a flood plain. It's pretty much abandoned warehouses and scrubland." Rizz crouched by the image. "Yeah. This makes sense, deserted but close."

Drake got to his feet. "We need to get down there." He ran a hand through his hair. "When I hear Rachelle on the phone, I'll know. They'll tell me when and where to deliver the D-44 info. I'll agree. As soon as the call ends, I make my move and we bring in the police. I get Rachelle and the kids out." He held a closed fist against the other palm. "Or I get myself between them and the bastards until the police jump in."

"I'm with you, Drake." Rizz stood up. "If we park in this lot we'll be hidden." He indicated a spot on the image. "We should be able to approach from behind the building."

"Grab your gear and let's go." Drake double-wrapped the two stoppered lab flasks he'd assembled in blue surgical towels. He secured them in a small backpack. A clasp knife was clipped to his belt and a two-foot-long pry bar lay in the backpack.

They exited the lab and went down the stairs. Drake's heart pounded and his palms were clammy.

As he made for his car, he stepped around the patch of asphalt stained with Jon's blood.

Chapter 69

Kristin's head drooped as she stood at the lookout post. It was time for Rachelle to awaken Shane to take another shift. It had been hours since she'd burned her hands free. The sun had been up for a long while. Exhaustion pressed like a massive weight. Her mind drifted.

Her innocent, beautiful children did not deserve to suffer. Wasn't God supposed to be just and kind?

Rachelle expected bad things to happen to her. She'd sinned, and her life had rarely been without heartache. Her happiness with Drake and the children was more than she'd ever imagined possible. And even that gift had arisen from deception. Inside was awareness that her happiness was stolen—a thing that she did not deserve with a price that would come due.

She'd almost expected it when just two days earlier she'd learned her and her family's dreams would be crushed.

* * *

When Rachelle had peered out the security peephole of the townhouse door late Tuesday morning, she bit her lip. Faith Reinhorst-Malar was never good news.

Faith said she dropped by to get Rachelle's signature on a document needed for NeurVitae business. Faith acted friendlier than ever before—uncomfortably friendly. When men were present, Faith barely acknowledged Rachelle existed. This morning she was all eye contact and compliments. And touching.

Faith always dressed provocatively, but this morning she flashed braless cleavage in an outfit that seemed more negligee than businesswear. Rachelle had never sensed this brand of sexuality in Faith before. The kids were at a friend's home for a scheduled morning play date.

Rachelle's unease grew.

Faith asked if Drake kept business or research information at home. Had Rachelle seen a form Faith had given Drake to review and sign? If it could be found, it would save her a trip.

Drake rarely brought business or research home, but Rachelle went upstairs to check.

The audio monitors were on. Rachelle always kept an ear on the kids as she did household tasks. Now, as Rachelle looked for the NeurVitae document, she heard the sounds of shuffling papers. *Faith was going through the downstairs desk!* Before Rachelle could respond, she heard the ringtone of a phone transmitted through the monitor. Faith's hushed answer came from the speaker.

"It's about time you returned my call. Are you Ohio people clueless?"

Rachelle felt uncomfortable eavesdropping, but Faith's words held her captive. *Ohio?*

"You found something for me?"

Rachelle made out the sounds of Faith moving into the kitchen. She put her ear to the speaker.

"Are you sure you have the right Drake Cody?".

Rachelle's breath caught and she stared open-mouthed at the speaker.

"A felony conviction!" Faith's delight broadcast from the speaker.

Rachelle dropped to her knees, weak and ill. Drake's secret. He didn't even know that she knew of his record. And Rachelle understood the consequences if others found out.

"A violent offence and time behind bars? Incredible." Faith sounded eager. "He has to have lied about that. God, I own him. Email the details to my office. I'll transfer your payment before the day is done."

Fear coursed through Rachelle as if it had been injected into her veins.

Faith would destroy Drake. She would end their dreams.

* * *

Rachelle had feared for their dreams.

Today she was afraid for their lives.

Rachelle touched Shane's shoulder to rouse him for his lookout watch. He snapped awake.

Kristin cried out from her perch. "Mommy! It's the van. The yellow one. She's coming."

Rachelle jumped. She lifted Kristin from the range. She hugged her tight as she set her down. Her little one's heart thrashed like the wings of a panicked bird.

"Get to your spots. Watch your step, babe." Kristin's shoes were now without laces.

"Kids, I need to put your gags back in."

Rachelle had removed the crude wrist bandages she'd made from her gag. She'd almost blacked out from the pain. She'd torn sections off the children's gags, making them smaller and more easily tolerated.

Kristin looked pale and her eyes were frantic. "Mommy, I'm not brave enough. We need Daddy."

Rachelle crouched to Kristin's eye level. "You can do it, sweetheart. You are Kristin Cody and you are brave."

Shane stood as straight as his bound arms would allow. He blinked and rocked from side to side.

"Just like we practiced, kids." She fed the torn rags into their mouths behind the plastic ties. The children sat on the floor side by side near the range closest to the walk-in cooler.

Rachelle ran to the cooler, entered it, and returned, getting ready. Her wrists flamed like burning paper. She put the pain elsewhere.

The freak was planning to kill her babies.

"Kids, I'll be holding my hands behind me so she'll think I'm still tied. Don't look at her and be ready."

She pushed the torn section of rag into her mouth behind the zip-tie. Her stomach heaved as she tasted the bandage's residue. She shook her weeping, blistered hands and charred wrists and prayed they could do what needed to be done.

She faced the galley door, standing with arms and back leaning against the end of the central prep table. The kids lay ten feet to her left and the chained doors at a diagonal ten feet to her right. Her chest hammered and her breathing accelerated.

She scanned the setup and her breath caught.

There was water on the floor. A series of puddles, the largest near the sink and smaller collections forming a trail to the cooler. If the woman noticed she'd be alerted. *Don't notice. Please don't notice.*

The sound of the heavy chain being pulled across the door handles sounded startling and loud. Rachelle's heart leaped to her throat.

Kristin whimpered.

Their captor had returned.

Rachelle gave the kids a confident nod, inside she quaked.

One of the doors pulled outward and the brim of a woman's hat peeked into view. Next came the damaged face. "Good you didn't try anything, Scar-Mommy. I know you have a thing for sneak attacks. I was going to kick your ass if you did." She shrugged. "I guess you learned who's boss."

Rachelle could not believe her eyes. The woman looked dressed for a debutante party, the hat and clothes as out of place as her smile.

"Oooh. Stinks in here. You're like barn animals. Must be bad because…" She waved a hand in front of her deformed nose as she took a few steps forward.

Rachelle held her breath as the woman passed by a small puddle. She stood within feet of a larger collection.

"Well, kiddos, did you like staying on the boat overnight? Pretty cool, huh?"

They directed their gaze downward.

"Not talking, huh? Cat got your tongues?" She gave a hick of a laugh. "That reminds me. Guess who wants to hear your voices this morning. Daddy boy, the cat crippler."

Both children raised their heads at the mention of their father. Shane nudged Kristin and they looked down once more.

"Who should I pick to talk with the wimpy, whining doctor? Hmmm. Scar-Momma or a little one?" She moved a couple of steps closer to the kids. "Don't want to look at me? I'm the best-looking woman you're ever going to see." She laughed. "I guess you're too young to appreciate womanly perfection."

The brute stood midway between Rachelle and the children.

Rachelle gathered herself. She signaled the kids with an exaggerated nod.

Shane exploded in a series of violent jerking movements accompanied by grunting utterances. Kristin clambered to her feet and scrambled to the corner away from him and their captor.

The woman stiffened, her back towards Rachelle.

Rachelle twisted and grabbed her creation from the prep table.

It looked like a baseball bat. She'd scrolled two of the plastic sheets lining the shelving in the walk-in cooler into a tube and used pieces of their gags and shoelaces to plug and tie off one end. Filled with water and placed upright in the chest freezer for the last few hours, it had frozen into a two-and-a-half-foot amalgam of ice and plastic.

In the minute before the chains rattled, Rachelle had pulled her weapon from the freezer and wrapped the remaining cloth fragment around one end as a grip. In the seconds before the door opened, she laid it along the prep table divider behind her back.

Rachelle spun, then took two large steps, cocking the ice-bat high. She swung with all her strength. The weapon struck the back of their captor's head, exploding in a high-speed collision of skull and ice. Rachelle felt the impact from her charred wrists to her teeth. Ice fragments rocketed across the galley.

The woman's head snapped forward, her body momentarily suspended. Then she pitched downward, face-first with arms limp at her sides. Her forehead and face impacted the floor with the sound of a dropped melon.

She ended motionless, her head twisted and facing sideways. A gaping laceration tracked like red lightning across her forehead. Her lids were half-open, eyes rolled back. The flowered hat lay in the puddled water, its crown collapsed.

Rachelle's hands shook.

Blood trailed down their captor's forehead, crimson oozing onto the partially exposed white of the left eye. There was no blink.

Their captor was unconscious…or dead.

Chapter 70

The Consultant threw the Capricorn logo pocket protector into an open door as he sprinted out of the ICU. He slipped his clipboard into a chart rack outside another room. He came to the confluence of four halls that met at the bank of elevators.

He turned left and entered the stairwell. His feet played a drum roll as he sped down three levels. He exited and walked unhurriedly down the long hallway of neurology ward 3C, his hat brim low.

He opened and slipped through the oversized door to the second room from the end. Mounted alongside the door hung a plastic placard that read Patient Mobility Equipment. The room looked unchanged from his earlier staging run, the walls lined with crutches, braces, walkers and canes. Against the back wall were several wheelchairs, both patient-propelled and electric.

He closed the door, then cursed and clenched his fists. Damn that doting nurse and the revved-up cop. He'd been so close he could almost feel the plunge of the ice pick. Just a few seconds more…

He put his disappointment aside. Evade and escape had become the imperative.

With any kind of break, the "miracle" patient might yet die.

The Consultant went to a wheelchair in the corner, and pulled out the brown paper package he'd stashed beneath it on his early a.m. staging visit. He removed a soiled Minnesota Twins sweatshirt and a pair of baggy, dark sweatpants. The pants gave off the ammonia-tinged odor of dried urine. He taped a dirty bandage at an angle across his forehead, almost covering his left eye and placed gauze packs inside his right cheek, deforming his face. He put on a battered hockey-style helmet, the type that some seizure patients wear.

A push on the toggle and the wheelchair rolled forward. He sat down, putting his Glock alongside his right thigh and placing a Budweiser windbreaker across his lap.

He assumed a slumped, head-bent posture. He laid his left arm on his lap, limp and flexed at the wrist as if a stroke victim.

He'd completed the change in less than ninety seconds.

He used his right index finger to toggle the switch forward and move out the door and into the hall. As he began to encounter people, they glanced at him out of the corner of their eyes and then self-consciously looked away.

Things had not gone as planned, causing him to miss the rush of using his pick. He killed for pay or necessity, but in either case, the thrill could not be matched.

If people needed to die for him to escape, he would oblige.

Chapter 71

Detective Aki Yamada burst out through the ICU doors. His arm burned like it'd been speared by a branding iron. It still moved but stiffened by the second.

Police and hospital security were mobilizing. Eight floors and two wings, over four hundred patient beds and all the offices, labs, ORs and utilities—it was a huge area to cover.

Aki set his radio to channel seven, which linked him with hospital security. He had both the radio and his cell phone. Minneapolis PD could be patched in when on site.

Hennepin-North Hospital and all major medical centers had worked with law enforcement to develop coordinated responses to threatening scenarios. Possible newborn kidnapping triggered a Code Pink, armed intruder triggered Code Orange, and so on.

The hospital had low-resolution video surveillance of main hallways, exits, the ER, ICUs and exits.

Aki spoke to hospital security control as he ran down the hall. "This is Detective Yamada in pursuit. Do you have visual contact?"

"Negative contact. Suspect entered sixth floor stairwell and exited on third floor. He headed east to three-C Neurology. We lost him there. Not showing anywhere on current surveillance. Is there a need to evacuate?"

"Negative on evacuation. I'm descending stairwell to third floor. What is the response status?"

"We're monitoring all exits. SWAT and police are mobilizing. Be advised—our staff will not confront. We do not want a hostage situation. Our security staff is unarmed. We want the intruder off our grid."

"Roger that. Can you patch me the on-scene police commander when you connect?"

"Ten-four, Officer."

Aki had his gun in hand but concealed in his left sport coat pocket. Normal hospital traffic passed him heading towards the elevators as he followed the signs indicating 3C. They needed to avoid panic. The security chief had it right—they had to get this guy out of the hospital. Aki's right arm no longer functioned effectively. If he had to shoot it'd be left-handed. *Shit.*

A former Marine and a homicide detective—who would guess that his pistol shooting skills stunk? He'd barely qualified each time he'd undergone the required departmental testing. Minimum acceptable score was sixty points and he had achieved a sixty-one. And that was with his right hand.

"Officer Yamada, this is control. Replay confirms subject passed down the Neurology three-C corridor minutes ago. We believe he entered one of the last rooms on the west wall. He has not been seen leaving. Copy?"

"Ten-four. I'm almost there." He shifted his grip on the pistol.

"Yes, we have you. There's been other traffic in the hall and our camera is positioned at the start of the corridor. We could have missed him."

"Ten-four."

Aki glanced into the open doors of patient rooms as he moved down the hall. He caught the odor of cleaning agents and musty bodies. The second of the last three doors stood closed.

He felt as he had when he made a high-altitude parachute jump in the service—not enough air and scared sick.

A placard was mounted next to the door: Mobility Assist Storage. He winced as he grasped the door's handle with his right hand. He launched into the room, landing on his knees with pistol raised. Nothing moved and he heard only his thudding heart.

Below the walkers and crutches, he spied a bundle of wrapping paper on the seat of a wheelchair. Resting his gun on the seat, he opened the bundle with his left hand. As he examined the contents he felt the pressure in the room change and heard the soft whoosh of the door opening behind him. He grabbed for his gun as he threw himself to the side, crashing into a phalanx of walkers. He brought the pistol up left-handed and pointing.

A long-haired, thin young man wearing scrubs swung his clipboard in front of himself as if a shield. The whites of his eyes flashed wide and a tongue stud showed in his open mouth.

"Police," Aki said, lowering his gun while shaking inside, unsure of how close he'd come to pulling the trigger. "What are you doing here? Did you see anyone?"

"You scared the shit out of me, man." The kid looked pale and his voice shook. "I'm just doing my job. I didn't see nobody. I didn't do nothing. For real."

"You know this room? Anything different?"

"This is our storage. I'm the physical therapy orderly. I help with crutches, walkers, everything." He looked around and checked his clipboard. "Someone boogied with a big one. We've been ripped off before. Pretty lame."

"What's missing?"

"A Kohler R-235. Toggle controlled, tight radius, silent drive. Worth a bundle."

"What's that?"

The kid looked puzzled, then brightened. "A wheelchair, man. An electric wheelchair."

"What's it look like?"

"It's a wheelchair," he said with a shrug.

"Come on. Color? Label? Anything?"

"Oh. I get it. It's blue. Right-hand toggle. It has H-N Hospital printed on the outside of the backrest."

Aki bolted past the orderly holding the radio to his mouth. "Control—intruder is disguised. Using an electric wheelchair. Blue color with H-N hospital printed on the back."

"Copy. We have you patched to police command. They're reading you."

He raced past a nurse's station, their heads turning. It came to him. As he'd come out of the stairwell from six, the folks moving to the elevator. A pathetic looking guy in a wheelchair, dirty, with a hat. No. A helmet. Aki had run right past him.

He spoke into the radio as he ran. "Control, I'm taking stairs. SWAT command—he's wearing a helmet and looks old. We need him clear of the hospital."

"Yamada, this is SWAT command. Assets are assuming position. Is the target hot?"

Aki did not hesitate. "That's an affirmative. Armed and has attempted to kill." He raced down the stairs, his footfalls echoing.

The radio spoke. "This is hospital control. We have a visual. First floor, main corridor. Heading toward west exit. Electric wheelchair, helmet." A moment of static. "West exit team. Observe and report. Do not engage. Repeat. Do not engage."

Aki reached the main floor, pulled open the door, and looked. He turned right and sprinted down the hallway.

The radio crackled. "West exit reporting. Your suspect just rolled out. Hospital label noted on chair but this individual looks like a handicapped individual. I repeat—looks like a handicapped individual."

Aki held the radio to his lips, keying it as he scrambled. "SWAT command, this is Yamada. Lock on and track. I will approach. Hospital security, maintain exit surveillance."

Aki entered the west lobby. Two security personnel stood next to the hospital exit. One held up a hand and signaled out the door to the left.

Aki ran left onto the hospital's asphalt parking lot feeling terrifyingly exposed. His senses buzzed. He moved past a large hedge on the margin of the lot and caught movement out of the corner of his eye. The wheelchair sat like a discarded shopping cart beside a blue Honda. A man in a dirty sweatshirt bent by the open car door. The man turned, raising his arm.

Aki threw himself sideways, snapping off two shots left-handed. He knew with dread certainty that he'd missed.

In the slowing of time that accompanied what he knew would be the moment of his death, he heard the *pfftttt* of a silenced round.

He hit the asphalt rolling and attempted to accelerate his tumble. The interval awaiting a bullet's impact stretched like a nightmare's never-ending fall.

A meaty slap sounded from the direction of the car. Aki came to a halt with gun outstretched but no target in sight. He got to his feet, heart in his throat. A silencer-fitted Glock lay on the ground. The man lay semi-upright, his back wedged against the open car door. Crimson flow pulsed from a jagged defect at the base of his neck. His jaw moved spasmodically, the eyes staring upward.

Aki looked up and saw the black-uniformed SWAT sniper rise with rifle in hand from his perch on the parking garage's third level.

Aki moved closer, his gun centered on the slumped man's chest.

The ashen face gave a slight upward nudge, the lips moving.

Aki bent and put his ear near. The words were just audible.

"I liked my odds."

The body settled.

Chapter 72

Drake glanced at the dashboard clock. Still more than twenty minutes before the kidnapper's scheduled call. Each passing minute added to his dread. He turned, following Rizz's car.

He'd never seen this pocket of the city, close to downtown, yet generally abandoned. Since their last turn-off, Rizz's vehicle was the only sign of human activity he'd seen. Old warehouses, in poor repair, sat along narrow roads of dirt and crumbling asphalt.

Rizz pulled into a dirt parking lot and Drake followed. He climbed out of his car and stood next to a rusted dumpster.

A dank odor greeted him and the intense but hazy sky lit without shadow. The one-story cinder-block warehouse facing them was covered with flaking white paint stained by splotches of rust. His plan would mean disaster if his family was not on the boat that was moored some 400 yards beyond the other side of the building. Emptiness gnawed at his stomach.

Rizz opened the laptop on the hood of his car and checked the wireless signal and function.

Drake called the 911 operator-technician and confirmed the tracked phone had not moved. *Be there and be safe!*

Drake opened his trunk. He removed an old pump-action, twelve-gauge shotgun and an empty duffel bag. The twelve-gauge shells he had were birdshot used for hunting pheasant in Ohio. The spread of small pellets could knock down a bird at twenty yards—it would not stop a man unless much closer. Inside of six feet, it would obliterate.

Drake fed a shell into the magazine then racked the pump action with a solid *sla-snakk.* He loaded two more, then checked the safety.

Rizz checked the shell box. "Birdshot—damn." He held out his hands. Drake handed him the weapon.

"It's old and looks beat to shit." Rizz hefted it. "But I like the feel."

Drake took the gun and slid it into the duffel. "I may leave it with you. When I make my move, I'll need speed and surprise. I probably won't be able to carry this thing."

He checked the time. Fifteen minutes until the kidnapper's call—if things went as scheduled. Fifteen minutes to figure out a way to save those who meant everything to him.

Rizz slung the duffel bag strap over his shoulder and picked up the laptop. Drake checked his small backpack, then put it on. They moved toward the rear of the warehouse.

A forty-foot-wide strip of open ground lay between the back of the building and the tracks. Rusted bolts, metal barrel tops, broken bottles, and other objects had embedded into the oil-blackened dirt like step stones in a garden. The odor of damp earth and creosote was joined by that of the river and a hint of wood smoke. Drake and Rizz viewed the river flats from behind a jumble of railroad ties and discarded wooden pallets.

The riverboat sat approximately three hundred yards away. The floating restaurant's overgrown parking lot, some scrub-covered wasteland, and the railroad tracks lay between. A growth of hardwood trees and thick bushes began on their right immediately across the tracks. The woods extended for some distance in that direction.

A yellow van stood parked near a small outbuilding. An awning-covered walkway connected boat to land. Gulls swooped and shrieked in the hazy bright sky. The air was hot, and dead still.

Drake sensed this was it. Rachelle, Shane and Kristin—he could almost feel them. He had the urge to sprint to the boat and race up the gangplank in a kamikaze rush.

"There's no cover," Rizz said.

From across the tracks and among the cluster of trees came faint laughter and voices. Rizz and Drake crouched deeper behind the pallets.

After a moment Drake signaled Rizz, then scrambled over the tracks into the trees and head-high brush. He advanced along a small worn trail. Rizz followed.

"This tastes mighty fine," said a nearby, slurred baritone.

Drake and Rizz froze.

"Hell, yeah," came a higher-pitched and likewise slurred response.

"This malt liquor is fine earth product."

"Give me another." The higher voice sounded sharper and no longer jovial. "Like right damn now."

"Easy, Coach." The sounds of a pop-top snap and gush. "I am the Captain and I make things happen. It's my mission."

Drake and Rizz turned to one another—*the Captain?*

Drake stepped past a last clump of bushes into a small clearing.

The Captain and a small, white guy with bird's-nest eyebrows and a ZZ-Top-like beard sat on upended five-gallon buckets next to an old cable spool. The smaller man wore grimy jeans and an ancient high school letter jacket. A case of forty-ounce cans sat on the spool table, with a number of empties on the ground. A pile of yellow foam insulation sat behind the table.

The drinkers clambered to their feet. The smoking remnants of a campfire fire lay nearby. The Captain's wire-framed, two-wheeled shopping cart leaned against the base of the nearest tree.

The Captain raised his arms with hands open and spread, his coats splaying wide. "Our mission is one of peace." His posture and the two hats stacked on his head made him look like a homeless archbishop.

"Captain, it's me, Doctor Cody. You know—Bones."

The Captain's posture eased and he squinted. He looked from Drake to Rizz. A smile, made lopsided by his stitches, spread. "It's Bones and Bones." His eyebrows rose. "I'm not at the hospital, am I? Did you arrive by transporter?"

"Captain, I'm on a mission."

"You have a mission?" The Captain said, wide-eyed.

Drake noticed several of the wooden pallets were configured into a hut in the bushes behind him. "Captain, have you seen people around the big boat on the riverbank last night or today?"

"I have not been in observation mode." He opened his hands. "Welcome to Outpost Alpha—the advance base for my mission. I've logged the coordinates with our orbiting drone." He pointed at Drake "You gave me sandwiches after you fixed my face. You helped my mission."

Drake moved to the edge of the clearing and peered through thick bushes toward the river. He bit his lip as his mind sifted and spun. He considered options and projected possibilities. The life clock was ticking and the lives at risk were those who meant everything to him. His mouth was dust dry and he tasted ash. *Please be safe!*

Drake moved back to the group. "Captain, will you help me with my mission?"

"We of my world like to help. It is our nature."

"Thank you." Drake unslung his backpack. "First I need to borrow one of your coats and a hat."

The Captain and Rizz looked at him with raised eyebrows and heads cocked.

Chapter 73

Morning

Rachelle once again felt driven to kill.

Their tormentor lay sprawled on the galley floor. Life showed only in the rise and fall of the chest. Rachelle wanted to wrap her hands around the thick neck and squeeze until the flesh was blue and cold.

Kristin whimpered.

Rachelle climbed on top of the range and looked out the porthole. Gulls swooped over the parking lot. The sky was hazy but so bright it hurt her gloom-accustomed eyes. The yellow van stood alone next to the walkway.

She got down off the range, then grabbed the downed woman's leather bag and dug into it. The wire cutters were near the top. *Thank God.*

She cut the children's restraints, and freed them of their cruel gags, each snip agony for her hands and wrists. They leapt into her arms, Kristin sobbing and Shane trembling. The smell of urine and body odor was no barrier to the wonder of the embrace.

The scream of a circling gull jarred Rachelle back. "Be ready, my babies. We have to get out of here."

Rachelle ripped back into their captor's bag, throwing to the floor the items of no value. A small bundle of the plastic zip ties, a plastic bag filled with orange M&Ms, a compact mirror, and a scrolled twenty-dollar bill held by a rubber band. The end of the bill was crusted with dried blood.

Her fingers settled around a set of keys. She pulled them out, her grip excruciating and clumsy—two keys on a clip with a car rental agency name displayed.

She held them up like a prize. "Now we run."

A last glance at the collapsed body showed no change.

Rachelle led with Shane's hand in hers and his bonded to Kristin's. They passed through the galley's swinging doors into what had apparently been the main dining room of the restaurant. Rachelle's nerves sparked, her senses hyper alert. The air smelled like wet dog and mildew. The room was large with a low ceiling. The three walls not abutting the galley had wood-paneled bases and upper halves of plate glass.

The mid-morning light penetrated only a short distance around the periphery, leaving the majority of the room in shadow. The space screamed *get out now* to Rachelle.

They stood next to a door that opened onto the deck facing the river below. Rachelle felt the wild urge to burst through that door with her children and jump into the water.

They *needed* to be off this boat.

As she looked for the exit she probed their captor's bag, which hung from the strap around her neck. When Rachelle had been carried onto the boat, she'd been dulled from her assault and panic attack. She spied a solid door on the forward wall. "Come on, kids."

Her fingers discovered the cell phone within the bag. She used her thumb to depress the 9, then the 1, while with her left hand she grasped the exit door's metal handle and pulled. With too little effort the door burst open, startling her.

A tall, blond-haired man pitched forward from the other side, his palm outstretched and surprise on his face.

He looked from her face to her hand and slapped the phone to the floor. "Get them," he ordered over his shoulder.

Rachelle sprang forward, clawing at the man's face. Kristin ran back towards the door to the galley, then stopped at the swinging doors. She covered her face with her hands and began to scream.

Shane took two steps away, then stopped and turned.

The blond man drove Rachelle back and knocked her to the ground with a blow to her face. Two thicker men emerged from the stairs.

Shane flew at the blond man, flailing blows that reached no higher than the man's stomach.

The man kick-swept Shane's feet out from under him, while throwing him to the floor.

Rachelle and Shane lay stunned. Kristin's wail sounded like the cry of a small animal.

"Shut her up," said the first man. One of the thicker men clamped a hand over her mouth.

The blond man stood over Shane, red-faced, with both hands raised and clenched. He moaned. A large vein stood out on his forehead, the tendons in his neck taut. "They have seen me." He clasped his hands to his temples. "No, No, No."

He dropped his hands. "Bring them." He glanced about, then gripped Rachelle's arm and dragged her through the swinging doors. He took a step into the galley, turned, then froze. His eyes grew wide.

Rachelle turned her head to see.

The woman knelt, head bent, with her face rising from the floor. She held one of the scrolled bills to her nose, a mound of white powder on the surface of the compact's mirror. Other items from her bag lay strewn across the floor.

Their captor looked up. The blood from the jagged gash across her forehead had clotted. Congealed blood circled her eyes like grotesque goggles. More blood, in a dripping paint pattern, covered her cheek, jaw and neck.

Her eyes were electric with madness, the whites radiating from the contrast of their crimson surrounding. Twin trails of white powder showed beneath her nostrils.

"Hey, Hein-dick. Let me guess? You want to bitch about something." She laughed, choked briefly, then hacked a dark clot from her throat. She raised the scrolled bill and gestured. "Alkylated coca ester in high concentrations is a potent neural stimulant. It's keeping this intellectual Ferrari flying."

The woman huffed at the blond man. "You know what, Heinie? If you'd have got nailed like I did, your prissy ass would be dead and gone."

Her lip curled as her eyes moved to Rachelle. "You're gonna pay, girly-girl."

The creature pointed the bloodied bill to the floor at Heinrich's feet. "Make yourself useful for a change, Heinie, and toss those M&Ms this way." She grinned, a spectacle of fright. "More fuel for the Ferrari."

Chapter 74

Drake Cody mimicked a drunken sway as he moved toward the riverboat.

The ash and earth of Outpost Alpha dirtied his face, hands and shoes. He wore a pair of the Captain's oversized wool pants and a full-length coat over his own clothes. Pulled low on his head over cheap sunglasses was the broad-brimmed fedora. He was sweat-soaked in the climbing heat and stillness.

Drake had run through the woods and exited the cover about one hundred yards downstream from the rear of the boat. He advanced, pulling the Captain's two-wheeled cart. Now he stood within twenty yards of the paddle wheeler.

He'd neither seen nor heard any activity on the boat. The kidnappers' call was overdue. His throat knotted. He was in position but the timing was out of his control. As he knelt by the cart, he spoke softly into the phone.

"See anything, Rizz?"

"Nothing."

"They should've called. It feels wrong. I can't wait. Start it happening. Make the first call."

"Good luck, brother, and look for me. I've got your back."

"Not too soon, Rizz. Get it started, but follow the plan. Wait for the cavalry."

The paddle wheel spanned the width of the vessel and rose from within the water to the level of the upper deck.

He moved to the edge of the concrete levee. Concrete pillars with linking mooring hawsers stood fore and aft. He positioned himself behind the nearest pillar. The structure hid him from the parking area and the canopied walkway.

He believed the Captain's garb would cover him if spotted along the bank. If seen while climbing onto the boat, there would be no surprise. And no chance for him to protect his family.

That was his strategy—get between the kidnappers and his family until the police arrived. He would safeguard them until the threat disappeared. His stomach clenched. It all seemed desperate and half-baked. The lives that meant everything to him depended on his actions. And he didn't know shit. *Please, God. Make it work.*

The river's surface churned twenty feet below the top of the concrete levee. The nearest edge of the paddle wheel lay thirty feet from the levee wall. The river here smelled of muck and dead fish.

Drake sealed the phone inside two plastic bags and pocketed it. Seagulls screamed as he looked and listened for evidence that Rizz and the Captain had initiated the plan. A cloud of gray smoke rose from the trees near the Captain's camp.

Drake quickly took off the Captain's coat and hat, then removed his pack from the cart and strapped it on. He climbed down and hung by his arms off the edge of the levee. Letting go, he plunged feet first into the water.

He opened his eyes underwater and could see nothing in the silt soup. Rising to the surface, he took one breath and submerged again, swimming underwater toward the paddle wheel.

As Drake grasped the edge of the wheel, he felt a buzz against his chest. Anticipating the kidnappers' call, he jolted as if shocked. Pulling himself from the water onto the blade, he clawed open his pocket. He pulled the vibrating phone from the sealed bags and connected.

Rizz sounded strained. "Our fire is cranking. Fire and ambulance are on the way. But things look bad. A black SUV pulled up one minute ago and three big guys in suits went up the walkway. Damn, hold on. I've got an incoming from our 911 gal. I'm putting you on hold."

Drake's breath came hard. His plan was turning to shit.

"Drake, you there?" Rizz clicked back on, speaking fast.

"Yes."

"911 just registered a call from the kidnappers' phone. A hang-up—no one on the line. Their protocol says call back and send a squad if no response. She held off and called us."

"Rizz, it's them. The call. Rachelle and the kids got to the phone. It has to be. I'll call Yamada. You activate Air Care. I'll be in position. When it's time, come like hell."

The wail of a siren arose from the direction of downtown. An unseen dog howled in response.

Chapter 75

Heinrich's head was ready to explode.

Meryl had allowed the mother and children to see him. Now they must die.

God damn the drug-sniffing American lunatic.

Up until the family saw him, his plan had been to have Meryl killed as soon as the exchange with the doctor was arranged. The family hadn't known Heinrich existed. With Meryl dead, he'd have been free and clear, with the D-44 information in hand. On his way to incredibly rich.

But not now. Everything was different now.

He heard the frenzied screech of gulls and a distant siren. Sweat soaked his shirt. He looked about the dimly lit main room, noting the flicker of the seagulls' shadows on the plate glass. The boat stank—among the odors the faint but distinct trace of fish. God, he hated the stink of rotting fish. He could taste it and felt the need to spit.

The doctor's wife and children were in the galley, bound and gagged. Meryl remained there, directing abuse at the woman who had outwitted her.

The mother and children had suffered cruelly at Meryl's hands. The coarseness and stupidity of the developments sickened him. The doctor's wife was particularly unsettling. She displayed a mother's courage despite her battered state.

And something more. It showed in her eyes—she knew what would become of them.

The doctor had to be anxiously awaiting the overdue call that would prove his family safe and trigger the exchange that would release them. Heinrich would make that call. He was taking over everything.

Everything but one brutal chore—that he would leave to the freak. He would not have the blood of innocents on his hands.

He found the voice scrambler on the floor near the swinging doors. He used Meryl's phone and entered the doctor's number.

He turned to the darker Doberman and pointed towards the galley. "Get the little girl out here. With her gag off. Now!"

The man nodded, but his face darkened.

"Uh, please. It's important."

The connection completed and ringing started.

* * *

The minutes clotted as Drake waited. If he didn't get the call soon he would have to risk charging in blind. The consequences of failure rimmed his mind like the edge of a black chasm.

The phone buzzed and Drake grabbed for it. He held himself with his legs scissored around a blade of the paddle wheel and cupped the phone with his hand. "Hel…hello."

"Do you have the information?" Although still electronically distorted, it was not the voice of the previous kidnapper.

"Yes. I have it. You're late. I was worried. I—"

"You will deliver the molecular identity and synthesis information now."

"My family. I need proof… you promised. I mean the last caller promised. I need to talk to Rachelle."

"Be quiet and listen." The static and buzz ended. Drake heard an undistorted but distant male voice, "Are your mommy and brother alive?"

"Yes." A sob. "Daddy! I want to go home. They—" Kristin's terror-shrill response cut off. The electronic buzz returned.

Drake's blink of relief at confirmation of his family's nearness flashed to fury.

"That is your proof of life. There will be no more. You will—"

"Don't hurt them. You bastards." His instinct to strike triggered, and the drumming began in his head. Heat flared. *No!*

They had his family.

"Calm down, Doctor. I am a professional. Do what I say and our exchange will concluded successfully. Anything else and they die."

This speaker sounded businesslike—ruthless but sane.

"I don't care about the drug. Don't hurt my family." His chest tightened.

"You'll deposit the information where I tell you. After it has been retrieved, I will review it. If it's satisfactory you'll be contacted with your family's location. Understood? None of this is negotiable. This is what will be."

"But I nee—"

"I repeat—none of this is negotiable." He dictated the drop demands. "Do you understand the instructions?"

"Yes, I understand. But—"

"You have one hour."

The line went dead.

* * *

As Heinrich pocketed the cell phone, a siren's wail came nearer. He and the Dobermans moved to the riverbank side of the room and looked through the glass.

Black smoke rose from the woods near the railroad tracks. An ambulance with lights flashing bumped along the dirt access road, its siren bleeping off abruptly. The flashing lights moved past the boat, through the overgrown dirt parking lot and into the waste area nearest the woods. Paramedics climbed out, unloading a stretcher and moving into the woods near where the smoke rose.

A fire—could things be any more out of control?

Heinrich reached to his back and pulled the silenced pistol from his belt. He pushed through the swinging doors.

Meryl stood near the sink. She had attempted to clean her face and plastered on more makeup. "I put the bloom right back on the rose, Heinie."

Heinrich stared. Her wet hair hung in Hydra-like clumps. A jagged gash tracked across her forehead above blackened eyes and her damaged nose. Worst of all were her eyes. If eyes were the windows to the soul, these needed to be barred with galvanized steel.

He no longer considered her human.

Heinrich approached her—away from where the bound family members lay. He spoke quietly.

"Because of your carelessness, they've seen us and have to die." He held the pistol towards her, butt-first, his hand wrapped around the silencer. She looked into his eyes and he looked away.

She gave a huff. "Another job you're too weak to handle." She placed her hand on the pistol's grip. "Once again, it's Meryl who takes care of business."

"This is not the time to keep score. Make it quick. I'll wait outside with the men."

"Don't you mean 'attack dogs'?" She snorted. "You're all gutless."

"You have two minutes. We need to get out of here. There's a fire and rescue vehicles near."

"I heard the sirens. Don't fret, Heinie. You won't get burned." She waggled the weapon in his direction in a come-on motion. "Was the doctor still whining?" Her eyes narrowed. "Where is he delivering the D-44 information?"

Heinrich sensed the risk. "I'll tell you after..." He nodded towards the bound family. "Finish the job and we'll make the pickup and be on the jet within an hour." He'd avoided eye contact but looked at her now. "We're going to be rich, Meryl. Incredibly, spectacularly rich—you've done it."

She grinned widely, the effect hideous. Heinrich looked away. She reached for her mirror and stash.

"Do you need to do that now? Meryl, you're not well. That stuff is going to kill you."

She chuckled as she dumped white powder on the mirror. "Don't worry. I'll do what needs to be done. I always do."

* * *

Heinrich's eyes skipped around those of the Dobermans and slid to the closed swinging doors behind them. "She's taking care of the family. Their blood will be on her hands." They stared at him without blinking. "I gave her my gun. Keep your weapons handy and be on guard for anything crazy."

He pointed towards the galley doors. "When she's done, I want you to take the gun away from her and get her restrained." He flushed warm. "Then I'll come in. I'm going to shove the gun into her mouth and," he raised a fist, "blast a bullet into her brain."

"We'll wipe down the gun and fit it back into her hand. The evidence will show her to be a drugged-up killer and subsequent suicide." He paused. "We'll pick up the drug information, then go directly to the airport." He looked from one to the other. "Can you do this?"

Their faces were stone. The darker one spoke. "It will be so."

"Wipe down everything you've touched. Leave no trace."

It would all work out. He would survive—a very rich man.

* * *

As the doors swung shut behind Heinrich, Meryl set down the cocaine-heaped mirror. She crept next to the doors, got on her knees and listened at the gap along the floor.

The fool underestimated her hearing, like everything else. What she heard was no surprise.

Gutless Hein-dick thought he'd outsmarted her. What a joke. He was like the rats she'd seen on the riverbank during the night—sneaky but dim-witted. She checked the pistol—fully loaded. He would blast a bullet into her brain? *Not hardly.*

Even now the arrogant German failed to recognize her infinite superiority.

She bent over the mirror. Thoughts whipped through her mind like snowflakes in a blizzard. Before the scrolled bill reached the powder, she had it figured.

She'd take out the attack dogs first. That would leave her free to spend time with Heinie. Meryl envisioned *persuading* him to tell her where the info drop site was. She smiled.

Next she'd handle the doctor's family. Meryl wouldn't hurt the kids. But head-case momma had hurt her. Hurt her bad. She probed her damaged nose and forehead. Maybe she'd deal with her barehanded. Meryl flexed her arms and shoulders. *Payment due, girlie-girl.*

Afterwards, she'd swing by and pick up D-44's molecular identification and synthesis information.

Fuck BioZyn.

Meryl would do what Faith, the double-dealing money slut, had tried to do. She would sell D-44 herself. *Ka-ching!*

A matchless mind and all-world body in synergy with wealth and the power of drugs. Fat, poor, and queer little Meryl had become a force without equal.

Damn, it's awesome being me.

Chapter 76

Both of Aki's shots had hit.

One hit the front grill of the Honda and the other hit the wheelchair three feet to the left of his target.

The intruder's silenced slug had left a ragged track just left of the chest pocket of Aki's new but rapidly aging sport coat.

The SWAT sniper's bullet had entered the target's neck just behind the collarbone, angling downwards into his chest. He could not have been saved if he'd fallen prepped and draped onto an OR table.

Aki sat on the curb next to the Honda as the paramedic assessed his injury. His upper arm pulsed with white-hot fire. Damn. He should have figured it out sooner. Doc Malar as a victim of random city violence had been too easy.

The big questions—who tried to have Doc Malar killed? And did he kill his wife?

The paramedic finished applying a bandage. "You need to get into the ER. It's not bleeding out, but it's swollen and hard. You're working on a hematoma in there. And there could be bone, arterial or nerve injury. Not to mention infection risk. We'll get a wheelchair and roll you over."

"I can walk." Aki felt his phone vibrate. Using his left hand, he extracted it.

"Yamada here."

"Aki, this is Drake Cody. My family is minutes from death. Kidnappers have them and say they'll kill them if I contact police. You must come with your best right now. They're being held in the old paddle-wheeler moored on the river. Do you know the place?"

"Whoa, doc. Yeah, I know the place but—"

"There's no time. I'm going in now. Get here with help. There are at least three men and a woman. Please. It's going down right now. My wife and two children. We have an ambulance and fire diversion on the scene and Air Care is being called in. Get my wife and kids out safe. Kill anyone who gets in the way. Don't worry about me. Get my family safe. Come with the cavalry. Full speed and right now."

"Doc, what's that about Air Care? I'm at the hospital."

"Get to the flight elevator—now! The flight will be activated any second. Come fast and bring help. Save my family. Please."

* * *

Drake had a good angle. There were three of them—the suits. Had to be the ones Rizz saw arrive. They stood in the hazy, bright light just inside the glass-windowed wall in front of a pair of swinging doors.

The tall, blond guy appeared intense as he addressed the other two. He gestured towards the swinging doors. The two men listening were hard-faced and thick-chested.

After Drake made the call to Aki, he'd climbed up the paddle wheel. He watched now, balanced on an inner strut where he was able to peek through unseen.

Where were Rachelle and the kids? *Please, be safe.* The swinging doors seemed to be the focus.

He didn't know if he could wait. It was their best chance but it felt wrong.

Gulls shrieked. Black smoke drifted in the air above the boat. Intruding now and growing louder was the sound of another siren. The distinctive tone and deep bass horn honks were that of a Minneapolis Fire Department pumper truck.

Drake watched the men inside turn to the sound. They moved towards the landward windows. The siren grew louder. Now Drake could make out the deep throb of the truck's engine. The men stood looking out.

He slipped through the gap between the paddlewheel blades and quick-crawled to the base of the windowed wall. His heart pounded.

A folding knife sat sheathed on his belt, and a wire-cutter was in the pack. He hoped that with these and the pry bar, he'd be able to free Rachelle and the kids from any restraint. He also had the two tightly stoppered flasks he'd assembled in the lab. He carefully removed one from the pack.

Pry bar wedged in his belt, flask in his right hand, he belly-crawled along the outside deck against the base of the wall, then advanced toward the door.

The siren went silent. The pumper truck's idling engine broadcast a deep rumble. The residue of the river water fouled his tongue and made his damp clothes stink. He lay two feet from the door.

A man's voice startled him. It came from just inside the glass window. Drake pressed himself like a coat of paint against the base of the wall. Gulls cried at one another just over the rail. Motionless, he held his breath. They were within feet of him.

Drake waited on the plan. *Come on.*

Three muffled reports came from somewhere inside the boat—like the sound of a man beating a rug.

Drake's stomach clutched and a sickening emptiness filled him.

Had he been too slow? *Please. No.*

* * *

The wooden pallets and the Captain's rubberized insulation material burned fiercely. Black smoke filled the sky. The heat and toxic fumes forced Rizz to back off.

The ambulance neared the woods. Rizz ran over to the paramedics as they opened the rear doors. He knew them both. He informed them of the situation and the lives at stake. They maintained appearances and moved with the stretcher into the woods.

The paramedics greeted the Captain as he took his place on the stretcher. Rizz commandeered the paramedic's radio and called Air Care dispatch.

"This is Doctor Rizzini. I'm on scene with ambulance 7-1-9. Activate Air Care scene run. A man down with serious burns."

"Roger that. We show west river flats. Any obstacles?"

"Power lines distant and north of railroad tracks, but river approach clear."

"That's a copy. Air Care activated."

Rizz wanted to share with Air Care the diversionary nature of the flight, but radio traffic could be easily monitored by the kidnappers. Additionally, having the med-evac copter on scene was legitimate. The thought that it might be needed for Drake or his family made him glimpse the shadow of a self-hatred beyond imagining.

Somehow, earlier, as he had stood next to Drake in the lab, it seemed as if his friend's plan to "get between the kidnappers and my family" could work. But the on-scene realities and the formidable looking men who had climbed onto the boat had erased any optimism.

He'd encouraged Drake to undertake a suicide mission. *Michael Rizzini, you're a worthless son of a bitch.*

His weakness had put them all in harm's way.

The fire truck's siren and horn brayed its approach, then silenced. "Jenna," Rizz called out to the tall senior paramedic. "You're scene medical control until Air Care arrives. Keep everyone down and back until the police clear the scene. Then come in fast. Bring a pediatrics bag—Drake's two kids are in there."

She gave a thumbs-up. The setting was unique, but paramedics standing ready to enter an uncontrolled, dangerous scene was commonplace. Rizz felt a flush of pride. His knowledge of the dedication and ethic of his EMS colleagues left no doubt they would be in the midst of it when needed—regardless of the risk.

Rizz shared that commitment—it provided him his strongest hope that he was something other than complete garbage.

He maintained calm on the outside, while guilt and self-loathing raged underneath. He picked up the duffel bag.

"Bones."

Rizz turned. The Captain sat on the ambulance gurney with an oxygen mask hanging loose around his neck.

The Captain's brow furrowed, his baritone rumbled. "It is your time. Your mission is now."

The big man's eyes made Rizz uneasy.

"And Bones," the Captain gripped Rizz's arm, "the human is the only earth creature that can cry tears." He released Rizz. "There's a reason for that."

The homeless man's gaze burned. Rizz had no idea what the words meant, but they felt right.

He scrambled off through the woods, following the track Drake had taken earlier. Drake, alone, against at least three men and a woman who were likely armed.

As Rizz broke out of the woods, he heard the first rumble of the incoming engines. The helicopter appeared upriver and high. It curled towards the riverboat.

It would take the least obstructed path to the river flats, just as Drake had figured when viewing the layout on Google Earth.

The helicopter would come in from over the river, then put down in the clearing near the edge of the woods. They would land in no more than a minute or two. Rizz reached into the duffel and pulled out the beat-up shotgun. He jammed additional shells into his pocket. Weapon in hand, he sprinted along the riverbank.

Drake had considered stealth and surprise as his best hope for saving his loved ones. Rizz figured by the time he joined the fray it would be balls to the wall. That was okay—restraint was not his strength.

Somehow the Captain had known. This was Rizz's mission. This was his time.

Chapter 77

The distant throbbing became thunder. The crimson- and flame-painted helicopter raced down the river, then flared directly over Drake, the air bursting with vibration and power. The pitch changed as the copter moved above the flats and hovered in anticipation of landing.

Drake had heard a “What the hell?” from inside the glass before the roaring engines and air-jacking rotor drowned all other sound. The power of the spinning blades air-hammered his chest.

He made the sign of the cross for the first time since his brother’s death, then sprang to his feet and ripped open the door.

The three men stood at the opposite wall, distracted by the descending helicopter. As Drake passed through the door, the light shadowed and one of the thicker-bodied men turned.

Drake held the seven-hundred ml lab flask in his right hand.

The first man started to reach under his coat as the other two turned their heads.

Drake rifled the flask, like a baseball, toward the man, aiming for the floor at his feet. The glassware shattered and the mixture of acetone and elemental sodium ignited instantaneously and a dense blue-orange ball of flame enshrouded the man.

Drake felt a flash of heat and heard a scream as he dove through the swinging doors.

He scanned the room. Rachelle and the kids lay face-down against one another on a plank floor, gagged with feet bound and hands trussed behind their backs. They were not moving. *God, no.*

He jammed the pry bar through the handles of the doors using the backpack’s straps to secure the tool as a crossbar.

Crouching with knife in hand, he scanned the galley. He ran down the room’s length, his nerves crackling like a downed power line. The main galley looked clear, and a look through the open door of a walk-in cooler revealed no threat.

He dashed to his family. The boom of a firearm penetrated from the parking lot.

Rachelle turned. Swollen and blackened lids surrounded deep brown eyes.

Drake slumped to his knees, his heart impaled.

Both kids moved, heads turning to face him. His surge of relief survived only an instant as the emptiness of their hollow-eyed expressions registered.

"I've got you, guys." He moaned, caressing their backs.

He reached and cut the plastic tie from Rachelle's mouth. He pulled the cloth gag free.

"Where is she?" Rachelle's eyes strobed wildly. "Where's the woman?"

Drake stopped and swiveled his head. "There were three guys. No one else."

"Drake, she was just here. Look out for her, she's…" her voice wavered. "She shot the gun three times. At first, the kids… I thought…" Her eyes continued to skip. "Where is she?"

He turned to free her hands, but stopped open-mouthed. "Your hands. Your wrists. Oh my God." He grit his teeth. The galley doors rattled. Drake leapt to his feet with the knife in hand.

"Drake, you there?" Michael Rizzini called.

Drake scrambled to remove the pry bar from the door handles.

Rizz burst into the room, holding the shotgun at the ready.

Drake moved back to Rachelle. "We've got to get them out of here."

Rizz surveyed the family. The weapon dropped to his thighs, his face sagged. "The suits came down the walkway just as I got to the boat. They were dragging one guy. One flashed a gun. I put him down but he got up." He gave the shotgun a lift. "Damned bird shot. They took off in the SUV."

Rizz took halting steps towards the kids, ending up between the family and the open door of the walk-in cooler. "Hey, little guys." His voice sounded tight. "You're safe now." He turned toward Rachelle. "Where's the freak?"

"I don't kno—" Rachelle's head jerked.

Drake saw her eyes widen at the same instant a metallic squeal sounded behind him. He whirled.

The door to the horizontal chest freezer at the rear of the open cooler stood open. Bursting upright rose a hugely muscled woman in a bloodied sleeveless top. She raised a blue-black pistol in a two handed marksman's grip. Her hair hung wild, her face ravaged and her eyes high-beams of insanity. She looked like a cadaver possessed. The gun barrel swung toward them.

Drake started forward.

Rizz launched. His body passing in front of the family as the pistol bucked twice, the silenced rounds sounding like angry jets of air.

Rizz cried out, thrusting the shotgun forward as he slammed to the floor.

Drake caught the weapon's grip in his right hand, swinging it toward the freezer.

The blast was a thunderclap. The expanding load of birdshot struck the woman like metal hail. Her hands and arms in the center of the spreading pattern. Her face and head recoiled as if she'd been slapped. Her crazed eyes still showed wide as her carcass slumped into the freezer.

Rizz was down, his breathing harsh.

Drake chambered another round and kept the shotgun trained on the rim of the freezer. He yelled ragged and loud, his ears keening. "Rachelle, you...the kids?"

"We're not hit, Drake," Rachelle said. "Don't let her—" Her voice choked.

Rizz grunted through clenched teeth. "Finish her, Drake."

Drake held the shotgun poised as he advanced into the cooler. He reached back and pulled the heavy door behind him to protect the others. It sealed with a thunk and a pressure wave he felt in his ears. The air hung dead and musty. A single bulb mounted on the wall above the freezer illuminated with dim yellow light.

Drake's heart thundered. He gripped the gun, his nerves and reflexes trip-wired and animal-ready. Rage consumed him—his children's faces, Rachelle's wounds—the woman's heartless cruelty.

He heard clumsy movement from the freezer, and her head rose into view. The furnace within him roared for her blood. His finger tightened…

He held the shotgun pressed to his cheek, finger on the trigger. From this distance, the bird shot would annihilate her. His every instinct screamed for him to pull the trigger

"Don't move," he shouted.

She ignored him and raised herself to where her entire face showed over the freezer's wall. Lifting her hands, she stared, as if curious, at injured fingers, two with shards of bone and pellet wounds oozing. She opened and closed her fingers, testing them, then *smiled.* Scattered pellet wounds marked her face and upper chest. A broken tooth showed from behind a flayed lip.

And still her eyes burned.

"Your whiney act had me fooled, Drake Cody. You're not the gutless pussy I thought." She gave a blood-flecked cough. "It's nice to find someone who's almost in my realm." Her grin repulsed him.

His trigger finger twitched. A trickle of sweat entered his eye. He blinked it clear. *Shoot her, damn it!*

From somewhere, mixing with his revulsion and rage, he felt something else. It was as if he'd come across an animal driven mad by horrific illness or injury.

"I was waiting for Heinrich and his boys to make their move, but you showed up." She shrugged. "I came up with a new plan. Hell of an entrance, huh?" She beamed as if expecting applause.

"I wasn't going to shoot you. We still have D-44 business to take care of. I aimed for your girly-girl. People who hurt me don't do well. Remember the last bitch who messed with me? The succinylcholine—whoever used that impressed me. But God, what a waste of flawless female."

The battered Amazon was breathing hard and swaying. She sagged and almost collapsed before righting herself. "And then you effing blast me."

Drake kept the gun trained on her but lowered it to waist level. "What do you mean, 'whoever used' succinylcholine? It was you. You killed Faith."

"Jesus," she shook her head. "Faith loved money, but she worshipped sex. On a scale of one to ten, naked orgasmic fun with her measured twenty. I'm gonna give that up?"

She turned her head and spit blood. "I mean, you're right. She had it coming, the double-crossing slut. No doubt, she deserved it." She coughed, winced and shifted.

Before Drake could react, she snapped the pistol up from below and fired. Heat punched deep into his shoulder. The shotgun roared as he fell back. The light bulb shattered, blinking the vault-like room to black.

He was lost in the utter blackness, his eyes flashing false glimmers. His ears registered pain and a continuous keening. He strained to sense her. Had he hit her? He got to his knees. His shoulder raged. A whiff of perfume.

Arms locked around his neck from behind—his airway and blood flow cut off as if he hung by a rope.

He clawed at the steel cables of her arms, his right hand useless. Surging to his feet, he thrashed and bucked. She rode him, her hold unyielding. He couldn't breathe and his mind faded as it starved for blood.

No air. No blood to his brain. His strength failing.

A flash of his brother—always battling, never beaten.

Drake labored to his feet, the woman's muscled mass riding his back, her arms crushing. He backpedalled blindly, accelerating.

A collision of wall, tissue and bone—her grip easing for only an instant before redoubling.

He powered upright, lifting his deadly rider once more. Consciousness waning, he exploded forward through the blackness. Twisting, he launched back-first into the air.

They struck the metal shelving like a train. Her hold broke, he gasped and spun.

They reengaged with the fierceness of fighting dogs.

His left hand found her throat. His right arm useless.

She encircled his neck with fingers of steel.

He powered forward pinning her in a corner. His left hand tightened, vise-like, her pulse throbbing beneath his fingers. Time stretched.

Her grip relentless—her strength inhuman. Too long.

The most primal of fears seized him. *I'm dying.*

His consciousness blurred. His life a guttering flame.

Chapter 78

Aki made it to the Air Care elevator just as the flight doctor arrived. They rode the elevator together and, by the time the doors opened to the roaring copter and vibrating flight deck, the doctor knew what was at stake.

This copter looked sleeker than those Aki had humped during his combat experience, but his feelings had not changed. The flying egg-beaters terrified him.

He felt the lurch, dive and rise of the take-off and controlled his urge to scream. He saw none of the city views from his strapped in, eyes-closed position in the rear compartment. The copter's noise drowned out the exchanges on his police radio. He hoped they spoke of forces converging on the river site.

Minutes later his stomach pitched as the craft hovered and stalled. He opened his eyes in a panic. The flight nurse flashed the OK sign. Aki clutched a support strap with his good arm as the craft rotated and descended touching down with a thump. He ripped loose his seat belt and exited the craft as if it were on fire.

The rotor wash and noise battered him. He bent so low he practically crawled as he scrambled to get clear of the copter's blades. His right arm spiked pain with every movement.

He scanned riverward and saw the boat about two hundred yards distant. A yellow van and a black SUV sat on the concrete apron next to the walkway. Closer to him and away from the river, firemen hosed down a pile of burning wooden pallets and foam insulation. Black smoke rose then was swept by the copter's turbulence as the idling engine continued its thought-jarring thunder.

A woman paramedic waved him over to the ambulance positioned near the woods.

As he approached he noted the gaunt, black man sitting on a stretcher next to the paramedic. Aki saw the tight row of black stitches across one side of his face. *It's the guy Doc Cody fixed. What the hell?*

The paramedic yelled over the engine noise. "Doctor Cody is onboard and Doctor Rizzini is on his way." She pointed toward the boat. "Rizz said come as fast as you can. The family could be killed any second."

Aki's gut flopped.

Two squad cars running silent with flashers off came into view approaching from a distance upstream.

He looked toward the boat and saw three men scrambling down the walkway. Dr. Rizzini appeared from behind a mooring pillar with a raised weapon. *Oh shit!*

A blast sounded and one of the men dropped. He regained his feet. The others assisted him and they clambered into the SUV.

Aki pulled his weapon and sprinted toward the boat. He yelled over his shoulder. "Stay back." The SUV began to pull away.

He pounded across the river flats as Rizzini disappeared up the walkway.

Aki keyed his radio and yelled into it. "Squad cars on west river flat. Black SUV heading your way. Three armed men. Shots fired. Take them down." He raced over the dirt parking area hitting the walkway at a full run.

Another blast sounded; this time from on-board and above.

He flashed on the earlier image of the tongue-studded orderly in his gun-sight. *Don't kill the good guys.* He quick-peeked around the corner at the top of the walkway.

Another report sounded. Aki jerked. The shot was muffled but definitely came from the upper level.

He opened a door and took the stairs there two at a time. He entered a large empty room. The stink of burnt fabric and something like paint thinner reached his nose. A patch of blackened carpet smoldered near the windowed wall.

He spied swinging doors and dashed for them. He slammed through, throwing himself to the ground with pistol raised. His injured arm screamed.

Four figures lay on their bellies on the floor. The stink of urine and gunfire. Two gagged and wide-eyed children's faces twisted to meet his, then turned back towards a large metal door.

The bound and battered woman cried, "Hurry! Help him!" *Drake's wife?*

"The cooler," yelled Rizzini from the floor, pointing. The doc lay unbound but his legs appeared anchored. "Now! It's Drake and the killer in there." Blood saturated his shirt over his lower back.

Aki moved to the side of the door. He grabbed the handle and yanked. The mechanism clanked and the heavy door swung open. Silence.

Aki stood with his back pressed against the outer wall – his heart hammering. A snap-peek showed only shadows. The odor of blood and decay welled from the darkness as if from a beast's den.

"Police." His shout came out a nerve-jacked screech. "Drake Cody?" No response. Aki felt piss-himself scared. He sprang into the door's opening with pistol extended. His eyes narrowed. His face blanched.

"Oh my God."

Chapter 79

Morning

Farley pushed himself away from the keyboard. *Damn.*

Faith Reinhorst Malar—had her cruelty been limitless?

What would the DA do with this information?

He swept the small mountain of junk food wrappers and pop cans off his desk and into the trash. When he felt stressed, he ate. Based on the number of empty chip bags and Snickers wrappers, he was headed for a nervous breakdown.

He put aside the printouts of his latest hacked findings and checked the time.

Earlier Farley had contacted the security guard at Faith Malar's office building and once again emailed him photos. Faith had been at her office the morning before she died. Anyone who'd visited her then was a prime suspect. The sex pad seemed a fitting site for the killing drug's unseemly delivery. The guard's return call should come any minute.

He'd sent the photos hoping for a lead that would keep the brass from shutting down the investigation: a newer image of BioZyn scientist and mania patient Meryl Kampf. An updated photo of Dr. Michael Rizzini. Had the hard-partying doctor been to her office that morning? A photo of the Malars' Mexican groundskeeper from a work-permit application. A photo of Andrew Reinhorst—the thought of her father and his daughter's hidden room sickened.

He'd also sent a photo of Dr. Drake Cody. The family shot had come from the hospital's e-newsletter when he'd arrived in Minneapolis—four years old, but good enough. He didn't know why he'd bothered to attach it. Without Dr. Cody's medical suspicions, the murder might never have been discovered.

The phone buzzed.

"Farley, Homicide."

"Detective, it's me, Steve from Sims Security. I eyeballed your photos. First off, there's a different picture of that same tall guy you sent me before. I didn't see him come in that last day."

Farley eased—he'd been hoping Dr. Rizzini wasn't involved.

"I saw two of the others you sent me."

Farley rocked forward on his seat. "*Two* of the others?"

"For sure. There's that muscled-up chick with the wild eyes that I told you about before. You sent me a newer picture, but that's her. She was here the morning you're asking about. Early. Stayed maybe an hour."

"And the other one?"

"Only one time. But it was the morning you're interested in."

"Which one?"

"Just kinda slipped in, a little after the muscle-chick left."

Farley frowned. "The silver-haired guy?"

"The old guy? Geez, no."

"The guy in the family photo?"

"Right shot—wrong person. I'm talking about the woman. She's a standout. Kept a low profile, didn't ask directions, just scoped the wall directory and got on the elevator. But no way a looker like that slips by me unnoticed." He chuckled.

What the hell? Farley swallowed. "Are you sure?"

"Detective, eight hours a day I sit here and watch people. Mostly fat business guys. I don't forget pretty ladies."

"Was she there long?"

"Hmmm. I'm not sure. I remember thinking she looked different leaving."

"What do you mean?"

"Looked like she felt sick or something. I couldn't swear to it. Maybe she was just in a hurry."

Farley's desk phone buzzed and a second light lit. "Thanks, Steve. I've got another call."

Still reeling, he hit the blinking light.

"Farley, get on frequency nine, now." It was Nancy, a friend of his working dispatch and she was talking fast. "Your partner's in the middle of something real bad at the hospital. SWAT is involved."

Farley patched in on his mobile.

Static, then someone breathing hard. "Target is hot," broadcast Aki Yamada.

Farley went to ice. *Aki's in a kill zone.*

Farley grabbed his sport coat and took off running for the vehicle lot. His shirttail resisted efforts to be tucked in. He pounded down the stairs, his belt-holstered Glock jabbing as his belly jiggled.

He exited the building with thoughts flying. Aki Yamada was only minutes away. Farley might get there in time. His mouth went dry.

Breathing hard, he made it to the lot and jumped into his unmarked. He fumbled with the key. The engine started and he hit the gas.

The car surged forward, and a uniform jumped out of the way.

Farley shrugged an apology.

His partner was in a life-or-death confrontation. Farley was a mile away and so shaky he could barely drive.

Newton Farley—homicide cop. *Who are you trying to fool, fat boy?*

He'd never truly fit anywhere. No one took him seriously—Farley the joke. It was his test smarts and computer skills that had won him the coveted Homicide spot. More than one of his fellow cops had voiced the opinion that he was a fat-ass desk jockey who didn't deserve a gold shield.

Working with Yamada on the woman's murder, he'd started to think that maybe he actually belonged in Homicide. He lit up the dash flasher as he exited the lot.

His mind jumped to the shocking info he'd just hacked from the insurance and pharmacy records of Faith Reinhorst-Malar.

During the questioning downtown, Yamada had asked the husband about children.

"I prayed but God did not bless us with children." Jon Malar's voice had broken and he'd turned his eyes away.

Throughout the interrogation, Farley had found himself sympathizing with the abused physician. The birth control prescriptions Farley found documented was evidence of one more cruelty wrought by the murdered wife.

Farley's next discovery had dwarfed that deceit.

He slowed, then powered through a red light.

Faith Reinhorst-Malar's pharmacy records revealed two instances where she'd filled prescriptions for two antibiotics and a painkiller. The first time three years back, and again in the spring of last year. The same physician prescribed on both occasions.

A Google-search of the physician's name yielded a mess of hits. He ran a Minneapolis abortion clinic.

Farley then searched "abortion procedure medications" and found the antibiotics Faith had filled were the standard medications prescribed post-procedure.

He accelerated and passed a truck on the left. Last, Farley had hacked into Faith's insurance record and checked the dates. Both were linked with entries of "OB/GYN procedure, unspecified—non-covered." There was no doubt.

Faith Reinhorst-Malar had aborted two pregnancies.

His heart pained once more for the soft-spoken physician. What could be more excruciating for the devout Catholic who prayed for the gift of a child? If Jon Malar learned of her actions, he could only feel she'd killed his babies.

Farley agonized. His hacking violated the laws governing legitimate search. Generally, he left it to the courts to determine what material was admissible. In this case, his conscience balked. He knew how the already guilt-convinced DA would use the information.

Farley wanted no part in a hasty conviction of Jon Malar—especially when politics and media pressure favored a rush to judgment.

The radio crackled. "Dispatch to available squads. Hospital is secure." Farley sagged in relief. "Divert to west river flats off Decatur Road, code two. Hostage situation at abandoned riverboat. A woman and two children being held. Suspects are three men and a woman—consider armed and dangerous. Officer Yamada en route. Paramedics and fire personnel on scene.

Son of a bitch! Farley could divert and be there in minutes. His stomach dropped. Responsibility and shame were pushing him away from where he desperately wanted to be; where his fat ass likely belonged—sitting behind his desk.

Perhaps the action would be over before he arrived? The tires squealed as he turned toward the river. He was very close. He swallowed hard and shook his head. Would a real Homicide cop ever feel like he might piss himself?

Chapter 80

"Hurry! Help him." The agony of Rachelle's burns and the degradation of her sexual assault were momentarily gone. Drake's safety was everything now.

As the policeman advanced toward the door to the cooler, Rachelle's memory flashed an image of the door to Faith's inner office the morning of her death. The fears that had driven Rachelle to that door had been eclipsed. To have Drake come out of that cooler alive was all that mattered.

Rachelle prayed so hard she shook.

* * *

Aki kept his gun trained on the linked bodies.

Drake's left hand appeared fused to the woman's throat. Her eyes bulged, sightless and horrific. Her ape-like arms aligned with his, the bloodied hands and fingers encircling the doctor's neck.

It was like an image Aki had seen of elk that had locked antlers in battle and fought to the end.

A grunt and the bodies shifted. Aki jumped, almost snapping off a shot. A cough was followed by a noisy gasp.

Drake Cody's chest heaved, and he writhed in the grisly embrace.

Aki crouched at Drake's side.

His eyes opened, wild and lost.

Aki pulled loose the dead clawed hands of the woman. Drake's left hand remained buried in her neck as if the flesh were made of clay. Aki attempted to free Drake's grip. It was a talon, the forearm rigid.

"No," groaned Drake, resisting.

"Doc, it's done. She's dead."

Drake's body shuddered. His hand came free, the fingers still curled. Deep imprints in the woman's neck remained. He tried to rise. "Rachelle, the kids, Rizz. Got to—" Blood welled from his shoulder and his eyes rolled back.

"Hold on." Aki keyed his radio. "Paramedics, now. Multiple injured. Second level."

* * *

Farley slowed on the cratered asphalt of the derelict road. He stopped where the paved road ended near the riverbank's edge. The paddle-wheel boat was visible several hundred yards downstream. He passed a rusted sign as he turned onto the dirt-packed access track that paralleled the river.

The radio crackled and a voice burst forth. "Heads up to the squad cars on the west river flat." Yamada was breathing hard. "A black SUV heading your way. Shots fired. Three armed men. Take 'em down."

Two black-and-whites kicked up dust about two hundred yards in front of Farley, heading towards the boat. A black SUV appeared, hurtling towards the squad cars from another couple of hundred yards ahead. Farley hit the brakes and looked over his shoulder for an escape. His reflex triggered a flare of self-loathing.

He threw the car in park, ripping free his seatbelt as he dug for his pistol. The edge of the Glock gouged his belly as he wrenched it loose. His hands were ice. *What the hell am I doing here?*

The black SUV plunged off-road, bypassing the squad cars at an angle. It blasted through the bushes and scrubby growth.

The SUV fishtailed back onto the road, catching air as it slammed over the railroad tracks.

Farley's unmarked car sat on the only way out. His breath caught. He wiped sweat from his eyes.

They were on a collision course.

His guts went to jelly. *Make the call, fat boy. Where do you belong?*

He slammed the car in reverse, swinging his arm over the seatback and looking out the rear window as he accelerated.

After thirty yards he cut the wheel and stopped—lodging the car across the road between the culvert on one side and the concrete abutment of an erosion levee on the other.

They would have to go through him.

He wrestled his bulk out of the car. He braced his fifteen-shot Glock in a two-handed grip on the car's roof. The big SUV rocketed towards him, its engine screaming.

Centering his weapon on the glint of the careening driver's side of the windshield, he started squeezing off shots. He recentered after each kick of the weapon. The vehicle closed impossibly fast.

He fired the last shot at five yards, bracing for collision as he did.

The windshield starred, and the SUV wrenched to the left. The vehicle tipped as it left the road and plunged into the culvert. Farley felt the gust of the vehicle's draft as it missed his car by inches and plowed into the culvert's muck and cattails. He pivoted, ejecting the empty magazine, then slammed home his backup as he ran down the road. He stopped, training his weapon on the steaming undercarriage and spinning wheels now fifteen yards away.

The door kicked open and a dark-complexioned man dove out, firing a handgun.

Farley, caught in the open, crouched in a shooter's stance. He squeezed once.

The man rocked and went down.

A voice screamed from the vehicle. "No, no, no! Do not shoot. I am a businessman. Do not shoot." A blond-haired man crawled out the open door, then clawed through the mud up onto the road. He knelt with his hands raised. "The bad ones are dead. This is a mistake. I am a businessman."

"Belly on the road or I blow your ass away," Farley yelled.

The man dove face-first to the dirt.

"Hands behind your head with fingers locked."

The squad cars braked hard to a stop on the other side of his unmarked. Another black-and-white approached from the asphalt.

Farley was a hot air balloon rising—the feeling indescribable.

He was alive.

And he wasn't a joke.

Chapter 81

As two of the coroner's crew wrestled the second body bag out of the culvert, the zipper gapped and the corpse's head and torso lolled into view. Aki saw Farley blanch. The nine-millimeter slug and crash impact had made a fright-show of the man's face.

Aki put a hand on the rookie's shoulder. "You did what needed to be done."

Farley nodded, but remained silent.

"Come on." Aki opened a mud-smeared wallet one-handed. "Let's find out what," he pinned the leather with his sling-bound arm and pulled out a business card, "BioZyn president Heinrich Pater has to say. I'll take the lead, okay?"

The German sat cuffed in the back seat of Farley's unmarked with the AC off and the windows up. Farley took the driver's seat while Aki opened the passenger-side rear door.

"I can explain!" The flushed and sweating prisoner began speaking as soon as the door was cracked. "I am a businessman. I am not a criminal. I—"

Aki winced as he adjusted his sling. "Shut up until I tell you to speak." The man's mud- and muck-soiled clothes reeked. "Turn on the AC will ya, Farley?"

The blower kicked on and the air began to move.

Aki turned on the recorder and read the Miranda warning.

"Do you understand your rights?"

"Yes, but I must speak. You need to know the truth." Heinrich looked from Aki to Farley. "I knew nothing of the kidnapping. What Meryl did sickened me. My colleagues and I were just readying to free the family from her when the crazy man on the boat threw a fire bomb at us. My colleagues have a history with war. I could not control their reaction."

"How do you explain Meryl Kampf's involvement?" Aki said.

"She had gone insane. It was all her." Heinrich stopped as if his words explained all.

For a foreigner, up to his neck in shit, it was a clever story. Could it be true? Aki looked to the front seat.

"Are you buying this tale, partner?"

Farley turned. "Her business card says she's BioZyn's Chief Product Development Analyst. You expect us to believe you had nothing to do with her actions?"

"I tell you, I behaved honorably. The documents proved the attorney woman to be the owner of NeurVitae's intellectual property. Neither I nor BioZyn played any part in Meryl's actions or anything criminal."

He swiveled his eyes between the two detectives. "Not until I arrived here did I learn what she'd done." He hung his head. "Meryl and this Faith were—" he raised his eyes, "were involved. Sexually and in illegal business."

"We're talking about murder and kidnapping—not sex." Aki pinned him with his eyes.

"I'm telling you everything." Heinrich said. "We paid $75,000 to secure the agreement. This Faith woman provided the D-44 research and was in line to receive millions. We were awaiting her delivery of the final and most critical drug information. That was when I learned that she, this American attorney-criminal, was secretly negotiating with another party to sell them *our* drug. I informed Meryl. One day later the woman drowned. I assumed accidentally. We had a contract giving us ownership of D-44. Meryl said all was in order and she had the final D-44 information, so I flew here to collect it."

"Just business as usual, huh?" Aki said.

"No. This is what I'm telling you. When I got here, I found Meryl was insane. She was sniffing drugs, and talked with hatred of Faith. I learned it was murder."

"Did she admit to killing Faith?"

"If you saw her, you know what she'd become. I had nothing to do with it." His eyes once more jumped from Aki to Farley. "Meryl did it all. I tried to help that mother and her children. I'm just a businessman."

Aki turned off the recorder. He looked at Farley who frowned and shook his head.

The German was slick. The story made some sense but…

"Nice try, Mr. Businessman. You're headed for a cell downtown. We'll see how your story holds up when we talk with the real victims."

***

Aki exited the ER into a main corridor. The ER folks had taken good care of him. The pick had penetrated but not broken the bone, and there was no nerve or artery injury. No cast needed, just a new bandage and sling. And some pain medication that had him feeling pretty damn good.

Maybe it was the drugs but he really appreciated the Emergency personnel. The paramedics, techs, nurses, and doctors were solid. They were like cops—ready to go whenever bad shit happens.

Aki's shoes squeaked on the glistening hospital floor. Earlier, he'd raced through these hallways, fear-sick and hurt, chasing a professional killer. Quick reflexes, dumb luck, and a deadeye sniper had kept him alive to travel these corridors again.

After depositing Heinrich in a cell, Aki and Farley had driven to the hospital and taken Rachelle Cody's statement as a young surgeon worked on her burns. She corroborated the German's story of Meryl Kampf's drug-fueled insanity, but gave a decidedly different account of "Good Samaritan" Heinrich's involvement.

The "businessman" was awaiting indictment for kidnapping, assault, and federal crimes. It did seem that his claim of no direct involvement with Faith's death was credible.

Faith's murder via the intimate delivery of the paralyzing drug singularly fit Meryl Kampf's pharmacology expertise, sick character and reported physical relationship.

What she'd put Rachelle Cody and the children through had been cruel and sick. He didn't want to think about what would have happened to the mother and children if the crazed woman had not been stopped.

Doctors Cody and Rizzini had engineered one hell of a rescue. Both of them were still in surgery.

Dr. Rizzini had been bleeding heavily as he was air-lifted out. The man was no saint, but based on Rachelle Cody's report, he'd come through when it counted.

Doc Cody's wound looked serious but not life-threatening.

Worry for the injured docs and not knowing who had tried to have Doc Malar killed chewed at Aki's gut. What did it mean when three ER docs he dealt with only in the line of work were as close to him as anyone other than his fellow officers? His ex-wife was right. The job had taken over his life.

The cell phone rang. Aki left-handed the phone free.

"Yamada here."

"This is Farley. I'm outside the Post Anesthesia Care Unit. They say we can have a minute with Dr. Cody if we go easy."

"On my way."

* * *

The afternoon's brightness backlit the closed blinds of his library windows as Andrew Reinhorst disconnected with the DA. An unknown man had been killed by police at Hennepin-North Hospital after a failed attack on Faith's husband. Who else could it be?

The Consultant had failed irrevocably this time. *How will I get my money?*

The smug bastard had stood in this room drinking Andrew's scotch less than twenty-four hours earlier. The image brought with it the prick's words: "If I disappear or have an accident, a packet of information will be electronically delivered to the police and media."

Would he really have set that up? Andrew's spine went to ice. *Shit!* The son of a bitch didn't bluff.

Andrew scrambled to his feet, grabbed his cell phone and hit a programmed number key. He paced as it rang.

"Reinhorst Air services."

"Fuel the Gulfstream." He checked his watch, noting his arm trembled. "Flight plan for Costa Rica—now. I'll be there straightaway."

He snatched up his Bible as he made for the door.

* * *

The post-op beds were occupied by patients in various stages of post-surgical sedation. Nurses, doctors, and techs hovered around the patients. It was quieter and more controlled than the ER, but Aki sensed similar intensity.

Dr. Drake Cody looked like death. The head of his bed was raised, leaving him sitting almost upright. He looked pale, but the whites of his eyes were blood red. Strangulation caused the surface vessels of the eye to burst. Every other time Aki had seen the grotesque finding, the eyes were those of a corpse.

Drake's right shoulder and chest were bound with dressings. His neck and left arm lay exposed. His throat was collared by dense purple and black bruising. A warming light shone yellow-tinged, illuminating IV lines and monitor cables.

Aki and Farley approached. They'd agreed Aki would do the talking. The nurse offered Drake water through a straw. He winced as he attempted to swallow. He thanked her, his voice weak and hoarse.

Aki bent close. "How you doing, Doc?" Near him, it smelled of clean linen and the coppery tinge of blood.

Drake straightened, grimacing. "Rachelle, the kids? Where—?"

The nurse leaned in, her hand patting his. "They're doing fine. You'll see them real soon. Rest easy. Please. Your family is safe."

She turned to the officers and spoke just above a whisper. "He keeps struggling and asking about his family. When he first came out of anesthesia he had to be held down. He's heavily medicated. Take it easy. Okay?" Her manner made it clear she was not asking.

Aki nodded. Her protective posture reminded him of the nurse watching over Dr. Malar in the ICU. There was something special about them.

The nurse moved off.

"Can you tell us what happened?" Aki asked.

Drake's brow wrinkled and he looked adrift for a moment.

"They took my family." He raised his head. "They wanted D-44." He strained forward, grisly eyes wide. "Are they okay? The kids? Where—"

"Easy, Doc. They're good. You saved them."

He settled back.

"Doc, who took them? Did they say anything about Faith?"

"A voice on the phone. It was a woman." He closed his eyes for a moment. "Cruel."

"Was there anyone else?" asked Aki.

Drake frowned. "The boat. Three men." He raised his good hand to his brow. "Rizz came." His face twisted. He turned his eyes to Aki and his voice rose. "Rizz was hit." Drake reached out with his left hand and clutched Aki's sleeve. "Is he okay?"

"He's alive." Aki glimpsed the nurse knifing towards them. They were supposed to keep Drake calm. It wasn't happening. "He's in surgery now. I don't know more."

Drake slumped back, eyes closed and breathing hard.

"That's enough," the nurse said in a fierce whisper. She slid herself between Drake and Aki, but Drake wouldn't release Aki's sleeve.

Drake's eyes flew open and he snapped forward, his neck muscles standing out. He pulled Aki close. "The woman," he rasped. His blood-painted eyes darted, the pupils tiny. "The one. Where is—"

"She's dead," Aki said. "She can't hurt anyone anymore."

Drake released his grip, falling back on the bed, chest heaving.

The nurse put a hand on Aki's shoulder.

"That's enough," she said steering Aki and Farley away from the bed.

"Aki," Drake said, still breathing hard.

Aki stopped and turned, still in the nurse's grasp.

“She talked about Faith.” Drake slumped back looking spent. “She said Faith deserved it.” His lids drooped. “Said she had it coming.” He nodded off.

Chapter 82

Burn Unit, late afternoon

The bandages got in Rachelle's way.

She wanted to comfort the kids without restriction. Her poor, brave little ones slept next to her on the oversized bed. She worried for them.

God, imagine that? She, Rachelle Cody, worrying. If it wasn't for the relentless pain, she might have smiled.

It made no sense, but the past few days had left her feeling more together than usual. Again she almost smiled—when it came to her history, that wasn't saying much. It occurred to her that throughout the ordeal she had not once thought about her "pills". She'd grown stronger.

She hadn't failed her children. And they would be okay. She would help them. There was nothing more important than that.

The nurses were kind. They'd arranged the special oversized bed so the kids could stay by her side. She couldn't bear to have them out of her sight.

They told her that Drake's injury was not life-threatening and she believed them.

This facility looked nicer and more high-tech than the burn unit in Duluth twenty years ago, but even so, she knew it was a place steeped in pain and sadness. The agony of her burned wrists and her hands mirrored the misery of her childhood hospital stay. Both places shared the signature odor. The scent of burned flesh mixed with the chemical tang of ointments and cleansing solutions brought her back as if it were yesterday.

Rachelle sniffed again. There was no trace of sweetness. Good. When infection developed in a burn unit, an odor like overripe fruit arose. She'd learned that it had to do with the bacteria that invaded burns. The sweetness had seemed a strange thing to her.

All through Rachelle's life, the doctors, psychologists and counselors believed they had her figured out. They'd looked at her records and hardly asked her anything. "The events of your youth were devastating. Post-traumatic issues are to be expected."

Even with no knowledge of the worst of what had happened, they "expected" that she'd be messed up. Did the truth matter after all this time?

She now believed it did. And if she shared—it might help. She would tell Drake. She'd tell him what she'd never told anyone.

Shane's and Kristin's chests gently rose and fell. Gazing on their faces, tears came to her eyes. She'd come so close to losing them.

There was one thing she could never tell Drake.

She'd been thrilled when she heard Jon had regained consciousness and his brain looked to have been spared. Her relief had been cut short. What might he say in his damaged state?

She looked from side to side as if checking to see if anyone might see her thoughts. The IV machine ticked like an old-style clock. The nurses at their station were a soft mutter. Rachelle was alone with the memory.

* * *

After overhearing Faith's heartless plan over the kid's audio monitor, Rachelle had struggled to control her panic. When she returned downstairs, she'd confronted the woman who threatened their world.

Rachelle bargained with everything she had.

She knew Drake would not give in to Faith's blackmail. He wasn't made that way. Faith would use his criminal record to destroy him and end their dreams.

Rachelle pleaded, pointing out that ruining Drake's life and career would not get Faith what she wanted. She assured Faith that she could deliver the drug information.

Faith agreed to give her forty-eight hours.

Rachelle then stood trembling as Faith stroked and kissed her. She'd begun to unbutton Rachelle's blouse. Rachelle felt the panic start. Her breathing had begun to race.

The ringing phone saved her.

The kids would be dropped off in a minute.

Rachelle had accepted Faith's demands. If Faith would withhold her blackmail of Drake, Rachelle would deliver the information—and herself. They would meet at Faith's office the following morning.

Rachelle had agreed but inside she'd known. Faith had to be stopped.

Rachelle would have to do the unthinkable—again.

* * *

Rural northern Kentucky, **twenty years earlier**

Big Joe worked in the stinky shed some days. No one else was allowed in there. He said it would "blow to hell" if there was "even a spark." He said over and over that he better never see us with matches or playing with fire. One time Billy picked up Joe's lighter and got punched in the face.

Rachelle had snuck a peek in the shed. The worn wood building used to be for storage and play. Since Joe, it stunk like toilet cleaner in there and made her nose sting. There was a table with boxes and bottles and lots of glass stuff. Joe put on a mask thing when he went in.

On a day soon after Billy got out of his cast, Joe was in the shed.

Rachelle took the jar candle from its hiding place behind the building. She shook so hard, it took almost the whole book of matches before she got it lit. She could hear the big man mixing and bumping around on his table right on the other side of the old wall. Rachelle shifted the loose board from the hole at the base of the wall. She slipped the candle inside onto the floor, crawled backwards, then stood and ran.

She got on her bike and bumped down the long dirt driveway. Her heart pounded all the way to her throat and she could barely breathe. She stopped near the road and waited for Joe to blow to Hell.

The back door to the house opened. Momma had Billy by the arm. He had on his ball glove. She looked mad. She dragged him toward the shed.

"No, Momma!" Rachelle screamed. She jumped on her bike and pedaled harder than ever before.

Momma pulled Billy into the shed. The door closed behind them.

Rachelle threw her bike down next to Joe's motorcycle. As she ran, she screamed, "Billy, no! Please, Jesus, please!"

Rachelle heard Joe curse and Billy cry out..

She grabbed the door and pulled.

And they all blew straight to Hell.

* * *

Rachelle's burn unit nurse approached. She checked the IV and adjusted the rate. Her eyes swept over the sleeping children, then back to Rachelle. She spoke just above a whisper.

"I can see that you're hurting. Let me set up your patient-controlled morphine pump or at least give you something now. Please."

Rachelle had accepted a morphine injection earlier as the doctor stripped away the dead tissue of her burns. In a case of lousy timing, that was when the detectives showed up. Among their questions they'd asked about her visit to Faith's office. She believed she'd answered safely. It seemed that they'd believed her about a needed signature as the reason for her visit to Faith's office, but the questioning had terrified her. She'd refused all pain meds since.

"No, but thank you. Don't worry. I'm okay."

The nurse looked doubtful. "Push the call button if you change your mind. Please." She adjusted a blanket and left the room.

Rachelle hoped exhaustion would push her into the numbness of sleep. Her pain gnawed mercilessly, but she would not risk the drugs.

Until the police ended their investigation, she couldn't risk being anything less than razor sharp.

Chapter 83

As Farley entered the Homicide room, the chatter and bustle of the dozen or so plainclothes and uniformed officers ceased. He was puzzled, then startled as applause and hurrahs broke out. People actually slapped him on the back. For a clumsy, chubby kid who'd never played on a sports team or heard a cheer, it seemed unreal. He felt his cheeks flush.

He waved them off in happy embarrassment and took a seat at his desk. His computer in-box icon signaled awaiting email.

A registered overnight delivery envelope lay on his keyboard. Farley picked up the envelope as he scanned the subject headings in his inbox.

Just three new emails—two were garbage and one odd.

The registered letter was postmarked Berne, Switzerland and was a communication he'd been waiting for.

> From: Ingersen Pharmaceutical, Product Acquisitions and Development division
> To: Minneapolis Police – attention Detective Farley
>
> Ingersen Pharmaceutical is not at liberty to share all business specifics, but is eager to cooperate within the constraints established by our legal department.
>
> Per one aspect of your inquiry, we can share that procurement and disbursement contracts for a promising pharmaceutical agent frequently exceed ten million U.S. dollars in initial payment. Breakthrough drugs addressing critical illnesses with no current therapeutics can result in disbursements many times that amount. Downstream payments linked to product revenues are typically significant elements of such contracts
>
> Ingersen Pharmaceutical negotiated with Faith Reinhorst-Malar, JD, as the documented controlling

entity of NeurVitae, LLC. We reached an agreement in principle and a good faith negotiation disbursement of $100,000 had been accepted by Ms. Reinhorst. A call to complete a subsequent wire transfer for a substantially greater payment went unanswered. We believe this is the call you referenced in your inquiry.

I hope this information satisfies your needs. This communication does not, in any way, discount the enforceability of our contract for the intellectual property of NeurVitae, LLC.

Ingersen Pharmaceutical is committed to developing and bringing to market this promising new drug. Please direct any further inquiries to our legal department.

Respectfully,
Ivar Zeiss, PhD
Vice President – Acquisitions and Development

Farley looked at the copy of the newspaper photo from the wedding day of Jon and Faith. Her incredible beauty had masked an ugly core. She'd been on the cusp of stealing the doctors' breakthrough—and collecting millions. At the same time she was double-crossing Meryl Kampf and BioZyn.

Betrayal, deceit, sexual debauchery, fraud, wanton greed, theft and the secret abortions of her unknowing and trusting husband's unborn children—those were just the things Farley knew of.

Meryl Kampf—brilliant, drug-crazed, mentally ill, greedy and violent.

Faith and Meryl—partners in sex and crime. What were the odds of two such damaged creatures finding one another? Farley rubbed his temples.

Drake Cody had revealed Meryl's words, "Faith deserved it. She had it coming."

Farley considered the law-office sex lair, the delivery route of the killer drug, and Faith's horrible death. Meryl had certainly given *it* to her treacherous partner.

Farley collected the printouts documenting Faith's procedures and post-abortion medications. What would be gained by revealing this ugliness now?

If Jon Malar learned of the abortions, it would only increase his suffering. Ignorance would be a kindness.

Farley fed the papers into the document shredder.

His high from the acclaim of the Homicide group had crashed with his thoughts of the much-abused doctor. They'd yet to find any clue as to who had tried to have him killed. Farley clenched his jaw. He would make sure that crime did not go unpunished.

He slid open his bottom drawer and pulled out a bag of Fritos and a warm can of Mountain Dew. A fistful of Fritos passed his lips as he turned to his computer.

The curious email was identified as an auto-mailing from "Catalyst Consulting." Most likely sent by a nut-job, as the subject heading was "In the event of my death." There were attachments.

One minute later, chewed Frito mash remained in his mouth, unswallowed. The mystery of Dr. Jon Malar's shooting unfolded as he read.

Chapter 84

Aki had yet to get a single answer from the attorney, political insider and murder suspect. Even though Andrew Reinhorst wasn't giving them squat, Aki wished Farley was along to watch the bastard sweat.

Internal Affairs had caught up with Farley and sent him home on administrative leave, as was standard procedure for all officer-involved shootings. At least he'd been around long enough to see Reinhorst hauled in wearing handcuffs.

Aki pointed his pen at the silent big shot, who sat alongside the Twin Cities' highest profile criminal defense attorney. "I'll ask one last time—how do you respond to the transcripts and digital recordings documenting your order and payment for the murder of Jon Malar?"

The silver-haired mogul sat, head bowed, hands resting on a worn leather-bound Bible. The acting DA looked at Aki and shrugged.

Just over an hour earlier, Farley had checked airport control logs and found that a Gulfstream jet registered to Reinhorst, LLC had been undergoing preflight fueling. He'd sent a squad car to the airport. The Minneapolis uniformed officers had apprehended Andrew Reinhorst in the private VIP lounge. His bags were already on board, with a flight plan filed for San José, Costa Rica.

"You maintain you were leaving town on business. Correct?"

Reinhorst's attorney leaned forward. "My client has made no statements as to his intent. Nor regarding anything else. That is my recommendation, and he understands the importance of having his rights protected. We have no comment."

Aki turned off the recording devices as he stood. "Okay, take him down and book him."

Reinhorst wouldn't make it easy, but the "consultant's" evidence couldn't be more damning if it'd been prepared by a prosecuting attorney.

They were going to nail the self-righteous prick.

"You'll look good in an orange jumpsuit, *Andy*." Aki savored the moment.

The "in case of my death" email materials documented that the DA had shared key details of the ongoing investigation with Reinhorst.

Reinhorst's stooge had been dismissed as DA. There was no doubt the ass-kissing hick would be disbarred. He'd be lucky to avoid jail time. Aki smiled. *Sayonara, douche bag.*

Maybe he'd send him an Origami jackass.

* * *

Aki's cell rang as he climbed the steps of the old, but timelessly ugly downtown Minneapolis police station. "Yamada, Homicide."

"This is Kip Dronen, superstar ME. If you're not too busy writing parking tickets or beating jaywalkers, I've got the quick and dirty on the truckload of stiffs you dumped on me."

Just the guy to kill Aki's high. He was still seriously pissed about the ME's media grandstanding regarding the killing drug.

"Yes, Doctor Genius. Are you sure you can reveal privileged information on an active investigation without a TV camera on you?"

"'Genius'—hey, that's more like it. Glad you've learned some respect."

Aki shook his head. This guy's ego blocked out the sun. "What have you got?"

"The yet-to-be identified guy taken out by SWAT at the hospital looks like their usual work—one shot and deader than dead.

"The foreign guys with the bad dental work were also slam-dunks. Both killed by a nine millimeter. One took a shot through the chin and into the base of the brain. The other a chest hit that shredded the aorta and pulmonary artery—adios. Looks like you and your colleagues had fun."

"There was nothing fun about it."

"Whatever. Boring cases—even our brown-nosing hack of a chief ME could've handled them. Now this last one—she's special."

"What's that mean?"

"The woman deserved my genius."

Aki sighed. "Just get to it."

"Excuse me all to hell for taking your valuable time, Mr. Civil Servant. Can this world-renowned forensic pathologist get you some fries with your autopsy report, sir?"

"Please just tell it," Aki said.

"First off, this wench is a study in anabolic steroid use—truncal acne, hair loss, the muscle development of a gorilla. And her sexual changes—ai-yi-yi."

"Too much information," Aki said, increasingly irritated by the ME's manner.

"She was also a world-class user of Peruvian marching powder. Her cocaine level came in higher than any I've seen before. Her heart was the size of a sumo wrestler's, she had advanced coronary artery disease, and her nasal septum had ulcerated. Her brain was— Well it's beyond you, but believe me, this chick was gonna blow a head gasket any minute." He laughed. "Get it? *Head* gasket. You know, as in brain."

Aki did not respond.

"Whatever. And all that was just her baseline. Here's the trauma she withstood." The M.E. spoke like an admiring sports fan. "Multiple face and scalp lacerations and contusions with a broken nose. Nineteen shotgun pellet injuries. Some were minor causing finger fractures, facial wounds, and shattered teeth, but also some major hits—penetration of her left carotid artery and a pneumothorax."

Kip practically cheered as he listed the damage. "On top of all that, she had a fractured skull with an epidural hematoma. Someone smashed her in the head with something like a baseball bat. A lesser creature would have been dead several times over." He spoke as if she deserved an award. "Like the old Timex watch commercials—takes a licking and keeps on ticking." He cackled. "It blows my mind that she continued to function."

"Her function was to torture and kill." Aki had reached his limit with the squeaky ME.

"Whatever. And after all that, life had to be choked out of her. Her larynx and proximal trachea were crushed. What you ignorant types would call the voice box was destroyed. Her hyoid bone was practically dust. I'd have guessed by a tool or power mechanical device, but I found finger lesions in the soft tissue—totally amazing.

Aki pictured the scene in the cooler and felt queasy.

"She is well and truly dead." The ME spoke slowly, and for the first time Aki heard something akin to sadness in the misfit's words. "But it took one helluva lot to kill her." He paused. "I gotta admit—I love this wench."

"You and you alone, Dr. Bizarre," Aki said. "Send me the report. I'll talk with you later—if necessary."

Aki pocketed his phone. He laid his hands flat on his desk. The ME seemed to revel in the ugliness of death.

Aki chose to focus on the positive.

Faith Reinhorst-Malar's killer was dead. Jon Malar was alive and his shooter would never kill again.

Andrew Reinhorst and the DA would be indicted.

Heinrich and BioZyn were in the FBI's grasp.

His Homicide cases were closed—righteously closed. Justice wasn't always the outcome in his work, but today was different. They'd taken care of business and it felt damn great.

This is as good as it gets for me. Am I nuts?

Chapter 85

Drake vaguely recalled seeing Aki post-op. Had there been someone with the detective? By the time Drake was moved to a room on the general surgery ward, he felt clearheaded. The nurse assessed him and emphasized his need for rest.

Five minutes later, Drake talked an orderly into helping him into a wheelchair. Over his nurse's objections, he made his way to the burn unit. Rachelle, Shane and Kristin were all in one oversized bed—asleep. He sat for some time, watching.

What he felt went beyond relief. The peaceful appearance of their sleeping faces gave him hope. He touched each one lightly.

He rolled to the elevator and hit the button for the sixth floor ICU.

Jon lay deeply sedated on the ventilator. The *click-hiss-blow* of the machine marched on. His prognosis had improved to guardedly optimistic. Drake held Jon's wrist, instinctively checking his pulse. The strong beat combined with the warmth of his skin made it real for Drake. His friend would live.

Tracy showed him a clipboard. "He's starting to write. It's scattered but, well, you know..."

Drake viewed the letters scrawled at odd angles across the clipboard. Several single words or phrases whose meanings were clear: *thank, cold, hurting, tube out?*

There was a second sheet. Drake flipped to that page. The writing was worse here. Drake squinted. Mostly illegible scratching but he could make out a few words: *NO…babies…lies…stop…sin…damned.*

From the Crash Room instant Drake had recognized the ravaged, pulseless body as his friend, he'd been carrying a heavy weight. He'd never fully believed that Jon could survive without profound handicap.

The ability to write was evidence of high level brain function. It was a strong predictor of recovery. For the first time he dared to think of having his friend back as he had been.

"I should have thrown that page away. It's nonsense," said Tracy. "It was the first stuff he wrote. He was totally out of it—agitated and fighting the ventilator." She took the clipboard. "I feel bad that I let him get so worked up. I should have upped the Propofol quicker." She reached and adjusted a sheet.

Drake took her hand in his. "You've been amazing. No one could have cared for him better." His voice caught. "Thank you."

Tracy flushed. "You too, Drake Cody." She gave his hand a shake. She straightened his sling. "You fought so hard to save him. I'm thrilled he's going to make it." She shrugged. "It's why we do what we do."

* * *

Recently transferred to the ICU after four hours of surgery, Rizz looked pale, yet awake and alert. Drake's friend seemed indestructible.

"I heard Jon is a miracle—just what we'd expect from our saintly friend." Rizz summoned a small smile.

"He's awake. His mind is there. Maybe sometimes God really does look after the good guys," Drake said.

"Does he know about me? Me and Faith?"

"I don't know." Drake looked away. "That's something I won't be sharing."

"I'm ashamed. From the first time I saw her. God, I could feel it. And she knew. She always knew."

The printer at the main nurses' station chattered to life. Drake rubbed his chin. Faith's death. He thought about all he now knew—Faith's treachery, the crazed BioZyn woman and what she'd said about Faith's death. *"She deserved it. She had it coming."*

And the rest: *"whoever used the succinylcholine" and "I'm gonna give her up?"*

"Rizz, when you were in the lab this past week, did you administer Vermex? Or take it out of the meds locker?"

"Huh? The suppository? Hell no, you know I leave all that animal care for you. Why?"

"Forget it. It's nothing." He swallowed and the ember of unease burning in his gut flared. Rachelle helped him treat the cats.

The nurse came into the room. "You okay in here?" They nodded. "Just hit the call button if you need anything at all." She slid the glass door shut.

Rizz stared at his hands and an awkward silence held.

"Rachelle and the kids—" Rizz's voice cracked. "Are they okay?" His guilt filled the room like a bad smell.

"They're sleeping. Rachelle's scheduled for skin grafts. More scars, but she'll heal. They say she'll be able to paint." Drake shifted in the wheelchair. "No one could have been braver."

"The kids? Are they…do they seem all right?"

"They're okay physically. The trauma counseling coordinator at Children's is lined up to see them. We're going to do all we can."

"Damn me to hell." Rizz shook his head. "This is killing me. I betray Jon. Allow myself to be blackmailed by Faith. And your family…" He wrung his hands.

"You needed to let me know what was happening."

"I know it now." He coughed and winced. "I thought I could figure a way out." His brow furrowed. "I seriously considered killing Faith. When I heard she died, I was happy." He shook his head. "How sick does that make me?"

"She hurt lots of people, partner."

Rizz's face twisted. "If Rachelle or the kids aren't okay…" His voice caught and he looked away.

Drake reached out and squeezed Rizz's forearm. "You took a bullet for us."

Phones sounded and nurses' voices murmured from the station desk. The IV pump continued its mechanical beat.

"What'd Rockswald say?" The chief of neurosurgery had operated on Rizz.

Rizz pulled his arm away, his eyes coursing about the room.

"He told me it was badness." He swallowed. "The bullet shattered the tenth thoracic vertebra. The fusion went well, so my spine will be stable." Rizz put his hand on the rolling tray at the bedside and moved it away and back with his fingers. "That's the end of the good news." He stared blankly as he spoke.

"My spinal cord is trashed. You know Rockswald. He doesn't bullshit." Rizz paused and swallowed once more. "The 'expectation' is that I'll have complete paralysis from… from," he skipped a glance into Drake's eyes and continued his roving, "from T-ten down. Said there 'isn't any reason to expect' I'd get anything back."

Drake caught Rizz's gaze, glimpsing bottomless pools of fear.

"I'm dead from my chest down," Rizz said. "I can't even feel my schlong. It goes from running my life to nothing." He fixed his gaze off to the side.

"Son of a bitch, Rizz. Jesus." Drake's shoulders slumped. He'd expected it but…

Rizz's IV pump beeped. "Fluid reset" flashed on the view screen. Before a nurse could respond, Rizz reached a lanky arm over, flipped open the control guard, re-entered a flow rate, and cleared the alarm.

"Shit, maybe I can get a discount?" He tried to smile. "I'm my own nurse."

Drake stood from the wheelchair and clasped Rizz's hand. "If there's anything you need—anything—you got it. Please know that."

Rizz winced, clearly still hurting above the level where the bullet had killed all sensation. His features knitted, he tilted his head, fixing Drake with a hawk's gaze.

"The drug, Drake. D-44. I need it now."

"You can't be serious." He let go of Rizz's hand, his mind staggered.

"Serious as paralysis, friend."

"C'mon, Rizz. The risks." Drake shook his head.

Rizz's gaze was steady. He shrugged. "And?"

A list of catastrophic potential side effects unfurled in Drake's mind.

"Drake, there couldn't be a more informed experimental candidate in the universe. I understand the risks. I want the drug. I need it. Don't make me beg."

Drake's stomach clenched. He looked down and away. His eye caught the yellow column of urine in the plastic catheter that ran from under the sheets to the collection bag

Rizz grasped Drake's wrist and pulled him closer, his grip a claw. His eyes laser-like.

"Drake—you're Florence Nightingale and Dudley Do-Right rolled into one. You try to protect and heal everyone, but it isn't up to you. Let me call my own shot. I think this is the way it's supposed to go down. Whatever happens—it's on me. Please."

"Damn it, Rizz. I can't do something that could kill you."

Chapter 86

Drake wheeled back to the surgical ward and his nurse checked him over, scolded him, and hung his medication. As the IV antibiotics ran in, Drake picked up the phone. Minutes later he disconnected. Patty, the ER charge nurse, had agreed to take care of things at the lab on her way in for her evening shift. He lay back.

* * *

After a brief but deep sleep, Drake mounted his wheelchair and made his way back to the burn unit.

Rachelle and the kids lay awake on the bed, with Rachelle's bandaged arms wrapped around each child.

Drake fit himself amongst them and they all embraced desperately.

Rachelle cried softly and the children pressed tight. His mind unknotted for the first time in days and his pain disappeared. The wonder and lightness of what he felt was beyond description.

He'd almost lost them all.

Fifteen minutes later, they were still cocooned on the bed. The kids had slipped back into an exhausted sleep.

He held Rachelle close. They didn't need words. It made him think of his brother.

He looked into her eyes. "Thank you for being so strong for the kids."

"I was a wreck and barely held together." She shook her head. "I need to get better. For you and them." She faced him. "And mostly for myself. I've hidden things inside forever. Terrible things I've done. And things done to me. I need to let it out." She bit her lip. "Does that make any sense?"

"It does to me." He shifted to his side. "I understand bad memories and painful secrets."

The lies and ugliness that scarred his past flashed like red-tinged snapshots.

"I don't have the courage to share mine. Or know if I should." He traced a finger over the scarred tissue of her neck. "I've been failing you and the children. If I'd lost you…" His voice failed.

Her eyes filled. They held each other tight.

The background murmur of voices and the chatter and trills of printers and phones carried from the nurse's station down the hallway. The air carried the distinctive burn unit scent.

Drake thought he noted a hint of sweetness.

The terrible apprehension that had arisen earlier gripped him again. Faith's death. A knot formed in his throat. The muscled woman's words "whoever used the succinylcholine." Drake's eyes went to Rachelle and their children. *No, she couldn't have.*

"Rachelle, did the kidnapper admit to you that she killed Faith?"

The IV pump's mechanical *tock-tock* marched. The breaths of their children sighed.

"She hated her, Drake." Rachelle leaned forward and twisted onto an elbow. Their eyes linked. "You said there are things you can't tell me." She winced and straightened her arm. "Our family is safe. Jon is alive. I need you to let it go at that. We need to focus on the living and do all we can for the kids, Jon and Rizz. Leave the rest of it. Can you trust me on this?"

Drake's mouth went dry.

He'd found the box of Vermex sitting out in the lab the morning after Faith's murder. He had not used it the previous day. The medication was a suppository used for de-worming the cats from the pound. Its outer shell was made of a time-release absorbable material.

Rachelle knew the combination to unlock the medication cabinet and opened it when she'd helped Drake with the cats. The sitter had watched the kids leaving Rachelle free the morning that Faith died.

His doubts surged. Faith's plan to steal D-44. What the insane woman had said in the cooler. Had Rachelle known? Could she have…?

He couldn't breathe. *Had the mother of his children killed Faith?*

A fierce pressure filled his head. *Please, God, no.*

He knew that the legal system could ruin lives. The law's involvement was not a guarantee of justice.

He could live without telling the police all he knew—or suspected.

But can I live without knowing?

"Rachelle, you don't have to answer but..." He swallowed and his chest constricted as if being crushed by a massive weight. "Did you go to the lab the morning of Faith's death?" He looked into her eyes.

She did not look away. "Faith was going to destroy us, Drake. I knew that."

Drake's heart thundered. His throat clenched.

"But I did not go to the lab that morning. I've never gone to the lab without you, Drake. Never."

Chapter 87

Tracy had been standing at the bedside when Jon Malar first opened his eyes. She'd laughed and practically danced around him. He'd squeezed her fingers and blinked on command. His brain worked!

She still hadn't got over the thrill.

Today Tracy charted good numbers. Temperature ninety-eight point seven—thank God no more need for the hypothermia. Blood pressure and pulse normal. No blood from the chest tubes and only a minimal air leak. Still intubated, but the ventilator settings were minimal. She checked his dressings.

Hopefully, the ET tube could come out soon and he'd be able to speak. Up to now it had just been nods, following simple commands, and a few words on the clipboard she held for him. Generally it seemed best if he remained sedated.

The past few hours, every time he lightened up from the medication, he bucked and fought. Nothing good could come from that.

He started to struggle again. The ventilator overpressure alarm sounded. The click-hiss- blow rhythm stumbled and her patient gagged and bucked. She winced and increased the rate of the Propofol drip. The discomfort of any of her patients distressed her and he, in particular, had endured so much. He settled as the drug flowed. She patted his arm and repositioned his pillow.

* * *

Jon floated in and out of consciousness as if pitched by cresting waves.

An unyielding foreignness violated his throat. His chest raged in synch with the mechanized sound of moving air.

With awareness came pain and flashes of dread-tinged recall. *Faith?*

His thoughts stuttered and a memory caught. Blackness enveloped him. *No, no, no.*

What she'd done. The babies—she'd killed their babies.

He cried out but heard only a hitch in the rhythm of the machines and a shrill beeping.

Recall continued to drift. Rachelle calling him as he worked in the lab that morning. She'd just left Faith's office. Faith had betrayed them all. She'd stolen the rights to the drug and would destroy Drake. All for money. All about her.

Rachelle begged him for help.

The beeping stopped. Someone stroked his arm.

Faith. After all that she'd taken from him, now she would ruin Drake. She had to be stopped.

The plan had formed in an instant. His heart turning as hard and cold as mid-winter ice.

That morning he'd administered Vermex to two cats new from the pound. It got rid of parasites.

He'd then opened another of the Vermex slow-release capsules, emptied it and refilled it with three times the succinylcholine needed to paralyze a two-hundred-pound man.

He arranged to meet Faith at home.

Keeping what he'd learned from her, he pretended the love that had never been anything but pretend from her.

Never before had he used a condom. He'd taken her savagely, with an ugliness that was not him.

And she liked it. Wanted it cruel and pain-filled. She laughed and drove him on.

It did not matter to her. He could have been anyone.

When he came, his quaking release fueled disgust—for her and himself.

He'd brought the succinylcholine to the bedroom. In his rough handling of her he inserted the drug.

After that, it was a matter of time. The capsule would break down and then…

He'd left without a word. There were no words.

Had it really happened?

Faith had mocked his love, killed the blessed gift of his babies, and planned to destroy Drake.

She'd needed to be stopped, but in his heart Jon knew he'd used the threat to Drake and his family to justify murder.

It was his hatred that had driven him to kill. *Please, God, forgive me!*

He had lost his soul.

Surely he was damned.

Chapter 88

Patty met Drake in the burn unit. She'd stopped by the lab and done as he'd asked. The animals were cared for. He thanked her and considered once again how lucky he was to have her as a friend.

The children awoke. After some preparation, the family made the pilgrimage to the ICU to see Jon and Rizz. Both Rachelle and Drake could stand, but they were weak. Hospital policy dictated wheelchairs. The kids pushed Rachelle.

Jon was deeply sedated on the ventilator. Rachelle climbed out of the wheelchair, laid her head on his shoulder, then kissed his forehead. Tears streamed down her face.

Drake stood and helped her into her chair, not surprised by the strength of her reaction to their kind-hearted friend.

They moved on toward Rizz's bay. The glass partition and curtain were open. Kristin smiled as she spied Rizz. She ran to the bedside and grabbed his hand.

Shane jumped forward. "Don't hurt him!" he said, his face twisted.

"I'm okay, Shane." Rizz extended his hand. Shane looked at the hand, then stepped forward and hugged Rizz's arm, burying his head against his shoulder.

Rizz closed his eyes as he held the children.

Shane's voice trembled. "Dad says you got shot to save us. Does it hurt?"

"No worries," Rizz said. "I'm fine."

Shane and Kristin stood big-eyed and silent.

Rachelle moved forward. She kissed Rizz on the cheek, and hugged him with her bandaged arms. "We love you, Michael. We'll always be here for you."

She ushered the children to the curtain and sat down in the wheelchair. "We'll see you again soon, Michael." The kids wheeled the chair out, looking over their shoulders as they left.

An oversized manila envelope with a red bow drawn on it and a small package wrapped in newspaper were left sitting on the bedside tray.

Drake stood. He clasped his free hand in Rizz's.

Drake had wrestled with Rizz's plea for D-44. He could not inject a potentially deadly experimental drug into his friend. Drake Cody could not assume responsibility for everyone. It was a decision he could live with.

"You came through for us, Rizz."

"Things would've never gotten that far if I wasn't such a decadent, gutless mutt."

The monitor beeped, a small column of blood backed up in the IV tubing. Rizz cleared the alarm.

"Rizz, it's sappy but—"

"Yeah, I love you too, brother." A near-smile flickered and then faded. "Drake, earlier I said it wrong. You're not a Dudley Do-Right or Florence Nightingale. That's how I feel Jon is—taking nothing away from him. He's somehow naturally pure. It's his nature to always do right. I can't relate to that.

"You're more of a trying-to-keep-it-together guy like me. You feel them—the nasty drives and instincts. The dark, primal hungers claw at you. That's why you impress me. The animal stuff is there, but somehow you hold on and always do the noble thing."

Drake frowned. *Not hardly, partner.*

Perhaps someday he could share fully with his friend. "Rizz, no matter what happens—I'm with you."

Rizz pulled Drake forward. They touched, forehead to forehead.

The noises produced by the delivery of intensive care hummed in the background. Tiny silver droplets of fluid dripped into the clear IV tube. The scent of clean linens and damaged flesh hung.

Drake straightened.

Rizz's eyes glistened.

Drake wrapped his other hand around their clasp. He shook it and released. "Do me a favor, brother, and look at your gifts straightaway." Drake pointed to the envelope and small wrapped box at the bedside. "The kids did the wrapping." He climbed back into the wheelchair. "I'll be checking in on you soon." He rolled himself out of the room.

* * *

Rizz blinked several times, then rubbed a hand over his eyes.

Half of his body was dead. His life changed forever. *Can I hold it together?*

His gaze found the wrapped gifts. He fingered the bed control and the servomotor hummed, raising him. Reaching over, he gathered the presents.

He opened the oversized envelope and slid out a cardboard-backed drawing—Kristin's picture of the black-and-white cat helping the stick-figure man stand. He propped it on the bedside table.

The second package, about the size of a cigar box, gave a slight fluid slosh when lifted. Probably booze, Rizz thought. Hell yes, why not?

Tearing off the wrapper, he found an unmarked box. He lifted the flap and gave it an angled shake, a three-hundred-milliliter fluid-filled IV bag and three feet of coiled IV tubing plopped onto his lap.

The administration bag was hand-labeled: "Protocol D-44, dosage based on specimen weight 86 kg." Taped to the tubing a note: "Earth product to help with your mission. It's your call. – Drake"

Rizz eyed the IV access port that lay next to his newly opened gift.

Acknowledgements

I want to thank all those I worked with and learned from at three incredible institutions. Hennepin County Medical Center (medical school rotations and internship wherein I was introduced to the specialty of Emergency Medicine), the University of Cincinnati hospital (three years of EM training and duty as an Air Care flight physician) and North Memorial Medical Center (eighteen years at this top-ranked Level one trauma and medical facility).

My special gratitude to the nurses, doctors, and many others at North Memorial Medical Center who were there for me when I needed them most.

I need to especially thank Jodie Renner, my outstanding editor (www.JodieRennerEditing.com). She went far beyond the call of duty in helping me get this book to press—she became a friend. I guarantee that any errors are the result of this author's wayward keyboard skills and an inability to leave a "completed" manuscript alone.

Thank-you to the writer-educators and staff of the Loft Literary Center for the years of instruction and support (Mary Carroll Moore, Ellen Hart, William Kent Krueger, David Housewright, the late Vince Flynn, and dozens more). The Loft has played a key role in my writing life.

Thanks to Michel (Sears) Stanley, author of the award-winning Detective Kubu Mystery series, for his generous guidance. I also owe world citizen, A.M. Khalifa, author of brilliant international thrillers, for his help..

Big thank-yous to my friends Tom Holker and Bruce Johnson - perceptive input and unwavering support. Yessah!

I want to acknowledge those who read and provided feedback on *Nerve Damage* in its early stages: Jane Combs, Anna Shovanec, Jerry Hendrickson, Michael Hamada, Tim Combs (also my resource for police action), Scott Fontana, Donnie Gibson, Terry Combs, Donna Hirschman, Connie Ekblad O'Brien, Dennis Kelly, Peter Kelly, Gary Gudmundson, Sonja Hutchinson, Melanie Peters, Scott Anderson, Gina Havenga, Alan Chaput, and members of Critique Circle.

Thank-you to Mike Lance, whose formatting, design, and technical expertise ensured that the book and eBooks reached you in good form (Mike@theLances.info)

The cover concept was executed by Travis Miles.

Thank-you to my wife, Michele, my son, Brian, and entire family for their support. Special thanks to my daughter, Kristin, for her encouragement and the chance conversation that gave birth to the character Meryl Kampf.

I must also take the opportunity to apologize.

I'm sorry to Minneapolis/St. Paul - for dramatic purposes I misrepresented aspects of my two favorite cities (e.g. we have no "projects").

I apologize to healthcare providers everywhere. For the sake of story-telling, I omitted or altered details of some medical procedures/practices and described behaviors unlike any I have witnessed.

I also want to make clear that while characters in this story suffered with mental illness, this is fiction. The behaviors described do not reflect upon those among us with mental health issues.

Before closing I want to share my gratitude for the gift of good health and the opportunity to write.

Finally a big thanks to you readers – I hope that my writing provides you the special pleasure reading provides me. I much appreciate any who will provide reiveiws on Amazon or elsewhere.

The next book in the series is on the way. I hope you're interested in spending more of your valuable reading time with me. Please visit at www.tom-combs.com

About the Author

Tom Combs' career as an ER physician provides the foundation for his unforgettable characters and riveting plots. His emotional engagement arises from 25 years of battling to help and comfort those facing illness, trauma and tragedy.

To earn his way to medical school, Tom worked jobs using jackhammers, chainsaws, and heavy machinery. He then shifted to laboratory equipment and, eventually, to the stethoscope, scalpel and other tools of the Emergency Medicine specialist.

His current weapons of choice are the keyboard and a dangerously fertile imagination.

Nerve Damage, his debut thriller, immerses the reader in high-level intrigue and edge-of-your seat suspense. The events are tomorrow's headlines credible with surprises unfolding to the final page.

Tom lives with his artist wife near family and friends in a suburb of Minneapolis/St. Paul. Visit his website at www.tom-combs.com or communicate via email at tcombsauthor@gmail.com

CPSIA information can be obtained at www.ICGtesting.com
Printed in the USA
LVOW10s1933201215

467322LV00023B/2717/P